A 'LOVE IN THE DALES' STORY

The Perfect Fit

MARY JAYNE BAKER

Mirror Books

Published by Mirror Books,
an imprint of Trinity Mirror plc,
One Canada Square, London E14 5AP, England

www.mirrorbooks.com
twitter.com/themirrorbooks

Mirror Books 2018

ISBN 978-1-9126-2407-2

First paperback edition

Typeset by Danny Lyle
DanJLyle@gmail.com

Printed and bound in Great Britain by
CPI Group (UK) Ltd, Croydon, CR0 4YY

Every effort has been made to fulfil requirements with regard to
reproducing copyright material. The author and publisher will be glad to
rectify any omissions at the earliest opportunity.

For Amy Smith,

my favourite tiny amdrammer.

Chapter 1

'Behind you! Peter! Peter, he's right *there*!'

Pip bounced on her seat, waving frantically at Peter Pan, who just couldn't seem to see the burly pirate lurking by his shoulder.

Peter cupped a theatrical hand to his – well, her – ear. 'Did you say something, boys and girls?'

'Can't you hear me?' Pip yelled, her voice soaring far above the other children. 'He's right behind you! He's gonna take Tinkerbell!'

Peter turned around slowly, the pirate mimicking her movements so he was still behind her back.

'Oh no he isn't!'

'He is! He is!'

'Quiet down a bit, eh, sweetie?' I whispered.

'But why won't he *listen*, Aunty Becky?' Pip asked. 'I've told him a *majillion* times, and he won't look round. And now there!' She clapped her little hands. 'I TOLD YOU!' Pip shouted as Captain Hook's henchman scampered away with Tinkerbell's tiny house under his arm.

I wondered whether I should have another crack at explaining that the panto was just pretend. That Peter wasn't a little boy who would never grow up but a *Hollyoaks* actress in her mid-twenties, and 'the lady with hair like Aunty Yo-yo's' playing Mrs Smee, the pirates' cook, was actually a six-three former Leeds United striker. Except I suspected, underneath her indignation, that Pip was having a great time.

'Serves you right! Serves you flippin' well right, you big *silly*!' she was shouting at Peter now. 'Doesn't it, Aunty Becky? He should've listened when I told him. I *said* the bad man would take Tinkerbell. And now she'll be all on her own and scared, coz of him not listening.'

'Don't get too upset about it, Pipsqueak. Peter and the Lost Boys'll save Tink, double-triple aunty promise.'

I held out my crooked little finger to seal the double-triple promise, but she was too absorbed to notice.

'If I was him, I wouldn't have let the man get even near a bit. I would've – oh my goodness, he's come back! Peter! *PETER!*'

And off she went again, standing up on her chair to get Peter's attention.

'Can you please calm your little girl?' a man sitting behind said. 'My grandson can't see a thing.'

I turned to flash him an apologetic smile. 'Sorry. My niece has never been to a pantomime before. She has a bit of an over-active imagination.'

'If you can't keep her under control, you really ought to take her home,' the man grunted as Pip waved her arms at the stage, shrieking her head off.

I frowned. 'Ok, no need to get in a lather about it. She's only five. Audience participation is all part of the fun, isn't it?'

'Yes, well,' he muttered. 'There's audience participation and there's plain disruptive. She's ruining it for the other children.' He sent me a pointed look. 'You know, the well-mannered ones.'

With a final glare, I tugged Pip's hand, whispering for her to get back in her seat. She grudgingly sat down, amid dark mutterings that Peter Pan must be either deaf or stupid not to hear her.

***

'So, how was it?' Cameron asked when I'd taken Pip home. She was snuggled between me and her dads on the giant floor beanbag while I gratefully supped a post-panto glass of wine the lads had been considerate enough to have waiting for me. 'Did you two girls have fun?'

I mouthed the words 'never again' over his daughter's head before slapping on a bright smile.

'Oh, we had a fantabulous time – that's a panto word, we learned it tonight. Didn't we, Pipsqueak?'

Pip's voice was still hoarse from shouting, but she grinned happily at Cam. 'It was brilliant, Daddy! I mean, er, it was fantastulous – that's a special pantomime word. Peter Pan was a total stupid! But I told him right off, didn't I, Aunty Becky?'

'You certainly did, sweetie,' I said. 'For two whole hours.'

'*And* I learned a new joke,' Pip said, puffing herself up. 'Better'n my dinosaur one, even.'

Tom pulled her onto his knee. 'Will it make me laugh?'

'Yup!' She shuffled on his lap to face him, looking sober as she prepared to deliver The Joke (TM). To Pip, comedy was a serious business. 'Ok. This is my new joke. Ready, Papa?'

'As I'll ever be.'

Her brow puckered with concentration. 'Why – right – why are pirates called pirates?'

'Dunno. Why are pirates called pirates?'

'Because they *arrrr!*'

Pip looked smug as Tom forced a loud belly laugh, suppressing the groan I could see hiding behind his eyes.

Cameron leaned round his husband's back to talk to me. 'Were they all like that?' he muttered.

'That was the best one. Two solid hours, Cam. Two. Solid. Hours.'

'Eesh. Sorry.'

'Come on then, Pips,' Tom said. 'Time for Lost Girls to fly up to bed.'

'You need fairy dust to fly, Papa.'

'Oh, do you now?' Tom swung her up onto his shoulders and jumped to his feet. 'Then what just happened?'

Pip giggled. 'Flying?'

'Yep. Dad magic, even stronger than fairy dust. Come on, kiddo, we can make up –' he paused – 'two whole stories, I think, before it's absolutely sleeptime.'

He shot an enquiring look at Cameron, who nodded slightly to show he was fine with two whole stories. Parenting code. After three years on aunty duty, I was just about starting to get how it worked.

'Yay, stories! Na'night, Daddy. Na'night, Aunty Becky,' Pip called as Tom flew her to the door and galloped away up the stairs. 'Don't let the bedbugs – argh!' She broke off into giggles when Tom dived her into an unexpected swoop at the top of the landing.

I sagged into the beanbag and held up my wine glass.

'That bad, eh?' Cam said, pouring me a refill.

'Worse. That kid of yours'll be the death of me.'

'Heh, join the club. Thanks for taking her, Becks.'

'My pleasure. And at least 43% of me really means that.' I smiled. 'Honestly, though, she was adorable. Couldn't convince her it was pretend.'

'Well, you've done your babysitting stint. Next month she can go to Aunty Lana and Uncle Stew. They need to be getting some practice in.'

'No news?'

'Nope. I swear Lana's started physically vibrating with the stress.'

'Think it'll be much longer?'

'Yeah, could be a while yet. They still have to go through a load of background checks, plus medicals and stuff.'

'How long did you and Tom have to wait till the adoption agency said you could move to the next stage?'

'Two months. Then another four of training before they finally started finding us a match. God, it was hell.' He smiled at the photo of the three of them hanging over the fireplace. 'Worth it though.'

'Poor Lana. I'll pop round on Monday after work, see if I can take her mind off it.' I sipped my wine with the relish that can only come from hours looking after someone else's kid. 'How was date night?'

'Honestly? You want all the gory detail?'

I shrugged. 'Might as well live my sex life vicariously through yours, since I'm getting bugger all.'

'Tom'll kill me for telling you.'

'What? Spanking? Whipped cream? Go on, I can take it.'

He fell back into the squishy beanbag. 'Sleep. Sweet, glorious sleep. I was out like a light within half an hour of the girl being gone.'

I laughed. 'Poor Tommy.'

'I know, he'd got massage oil and everything. Still, think he appreciated the peace and quiet. That's the ultimate aphrodisiac for us these days.'

'Come on. Don't pretend you're not loving this.'

'Yeah,' he said with a sigh. 'I'm knackered, but I know Pip's the best thing we ever did.'

'No arguments here.' I gave his arm a squeeze. 'And I'm trying not to be jealous, honestly. Even if my baby brother is ahead of me in the real-life Game of Life.'

'You know, they actually just call that life.'

I sighed. 'Wish I knew when my turn would come. Over two years now me and Cole have been talking about getting married and starting a family.' I held up the finger that bore my engagement ring and watched as the light danced from the heart of the diamond. 'I never thought we'd still be at the pre-planning stage by the time we reached our mid-thirties.'

'Pre-planning? God, you make your life sound like a PowerPoint presentation.' Cam leaned on his elbow to look at me. 'It'll happen, Becks. You're home, aren't you? Moving to Egglethwaite was supposed to be the first step.'

'It is nice to be back where there's wide open spaces,' I admitted. 'We wouldn't have been able to keep a hamster in that Finsbury Park matchbox, let alone a baby.'

'Exactly. And now all the other life goals can follow.'

'Ugh. Life goals. Have you been watching *Loose Women* again?'

'I find it empowering,' he said, tossing his head. 'I'm right though, aren't I? Step one: The Big Move. Step two: The Big Wedding. Step three: The Big Bouncing Baby. Or the other way round, if your biological clock's giving you gyp.'

'Hmm. You seem to be forgetting I haven't actually got the necessary equipment to hand for bouncing babies, since Cole and all his attached baby-making apparatus is still down in London.'

'You want to borrow Tommy for the night?'

'Will he bring his massage oil?'

Cam shrugged. 'Yeah, if you want. We're not having a fry-up tomorrow.'

I laughed. 'Best not, eh? I don't fancy explaining that one to Dad and Cynthia, keen as they are for another grandkid.' I put my wine down. 'Right, I'd better go.'

'Why, have you got plans?'

'Yep. PJs, pinot, early night. Bliss.'

Cam shook his head. 'Can you stop being so bloody old? It's half-eight on a Friday night. Stay and have a few drinks with us.'

Chapter 1

I hesitated. It did sound tempting.

'Well... half a glass,' I said. 'But then I really have to go. Cole's due to ring at nine.'

'It's not healthy, you know,' Cameron said as he topped up my wine.

'Cam, you're doing that voice again.'

'Well, honestly, you can't keep this up. You here, fiancé at the other end of the country. Shutting yourself up like a nun every night while you wait for him to call. I thought the pair of you were moving here to build a new life. You know, get out and be part of things?'

'We have to talk, don't we?' I said, trying not to sound defensive.

'Every night though?' he said. 'We wouldn't mind seeing you for an evening now and again. How about quiz night at the Fox on Thursday with Stew and Lana? Come on, we could use another brain.'

'Well... maybe. If Cole doesn't mind.'

'Seriously, you have to get permission before you're allowed to play out?'

'No. I just don't want to hurt his feelings.' I sighed. 'Look, I was the one who convinced him moving here was a good idea. I can hardly complain if his job means he has to stay in London a while, can I? We can't afford for either of us to be out of work if we're hoping for a wedding next year.'

'But how long can you live like that?'

'It won't be for long. Just until there's a job opening within commuting distance.'

'And when's that likely to happen? This isn't London, there aren't just art lecturer jobs for the asking.'

'We need to be patient, that's all.' I downed the last of my wine. 'Right, I really have to go. Tell Tommy I said bye.'

Chapter 2

I frowned at the door handle of the old Victorian terrace I rented at the bottom of Egglethwaite's cobbled main street. Something wasn't right.

In the three months I'd lived there I'd become accustomed to the handle's severe case of brewer's droop, and after locking up I'd got into the habit of pushing it upwards until it stuck in a jauntier position. Well, it looked so pathetic, sagging about. Life was depressing enough without suicidal door handles.

I always pushed it up. Always. Yet there it was, flopping miserably. Who'd been fiddling with it?

I waggled it, in a momentary panic about burglars with stripy jumpers and swag bags, but the door was still locked.

Hmm. Joggled by the postie, maybe.

'Hello?' I called as I went in, just in case my dad and stepmum, the only other people with a key, had called round.

No answer. I flicked on the living room light and breathed a sigh of relief to see everything as it had been that morning – TV, laptop, furniture, all right where I'd left them. Just a minor attack of paranoia.

I jogged upstairs to my room and chucked on a clingy black top and pyjama bottoms – not much point tarting myself up from the waist down for FaceTiming – then did a rush job on my make-up. Lippy, eyeliner, mascara...

I wanted to look like I'd made an effort. Our daily phone calls were the closest we got to dates these days, apart from the rare occasions Cole came up for a weekend visit. We tried to limit those though. Train tickets from London weren't cheap, and we had a wedding to save for – a family soon too, if everything went to plan. A lot of what had been in the pot had been reallocated to the move up to Yorkshire, so there was a bit of catching up to do.

I popped my phone in its dock and sat staring at the screen. As usual, it lit up with an incoming video call at nine on the dot. I beamed at it. He never forgot and he was never late, which showed that no matter how far apart we were, Cole was thinking about me.

'Hello, beautiful,' a gentle, cut-glass voice said when I'd swiped to answer the call.

'Hiya,' I said, waving manically at the boyish face with its rumpled blonde hair and slightly bewildered-by-life expression smiling back at me. 'Bang on time, as always.'

'A date's a date.' He stared out of the glass at me for a second, taking in my appearance. 'You look pretty. Have you been out?'

'Yep. To the theatre, no less. Get me, eh?'

He blinked. 'The theatre? You?'

'All right, no need to sound so surprised. I'm cultured. I do culture.'

'Since when?'

'Hey. Like five times I've watched *The Sound of Music*.'

He laughed. 'Ok, so you're cultured. What was the play?'

'*Peter Pan*.'

'Oh.'

I smiled at his puzzled expression. 'Go on then, I'll come clean. It was a pantomime. I went with our Pip while her dads grabbed a bit of couple time.'

'Did you have fun, darling?'

I shrugged. 'Bit naff, to be honest. I mean, even for a panto it was naff – not a patch on the ones we used to have in Egglethwaite when me and Cam were kids. But Pip enjoyed herself.'

'You have them in the village?'

'We did, at the temperance hall. Amateur productions, but they were pretty awesome. Didn't you?'

'Not where I grew up. The masters used to put one on at school every once in a while.'

'Really? Wouldn't have thought they'd have anything as frivolous as a pantomime at Posh School.'

'Oh, even we were allowed to take the frock coats off and let our hair down at Christmas,' Cole said. 'Mind you, it always seemed rather foolish to a studious little scholarship boy like me. I thought I'd die of embarrassment the day I first saw our Latin master in his big flouncy dress and Marilyn Monroe wig.'

'Well, that's public school for you. Taking prep, was he?'

He looked puzzled. 'No, he was the dame.'

'I know,' I said, smiling. 'Joke, Cole.'

'Oh. Ok. I knew that.' He wiped a palm over his eyes. 'Tired, that's all. Sorry, Becky.'

'Rough day at college?' I asked gently.

Cole was a landscape painter, but like many a talented young artist, he'd discovered that while flogging canvases was good for pocket money, it was no way to pay the bills. On weekdays he lectured in art history at an adult education college.

'No worse than usual,' he said. 'It's getting ready for this exhibition that's really taking it out of me. There's still so much to finish.'

'Poor Cole. Here I am moaning about a lack of quality panto while you've been painting your little socks off at all hours.'

'My socks are a good, manly size, thank you.'

I smiled. 'Wish you were here, love.'

'So do I.' He kissed his fingertips and touched them to the screen. 'It seems like so long since I was able to hold you at bedtime.'

'How long will we have to do this, Cole? I miss you.'

'Just a little while, that's all. I'm selling more now, since the last exhibition at Ryder's gallery. And just as soon as a lecturer position opens up in Yorkshire, I'll be there like a whippet up a trouser leg.'

'Offensive,' I said, raising my eyes. 'Anyway, that's ferrets. Check your stereotypes, Lord Snooty.'

Cole laughed. 'Sorry. I'll be sure to do some revision before I move.' He softened his voice. 'Are you very lonely without me, darling?'

'Sometimes,' I admitted. 'I mean, I've got my family, but I've been away from the village so long, it almost feels like I'm an outsider again. Not that I'm not glad to be back,' I added hastily. 'I do think it was the right decision for us – or it will be, when we can be together.'

'It'll be soon, I promise.'

'Cam thinks I should get out more. Him and Tom want me to join their quiz team at the local pub.'

'And are you going to?'

'I don't know, what do you think? It'd mean missing our Thursday night date-call.'

He smiled. 'Well, it's not very fair to keep you all to myself. Your brother's right, you should have more of a social life than just chatting to me.'

'I like chatting to you.'

'Still. We planned for a life in Egglethwaite because we wanted to build a future there. That really should mean becoming part of the community,' he said. 'Go out and have fun,

Becky. Join a club or something perhaps, make friends. I feel awful thinking of you alone.'

'It's not your fault. I knew this was the way things would have to be for a while.' I sighed. 'But I do feel a bit isolated. You sure you don't mind me going out without you?'

'Of course not, darling. We've never exactly lived in each other's pockets, have we? I can console myself with a goodnight text in lieu of a phone call.'

I smiled. 'You're the perfect man, you know that?'

'I know.'

'And quite touchingly humble.'

'I know that too.'

I reached out to touch the phone screen. 'Hate thinking of you so far away.'

'Then don't,' he said, with the hint of a smile. 'Just a minute.'

Cole stood up from whatever he'd been perching on, and a second later the screen went dark.

'Cole?' I tapped it a few times. 'Cole? You still there?'

'I'm still here.'

I stared at the screen. But this wasn't a tinny, muffled phone voice. Slowly I turned my head.

'Oh my God!'

I blinked a couple of times to make sure he wasn't going to disappear. Yes, it was really Cole: gorgeous, rumpled and most importantly life-sized, filling my bedroom doorframe. It felt like so long since I'd seen him, he'd almost become a dream. And now here he was, as solid as ever and beaming at me.

'When did you get here?' I managed to gasp. 'How did you get in? Where did you call me from?'

'Right before you got home. Spare key under the shed door, same place you always hide it. And the attic, respectively.' He glanced down my body and laughed when he took in my strappy top and baggy lounge pants. 'So this is what you wear to FaceTime me, is it? And to think I always imagined you in lacy hotpants.'

'I can't believe you're here,' I whispered. 'Why did you come, Cole?'

He came and crouched in front of where I was perched on the bed, putting his arms around my waist. 'To surprise you.' He glanced up towards the ceiling. 'And on a more prosaic note, I wanted to have a look around that attic space to see if it would be suitable as a studio. A little small, but I think it will do.'

'How long can you stay?' I asked, nuzzling into his neck to absorb his familiar scent.

'Only until the morning,' he said with a guilty grimace. 'I'm sorry, Becky. I know it's an expensive trip for just one night together, but I have to put in some painting this weekend if I'm going to be ready for my exhibition.'

'You sure you can't stay longer?' I looked up from his neck to give my eyelashes a suggestive flutter. 'I can ask my stepmum if she could man the shop for me tomorrow. We could stay in bed all day.'

He smiled. 'Harlot.'

'That's why you asked me to marry you,' I said, smiling. 'You can leave it till tomorrow night, can't you?'

'I really can't stay that long.'

'The afternoon then.' I sighed, casting my eyes upwards in my best wounded martyr pose. 'You wouldn't want me to become one of these poor frustrated housewives, would you? Forced to get her kicks from travelling plumbers and milkmen?'

'Well... if you're determined to fight dirty, midday then. But absolutely not a second longer.'

'Three o'clock.'

'Two.'

'Done,' I said, shaking his hand. I glanced over my shoulder at the bed. 'So that gives us just over sixteen hours. Better make a start, eh?'

Cole rolled his eyes. 'Oh, the windswept romance of it all.'

'What can I say? I'm a romantic.'

He got to his feet and pressed a gentle kiss to my fingers, just over the engagement ring he'd given me nearly two years ago now.

'Still my girl, Becky Finn?' he asked softly.

'Always,' I whispered, pulling him down onto the bed.

Chapter 3

'You're glowing today,' Tom's sister Lana said when I dropped into her restaurant the following Monday.

'Yeah.' I stifled a yawn. 'Treated myself to a pamper weekend. Really seems to have done the trick.'

'What sort of pampering?'

'Oh, you know. Duvet day, face mask, good book.'

'That's your story and you're sticking to it, are you?'

I frowned. 'You what?'

She smiled for a customer who'd approached the counter. 'Here's a menu, sir. Specials are the game pie, chicken and leek pie or the Man vs Pie pie. Just take a seat, someone'll be with you in a minute.'

When he'd gone, she turned back to me. 'It's just, I heard from Yo-yo who heard from Rita who heard from Valerie that "some blonde beefcake" – direct quote, as if you can't tell – was seen sneaking into your place on Friday night.'

'Is nothing private in this village?'

'Not while the Ladies Who Lunch gossipvine's in operation. So Cole was up, was he?'

'Just for the one night. He had to get back to London.'

'You should've brought him over,' she said. 'I'm sure me and Stew could've found you a nice, quiet table in lovers' corner.'

I cocked an eyebrow. 'What, our first night alone together in months and you want me to drag him to this place for pie and peas?'

'Why not? Very romantic, pie and peas.'

I grinned. 'Was never going to happen anyway. We didn't leave the bedroom till half an hour before his train was due on Saturday.'

'Nympho.'

'Yep.'

'Come on then, let's have a few details.'

'Certainly not,' I said, tilting my nose. 'A woman's mucky weekend with her fiancé is her own personal, private business.'

'Aww, go on. Just an overview to liven up my shift.'

I nodded to the man she'd just directed to a table, who was approaching the counter with a black look on his face.

'Oh look,' I said. 'An angry customer.'

'How very convenient for you.'

She slapped on a bright smile as I sidled away to the bar.

'Excuse me,' the man said. 'Is this the only menu?'

'Just that and the specials,' Lana said. 'Is there a problem?'

'Well, yes. There's nothing on it but pies.'

'That's right. This is Pie and a Pint. I mean, that's literally the name of the restaurant.'

There was a lad leaning against the bar at my side. 'These're always worth watching,' he said, bending to whisper in my ear.

'I know the restaurant's called Pie and a Pint, but I didn't think that was all you'd have,' the customer told Lana stiffly.

'Why didn't you?' she said. 'It's right there above the door. Pie. And a pint. In big, shiny letters, with a picture of a pie and another of a pint. The last thing you could accuse us of is false advertising.'

I nudged the man next to me. 'She's unleashing the sarcasm. Could be fireworks.'

'Right then,' the customer snapped. 'One game pie, if that's really all you've got, and a small red wine.'

'I'm afraid if you want wine, you'll have to order it by the pint,' Lana said. Cruelly deprived of sordid details about my sex life, I could tell this was the highlight of her afternoon.

The customer's eyebrows rocketed up. 'You're joking. Are you really telling me all you do in this place is pie and a pint?'

'No, we're pretty broad-minded. If you don't fancy pie and a pint, we're quite open to serving you the pint first and then the pie.'

'Stew!' the bloke next to me called to the good-looking blonde man tending bar. 'Your missus is getting herself into bother.'

'Oh God, not again.' Stewart groaned and put down the glass he was polishing. 'Watch the bar a sec, Marcus. Honestly, she's been primed to go off ever since we put our adoption application in.'

Stewart hurried to the counter, and we heard him trying to explain his wife's idea of a joke to the poor customer while Lana, smirking, came to join us.

'You don't serve wine by the pint,' I said.

'Course we don't. I just thought a bit of mischief might cheer Stew up. He's been so tense since the adoption application went in.'

The man called Marcus grinned at me. 'Déjà vu, eh?'

'So you two've met, have you?' Lana said.

'We're about to.' He shook my hand. 'Marcus Teasdale.'

'Becky Finn.'

His gaze flickered to the diamond sparkling on my left hand. 'Ah, shame. Hope he's worth it.'

I smiled. 'He is.'

'Marcus is Deano's brother,' Lana told me.

My eyes widened. 'Bloody hell, there's more than one of them?'

It'd never occurred to me that Pie and a Pint's eccentric chef Deano had relatives. I'd always assumed he was the result of some bizarre DNA experiment in a Play-Doh factory.

'Yep,' Marcus said, grinning. 'My parents were obviously lulled into a false sense of security when I turned out all right, so like fools they went on to have Deano.'

'Marc's a wizard, you know.' Lana glanced at the counter, where Stewart, having dealt with the difficult customer, was staring morosely into the distance. 'Can you guys watch the bar while I see if Stew's ok? Poor lamb, he's struggling at the moment.'

'When'll you hear?' Marcus asked.

'Could be months till the background checks are done.' She sighed. 'So much riding on it.'

She went to Stewart and put a loving arm round his waist. He smiled, bending to plant a kiss on her dark curls.

'Sweet couple,' Marcus said. 'What's your connection?'

'Sister-in-law.' I frowned. 'Or sister-in-law once removed, if that's a thing. My brother's married to Lana's brother.'

'Ah right, you're Cam's sister. He told me he had one, but I thought he was just making it up to sound cool.'

'So how about you?'

'Oh, I've known them since the Dark Ages. Deano was working here back when the place was still a medieval restaurant.' He nodded to Galahad, the suit of armour Lana kept propped against the bar for old times' sake.

'What is it Lana thinks you're so wizard in then? Kitchen, garden, bedroom?'

'Well definitely not the first two. Deano got all the cooking genes and I've killed off three spider plants and a peace lily so far.'

'Third one?'

He grinned. 'Not really for me to say. Happy to give you a demo though, if the fiancé's ok with it.'

'So what are you a wizard at?'

'Magic. I mean, I'm an actual wizard. Card-carrying.'

Oh God. So he was one of these New Age Wiccan types, was he? All pentangles and healing crystals, probably. I should've known there was something wrong with him when he'd started flirting with me.

He laughed at the look on my face. 'Ok, so I'm not technically a Hogwarts graduate. I am a magician though. Professionally, that's what I do.'

'Seriously?'

'Yep.' He smiled. 'What? Some people have to be magicians.'

I sized him up. Marcus was tall and lean – so far, so magiciany – but he was a long way from a David Blaine, or even a Dynamo.

His hair was longish, the tight black curls twisting together into spidery fronds. He was dressed casually in jeans and a grungy white t-shirt that contrasted with the rich mocha of his skin, and his relaxed, don't-care attitude, his easy one-sided smile, as he leaned against the bar seemed calculated to put people at their ease.

'You're too good-looking to be a magician,' I told him flatly. 'And too ordinary.'

I don't know why it popped into my head to say that. It was the sort of crack I might make to Lana or Cam, who knew me well enough to know when I was joking, but this guy was a virtual stranger.

Marcus didn't look offended though.

'Yeah? What's your job then?' he said.

'I run a costume shop in Skipton. Fancypants.'

'Ah, right. That'd explain the outfit.'

I laughed. '*Touché.*'

'So, do you believe me? I am a 100% bona fide magician, I swear.'

'Hmm. Not sure,' I said, squinting one eye. 'You haven't even got a beard.'

'They're not mandatory, you know. The Magic Circle's very open-minded about the whole beard thing nowadays.'

'Prove it. Do me a trick.'

'All right. Bet you 50p I can make your breasts move without touching them.'

'That's not a trick, it's an off-colour chat-up line. Go on. You must have a pack of cards stashed somewhere.'

'Sorry. Left them in my other, more magic jeans.'

'Ha! Typical. No beard, no cape, no cards. Bet you haven't even got a proper magician name.'

'Such as?'

'Dunno, The Great Awesome-o or whatever.'

He laughed. 'Nope, just Marcus.' He gestured to Lana, heading back in our direction. 'Here's your sister three times removed or whatever. I'd better drop in on Deano and get off.' With a nod of goodbye, he walked off.

'You two looked like you were making friends,' Lana said when she joined me.

'Seems a nice lad. He's not really a magician, is he?'

'Yep, kids' parties. We're thinking of booking him for Pip's birthday barbecue.'

I watched Marcus disappear into the kitchen, wondering how he'd look in a top hat.

'Hey, want to hear a joke?' Lana asked.

'Ugh, not more jokes. Got enough of them at the pantomime.'

'It's a good one. Why are tables called tables?'

'Dunno, why?'

'Because they *arrr*.'

I laughed. 'I see Pip's been round.'

'Yeah, Tom and Cam brought her over on Saturday to tell us all about the panto. In quick succession I got why are pirates called pirates, why are tables called tables, why is Uncle Stew called Uncle Stew, all with the same punchline.'

'She's a cutie,' I said with a fond smile.

'Hey, why don't you and Cole take her out together next time he's up? It'll be good practice for you.'

'Yeah, good idea. Cole's not really spent much time with kids. Probably should ease him in gently to the parenthood thing.'

'Well, you've got a while yet. He needs a job before you start thinking weddings and babies.'

'I just hope it's not too long a while, that's all.' I flicked a fingernail against the service bell on the bar. 'I'm thirty-four, Lana. There's only so long I can keep telling my body clock to shut up.'

'When is he next up?'

'Next month.' I sighed. 'It feels so empty in the house, just me.'

'Then get yourself out. You can't sit at home every night just because you feel guilty.'

I stared at her. 'How did you know I feel guilty?'

She shrugged. 'Obvious.'

'Cole was saying I should join a club or something.'

'There you go then. Hey, you busy tonight?'

'Not really,' I said cautiously, wondering what she was planning. Twice since moving up I'd let her lure me to the pub for a girls' night, and both times it hadn't been pretty. 'You're not going to get me drunk again, are you?'

'Why don't you come to the village society meeting with me and Tom? I can always get you drunk after.'

I frowned. 'What, those old fogies?'

'Why not? They're a good bunch, and we need young blood,' she said. 'Ok, so it's not hours of endless fun, but it's right at the heart of the village. You get to know everyone.'

'Do you?'

'Absolutely. And Gerry and Sue will be there. Yolanda too.'

'Heh. Yo-yo.' The image of my old Brownie leader, magenta-haired and larger than life, appeared in my mind. 'Not seen her for years. She's a member too, is she?'

'Yep, one of the lifers.'

I thought about it. The meetings sounded pretty tedious, but Lana was right, it would be a good way to get back into the swing of small community life. And no group that included Yolanda Sommerville could ever be truly boring.

'Ok, go on,' I said at last. 'I'll see you there.'

Chapter 4

'So what happens at these things?' I asked when I'd taken a seat between Lana and Tom in Egglethwaite Temperance Hall's meeting room. We were the first three there – well, four if you counted Lana's border collie Flash, an honorary village society member, who was asleep under the table.

'Roger Collingwood witters on for a couple of hours, then we all go for a pint at the Fox to recover,' Lana said. 'That's basically it.'

'Sounds fascinating.'

'We keep ourselves amused.' She leaned round me to talk to her brother. 'Ok, a Guinness on Rodge to mention his villa in Provence.'

'Do I get innuendo siren then?'

'Yep. Bag of peanuts for one innuendo, beer for two.'

'What are you two going on about?' I asked.

Tom grinned. 'Just a few games.'

'How'd you get roped into this anyway?'

'Our dad was a member. When he died, felt like it was our turn to start putting something back.' Tom reached over me to prod Lana. 'Brought the average age of the society down by about 20 years, didn't we, sis?'

'Yep,' Lana said proudly. 'The only members under fifty.'

'When did you join?' I asked.

'Four years ago, after the Grand Départ came through Egglethwaite. We worked really hard to get our viaduct reopened for that. Felt a bit lost afterwards without something useful to do.'

'I won't lie, it's not exactly enthralling. But it is important.' Tom gestured around the room. 'Keeps this place standing, for a start.'

I took in the fading tangerine paint, the worn carpet tiles covered in black blobs of old chewing gum – the same tiles I'd stood on when I'd used this room for junior karate class nearly 25 years ago. It might even have been my gum.

'Looks like it could use some TLC.'

'It is going through a rough patch,' Lana said, looking glum. 'The council slashed pretty much all our funding in the last round of cuts.'

'That's not good –' I began, but Tom batted a hand to indicate we should shush. I glanced over my shoulder to see more folk filing in.

First was Roger Collingwood, the stern-looking chair and conductor of Egglethwaite Silver Band. Then came farmers Gerry and Sue Lightowler, Lana and Tom's surrogate parents, who'd helped their dad bring them up after his wife died young. After them, Yolanda Sommerville, chair of the WI – now re-branded as Ladies Who Lunch – flounced in. She was shrouded in scarves and clinging tightly to her new fiancé Billy, landlord of our local pub the Sooty Fox.

Gerry and Sue I knew well, but the others... it was strange, seeing them smiling politely with no glimmer of recognition. I remembered them all so clearly from when I was a kid. I felt like I ought to belong, but to the villagers who barely remembered me I was just another outsider.

'Don't be nervous,' Lana whispered. 'Honestly, everyone's dead friendly.'

'Well, shall we start with introductions?' Roger said, beaming at me. 'I see we have a new face at the table.'

Chapter 4

I smiled nervously. 'Hi. Becky Finn. I, um, just moved back. I used to live here, a long time ago.'

'Oh, we remember you perfectly, darling,' Yolanda said with a condescending smile.

'Do you?'

'Of course. You were one of those dreadfully sticky children, weren't you? We always had such a time getting the jam out of your hair on pack holiday when I was your Brown Owl.' Her gaze flickered up to my short, choppy blonde hair. 'You did get it all out in the end, didn't you?'

I flushed scarlet. 'Er, yes. I think so.'

'No teasing the poor girl, Yo-yo.' Sue smiled warmly at me. 'Glad you decided to come along, pet. Liven us oldies up a bit.' She held up a hand to Yolanda, who'd opened her mouth to object. 'Not you. You're lively enough for three of us.'

'The old girl prefers "of unknown antiquity" these days,' Billy said, blowing his betrothed a kiss.

Yolanda flashed him a dirty look. 'Why I was ever talked into accepting you, I'll never know.'

'Someone was bound to make an honest woman of you eventually.' He nudged Gerry. 'Not quite sure how I ended up drawing the short straw,' he muttered.

Lana grinned. 'How's it going, Billy? You look a bit tired.'

'Don't you believe it, love. Sexual prowess of a man half my age.' Billy shot a wary look at Yolanda. 'Good thing too.'

'Is it always like this?' I muttered to Tom.

'No, they're just trying to impress you. This is the softcore banter we save for newbies.'

Roger cleared his throat in best headmaster style. 'If you've quite finished with the usual pre-meeting japery, perhaps we can get on.'

He passed me an agenda, and I skimmed down the list of items.

Lana was right, it was riveting stuff. Village problems to be discussed included the impact of randy bulls on drystone walling, whether Kit Beeton's new hot tub was lowering the tone of the neighbourhood, and finding a Santa for the Christmas Fair after one too many sherries had sent the previous incumbent off to the great elf workshop in the sky. Fundraising for the temperance hall was the last item on the list.

By nine, after over an hour of Roger's monotonous drone, I was half nodding off. Lana kicked me under the table.

'You listening?' she whispered. 'This is racy stuff. You're missing all the action at Kit Beeton's hot-tub parties.'

I stifled a yawn. 'How come Flash is allowed a nap and not me?'

'He's earned it through years of long service playing Santa's reindeer at the Christmas Fair.'

'All right, next item,' Roger said. 'Father Christmas. Sadly, following the death of Eric Spiggott in January, we now have a full complement of elves, one reindeer –' he nodded at Flash – 'but not the old gent himself. So if anyone can recommend a mature male character actor able to provide his own rosy cheeks and belly, I'm sure we can dig up the requisite uniform.'

'Oh! I can help with that,' I said, pleased to finally have something to contribute. 'I run a costume hire place. More than happy to supply a Santa Special at no charge.'

Roger smiled. 'How kind, my dear.'

'You've just said his favourite words,' Tom whispered. 'Roger gets the same thrill from "no charge" that most of us get from sex.'

'I heard that,' Roger said, frowning.

'Why don't you do it, Rodge?' Sue demanded. 'You're the oldest.'

'He hasn't got the stomach for it,' Billy said, glancing down Roger's skinny frame. 'Gerry's our man, if you ask me. Save us a bit on pillows.'

'Oi. Fuel tank for a sex machine, lad.' Gerry patted his over-spilling beer gut proudly, ignoring Sue's snort.

'Woowoo?' I heard Tom say under his breath.

'Not an innuendo,' Lana muttered.

'Aww.'

'As you all know perfectly well, I'll be unable to attend the fair,' Roger said with exaggerated self-importance. 'Irene and I will be in Provence.'

Lana shot Tom a grin that even I could tell was code for 'you owe me a pint'.

'Well I'm not doing it,' Gerry said, folding his arms. 'Red's not my colour.'

Sue nodded. 'Clashes with the blood vessels in his nose.'

'Come on, Gerry, why not?' Tom said.

'I'll look daft, that's why not.'

Lana snorted. 'And yet you and the Egglethwaite Morrismen'll happily attach bells to your arses every first of May.'

'That's different. We have to do that to summon the summer.'

'This is Yorkshire, Gerry. We don't get summer.'

He shrugged. 'Never said we were any good at it.'

'Go on, Uncle Gerry, do it for Pip,' Tom said. 'She'll be gutted if I tell her Santa's not coming to the fair.'

'Oof!' Gerry said as Sue dug him in the ribs. 'All right, all right. If I'm getting a battering off the wife and uncled by the kids, s'pose I've got no choice.'

'Excellent.' Roger ticked the item off his agenda with a satisfied flourish.

'I'd better get free mince pies though,' Gerry muttered.

Roger's face assumed a serious expression. 'And now, the most important item. The hall's finances.' He glanced up from his agenda. 'It's not looking good, folks.'

'How serious is it, Roger?' Yolanda asked quietly, concerned enough even to drop her usual affected 'darling'. 'Will we make another year?'

'We... should,' Roger said cautiously. He passed around a printed spreadsheet. 'It really depends on how we weather the winter. Flood damage, closure due to snow – one disaster and we could be shutting our doors permanently in the new year.'

'Oh my God,' I m§uttered, staring at the spreadsheet. The final balance showed a far from healthy £1,500 in the bank, and income from the groups who used the place was barely covering outgoings. 'I had no idea things were so desperate.'

Roger flashed me a sad smile. 'Yes, for some time now. And there's no hard and fast fix, I'm sorry to say.'

'Ok, that innuendo you can have,' Lana whispered to Tom.

'But how did it get like this?' I asked. 'The Temp was thriving when I was a kid. Karate, ballet, Scouts, tea dances – there was always something on.'

'And so there is still,' Roger said. 'The hall is very much the soul of the village. It would break people's hearts to see it go.'

'But have you tried everything? What about increasing rents?'

I flushed when I noticed Billy roll his eyes.

'Sorry,' I mumbled. 'I'm new, what do I know? The Temp meant a lot to me when I was a kid, that's all.'

Sue reached across to pat my hand. 'Pay no attention to them, love. We could use some fresh perspective.'

'Increasing rents was the first thing we did when the place got into difficulties,' Roger said. 'People knew we'd lost our funding, and they were understanding for the most part. But it wasn't enough. This building's over 170 years old, it costs more every year to keep it in good repair.'

'We couldn't increase rents that drastically again,' Yolanda said.

Chapter 4

'What she means is, we don't want to price anyone out,' Tom said. 'It's the people on the lowest incomes who benefit most from the place.'

'That is true.' I thought back to my family's early days in the village, when Dad was struggling to make a go of the chippy he ran with his partner Cynthia. Money had been tight, and the Temp had been a lifeline for me and Cam. 'But raising rents has to be better than shutting the place down so no one can use it.'

'I agree,' Roger said. 'However, rent increase does need to be a last resort. People would never forgive us if costs forced their group to close.'

Sue had been watching me the whole time we'd been talking. I had an odd sensation she was reading my thoughts.

'You said the Temp was important to you,' she said. 'Tell us why.'

'I suppose with the village being so tight-knit, it gave me a way in,' I said. 'I was seven when we moved here, and the kids at school had their own little cliques already. It was the stuff I did at the Temp that helped me feel I belonged. Youthie – that's what we called the Youth Club – karate, Brownies...' I laughed nervously, dropping my gaze in the face of their stares. 'And here I am again. Hoping the place'll help me find another way back in.'

Sue was silent a moment. Then she turned to Roger. 'So what can we do about it then?' she demanded. 'We need to make money, shore up our reserves.'

'Cake sale?' Yolanda suggested brightly.

Sue tutted. 'Not every problem in life can be solved by bloody cake sales, Yolanda Sommerville.'

'That depends very much on who's baking the cakes.'

'How about another beetle drive?' Tom said, interrupting before an argument kicked off. Even when I was a kid, Sue and Yolanda's caking rivalry had been notorious. 'Those always go down well.'

Lana shook her head. 'The last one didn't, we only made £45. I think we've glutted demand.'

'Band concert?' I suggested.

'Did one last month.' Lana sighed. 'It's the same old things, isn't it? People want to support the hall, but let's face it, they're bored rigid of the band and the morrismen and the Ladies Who Lunch cake sales, and they've had it up to their jugulars with bloody beetle drives. We need to think of something new.'

'This place didn't get council funding back in the eighties, did it?' Billy said.

'No,' Gerry said. 'It was all paid for through rents and fundraising.'

'So how did it make ends meet in those days?' I asked.

'Same really. Beetle drives and so on. There was less to pay for back then.'

'Still. Must've been a lot to raise. What was the biggest earner after rents?'

Gerry shrugged. 'I wasn't in the society then. Couldn't say.'

'But Yolanda and I were,' Roger said.

Yolanda shot him a look. 'Yes, thank you, Roger Collingwood. I'll have everyone know I was very much the juvenile member in those days, a mere slip of a girl.' She turned to me. 'It was the annual pantomime. The Egglethwaite Players staged it every Christmas, and it raised hundreds.' She sighed. 'I always played principal boy, and then fairy godmother when I got too – when it seemed only fair to give somebody else a chance. I do miss it.'

'I remember the pantos,' I said. 'They were really good. Whatever happened to the Players?'

'The young ones grew up and moved away, or started families, lost interest. Some of the older ones died.' She cast her eyes down. 'Some of the younger ones too.'

'She means our dad,' Lana told me quietly. 'He was their star turn in the Simple Simon-type roles. The Slapstick King, they called him. I think once he was gone, no one had the heart to revive it.'

'Couldn't we though?' I said.

'It's a wonderful idea,' Roger said, 'but I don't know anyone in the village who'd have the necessary experience. Yolanda's the only Players alumnus left.' He glanced at me. 'Unless you have a theatre background?'

I felt almost guilty, he looked so hopeful. 'No, my background's in photography. Sorry, Roger.'

'Oh well,' he said with a sigh. 'In that case, I suppose another beetle drive is the best we have.'

Chapter 5

I was woken next morning by the buzz of my mobile. I blinked myself awake and glanced at the screen.

It was Cole. I answered, wondering what could be so important that he was calling at 7am.

'What's up, love?' I mumbled. 'It's first thing in the morning.'

'I'm sorry, did I wake you? I wanted to catch you before I went to work.'

'Why? What couldn't wait?'

'My news.'

'News?' I said, curiosity conquering drowsiness. 'Is it about the exhibition at Ryder's place?'

Ryder Sherlock-Steele was an old schoolfriend of his who ran a gallery in East London.

'No.' I could tell from his tone that he was smiling. 'I got a job.'

'You're not serious! A lecturing job?'

'That's right. I just got the email from the head of the faculty,' he said, barely suppressed excitement tingling in his voice. 'It's in York, Becky. St John's had a vacancy.'

'Arghh! That's amazing! You never told me you'd applied for something.'

'I didn't want to say anything until I'd heard, just in case I got your hopes up over nothing,' he said. 'I'm afraid that was a fib about needing to get back to London last weekend. They wanted an informal meeting before they made the official offer.'

'You sly thing.' I pushed myself up straight, beaming. 'This is wonderful, Cole! When do you start?'

'I'm giving my notice today. Just another month of long distance, then we can be together.'

***

'So how was the meeting?' Cynthia asked in her sharp Vermont twang, only slightly mellowed through decades in England, as I sat sipping tea on her and Dad's sofa. Even after all these years, she still insisted on serving the milk separately and a wedge of lemon on the side. All mine and Cam's attempts to convince her this was a tragic waste of citrus fruit, which always ended up unsqueezed in the bin, had fallen on deaf ears.

'Long. Mostly boring. Still, I'm glad I went,' I said. 'Tom's right, this stuff is important. Not sure I realised when I was little just how much work went into keeping the village running.'

Cynthia laughed. 'Kids always think these things just fall out of some grown-up's rear end.' She patted my arm. 'Well, good for you, sweetie, paying it forward. It helps keep it going for Pip. And your own children, when you have them.'

Ugh. This again. It felt like friends, family and my ovaries were ganging up lately to remind me I was still barren-wombed and hurtling towards my mid-thirties. As if I could bloody forget.

'Where's Dad today?' I asked.

She nodded towards the study. 'In there. He's writing his memoirs.'

'Since when?'

'He caught some literary bug during a late one at the Fox last week. Came back full of his glory days and how he should commit them to paper while – oh God, here he comes.' She lowered her voice at the sound of Dad rising from his swivel chair. 'Don't mention the hair, ok?'

'The hair? Why, what's he –' I broke off as Dad came in.

'All right, only daughter and light of my life?' he said, grinning. 'Everything ok?'

I couldn't answer. I was too busy staring at his hair.

As long as I could remember, it'd been grey. He'd even been proud to dub himself a silver fox, usually to a derisive snort from Cynthia. But no more. Just weeks after his 60th birthday, my dad had become an overnight blonde.

And not just any blonde. A bleach blonde. There was enough dye on his head to trigger a nationwide peroxide shortage.

Cynthia shot me a look and I pulled my eyes away.

'Yes. Fine,' I managed to mumble.

'Well, come here,' Dad said. I stood to give him a hug. 'We heard all about the panto from Pip yesterday.'

'Erm, yeah,' I said, still a little shellshocked at his appearance. 'She had a fab time.'

'And she told us a new joke. Why are grandads called grandads?'

'Think I've heard it,' I said with a smile. My brain prodded me, reminding me why I was there. 'Look, can you guys sit down? I actually came with some news.'

I wasn't sure why I should feel anxious about breaking the news that Cole would finally be joining me, but I did.

Dad took a seat next to Cynthia, looking concerned. 'Nothing bad, I hope, Boo?'

My face relaxed into a smile at the childhood nickname. It always made me feel safe, even if my dad currently looked more like an ageing Bros reject than himself.

'No, good. It's Cole. He's moving up at last.'

'Oh, fabulous!' Cynthia said, beaming. She accidentally-on-purpose stepped on Dad's foot. 'Isn't it, Danny?'

'Of course it is,' Dad said, a bit too quickly. 'Lovely lad, Cole.'

My face fell. 'You aren't happy.'

'No! No, we are,' Dad said. But I couldn't help noticing the flicker of guilt. 'If you're happy, we're happy. That's how it works.'

'Then why're you doing that face? You like him, don't you?'

'Honest answer? No idea,' Cynthia said with typical Yankee bluntness.

'How do you mean, no idea?'

'Well, how long have you two been together? Three years? That whole time we've met him about five times, by my reckoning.'

'We were down south.'

'But he hardly ever came up with you from London,' Dad said. 'We thought it might be different after you moved, but...'

'Three times I've asked him to Sunday dinner when he's been visiting,' Cynthia said. 'And three times he's made some excuse.'

'He's busy,' I mumbled. 'He is working two jobs.'

'Still, he's never seemed particularly interested in getting to know us.'

'He's just shy. It'll all be different once he's here.'

'Well, I guess you know best.' Cynthia stood to hug me. 'I am happy for you, sweetie, honest. I know how much you've been looking forward to this.'

I looked at my dad, or as near as I could without squinting in the glare. 'What about you? Have we got your blessing?'

'Since when've you needed that?'

'Since never. But I want you to be happy about it.'

'Oh, all right. One blessing, duly administered.' He came over to give it me in the form of a hair-ruffle. 'Don't use it all at once.' He grabbed a leather jacket – another element in his new look, apparently. 'Right, I'll leave you ladies to set the world to rights. I'm meeting Gatesy.'

'Do you have to?' I said. 'Thought we might head up to Pagans' Rock for a walk before I open the shop.'

'Sorry, love. I promised I'd help him move house today.'

'There's no big hurry, is there?'

'He has to get the hire van back by five. I'll see you soon, eh? Love you both.' He bent to give me a kiss, planted another on Cynthia's cheek and strode out of the room.

I shot a questioning look at Cynthia, who shook her head. 'Don't ask.'

'Nothing wrong, is there?'

'I'll make more tea,' she said, heading to the kitchen.

'Hold the lemon!' I called after her.

When our tea had brewed, she handed me a fresh cup and sank back onto the sofa. I went to sit beside her.

'So come on,' I said, reaching for the milk jug. 'What's with the hair?'

'You had to ask.' She sighed. 'Your dad's going through a difficult time at the moment, Becky. You know he's been kind of down since he turned sixty.'

'I know. He seemed bright enough today though.'

'Oh, he's bright. He's so bright I'm ready to damn well strangle him sometimes – the days I know where he is.'

'What?'

'He's out most nights. It feels like I'm barely keeping track of him.' She fixed me in an earnest gaze. 'Listen, sweetie, I know you've got your own stuff going on. But... just be there for him, can you? I'm worried.'

'What're you worried about?'

'Ok, look.' She put her tea down and placed a hand on each of my shoulders. 'We never told you this, you and Cam. Well, there didn't seem any point worrying you till we knew, and then you were in the middle of the big move, we figured you didn't need the stress...'

'What, Cyn?' I said, alarmed. 'Is something wrong with Dad?'

Chapter 5

'No. But... there could've been. Your dad had a bit of a scare, a few months ago. Found a lump somewhere a lump shouldn't be.'

'Oh my God!'

She gave my shoulders a comforting squeeze. 'No need to freak, it was just an inflammation. But I don't mind telling you it frightened us both rigid. We got our wills done and next thing I know, your dad's locking himself in the study reminiscing about his youth and the bathroom cabinet's full of Just for Men, Billy Idol Special Edition.'

'Oh God. The textbook mid-life crisis.' I patted her arm. 'Well, we'll get him through it. Just be grateful he hasn't blown your savings on a sports car.'

'It's not his behaviour. Lord knows, I could cope with that.' She cast her eyes down. 'It's the late nights. I'm scared stiff, Becky. Scared he's – that there might be someone else.'

'Don't be daft. He loves you to pieces.'

She gazed at her ringless left hand. 'And yet...'

'Come on, you know he does. You two've been together –' I did a quick calculation – 'God, thirty-one years. He'd never do anything to jeopardise that.'

'But it's not really about how he feels, is it? It's about getting old. The fear you'll never get another chance to experience the thrill of being with someone new. It's not unheard of for men to try to cure ageing with sex.'

'Not my dad,' I said firmly. 'He'd never do that.'

'He did it to your mum.'

I almost splurted tea across the room. 'He *what?*'

She sighed. 'Should've told you this years ago really. It wasn't your cousin's graduation party where we first got together, Becky.' She held up a hand to stop me interrupting. 'I know, that's what we said. But we'd been seeing each other for nearly a year by then, while your parents were still married. Secretly.'

'Shit! Did Mum know?'

'She suspected, I think. She and Danny both knew it was over by then, but still... it was wrong.'

I gazed into the distance while I tried to process this new information. Cynthia had been mum to me for so long, she was the only one I remembered. My real mum had died before I'd even had time to form a picture of her. But it would never have occurred to me that my dad, loyal, loving, laid-back Danny Finn, was capable of being unfaithful.

'It's... done now,' I said, fighting down my shock. 'And you were his soulmate, in the end.'

'But it wasn't right. I'm sorry, Becky.'

I summoned a smile. 'Well, no good crying over spilt adultery, eh? We're here now. You're in love, you're happy. You've got a partner, a son, a granddaughter, not to mention the sort-of daughter that came free with the rest. Happy families. Focus on that, not something you can't fix now.'

'Nothing sort-of about this daughter,' she said, smiling back.

'Dad wouldn't cheat on you, Cyn. I know it.'

'Wish I could be certain. It's such a funny thing, getting old,' she said with a sigh. 'Just be there if he needs someone to talk to, won't you?'

'I always am, he knows that.'

She squeezed my arm. 'Thanks, Becky. You're a good girl.'

Chapter 6

The bell over Fancypants' door jangled about ten minutes before closing time.

'Oh,' I said when Lana walked in, decked out in her Egglethwaite Silver blazer. 'Thought you were a customer.'

'Who says I'm not?'

'Looks like you've got your fancy dress sorted,' I said, nodding to the maroon blazer with its gold epaulets. 'Hey, I've got some flaming batons in the accessories section if you're interested?'

'Oi. Lay off the uniform.' She dumped her trombone case and threw herself into the armchair by the changing rooms. 'I get enough of that off Stew.'

'Where've you been playing?'

'Outside the castle. Bit of a busk for market day.'

'Again?'

'Yeah. Roger's been working us extra hard lately, putting collecting tins for the Temp out at every gig. I'm jiggered.'

'Did you make much?'

She shrugged. 'Not enough to turn the tide. Still, every little helps.'

I nodded to the trombone case. 'Can I have a go?'

'Help yourself.'

She smirked as I opened the case.

'What?' I said.

'Nothing. I should just warn you, it's harder than it looks.'

I put the instrument to my lips and blew into it, puffing out my cheeks. Lana laughed as a slightly amplified version of my own breath emerged.

'Here, try it like this.'

She demonstrated the right technique, poking the tip of her tongue between her lips then withdrawing it sharply.

I tried to imitate her, punching a breath into the trombone, and a fat, flatulent rasp filled the air.

I shot Lana a delighted grin. 'I did it!'

'Yeah, not bad for a first go,' she said, smiling.

I was well away now, marching around the shop, yanking the slidey bit about as I tooted. There was something incredibly satisfying about the cat-murdering din I was managing to conjure.

'Ok, ok,' Lana said, putting her fingers in her ears. 'Stop, before your neighbours form a lynch mob.'

Reluctantly I put the trombone away again, feeling strangely cleansed by my foray into the world of brass.

'Here, brought something to show you.' She reached into her handbag. 'You got me all nostalgic in the meeting last night. Went home and dug this out.'

'What is it?' I asked, examining the small leather album she handed me.

'It was my dad's. Old photos of the Players. He kept pictures and press cuttings from every production.'

I opened it at a photo of a handsome, dark-haired man in his 30s, wearing a blue uniform with gold trim. He had an arm each round a little girl and boy who I recognised as the young Lana and Tom.

'He was Buttons that year,' Lana said, smiling fondly. 'Here.' She took the album, flicked to the first photo and handed it back. 'First panto the Players ever did. '77, I think. Cast photo Dad cut out of the paper.' Lana pointed to a pretty, if rather smug, young woman with Debbie Harry hair. She was in long leather boots and the shortest of principal-boy tunics, obviously very proud of her shapely legs. 'Look familiar?'

'Bloody hell! Yolanda?'

'Yeah, before she got too old and they moved her into the good fairy parts.' She pointed out some of the others. 'My dad again, playing Simple Simon. He wasn't long over from Italy then. Eric Spiggott as the dame – he was the last Player apart from Yo-yo, till he passed away last month. Principal girl, don't know her name. She moved away for university, never came back.'

'Who played the cow?'

'Heh. He wasn't a Player, but I know Rodge was in the back end. Always fun to remind him his greatest service to the village was the time he was a cow's arse.'

I gazed dreamily at the snapshot of the past. Everyone was grinning, standing in front of a giant beanstalk made of old curtains. They looked like they were having the time of their lives.

'It's a shame, isn't it? Not just for the Temp, for the kids too. Me and Cam used to love the pantos.' I looked up from the album. 'You know, that big one I went to with Pip wasn't a patch on the old Egglethwaite ones.'

Lana laughed. 'Now come on. I'm as loyal as the next villager, but we're hardly competition for the £20-a-ticket jobs.'

'I mean it. Ok, so they've got impressive sets and special effects. Couple of biggish names on the bill. But apart from that, it was a bit rubbish. Awful script, dire acting –'

'It's supposed to be dire, it's panto.'

'This was dire even by panto standards.' I paused, trying to put my finger on just what'd been wrong. 'It had no heart. It felt like the actors wanted to be somewhere else.'

Lana cast an affectionate look at the photo of her dad and the other Players.

'You could never've said that about ours, for all our shoddy beanstalks.'

'Exactly,' I said, warming to my subject. 'Ours had heart because the actors cared. The audience cared. We all cared, because it was for the Temp.'

She smiled. 'You really love that place, don't you?'

I grabbed her arm, my eyes kindling. 'We can bring it back, Lana!'

'What, us two?' she said, frowning. 'We don't know anything about pantomimes.'

'You didn't know anything about viaducts but you got ours opened up, didn't you?'

'Yeah, and it was a lot of hard work.'

'Worth it?'

She pulled her blazer sleeve back to look at her silver charm bracelet, fingering a tiny train dangling from one link.

'Best thing I ever did,' she said quietly.

'Then let's try it.'

'But where do we even start?'

I hesitated.

'Is there really nobody in the village with theatre experience?'

Lana grimaced. 'Oh God. I'm going to regret telling you this, but... yes. There is one person.'

***

I rapped on the door a second time. There was no answer, but I could hear voices round the back so I knew there was someone in. Eventually I wandered round the side of the house to find them.

I followed the chatter to an open garage. An old, bug-like Morris Minor in British racing green was parked inside, the kind with wood detailing round the wheel arches. A pair of legs stuck out of each side.

'I can't believe you didn't get spark plugs,' the left-hand pair was saying.

'Because it doesn't need a spark plug. Do you even know what a spark plug is?'

'It's... a plug,' Deano said. 'A sparky one.'

'And yet he knows fifty ways to make pastry,' muttered the voice I recognised as Magical Marcus.

I tapped one of the legs and Marcus's oil-smudged face appeared.

'Oh. Becky. Hi again.'

I nodded a greeting. 'Great Awesome-o. Hey, did you know your car's sprouting legs?'

'Believe me when I say this is very much not my car.' He got to his feet. 'I'm helping Deano work on it in exchange for storing my bike here.'

He pointed to a motorbike resting against the wall.

'That's yours?'

'Yeah.' He smiled at my expression. 'What?'

'Magicians aren't allowed to ride motorbikes.'

'Well, the shop was fresh out of broomsticks.' He raised his voice. 'Deano! We've got a visitor.'

Another oil-stained face, this time with a shock of bright scarlet hair on top, popped out. 'Becky with the good hair. Heyup. To what do we owe this honour then?'

'Came to ask you about something.'

He got up. 'Ask away.'

'Well, Lana told me – sorry, Deano, I have to know. Why're you doing up a Morris Minor?'

He gave the car a fond pat. 'She's a beauty, isn't she? 1969 Traveller, a real classic.'

I ran my eyes along the car's humped, bulbous curves. 'She's certainly... in great condition. But why a Morris? Could you not've gone for something a bit more Greased Lightning?'

'Trust me, this old girl can pussy wagon with the best of them.' He trailed his fingers lovingly over the bonnet. 'Can't you, you sexy beast?'

'So what was it you wanted?' Marcus asked. 'Something for Lana?'

'No, something for me. She told me – Deano, can you stop stroking the car, please? It's creepy.'

'Sorry,' he said, bestowing a last lingering look on his Morris. 'Go on, Becks.'

'Lana told me you once tried to stage an amateur production of *HMS Pinafore* at your catering college.'

'That is 100% true.'

'She said the entire cast and crew walked out.'

'That is also 100% true.'

'Why?'

'They couldn't handle my vision. Philistines.' He paused. 'Plus I may have overworked them ever so slightly. They left me an open letter saying I was too much of a perfectionist. Well, I think the actual phrase they used was "utter, utter bastard".'

Marcus laughed. 'Every one of them swore they'd never work with him again,' he told me. 'Mum was so proud. She had the letter framed and hung it in the downstairs loo.'

'Why were you trying to stage Gilbert and Sullivan at a catering college?' I asked Deano.

'Same reason he's trying to do up a Morris Minor when he doesn't know what a spark plug is,' Marcus said.

Deano grinned. 'Love a challenge.'

'What's your interest, Becky?' Marcus asked.

I eyed Deano warily. 'Not sure I should say now. What was your role in this opera?'

'Director.'

'And you got pretty far along, did you?'

'Yeah, we were only a week from opening when everyone abandoned me. Bunch of knobs.'

I drew a deep breath. 'Well, all right, since you're the only one round here with experience. Me and Lana were thinking of reviving the Egglethwaite panto to raise money for the Temp.'

Deano's eyes glittered. 'And you want me to direct?'

'Well, we haven't got that far yet. I just came to ask if you had any advice for –'

'I'll do it. Sign me up.'

'Bloody hell! Thought I'd have to work on you a bit more than that.'

'Are you kidding? I live for stuff like this.' He threw himself at me for a hug. 'Arghh, this is going to be great! I have to go ring Mum, she'll be well chuffed.'

Marcus laughed. 'Tell her to clear a bit of space on the wall of the downstairs loo, eh?'

Deano strode off towards the house. 'Hey, what panto we doing?' he called over his shoulder.

'Dunno yet!' I called back. 'I only had the idea today.'

'You should talk to Marc. He's got stage experience.'

'You'll have to watch him,' Marcus said once his brother had disappeared. 'He gets a bit... intense.'

'I'd noticed,' I said drily. 'Honestly, I only came round to see if he knew how to get the ball rolling. One word and it's Thunderbirds are go.' I glanced up at him. 'Have you got stage experience?'

'Oh. Yeah. Sort of.'

'What was it?'

'Student review I was in. Sketches, variety, that sort of thing. One guy did a filthy ventriloquist act, there were a couple of stand-ups, and we had a lass who sang jazz numbers.'

'And you?'

'My thing was magic tricks that went wrong. Ripped off from Tommy Cooper mainly, but I wrote the patter myself. It was a big hit down the student union.'

'So that was how you got into magic?'

'Yeah. My degree's in geology, but it was performing I got passionate about.'

'Do you really make a living from it?'

'Just about. Actually my biggest earners are the circus skills workshops I run for kids' groups.'

Stage experience, circus skills, used to working with kids... he sounded like a useful man to get on board.

'You don't fancy being involved, do you?' I asked.

He hesitated.

'Oh, sorry,' I said. 'It's your job to do that sort of thing. You won't want to be giving your time for free.'

'What did you say it was for?'

'Our community centre. It's fallen on hard times lately.'

'Important to you?'

'Yeah. It's a lifeline for a lot of people in the village.'

He shrugged. 'Ok, if it's for a good cause. Could be fun.'

I flashed him a smile. 'Thanks, Marcus. One tiny question though.'

'What?'

'What the hell do I do next?'

Chapter 7

I spent the next few weeks doing research, reading anything I could find on how to stage a panto. Marcus suggested our next step should be an open meeting for anyone who'd like to get involved, which we pencilled in for the following month.

My social life saw a dramatic improvement. I spent more and more nights at the pub with Lana, Stew, Deano and Marcus, who'd drifted together to form the unofficial panto-organising committee. I joined Cam's quiz team too, and became an official member of the village society. It didn't seem so important to stick to our nightly FaceTime dates now I knew Cole was on his way to me.

I'd started checking off the days until he got here on the desk calendar in my shop. Three weeks, two, one...

We kept the posters advertising the panto meeting simple.

Do you remember the Egglethwaite Christmas Panto? A group of villagers are hoping to revive this lost tradition! If you'd like to get involved, please come along to a meeting at the Sooty Fox!! 7pm, Friday 9th March. No acting skills required!!!

We let Deano run free with the exclamation marks, but his suggestion of adding 'No slackers' at the bottom was firmly vetoed.

When I got to the Fox on meeting night, the other four were already there. I sat down behind a glass of wine that seemed to be for me.

'Cutting it fine, aren't you?' Deano said.

'I'm ten minutes early, Deano.'

'Exactly. Some of us have been here ages.'

I turned to Marcus. 'Go on, what time did he get here?'

'Six. Would've been earlier if I hadn't put my foot down. He's been pulling at his lead all afternoon.'

'Well, thanks for the wine, whoever got them in,' I said, taking a sip.

'You staying for another one after, Becks?' Marcus asked. 'I owe you a thrashing on the quiz machine.'

'Not tonight, I have to rush off.'

'Her fiancé's moving in tomorrow,' Lana said with a grin. 'She has to go iron her lacy knickers.'

Marcus laughed. 'Lucky feller.'

Stewart sat in silence while this conversation went on around him.

Lana nudged him. 'What's up with you?'

'Worried, that's all. What if nobody turns up, guys?'

'They will.' I tried to sound more confident than I felt. 'There must be loads of people who'd love to see the panto back.'

'Wanting to see it back and actually getting off their arses and doing something about it are two different things though.'

'We don't need loads of volunteers.' Deano looked perfectly calm, the hamsters that operated his brain obviously in mellow mood. 'We're talking, what, fifteen minimum for cast and crew? Easy squeezy.'

'Hmm.' Stew didn't look convinced.

'It'll be fine, fellers, on my word as a culinary genius. We're only after helpers tonight. Auditions for actors come later.' He nodded to the door. 'There you go. A volunteer.'

I looked round to see Yolanda scanning the pub for us.

'Should've known she'd be first here,' Lana muttered. 'There's been a hole in her life ever since she hung up her sparkly tutu.'

'Evening, my lovelies,' Yolanda said when she'd joined us. 'I'm so pleased we're doing this. The village has been tragic for lack of greasepaint these ten years.'

'Well, let's not get ahead of ourselves, Yo-yo,' I said. 'We don't know for certain it's going to happen. You're the first one here.'

'Oh, there'll be others on their way. I told all the girls about it.' By 'the girls' I knew she meant the members of Ladies Who Lunch, formerly Egglethwaite Women's Institute.

She rested a flirtatious hand on Marcus's arm. 'Would you be a treasure? I'd love a gin and slim.'

'You know, your fiancé's right there behind the bar,' Stewart said. 'Glaring.'

'Good. I like to keep him on his toes.' Yolanda sent the pissed-off-looking Billy a little wave.

'Ok, I can take a hint,' Marcus said. 'I'll do another drinks run.'

By the time he'd got another round in, he'd lost his seat. Following a sudden influx of interested panto fans, our table had grown by ten.

He grabbed a stool from another table and plonked it down next to me.

'Hey, it's looking good,' he whispered. 'This might actually happen, Becks.'

'I know, brilliant,' I whispered back. 'Go on, get things started.'

He shook his head. 'Your idea, your show, love.'

'Ugh. Ok.' I raised my voice. 'Um, hi. Right, so as you know, well, probably, Egglethwaite used to have a Christmas pantomime in the olden days, to raise money for the temperance hall. And, er, those of us who were kids here loved it. So we were thinking it'd be nice to bring it back. If we can. Um.'

'Highly laudable, my dear,' said Roger Collingwood, seated at the head of the table like that was the only natural place for him. 'But do we have the know-how? As someone who's been involved in the past, I can tell you a pantomime's no little thing to organise.'

'Finest cow's backside in the business, Rodge,' Lana said, toasting him with her Guinness.

'We don't need skills so much as we need commitment,' I said. 'I'm willing to offer that, if others are.'

There was a hum of agreement round the table.

'I'm sure we'll give our all,' Roger said. 'I'll even postpone my holiday to Provence, if it's for the temperance hall.'

Lana nodded to Yolanda, who was making notes. 'Minute that, can you, Yo-yo? Our Tom owes us a pint.'

'Anyway, I've been doing some research,' I said, warming to my subject. 'It's not as onerous as it sounds, really. I've put together a list of roles we'd need to fill, other than the actors.' I pulled a sheet out of my document wallet. 'Director – Deano's volunteered for that, he's got experience. Music – Roger, you're a band conductor. Reckon you could manage that side of it?'

'I believe so, if it's a case of sourcing a score. And Sue Lightowler will play piano for us, I'm sure.'

'Ok, great. And then there's choreography, we'd need someone for that. Costumes you can leave to me, I can get them at cost through my shop. Set design – my fiancé's a painter, he might be able to help us out with backdrops. Lighting. Then there's props, make-up, and finally the script. That's not too bad, is it?'

'Some of those things are kind of big, Becks,' Marcus said. 'Bigger than you're making them sound. Writing a script, for a start.'

'It doesn't have to be written from scratch, you can buy them online. Then it's just a case of customising it with some local references and zeitgeisty gags.'

'And who'd do that?'

'Well, I thought you might. You did say you wrote the patter for your magic act.'

'I don't live here though. It really needs someone local to give it that Egglethwaite vibe.'

'I'll help. I'm usually good for an innuendo.'

He shrugged. 'Go on then. Between us I think we can manage it.'

I glanced round the table. 'Anyone else?'

'I can do make-up. I always did in the old days.' Yolanda nodded to one of the women from Ladies Who Lunch. 'And Rita here can help with choreography.'

Rita laughed. 'As long as it's line dancing. I run the weekly class at the temperance hall.'

'Sounds good to me,' Deano said.

'Seriously, line dancing in a pantomime?' Stewart said.

'Why not? We want to make it unique, don't we?'

'What do you think, Becky?' Marcus asked.

'Deano's right. It needs to say Egglethwaite, never mind the done thing.' I nodded to Yolanda's friend. 'Rita, reckon any of your class would be interested in joining the chorus?'

'Oh yes, I'm sure they would. We so rarely get a chance to perform.'

'What about props?' Marcus said.

'We could ask some of the children's groups to make them,' Roger said. 'It couldn't be anything very complicated though.'

'What was the last panto the Players did?' I asked Yolanda.

'Gosh, it was over a decade ago, I'm not sure I – oh! Yes, I remember. It was a revival of our very first show, Jack and the Beanstalk. That seemed a fitting note to go out on.'

'And a fitting note to come back in on,' I said. 'Would there be any of the old props still around?'

'There might be a beanstalk in storage under the hall,' she said. 'And we made a giant foot out of papier mâché. It swung down onto the stage via a rope and pulley for the finale, very impressive. A coat of paint and it could still be usable.'

'Right, great. I'll do a recce tomorrow.' I looked round. 'What do you reckon, guys – Jack and the Beanstalk? The first, the last, the resurrection?'

There were hums of assent. They were certainly a cooperative lot.

'What about the actors?' one of the other Ladies Who Lunch asked.

Yolanda jumped in immediately. 'I'll be the fairy. I'm always the fairy.'

'Not so fast, Yo-yo,' Lana said. 'We can worry about auditions when we're further down the line.'

She looked scandalised. 'You wouldn't make me audition? I've been playing the fairies since –' She stopped herself. 'For quite a while,' she volunteered cautiously.

'Everyone has to audition if I'm directing. Even you.' Deano winked. 'But I wouldn't worry, gorgeous. I'm sure you've still got it.'

The flirting seemed to mollify her.

'Well, at least we know the perfect person to ask for advice.' She turned to Stewart. 'You can get him for us, can't you, Stewpot?'

Stew shook his head. 'Oh no. We're not involving him again.'

'Sorry, am I missing something?' I asked. 'Who're you talking about?'

'Harper Brady, of course,' Yolanda said.

'Oh. Him.'

Harper Brady was Stewart's TV-star cousin. I knew he did stuff for the village sometimes, as a favour to Stew and Lana when they needed some celebrity pull for a fundraiser. He was big though, increasingly so since he'd won a BAFTA. I couldn't imagine he'd want to get involved with our tiny panto.

'Would he be part of this?' I asked Stew. 'I mean, obviously he's not going to star or anything, but a bit of advice wouldn't go amiss.'

'Trust me, you don't want Harper involved.'

'Why not? He's been in pantos. Big ones too.' I turned to Lana. 'He's ok, isn't he?'

'Harper's...' She paused, choosing her words carefully. 'Harper's... special. Once you get him involved, you have to be prepared to provide a couple of babysitters.'

'A couple?'

'One for Harper, one for his ego. It's got a mind of its own.'

'But it would be such a wasted opportunity not to ask the only professional we know for help.' Yolanda turned to Roger for backup. 'Don't you think so?'

'It couldn't hurt,' Roger said. 'I hate to bring doom and gloom into an otherwise positive discussion, but the temperance hall very much needs this to be a success. Anything Mr Brady was able to do would be appreciated.'

Stew let out a sigh of defeat. 'Fine. I'll ask if he'll come along to the auditions, give us some tips.'

'Thanks, Stew. Here.' I kissed Lana's cheek and she leaned over to pass it on to Stewart, upgrading it to one on the lips.

He smiled. 'Cheers, Becks.'

'Ok, this is awesome. We've got a plan, we've got a panto and we've got a crew.' I beamed round the table. 'All we need now are some actors and we're good to go.'

'She makes it sound so simple,' Marcus muttered.

***

As soon as the meeting was over, I rushed off. Cole was due tomorrow, and I wanted to run the hoover around before he arrived. I couldn't wait to spend the night together as an officially cohabiting couple.

The door handle was drooping pathetically again, but I didn't think anything of it. Cynthia had said she'd pop round with a fruit basket from her and Dad as their way of saying 'welcome to the family'. For my sake they seemed determined to make a real effort with Cole, and the thoughtful gesture was typical of her.

But when I got in, I realised there was something else going on. The place reeked of burnt onions, and a flickering orange glow illuminated the kitchen doorway.

'Cole,' I said, smiling when I found him reading at the dining table. 'I thought the place was on fire.'

'Ah, there she is at last. My perfect woman.'

He came over, lifting me off the ground as he kissed me.

I laughed breathlessly. 'How come you're early?'

'I thought I'd surprise you with a romantic meal. Being the romantic soul I am.'

'You're sweet,' I said, kissing the tip of his nose. 'Wish you'd said something though. I haven't tidied.'

'There's no need to tidy for me. I already know you're a scruff.'

'And you're a cheeky git.' I nodded to the table, an army of tealights flickering next to a bottle of wine. 'What's all this?'

'I told you, it's a romantic meal.' He went to the hob and started ladelling something onto plates. 'Only it's a little dry now. I thought you'd have been home ages ago.'

'Sorry,' I said as I took my seat. 'Been in the pub. You should've said you'd be back tonight.'

'But that would have spoiled my surprise.' He served up the food, sat down and reached across the table to take my free hand. 'I decided I couldn't wait until tomorrow for our first evening living together as northerners so I rushed up straight after college.'

I smiled. 'Sorry, afraid we don't just dish out northerner status to anyone who moves here. There's a saying round our way that if you move in from outside the area, your children's children will still be offcumdens.'

He frowned. 'They'll be what?'

'Offcumdens. Newcomers.'

I had to laugh at his expression.

'You'll get used to us.' I glanced down at the meal he'd prepared. 'Er, what're we having?'

'Risotto. Leek and spring onion.'

'Oh. Yum.'

'So how was the pub?' he asked as I prodded the lumpy mess with my fork.

'Good. It was the open meeting about our pantomime.'

'Well-attended?'

'Mmm, very.'

There was silence for a moment as we both tried to swallow a mouthful of stodgy risotto.

'Perhaps you should leave them to it, if there were enough to manage without you,' Cole said. 'It's going to be a lot of work.'

I shrugged. 'Keeps me off the streets. Anyway, me and Cam enjoyed them when we were kids, seems only right we should pass that along for Pip's generation. And it feels good to be part of the community again.' I glanced up from my plate. 'Hey. Maybe you could get involved too. We could work on it together.'

I could tell from the look on his face that this was far from Cole's idea of a good time.

'No, darling, I don't think so,' he said. 'I've never understood the whole pantomime thing really. I know it's an old tradition, but even as a child it seemed rather absurd to me.'

'Ok,' I said, trying not to feel too disappointed.

'Have you made any new friends?'

'I've got to know Lana's best mate Deano a bit better. And his brother Marcus is a good lad too.'

He laughed.

'What?' I said, smiling.

'Can't leave you alone for a moment, can I?'

'Sorry?'

'Well, I can't help noticing that these new friends of yours are all men.'

'Oh. Yeah, suppose they are. I mean, not that I've looked.' I looked up from the wine I was using to lubricate the hard-to-swallow risotto. 'Not jealous, are you?'

'Of course not, darling. I trust you.'

I squeezed his hand. 'I know you do.'

'So what will your role be in this pantomime? Are you going to act in it?'

'Dunno. I hadn't thought about what I'll do if we actually manage to get it going.' I paused with fork halfway to my mouth. 'Wonder if I can act. Never tried.'

I forced down another mouthful of risotto, trying hard to stop myself grimacing.

Cole burst out laughing.

'Gosh, I'm sorry, Becky. It tastes like school dinner rice pudding, doesn't it?' He glanced down at his plate. 'It looks like school-dinner rice pudding.'

'No, it... it's delicious, honestly,' I said, swallowing hard.

'Admit it. You wouldn't feed this horror to a homeless dog.'

'Ok, no. I'm quite fond of dogs.' I started laughing too. 'You daft sod. Tell you what, why don't we get takeaway and eat it snuggled on the sofa? I'll go round my dad's shop for some fish and chips.'

Chapter 7

'That sounds perfect. You're my favourite person to slum it with.' He leaned across the table to kiss me. 'I am sorry, Becky. I'm a terrible cook but I love you.'

'Love you too.' I ran a finger down his cheek. 'You know, we don't have to wait till after the wedding,' I said in a whisper. 'We could start right now, tonight. Who knows how long it'll take?'

'Trying for a baby, you mean?'

I smiled. 'Well I wasn't suggesting getting a budgie.'

'There's plenty of time, Becky.'

'I know. It's just... watching Cam and Tom doing the parent thing, and Lana and Stew about to join them, I've been thinking about it more lately. They're all younger than me. I'm starting to feel depressingly like the aged aunty of the family.'

'At thirty-four?' Cole said, laughing. 'I haven't unpacked yet and already you're planning babies. One thing at a time, ok, darling? Let's do things the old-fashioned way, just this once.'

'If that's what you want.' I left a lingering kiss on his lips and grinned. 'No harm getting some practice in though, is there? How about bed first, then chips?'

He smiled. 'You read my mind.'

Chapter 8

'All right, where is he?' Cynthia demanded when I arrived in her and Dad's garden for Pip's sixth birthday party.

'Lovely to see you too, Cyn,' I said, bending to kiss her cheek.

Cameron was next to her sipping something bright pink out of a champagne flute, and I grabbed him for a hug. 'Hiya, bro. Made a start on the cocktails already?'

He laughed. 'It's cherryade. Mum let me have it in a big-boy glass.'

'I don't know how you can drink that stuff, Cam,' Cynthia said. 'It's nothing but e-numbers.'

'Mmm. E-numbers.' Cam took another sip and poked his tongue out to show us what a fetching shade of Yo-yo-hair pink it'd turned.

'Anyway, don't change the subject.' She turned back to me. 'Where's Cole, Becky? Me and your dad were all set to make a big effort with him.'

'He is coming,' I said. 'He'll just be a bit late. Something urgent he had to get finished.'

That's what he'd told me anyway, some commission that had to be completed by the end of April. He was spending so much time in his attic studio, it felt like I'd barely seen him for the last month.

I scanned the bunting-strewn garden for Dad. 'Where is Annie Lennox anyway?'

'God knows,' Cynthia said. 'He'll be somewhere about.'

Chapter 8

'Garden looks great, Mum. Thanks for doing this.' Cameron glanced around, taking in the bouncy castle, the piñata, the giant Jenga and other games Cynthia had hired. 'You know, you spoil her.'

'Granny's prerogative.' She smiled at Pip, who was sitting on the bouncy castle with an assortment of human and teddy friends, plus a puzzled-looking Flash, earnestly explaining to them how a potato masher worked. 'She's a strange little thing. Wouldn't swap her for worlds.'

'Where'd she get the potato masher?' I asked Cam.

'She stole it from the kitchen. Honestly, the kiddy quad bike we got her's barely getting a look-in.'

'Oh, there's Dad,' I said, spotting a mass of peroxide blonde in the throng. He was deep in conversation with Yolanda near the barbecue, currently being manned by Tom and Stewart. Yolanda was sipping something from a champagne flute that definitely didn't look like cherryade, resting her fingers on Dad's arm.

Cynthia followed my gaze. 'So he is. With Yo-yo Sommerville.'

Cameron put his arm round her shoulders. 'Don't worry, Mum. He's too old for her.'

'They're the same age, practically.'

'Exactly. So he's about thirty-five years too old for her.'

'Hm. Think I'll just go get a burger. See what it is they're talking about.' She wandered off to the barbecue, looking anxious.

'She thinks he's having an affair,' I said to Cameron when she'd gone.

'I know. Do you think he is?'

I snorted. 'With Yo-yo? You must be joking.'

'You don't think he would, do you?'

I thought about what Cynthia had told me: how her and Dad had first got together. It didn't sound like she'd shared that information with Cameron, and if she hadn't I certainly wasn't going to. It might upset him. It'd certainly shock him. I was starting to think there was a lot about Dad we'd never suspected.

'Dad? Nah,' I said, trying to sound casual. 'He'd never have the initiative.'

Cam snuck a worried glance at Dad. 'Still, there's something going on with him.'

'He's just panicking about getting old. He'll get over it, once he's adjusted to his new status as a sixtysomething.'

'Hope so. Mum's worried sick about him. Apparently he stayed out all night last Saturday.'

'God, really? That's not like him.'

'I know.' He shook himself. 'Well, let's not worry about it today. It's Pip's day. You know Lana and Stew hired her a magician?'

'Marcus Teasdale. Lana said she was going to.'

'That's him, Deano's big brother. Do you know him then?'

'Pretty well. He's one of the panto gang.'

'Going ok?'

'Early stages, but yeah. I found this company online that sells scripts, got us a Jack and the Beanstalk. Marc's going to come round next week so we can start making it a bit more Egglethwaitey.'

'What does Cole think about it?'

'He's not that interested really. I get the feeling he thinks pantos are a bit daft.'

'I mean about you spending time alone with another bloke.'

'No need for him to be jealous, it's just panto business. Ok, there'll be a fair bit of innuendo flying around, but I'm sure a few gags about the dame's dumplings boiling over won't have us overcome with insatiable lust.'

'Good-looking lad, Marcus Teasdale.'

'Yeah. Shame you're married, eh?'

'Funny.' He was staring at me, one of the knowing looks he'd inherited from Cynthia. 'So you haven't noticed then.'

I shrugged. 'Maybe. Academic, isn't it? When you're single you notice things one way, when you're in a relationship you notice them another. With a little voice that whispers "off limits".'

Someone tapped me on the shoulder, and I turned to find Deano and Marcus behind me with a pair of matching grins.

'Teasdale-dum and Teasdale-dee,' I said, nodding. 'We were just talking about you.'

'Good things?' Deano asked.

'Suppose. My brother thinks me and Marcus are using the panto as cover for our torrid affair.'

'Suits me,' Marcus said. 'Oh, but I can't do Tuesdays.'

'Sorry then, no go,' I said. 'If you're going to be my bit on the side I expect 100% commitment, seven days a week. I'm a hot-blooded woman, you know.'

'You should try Kit Beeton,' Cameron said. 'These late-night hot-tub parties up at Coplowe Farm sound like they're turning into all-out orgies.'

'How do you know?'

'There was a post about it in that Egglethwaite Residents Facebook group Yolanda runs.'

Deano shook his head soberly. 'It's come to a sad pass if you can't even run a knocking shop in this village without Yo-yo Sommerville writing it up for the online equivalent of the parish newsletter.'

'Don't remember you complaining about the write-ups she gave you,' Marcus said, nudging him.

'Ships that pass in the night, brother o' mine. Anyway, shut it. If you start reminding Billy about that little dalliance, he might decide to dilute my bitter with extra saliva next time I'm in the Fox.'

'Serves you right for shagging old ladies,' Cam said.

Always the last to know, I finally cottoned on to what they were talking about.

'Oh no, Deano,' I said. 'Not Yolanda. She was my Brown Owl.'

He shrugged. 'We all have needs, even Brown Owls.' He glanced at Yo-yo. 'And some of us have more needs than others.'

'No shame, eh?' Marcus said to me. 'Looks like it's up to me to uphold the family name.'

'Listen, lanky, I can uphold the Teasdale name with the best of them,' Deano said. 'Ask Yo-yo.'

Cynthia came back to join us, clutching a burger. 'All innocent. They're just gossiping about Kit Beeton's hot-tub parties.'

'It's this season's hot topic.' Cam gave her a squeeze. 'You ok, Mum?'

'Yeah. Just being silly.' She passed the burger to Cam. 'Here, you can have this.'

'Ooh. Cheers.'

'What have you guys been talking about?'

'Deano's sex life and Becky's pantomime,' Cam mumbled through a mouthful of burger. 'Oh, and Kit Beeton's hot-tub parties.'

Cynthia shook her head. 'I'll never get the British pantomime tradition. Still remember the first time I saw one. I thought you must be slipping psychedelic drugs into the tea.'

'It's not that weird, is it?' I said.

'You've got a woman who's really a guy, a guy who's really a girl, an audience of little kids but jokes dirty enough for a working men's club, and costumes that wouldn't look out of place in a drag show. All under the banner of wholesome family entertainment.'

Deano shrugged. 'Your point?'

'Didn't you have anything like that in America?' Marcus asked.

Chapter 8

'No. In the States pantomime means, you know...' She jiggled her palms and bobbed her head from side to side.

I squinted at her. 'It means having a seizure?'

She tutted. 'Mime, silly girl. That was my best "trapped in a glass box" there.'

'Was it? Bloody hell, Cyn, don't give up the day job.'

'Right,' Marcus said. 'I'd better go. I'm due to do my act for the kiddies.'

'Where's your costume?' I asked.

'Haven't got one.'

'You haven't even got a costume?' I shook my head. 'Worst magician ever.'

He grinned. 'You'll see.'

Chapter 9

'Is he any good?' I asked Deano when Marcus had gone.

'He'll surprise you.' He nodded to Marcus approaching Pip and friends by the giant Jenga. 'Go watch.'

I was curious to see how this magician with no costume, no magician name and a geology degree was planning on entertaining a gang of hard-to-please five- and six-year-olds.

'Come on, bro. We can watch while I queue for a burger, yours is making me hungry.' I grabbed Cameron's arm and dragged him to the barbecue.

I expected Marcus to gather the kids into an audience, but he didn't. He just wandered over to Pip and nodded.

'All right?'

The little girl eyed him warily. 'Hello.'

He sank down opposite her on the grass.

'It's your birthday today, right?'

'Yup.'

'How grown-up are you then?'

'You go first.'

'Thirty-three.'

Pip looked impressed. 'That's lots.'

'Thanks. What about you?'

'Six.'

'That's hardly any.'

'It's one bigger than yesterday.'

'Well, that is true.'

Chapter 9

He jerked his head towards the boy next to her, who'd been granted the honour of being allowed to look at her potato masher.

'This your friend?'

'Yes. S'Harry.'

'Does he like onion rings?'

She giggled. 'Dunno.'

'Do you?' Marcus asked Harry. The little boy shook his head slowly, staring at Marcus in wide-eyed wonderment.

'Right, great. You won't mind if I have this one then.' Marcus pulled a fried onion ring from behind Harry's ear and popped it in his mouth.

Pip let out a delighted shriek as Harry blinked and felt behind his ear to see if there were any more battered food products there. Other children were gathering now, alerted to the fact there was something going on.

'He is good, isn't he?' Cameron whispered as Marcus started showing Pip how to levitate a fiver. 'That lad Harry's dead shy. His mum was worried it'd end in tears when I said we were having a magician.'

'Because he's so relaxed,' I said, taking a burger from Stew. 'He doesn't do it like a show, just lets them come to him.'

I was chatting to Tom near the bouncy castle when Marcus joined us a while later. Cam had relieved Tom on the barbecue and Cynthia had gone to sort out drinks for Gerry and Sue, who'd just arrived.

'So how'd I do, guys?' he asked.

'We decided you earned this,' I said, handing over a glass of prosecco.

'That was ace. Cheers, Marc,' Tom said. 'Pip was loving it.'

'Thanks, mate.' He lifted his eyes to the sky. 'Because there're some people round here who in the not-too-distant past have cast doubt on my magical abilities.'

'Well, when a man doesn't even have a goatee...' I said, shrugging. 'That was great though. Interesting act you've developed.'

'Yeah, I like to keep it informal. Too much showmanship puts the shy kids off joining in.'

I felt a tug at my jeans. Pip had sidled up to my leg.

'Hello, little birthday person,' I said, lifting her up. 'Come to see us?'

'Yes,' she whispered, eyes fixed on Marcus.

'Not bored of your party already, Pipsqueak?' Tom said.

'No, Papa.'

'See, she's gone all shy now,' Tom said to Marcus. 'Too much jelly and magic.'

'Aunty Becky,' Pip whispered. 'Ask the man how he made the money fly.'

'Pip says, how did you make the money fly?' I said to Marcus.

'Just a bit of fairy dust.'

Pip nodded. 'That means it's *real* magic,' she told me excitedly. 'Because he knows that's the proper way.'

'Ah, I see. It was a test.' I smiled at Marcus. 'And you passed, apparently. Well done.'

'Here, kid. You know, you really shouldn't keep those in your nose. You might sneeze chocolate over everyone.' He reached out to extract a tube of Smarties from Pip's nostril and handed them to her.

She giggled and jumped out of my arms to show her friends what she'd got.

When she'd disappeared, Marcus shrugged. 'On the house.'

I narrowed one eye at him. 'Were you standing there with a packet of bloody Smarties up your sleeve this whole time?'

'I conjured them from the ether, I'll have you know. One day you're going to have to accept I'm just more magic than you.'

Chapter 9

'Were you though?' Tom asked.

'Yeah. In case of emergencies.'

I jumped when I felt someone kiss my neck from behind.

'Jesus, Cole!' I said, patting my heart. 'You scared the life out of me.'

'Oh. Sorry.'

My face relaxed into a smile. 'Well, I'm glad you made it.'

'I promised, didn't I?' Cole nodded to Marcus and Tom. 'Are you going to introduce your friends?'

'We've met before,' Tom said. 'Tom Donati.'

'Ah. Of course. Um...'

'My brother-in-law?' I shook my head. 'You really are dreadful with names.'

'Marcus Teasdale,' Marcus said. 'Nice to meet you finally. Becky's told me all about you.'

'Don't believe a word of it,' Cole said, smiling as he shook hands. 'What did she tell you?'

'You're a painter. Er, that's about it actually.'

'That's right. A busy one at the moment.' He turned to me. 'I'm sorry, darling, but I can't stay long. I just stopped by to say happy birthday to Pippa.'

'Still working on that commission?'

'Yes. I want to have it finished before our anniversary. Then we can enjoy the evening together without it weighing on my mind.'

'Anniversary... oh! Did you book a restaurant yet? Because I really want to try that new tapas place.'

'Leave it with me. I won't forget.'

'You don't really have to go, do you? Dad and Cynthia were looking forward to seeing you.'

'I really must get the painting finished. There's so much still to do.'

67

Pip came bouncing over, her little face flushed with excitement and sugar.

'Papa, can I go to Evie's for tea and stay for a sleepover?' she gabbled in one breath. 'Daddy says to ask you.'

'You still want tea after all that jelly and ice cream?' Tom shook his head. 'You little porky piglet.'

'Please, Papa! Evie's mummy says we can get pizza and watch *Moana*.'

I nudged him. 'Go on, Tommy. It's her birthday.'

'Oh... all right. But don't eat anything else now until teatime, Pips.'

'Ok.'

'Promise?'

She held up her potato masher solemnly. 'Promise.'

Tom nodded to Cole. 'Say hello to Cole before you go rushing off again.'

Pip turned guileless grey eyes up to Cole. 'Hello.'

'Hello, Pippa. Happy birthday.'

'Pip.'

'She prefers just Pip,' Tom told him.

'Oh.'

Cole looked a bit lost for what to say next. I helped him out.

'Pip loved the present we got her.'

'Did she? Wonderful.' He lowered his voice. 'What was it?'

'Cupcake-maker.'

'Right. I'm glad you liked it, Pip.'

'Say thank you,' Tom instructed her.

'Thank you,' she echoed dutifully.

'You're welcome,' Cole said. 'Um, why have you got that potato masher?'

'Coz it's my 'tato masher,' she said, rolling her eyes. Her face suddenly lit up. 'Hey. I haven't told you my new joke.'

Chapter 9

Tom laughed. 'Think you're the last person in the western hemisphere, mate.'

'Ok, go on,' Cole said.

Pip fixed her face into the sober expression she always used for comedy. ''K, right. Why is Aunty Becky called Aunty Becky?'

'I don't know.'

'Because she *arrr*!'

Cole frowned. 'I don't get it.'

'Because,' Pip repeated slowly, as if she was talking to a slightly dim toddler, 'she *arrr*.'

Cole looked at me helplessly.

'Just laugh,' I whispered.

'Er, haha.'

Pip giggled. 'Ok, bye.' She ran off to join her friends, still brandishing the beloved masher.

'Do I sense you're not used to kids?' Marcus asked Cole, smiling.

'Yes, they're a bit of a mystery. I've not really spent much time with them.'

'Soon fix that when we have one of our own though,' I said.

'Is that on the cards then?' Marcus asked.

I glanced at Cole. 'That's the plan.'

'But there'll be plenty of time to think about that.' Cole gave my waist a squeeze. 'We've got a wedding to plan first.'

'Come on, let's go see my parents,' I said to him. 'They're in the conservatory with Gerry and Sue.' I nodded to Tom and Marcus. 'See you in a bit, guys.'

Cole took my hand as he followed me towards the conservatory. 'You're not too disappointed I can't stay, are you, darling?'

'A little,' I confessed. 'I was looking forward to showing you off to the family. You've been here over a month now and it still feels like they hardly know you.'

'There'll be plenty of time for that.'

'You know, that's starting to become a catchphrase,' I said impatiently. 'It just feels like there's always some reason to be putting things off. I thought once you were here it'd be the start of our exciting new life, but I've barely seen you.'

'This is the last big job, Becky, I promise. Then I'm all yours.' He lifted my hand and kissed it.

'Hmm. Ok.' I glanced back at Marcus and Tom, remembering what else I wanted to talk to him about. 'Cole, can I ask a favour?'

'If it will get me back in your good books.'

I stopped outside the conservatory and turned to face him. 'I know you're super busy, but I was wondering if you might find time to paint a couple of backdrops for the panto. Nothing fancy.'

He laughed. 'You're not serious?'

'Course. Why wouldn't I be?'

'My landscapes sell for hundreds, Becky. You can't really want me to give my time for free?'

'Well, yeah. I'm giving mine. I'm sorting costumes through the shop at cost.' I nodded to Marcus. 'That guy's a professional children's entertainer, but he's doing the panto for nothing. Everyone is, because it's for the Temp.'

'That's hardly the same.'

I frowned. 'Why isn't it the same? Because your job's proper and ours aren't?'

'That isn't what I'm saying. I only mean, my time has a certain value attached to it. I have to be careful how I spend it. And how much I let it take me away from the other important thing in my life.' He drew me into his arms. 'Let's not fall out over it, darling. I didn't mean to offend you.'

'So will you do it?' I asked, slightly appeased.

'I'll see what I can fit in. How's that?'

'Perfect.' I stood on tiptoes to kiss his nose. 'Come on, let's go in to the old folk.'

***

'So that was the future Mr Becky,' Marcus said when Cole had said a quick hello-goodbye to my parents and gone home to his painting. I'd spotted Marc eating alone near the bouncy castle and wandered over to steal a chicken goujon.

'Yeah. What do you think?'

'Seems nice,' Marcus said. 'Plummy, isn't he? Where'd he get an accent like that?'

'Oh, some little comprehensive near Slough,' I said airily, nibbling my goujon. 'Doubt you'd have heard of it.'

I watched his eyebrows raise as he caught my drift.

'You're not serious! Eton?'

'Yeah, scholarship boy. Don't say anything though. He's got chronic posh-lad guilt.'

'He sounds like he should be dating a Middleton sister or someone. How'd he end up with you?'

'Thanks, Marc,' I said, lowering my gaze so he couldn't see my face crumple. 'You know, there's teasing and there's teasing.'

'What, you thought that was an insult?' he said, blinking.

'That you think my posh fiancé's better off with some peachy-arsed minor royal than slumming it with a pleb like me? Erm, yes.'

'I didn't say he'd be better off.' He squeezed my arm. 'It was a compliment, Becks, I promise. I bet you're ten times more of a laugh than Pippa Middleton. Prettier too.'

I smiled. 'You know, you're just digging a bigger hole for yourself.'

'Honestly, it really was a compliment. I'm crap at compliments.'

He made his eyes wide, fluttering his eyelashes until I couldn't help laughing.

'Badly phrased, but all right.'

'I just wondered how it happened, that's all,' Marc said. 'No offence, but you don't seem like you hang out down the local pony club. How did you meet?'

'It was three years ago. His mate Ryder had just opened this new gallery and he hired me to do the photography for the launch event.'

'You? What for?'

I shrugged. 'That's what I do – well, some of the time. I'm a professional photographer.'

Marcus looked impressed. 'Never knew you were so multi-talented.'

'You still trying to dig yourself out of that Pippa Middleton thing?'

'Maybe a bit,' he said, grinning.

'Anyway, Cole was there, and we got chatting. There was a Westminster scene of his on display I was admiring. Next day, it arrived at my flat by cycle courier with a note asking me out. Romantic, right?'

'Fairytale. Bit of a catch really, isn't he?'

'I know. Never quite worked out what he sees in me.' I slapped his arm. 'Right, I'm off to get a drink and make good with the mingling, as befits the hosts' daughter. See you in a bit.'

I left him and made my way to the trestle table where Cynthia had laid out drinks.

There was a woman I didn't recognise there, youngish and quite pretty, and she stood aside to let me serve myself.

'Oh no, you were here first,' I said, nodding Britishly to the wine.

'Thanks.' She smiled at me as she topped up her prosecco.

Chapter 9

'Are you one of the mums?' I asked, helping myself to a glass of white.

'No, I'm a friend of Stewart and Lana's. Carol. How about you?'

'Becky. My niece is the birthday girl.' I indicated Pip on the bouncy castle, bouncing hand in hand with Lana.

'Ah, ok. You know them then.'

'Yes, very well.' I took a sip of the warm-but-welcome wine. 'Have you known them long?'

'Not too long. They seem a lovely couple though.'

'They are.'

'Nice family too,' she said, glancing at Tom and Cam, who were standing with their arms round each other, watching Pip and Lana bouncing.

'On the Donati side,' I said, smiling.

'Sorry?'

'Well, there's Harper Brady on the McLean side. Never met him myself but he sounds a bit of a handful.'

She frowned. 'Not Harper Brady off TV?'

'Oh, sorry, didn't you know? God, I must sound like a right name-dropper.'

'What relation is he to Stewart?'

'Cousin. But they're more like brothers really. Stew's mum and dad half brought him up.'

'He's got quite the bad-boy reputation, hasn't he?'

'Yeah. Stew and Lana are very fond of him though.'

'Wasn't there something about a three-in-a-bed romp with a couple of sex workers a while back? It was in all the tabloids.'

'He's calmed down a bit since then, from what I've heard. He helps out with charity stuff in the village sometimes.'

'What, a big star like him?' Carol said. 'Must be exciting for a sleepy place like this.'

I laughed. 'Don't you believe it. You should hear about Kit Beeton's Friday-night hot-tub orgies.'

'Blimey! Really?'

'Absolutely. They're the talk of the village.' I took another mouthful of wine. It was slipping down very easily. 'And Lana and Stew have had their wild days too, you know.'

'Oh?'

'Mm-hmm. They once posed nude for a calendar.'

'Did they?'

'Yep. Nothing left to the imagination. And Lana once said the f-word to a bat conservationist live on TV.'

'She didn't!'

'Her sense of humour's a bit wicked.' I drained the last of my wine. 'Oh, sorry. Wittering on, aren't I? What is it you do?'

'I'm a social worker.'

'That sounds interesting. What sort of thing?'

'Kids, mainly. I work for an adoption agency.' She nodded to Lana. 'That's how I got to know them. I'm one of their assessors.'

Chapter 10

I stared after Carol as she wandered away.

'What's up with you?' Marcus asked. I spun round to find him helping himself to a beer.

'I just – oh God, Marc, think I just –'

'You just what?'

'Did you know there was someone here from the adoption agency?'

'Yeah, Lana invited her so she could see them doing some aunty and uncling. Why?'

'Well no one bloody told me!'

He examined my face. 'What's wrong, Becky?'

'I just got chatting to her. Had no idea who she was, or I wouldn't... would never have...'

He frowned. 'What did you talk about?'

'Hot-tub orgies. Nudity. The costly and colourful sex life of Harper Brady OBE.' I buried my face in my hands. 'Oh God. I've fucked it, Marc. Haven't I? Their last shot at being parents and I've fucked it for them.'

'Come on, you were only joking. The adoption lady'll know –' He broke off. 'Hey, can you smell that?'

I sniffed, and my eyes went wide. 'Is that what I think it is?'

'Who the hell's smoking weed at a kids' party?'

'Oh my God! If Carol gets a whiff of that then it'll really be game over.' I grabbed his arm. 'Come on.'

'Who could it be?' he said as we moved through the garden inhaling the heavy, sickly-sweet scent of cannabis. 'Surely not a parent?'

'It's not your Deano, is it?'

'Don't be daft. What makes you think Deano smokes weed?'

I shrugged. 'The look in his eye?'

'All my brother's hallucinogens are 100% natural and provided by the gremlins in his brain.' He stopped outside the garden shed. 'It's coming from in here.'

I opened the door and poked my head round, blinking in the gloom. 'Hello?'

'Shit!'

There was the sound of moving plant pots, then an overhead lamp flicked on.

'Hiya, Boo. Um, were you looking for me?'

'Jesus! *Dad?*'

'Oh my God!' Marcus said. Then I heard him snort.

I turned to fix him with a stern look. 'Not funny, Marcus.'

'No. Sorry.' He made an effort to straighten his face. 'I'll leave you two to talk.'

'Yeah. Listen, can you do something for me?'

'What?'

'Can you find my stepmum and keep her busy? And if you see the adoption lady, try to pass the smell off as muck-spreading or something.'

He saluted. 'Roger that. Try not to be too hard on your old man, eh?' He disappeared, and I closed the shed door behind me.

I turned to my dad, arms folded. 'Well? What've you got to say for yourself?'

'Not guilty,' Dad said quickly.

'Not guilty of what?'

'Of, er... whatever it is I'm supposed to have done.'

'You're guilty as sin, mate.' I nodded to an upturned plant pot. 'There's a joint under there.'

He winced. 'It's just a roll-up.'

'The hell it is. It reeks.' I shook my head. 'God, the state of your pupils. You look like a fucking Manga cartoon.'

'Oi. Language, young lady.'

'Oh, no. You do not get to play grown-up today, Danny Finn.' I pointed to the plant pot. 'Put that thing out properly, before the lady from Lana and Stew's adoption agency smells it.'

He grimaced as he turned over the pot and stamped out the smouldering joint. 'Shit, is there someone here from the agency?'

'Yes there is. And she already thinks this village is a hotbed of group sex thanks to me. We don't need you adding drugs to the menu too,' I said. 'Now come on, Father, where'd you get the weed?'

'I told you, it's just a...' He sighed. 'All right, I'll come clean. Off Pagey.'

My eyes widened. 'Mr Page? My old drama teacher's selling you drugs now?'

'No, he gave it me. Confiscated it off one of his Year 11s.'

'What the hell do you think you're playing at?' I exploded. 'It's your granddaughter's birthday, for Chrissakes! I knew you were going through some stuff, but I never thought you were such a selfish bugger you'd sabotage a little girl's party for the sake of a quick high.'

He looked ashamed, as well he should. 'I'm sorry, Becky. Thought I could sneak off for a sly smoke without anyone noticing. It's been a stressful afternoon, I wanted a time-out.'

'Without anyone noticing, are you kidding? I don't know what breed of skunk Mr Page has been confiscating but it stinks to heaven.'

Dad cast an appreciative glance at the flattened joint. 'Yeah, it is good stuff. Couldn't afford that kind of quality when I was sixteen.'

'Are you a connoisseur now?'

He shrugged. 'Back in the day. In the seventies we used to sneak it into gigs in film canisters. God knows how kids manage now, with just their cameraphones.' He let out a wistful sigh. 'Happy days.'

He looked so miserable, I couldn't help relenting a bit. I took a seat in his manky old armchair, indicating a stool opposite for him.

'Talk to me, Dad,' I said in a gentler voice. 'What's this all about?'

He sat down and leaned on his knees, digging his fists into his cheeks. 'Oh, you know. Worry I've let life pass me by. One last chance to grab it by the balls. You'll understand when you get to my age.'

'But it hasn't passed you by,' I said. 'You've got two kids, a partner, a granddaughter who loves you to bits. You're captain of the darts team. What more do you want?'

'I don't know,' he said in the same flat voice. 'Just to be doing something that matters. One final thrill before it's too late.'

'Now you're being morbid. You're only sixty. It's the new forty, isn't that what they say?'

'Still. It's an age that makes you think.'

I dipped my head to catch his gaze. 'Cyn told me about the health scare,' I said quietly.

'Did she?'

'Yeah.'

He sighed. 'You get so used to your body being yours, don't you? Doing what you tell it, Old Reliable. Until the day you realise there's a traitor in your midst. Bloody terrifying.'

'It was just a scare, Dad. You're ok.'

'But I might not've been. And one day it won't just be a scare, will it? It'll be the real thing.'

'You could've talked to me, you know.'

He smiled sadly. 'No, love. I might be a bit of a fuck-up, but I'm still your dad. Have to protect you and Cam from the big bad world, don't I?'

'We're adults. We protect each other now, all of us. And you're not a fuck-up.'

'Maybe not in one way.' He reached out to squeeze my wrist. 'I've given two things to the world I'm obscenely proud of.'

I smiled. 'Thanks, Dad.'

'It's a funny thing, life. Every day follows every day, and you keep thinking there'll be a tomorrow when it gives you everything you need. But John Lennon had it right, I think. Life is what happens when you're making other plans.' He laughed. 'God, I'm a depressing bastard.'

'You are not. You're my dad.' I took his hand. 'What about your family? Did we happen while you were making other plans?'.

He smiled. 'You were the times life did give me what I needed. You and your brother, and little Pip. But after the scare, I just felt so... empty. Aching.'

'Oh... Dad.' I gave the hand I was holding a squeeze. 'You know I love you. Hate seeing you like this.'

'Don't worry about me, Boo. I just need this little time to find where I'm going, that's all. My head's so full I can't sleep.'

I shot him a worried glance. 'Is that why you've been staying out so late? Cyn's worried sick about you.'

'No,' he said, avoiding my gaze. 'No, that's... something else.'

'Dad?'

'Yes, sweetheart?'

'You do still love Cyn, don't you?'

'Course I do. Nothing that's going on in here can change that,' he said, tapping his temple.

'Only some men your age, when they get to feeling a bit... well, mortal, they start thinking back to their youth. Getting full of the joys of spring, if you take my meaning.'

He frowned. 'Eh?'

'Cyn thinks you might be sleeping with someone else.'

He snorted. 'Does she? The daft cow.'

'Don't laugh,' I said, frowning. 'She's really worried. And I'm not going to have a go at you about it now, but I know you've got history in that department. My mum?'

He flinched. 'Cyn told you about that, did she?'

'She did.'

'That was different though. Me and your mum, we knew our marriage was over long before I met Cyn. Then when I did it was just, bam, you know? I knew she was the one, right away.'

'Yet you've never asked her to marry you.'

He shrugged. 'I tried that once. If it taught me anything, it's that marriage is nothing without love. And if you've got love, why bother with marriage?'

'What about what Cyn wants?'

'She never said she wanted to get married.'

'No. But I think she might've liked to be asked,' I said. 'So if it's not another woman, where have you been going?'

He looked embarrassed, scratching at the paintwork on the old stool with his fingernail.

'Just a little project. Old hobby I'm getting back into.'

'At two in the morning? What is it, bat-watching?'

'All right, Boo, I'll tell you. But only if you promise you won't take the piss.'

I frowned. 'Why would I take the piss?'

'Because you're my daughter and it's your favourite thing.'

'Oh Christ. What is it?'

'I've been in Pagey's garage with Billy and a few lads from the Fox.'

'What, smoking weed?'

'No. Well, sometimes.' His half-stoned eyes sparkled. 'It's just, me and the boys... we're putting a band together.'

'Oh, you have *got* to be kidding me.' I buried my face in my hands, half laughing, half weeping, till the tears stung my eyes.

***

'Becky!'

The voice had been calling my name for a good minute.

'Becky Finn! Where are you?'

The wall felt cool against my hot forehead. I groaned softly. I was quite content where I was, alone in my dad's shed. If the voice would only go away.

'Must've gone home, Marc,' a Deano voice said. 'Come on. We're the last ones.'

'She would've said goodbye.' There was a pause, then a soft knock at the door. 'Becks?' a voice whispered. 'You hiding?'

'Go 'way. Becky's not here.'

'There you go,' Deano said. 'Told you she went home.'

'You're a funny boy, Deano. Go say bye to Danny and Cynthia, I'll be out in a minute.'

The door opened a crack, and Marcus slid himself in.

'Dark in here,' he observed observantly.

I shot him a thumbs-up, not moving my head from its resting place. 'That's what I like about you, Marc. Never afraid to state the bleeding obvious.'

He stumbled around until he located the overhead lamp and flicked it on.

'How's the wall, Becks?'

'Awesome. Top wall. Best wall I've leaned my head against while groaning pitifully in, ooh, weeks.'

'Want to tell me what's up?'

'Ok.' I stood up straight and turned to face him. 'My future husband seems incapable of making a good impression on my parents, no matter how much I force him into their company. I may have made Egglethwaite sound like Yorkshire's answer to Sodom and Gomorrah to a social worker responsible for deciding whether it's a suitable place to raise a child. Oh, and my sixty-year-old father's become a weed-smoking rock-and-roller with embarrassing hair. That enough?'

'You've had some afternoon, haven't you?'

'Mmm. One for the family album.'

'Here.' He sat on the arm of the comfy chair and patted the cushion. I sank into it with another deep groan.

'Want to see some magic?'

'Not the time, Marc.'

'Sure it is. It's always the time for magic.' He reached into his pocket for a pack of cards. 'You once asked me to show you a card trick. Seems only fair, now I've got the necessary equipment.'

I gave a sigh of resignation. 'All right, Gambit, if you must.'

'Here's one you'll like.' He shuffled the cards, then fanned them out in front of me.

'Pick a card, any card, right?'

'You've done this before.'

I extracted a card and glanced at it.

'Now put it back anywhere in the pack,' Marc said.

I did as he asked, and he started shuffling again.

'Erm, Marc?' I said after a minute of him shuffling absently.

'Hmm?'

'Is that it?'

'Oh, right, yeah.' He nodded to an upturned plant pot. 'Look under there.'

I went to the pot and lifted it. Sure enough, there was a playing card underneath.

'Three of Diamonds,' I said, picking it up. 'Bloody hell.'

'Your card, right?'

'Um, yeah.' I stared at him. 'How'd you do that? You never even moved!'

He shrugged. 'Easy when you know how.'

'Come on, tell me.'

'Sorry. Trade secret.'

'Please. I won't tell anyone, cross my heart.'

'Nope. If I start revealing my secrets to girls I'm trying to impress, I'll lose all my sexy magical mystery.'

I took my seat again, fixing him with an impressed gaze. 'Ok, I take back anything I ever said about you not being a proper magician.'

He smiled as he put the cards away. 'And you feel better, right?'

'I do a bit. Thanks, Marc.'

'It's really not so bad, you know. What happened today.'

I sighed. 'It's pretty bad. If I've ruined Lana and Stew's adoption chances, I'll never forgive myself.'

'What did you actually tell the adoption lady?'

'I told her Stew was tabloid bad boy Harper Brady's cousin. I told her Kit Beeton's hot-tub orgies were the talk of the village. I told her Lana and Stew once posed nude for a calendar... oh God.' I buried my face in my hands. 'Ok, now I feel worse again.'

He flicked a hand dismissively. 'That's nothing.'

'How can you say it's nothing?'

'So Stew's got an embarrassing relative. Not his fault. Anyway, they'd have found that out from the background checks.'

'What about the other stuff?'

'Well, the calendar was for charity. It's not so shocking nowadays, is it? Loads of respectable people take their clothes off for calendars. And she'll know the thing about Kit was a joke.'

'Will she though?'

'Even if she doesn't, she's not going to write them off based on the word of somebody she got chatting to at a garden party. They'll make great parents. That's all she cares about.'

'What about my dad?'

'Oh, he'll get over it. To be honest, his mid-life crisis symptoms are pretty mild.'

'Doing drugs at a children's party? Are you kidding?'

'My dad went through something similar a few years ago. Blew his and Mum's savings on a trip to Thailand to "find himself".' He paused. 'Then he met someone else out there and decided to move permanently.'

'Shit!'

'Yeah,' he said, casting his eyes down. 'Tore the family apart. Me and Deano don't really talk to him now.'

'I'm sorry, Marc.' I took his hand and gave it a squeeze. 'Bet that was tough.'

'On Mum it was. God, we would've loved it if he'd just rolled a few joints and locked himself in the shed.' He glanced around. 'Speaking of sheds, we should really get out of this one. There's a fat spider over there looking at us like we might make a tasty snack.'

'I'll see you next week, won't I? Our first script meeting?'

'Looking forward to it. Hey.' He stood up and pulled me to my feet. 'Before we go.'

Chapter 10

He drew me into his arms for a hug. It was a good hug. Sort of bearish and unrestrained, his arms wrapping firmly across my back to squeeze me tight. An appreciative sigh escaped me.

'No more worrying, ok?' he whispered. 'You had a lot to deal with today, Becks. I was proud of you.'

'Yeah. Thanks, Marc.'

Chapter 11

'You look pretty,' Cole said when he discovered me in the kitchen one evening, distributing maize-based snacks into bowls. He fingered my strappy top. 'Is this for my benefit?'

'Sadly not. Marc's coming round to work on the panto script.'

'That's a shame. I thought I could take a night off and we could spend the evening together.'

I turned and put my arms around him. 'I'm sorry, love, you should've said. It's too late to reschedule now, he'll be here any minute.'

'No, my fault. I shouldn't expect you to be free at the drop of a hat now you're such a pillar of the community,' he said, smiling. 'Still...'

'What? I know that voice.'

'I do think they ask rather a lot of you, Becky.' He ran a finger under my eye. 'You look exhausted.'

I was tired, but it wasn't the panto causing the sleepless nights. It was Dad. He was still out till all hours, poisoning himself with booze and God knew what else. The family were worried sick.

I hadn't confided my worries to Cole though. When it came to the law, he was always so... upright. For Cole, just the word 'drugs' was enough to conjure *Trainspotting*-esque images of filthy smack dens and crumpled tinfoil. I couldn't help feeling he wouldn't understand.

'Who are "they"?' I asked.

'Well, you know. The pantomime people.'

'I am the pantomime people. It was my idea.'

'The people who run the village hall then.'

'That's me too. The village society are trustees of the hall, and I'm a member of the society,' I said. 'There isn't really any "they". Just volunteers, same as me. It's no good trying to make it someone else's problem: the Temp belongs to us all.'

He smiled. 'When did you get so public-spirited?'

'Hard-working people ran the hall when I was a kid. Now it's my turn.'

'You know you're pretty amazing?'

'I know,' I said, smiling. 'But I like it when you tell me.'

He glanced at my fancy top again. 'You don't really need to dress up just for Marcus, do you?'

I shrugged. 'Don't want him thinking I'm a closet slob.'

'What's all this?' he asked, indicating the food.

'Nibbles. We'll need to keep our energy up.'

He laughed. 'If I didn't know better I'd think you were getting ready for a date.'

'Cheeky.' I tapped the bridge of his nose. 'You know you're welcome to join us, love. Innuendo contributions all appreciated.'

'No, I'll get some painting done. Shame to waste the evening. If I think up any good innuendos I'll shout them down.'

'Ok,' I said, giving him a kiss. 'Oh, here. You'll need to keep your energy up too.' I handed him one of the snack bowls.

He frowned at it. 'What on earth are these?'

'Wotsits. Don't tell me you've never tried them?'

'These are food? They look like crunchy tangerine maggots.'

'Yeah.' I popped one in my mouth. 'Delicious bastards.'

'Oh, that reminds me,' he said, trying unsuccessfully not to let his distaste show as he put the Wotsits back down. 'Are we free the last Friday of next month?'

'Think so. Why?'

'I was chatting to Patrick today, the classics lecturer at college, and I sort of accidentally invited him and his wife over for a few drinks. Sorry.'

'No need to be. I'm thrilled you're making new friends. I still feel guilty about dragging you away from your arty set down south.' I smiled. 'Tell you what, I'll cook, shall I? We'll make it a proper dinner party.'

'I was hoping you'd say that.' His guilty grimace deepened. 'Because, er, I kind of accidentally invited Ryder and Ali too. They're coming up from Kensington.'

'Oh.'

Cole was a smart lad. Actually I'd long been convinced he was some kind of super-IQed mega-genius, easily capable of advanced calculus or brain surgery if he wasn't so committed to his art. So it seemed odd that with his huge brain, he'd never noticed how much I found his pretentious friend Ryder and his snooty wife hard work.

I summoned a smile. 'That's... great,' I lied. 'You won't mind me inviting a couple of people, will you?'

'Of course not. Who did you have in mind?'

Oh God, anyone to save me from the monotony of a night tête-a-tête with bloody Ryder Sherlock-Steele...

'It'd be nice to ask my brother and Tom,' I said. 'And Lana and Stew. I'm sure my parents won't mind babysitting.'

I was glad to have an excuse not to suggest inviting my dad and Cyn. Already unconvinced by Cole, I couldn't see an evening in the company of his braying tit of a best mate doing much to pour oil on troubled waters.

There was a knock at the door and I went to get it, Cole following.

'Hi Becks,' Marcus said when I answered, kissing my cheek. He brandished a few sheets of A4. 'I'll show you mine if you show me yours.'

'Come on in. I've cleared a space at the coffee table.'

'All right, mate?' Marcus said, nodding to Cole. 'You script-doctoring with us?'

'Hello Marcus. No, work to do I'm afraid.' He clapped Marc on the shoulder. 'Look after Becky for me.'

'Bloody hell, you're honoured,' I said when Cole had disappeared.

'Am I? Why?'

'He remembered your name.'

'Bad with them, is he?'

'Yeah. Spends too much time in his head with imaginary landscapes. Here, come through.'

He followed me into the living room and we took a seat on the sofa.

'So what have you written?' I said.

'Just a brainstorm really, a few jokes. Thought we could work them into suitable scenes.'

He passed me a sheet and I started reading. I was soon smiling at the cheesy gags.

'Ok, what's making you smirk?' he asked.

I pointed to a bit of dialogue. 'That's pretty funny.'

'Christmas cracker stuff,' he said, shrugging. 'Want to perform it with me?'

'Ok.'

'Go on then, you start.'

'Right.' I assumed a deadpan expression. 'Gee, secondary pantomime character. It's at times like this I wish I'd listened to what my mother used to tell me.'

'What did she used to tell you, primary pantomime character?'

'I don't know, I wasn't listening. Badumtish.'

He laughed. 'Hey, you've got pretty good comic timing.'

'Thanks. You've got great hair.'

'Will you audition?'

'For Jack?'

He picked the script up from the table and flicked through. 'I'd go for Jill, the principal girl. She gets better lines.'

'Maybe I will.' I looked him up and down. 'What about you? I can see you in an outrageous dress and a couple of massive fake knockers.'

He laughed. 'What, the dame?'

'No. I can just see you in them.'

'Was thinking I might audition actually. There's bound to be a dimwit sidekick part with my name on it.'

I took the script from him and turned to the character list. 'Yeah. Sleepy Steve, Jack's brother. Would you do tricks?'

'If I get the part. Might as well play to the cast's strengths,' he said. 'Oh, and I could juggle too, that always goes down well with the littlies. Especially with something breakable.'

'What, you juggle?'

'I have a full set of circus skills, luvvie,' he said, tossing his head.

'Hey, could you teach me? Pip'd be well impressed.'

'I could give it a go. Got any balls?'

I raised one eyebrow. 'We onto the innuendo already?'

'It's never too early.' He reached for his pen. 'I'm writing that one down. Sleepy Steve can use it on the principal boy.'

'I'll fetch some apples.'

I went to the kitchen for the fruit. Marcus stood to take them from me.

'Ok, Becks, nothing to it.'

He started casually tossing apples into the air, catching each one with consummate skill as another sailed upwards. His movements were so fluid and self-assured, he made it look like the easiest thing in the world.

'Here.' He caught the three airborne apples deftly and held up two. 'Start with just a couple. Trick is, you chuck one in the air and when it's at the halfway point, you send the next one up with the same hand you then use to catch the first.'

'You do what with the what with the what?'

He smiled. 'All right, come here. This is how I learned.'

He moved so he could put his arms around me from behind, moulding his body to mine.

'Ok, watch my hands,' he said, his breath against my ear. 'Then try to shadow my movements.'

'And this is how you learned, is it?'

'Yep.'

'From a sexy girl?'

He laughed. 'Big, burly lad from Rotherham actually. It's quite a skill, learning to juggle with some bloke's beard tickling the back of your neck.'

'Enjoy it?'

'Not as much as he did, lucky bastard.'

He started chucking the apples up, catching them skilfully, and I tried to mimic his movements.

'What's going on in here?'

'Shit!' Marcus said as one of the apples crashed to the floor. He let me go quickly and turned to face the speaker. 'Hi, Cole.'

'Just a juggling lesson,' I said, retrieving the fallen apple from the carpet.

'Ah, ok,' Cole said. 'I'm out of turps so I'm popping to the supermarket. Do you need anything while I'm out, darling?'

'No, we're good, thanks.' I looked at the bruised apple. 'Oh, actually. Could you pick up more apples?'

'Is he always this understanding when he finds you in another man's arms?' Marcus asked when Cole was gone.

I shrugged. 'Well it's not like it happens every week.'

'Flattered you're so picky.'

'You should be. It's not every bloke I let come up behind me and juggle my juicy fruits.'

'Ha! Nice one.' He grabbed his pen off the table. 'We'll have that for the dame.'

'Nothing to it, is there?' I said as he scribbled my juicy fruits line down. 'All you need is a filthy mind.'

'It can't be all dirty jokes though. We need some lines that won't go completely over the kids' heads.'

'Yeah, you're right.' I sank back onto the sofa. 'Come on, let's do some work. We can have juggling and innuendo for afters.'

'Ok, so what do children find funny?' Marcus asked, sitting beside me.

'Oh, slapstick. Farting, willies, bums. Anything toilet-related.'

'Kids're disgusting.'

'Cute though. You get fond of them after a bit.' I looked up from my notes. 'Think you'll have any?'

'I'd love to be a dad,' he said. 'I need to meet the right person first though. And let's face it, time's getting on.'

'Tell me about it. What're you, thirty-three?'

'And a quarter.'

'See, I'm a year older. I've reached that age where every friend and relative considers it their solemn duty to remind me that neither me nor my womb are getting any younger.'

'When were you and Cole planning to start trying for a baby?'

'Soon, I hope. It feels like for years there's been some reason to put it off. Not enough money, not enough space in our old flat, no family close by for support...'

'But not any more, right?' He glanced around the spacious terrace we were renting, less than half the cost and five times the size of our poky London flat. 'Looks like conditions are perfect for bringing a little Becky or Cole into the world.'

'Cole wants the wedding first. He's traditional like that.'

'How about you?'

'Not so much.' I sighed. 'He's right, you can't rush these things. But I can't help thinking about it, now I'm seeing so much of Pip.'

'Great little lass, isn't she?'

I smiled. 'Yeah. She's perfect.'

'It'll happen for you, Becks,' Marcus said earnestly. 'Sixteen years from now, you'll be the fun, pretty mum all your kid's friends are a bit in love with.'

'If it can happen.'

Marcus frowned. 'Why shouldn't it?'

'Maybe I can't have kids. I mean, I guess I can, but...' I glanced up to meet his eyes. 'It's just that there was another time it nearly happened for us – me and Cole. Back when we were first together.'

'What, you mean...'

'Yeah. Early stages, but I was late so I did a test and... it was positive.' I laughed. 'God, I was terrified. We'd only been together a few months. I was earning a pittance with my photography, credit card maxed out, sky-high rent I could barely keep on top of. London, right?'

'Jesus, Becks...' Instinctively, he stretched a comforting arm around me.

'I spent so long wrestling with whether I could afford to go through with it. But after two weeks, it...' I blinked hard. 'Let's just say it worked itself out.'

'Shit. You mean you... oh God, poor Becky.' He leaned round to look into my brimming eyes, his face full of sympathy.

'It's no big deal,' I said, wiping the tears away. 'Loads of women go through it. Nearly half of pregnancies end in miscarriage.'

'It's still a big deal.' He gave my shoulders a squeeze. 'I'm sorry, Becks. Does Cole know?'

'No. I never told anyone. Just pushed it down and got on with sorting my life out so the next time... I'd be ready. But I can't help worrying there's something wrong.' I looked down at my notepad, the squiggly panto notes blurring behind more tears.

'It doesn't necessarily mean that,' he said gently. 'It's common, like you said. If you're worried, see a doctor.'

'Perhaps I'm scared of what they might say. I'd rather find out the old-fashioned way.' I looked up to meet his gaze. 'I've never told anyone about that before.'

'You know I won't say anything.'

I summoned a wobbly smile. 'I know.'

'How's your dad doing now?' he asked. 'Any better?'

'Well, I convinced him to talk to Cynthia, so at least she knows it's not another woman keeping him busy at night.' I shook my head. 'This band thing though. I don't know what to make of it.'

'It's good, isn't it? Something to keep his mind away from the dark places?'

'Maybe. Just not sure it's healthy, staying up to all hours. Smoking weed. Drinking too much. I mean, his mind might've regressed to seventeen but his body's still sixty.'

'Are the band any good?'

'Dunno. In his mind they're bloody Status Quo though.' I twiddled my pen absently. 'There's no point dwelling on it, is there? He's a grown-up. I just need to be there for him.'

He examined my face. 'And are you ok? You don't look like you've been sleeping so well.'

'I'm fine. Just worried.'

'You know I'm always here if you want to talk to someone, Becks.'

'Yeah. Thanks for listening.' I flashed him a smile. 'You know, I'm glad I met you. Best thing that's happened since I came home.'

Chapter 11

He grinned. 'All right, love, enough trying to get in my pants. Let's do some work.'

'Why, what's in your pants that's so exciting?'

'The Three of Diamonds. That's for my after-dark routine.'

I picked up the script. 'So we'll need to customise this a bit, won't we? Add in some local stuff. Any ideas?'

'Where me and Deano grew up, the panto was always full of jokes about neighbouring villages having improper relationships with sheep and so on. Pretty racy, I don't know how they got away with it.'

'We can't do that,' I said. 'People come from neighbouring villages to see the show. Half the audience'll walk out if we're too insulting.'

'Ah, but that's where you have to be smart,' he said, tapping his temple. 'Where we lived, they used a village six or seven miles away rather than the ones either side. Close enough that everyone would get the joke but far enough away that it was unlikely they'd be in the audience. Always the same place, it became a running gag.'

'Devious. What was the village?'

'Oh, nowhere,' he said casually. 'Just some little place with ideas above its station.'

I narrowed one eye. 'It was here. Wasn't it?'

'Yeah,' he said with a grin. 'If it helps, I've discovered since Deano moved here that your relationships with sheep are entirely species-appropriate.'

'Well, not sure about Gerry Lightowler.'

'Mmm. He is very attached to them.'

By the time Marcus left at 11pm, we had two pages of innuendo, several jokes about the folk from nearby Pogley being unduly fond of their livestock, and some very mushy apples. I'd just about mastered the art of juggling with two balls, and Marc reckoned that if I practised I could soon be ready for three.

Cole was in bed reading when I made my way upstairs.

'Did you have fun tonight?' he asked as I crawled into my PJs.

'Yeah,' I said, sliding into bed and snuggling into him. He was warm and smelled slightly of turps, a scent I'd come to associate with safety. 'It was a good laugh actually.'

'I'm glad.'

I looked up into his face. 'You don't mind me doing this without you?'

'Of course not, darling. It's good for you to have your own hobbies and friends.'

'I guess. But you know I'd love you to be involved.'

This was the third time I'd dropped the same hint. But if I sounded hopeful, Cole didn't pick up on it.

'Don't be silly. This is your project, you don't want me muscling in. And I told you, it's not really my scene.' He pulled me to him for a kiss. 'Still, I'm glad it's making you happy.'

Chapter 12

The script was in progress, the props under construction and the crew all assigned jobs. The only thing we didn't have now was a cast. Which, I was reliably informed, was quite important if you were planning on staging a panto.

Auditions were advertised for the last week in April. We were aiming for a week-long run in mid-December, and even for newbies, seven months seemed a reasonable bit of rehearsal time.

On audition day, I called at Pie and a Pint for Lana. She was talking in a low voice to Tom, who'd come to relieve her shift.

'What're you two whispering about?'

'Oh, nothing important,' Lana said airily.

Tom nudged her. 'Go on. You know you're bursting.'

'What?' I said, looking from one to the other. 'What's the nothing important?'

'Only this.' She waved a piece of paper at me, the grin she'd been suppressing finally escaping.

'Oh my God!' I said, snatching it from her. 'Is it from the adoption agency?'

'Yep. We're through to stage two.'

'Arghh, amazing!' I threw my arms around her. 'God, and being completely selfish here, but what a relief.'

I'd confessed to my conversation with Carol the day after Pip's party, and although Lana and Stew had done their best to reassure me, I couldn't help worrying. I hadn't admitted my dad's pungently illegal shed-based activities, which had been another weight on my mind.

'What happens now?' I asked.

Lana groaned. 'Four months' training and assessment. New hell, same as the old hell.'

'So it's still not a done deal?'

'I don't think it's a done deal till they actually give us a kid.'

'It'll happen.' Tom gave her a squeeze. 'And trust me, sis, when it does, all the sleepless nights'll have been worth it.'

'I know.' She grabbed her handbag. 'Right, me and Becks had better get off to Egglethwaite's Got Talent. See you, Tommy.'

'Where's Stew?' I asked as we walked to the temperance hall.

'Gone to fetch Harper. We usually sneak him up through the cellar entrance. It's a good idea to keep him under wraps till we get started.'

The panel for judging the wannabe actors consisted of me, Stew, Lana, Marcus, Deano, Harper Brady, Yolanda and Billy, who I suspected had only volunteered so he could have a perve at the potential principal boys' legs.

There was some crossover between the panel and the auditionees. Yolanda was ready to bitch slap any other contenders for the part of the Good Fairy, I was going to take a probably doomed shot at principal girl, and Marcus was trying out for gormless sidekick Sleepy Steve. We couldn't vote for ourselves though, and Deano had made us swear an oath we'd be strictly impartial. An actual oath, he'd done printouts. I was starting to understand how the cast and crew of *HMS Pinafore* 2010, Sheffield College Catering and Hospitality Department, must've felt.

'Bloody hell!' I whispered to Lana when we arrived.

The place was packed to the gills with people. They couldn't all be from Egglethwaite. If there were that many aspiring thesps in the village, someone would've revived the pantomime years ago.

'We'll be here till midnight if they're all going to audition,' I said.

'Most of them'll clear out when they've seen Harper,' Lana whispered back. 'Happens every time. That's why we always allow half an hour for him to do autographs at the start.'

A row of screens had been dragged together to close off the area in front of the stage and I followed Lana behind. In the screened-off section were two tables, pushed together to make one long one, with eight chairs behind facing the stage.

'Hey, this is a bit telly,' I said. 'We haven't wandered into the first round of *X-Factor* by mistake, have we? Because I'm not sure I can cope with Simon Cowell telling me I'm shit on top of you lot.'

She laughed. 'Nervous?'

'Terrified.'

'You've practised, haven't you?'

'A bit. Marc's been coaching me and I've been helping him with his Sleepy Steve lines.'

'See? You'll be fine,' she said, giving my elbow a reassuring squeeze. 'How's Marc's acting?'

'Great. That lad was made for panto. Never seen someone improvise a sausage-based innuendo while performing a four-ball juggle before.'

'You two getting on ok?'

'Yeah. Feels like I've known him years.'

'I actually meant with the script,' she said, shooting me a curious look.

'Oh. Right. Yes, we've nearly finished,' I said. 'You'd better fetch Brady and get the ball rolling. I'm going out for some air.'

I hurried outside and leaned against the sooty wall of the Temp, gulping down mouthfuls of sweet, fresh air. I didn't know if it was the unexpectedly big crowd or a sudden attack of stagefright, but I was feeling seriously claustrophobic.

I'd not been alone with my thoughts two minutes when a woman hurried through the door, eyes darting to both sides as if something was chasing her. She leaned against the wall and exhaled slowly.

'Do you vape, sweetness? Mine's at home and I'm gagging.'

'Um, no,' I said, blinking. 'Sorry.'

She seemed familiar, though I couldn't work out why. Late twenties probably, very tall – nearly six foot in her flats – and indecently attractive, *Baywatch* attractive, in a well-cut trouser suit with long, blonde hair flowing over her enormous chest. She didn't suit the cobbles at all.

She didn't suit me much either. I felt a sudden, over-whelming insignificance in the face of this perfect specimen of womanhood.

'Are you here to audition?' I asked.

'Yes. Well, more a formality really. My hubby knows one of the organisers.' She let out a tinkling laugh. I should've known she was a tinkler, you could tell from the cheekbones. 'You feel sorry for the other girls, don't you? But all's fair in love and amateur dramatics.'

What organiser? All the organisers there were so far apart from me were Lana, Stew, Deano and Marcus, and none of them had mentioned anything.

'Oh, I am sorry,' she said. 'Were you here for the part? They really should've told you so you didn't need to waste your time.'

'No, I – sorry, which organiser does your husband know?'

'Stewart McLean. You heard of him? He's a cyclist. Well, he was. He's retired now.'

'Stew? Er, yeah. How does he –'

Chapter 12

'Oh God,' she hissed, grabbing my arm. I followed her gaze to a man with a handheld video camera making his way out of the hall. 'You see what I have to put up with? This is what I was hiding from.'

'Is that your husband?' I asked, more confused than ever.

She tinkled again. 'Him? I wouldn't widdle on him if he'd been stung by a flock of jellyfish then set on fire.' She turned to the man. 'Honestly, Gavin, must you follow me round with that thing like a horny puppy? I'm not making gripping TV while you aren't looking, cross my heart.'

'Mr Brady says not to let you out of my sight,' the man mumbled, training his camera on the pair of us.

'You don't mind, do you?' she said to me. 'Harper's idea. He's got us doing one of those "at home with" reality shows. Pain in the hole, but I figure he knows what he's doing.'

'Oh my God!' I said, suddenly realising why she looked familiar. 'You're Maisie Moorhouse!'

'Maisie Brady, lovely. Thought we'd go a bit tradish, you know? Good for the public image, Harper says.'

I couldn't believe I hadn't recognised her – although to be fair, I'd never seen her with all her clothes on before.

Maisie Moorhouse was a glamour model known for the 'natural look': no implants, in other words. She'd been the darling of the trashier tabloids but pretty Z-list generally until she'd married Harper Brady two months ago. Then there'd been a flurry of photoshoots, magazine spreads, and for a while she'd been everywhere, until the next celebrity couple had come along. Why she was auditioning for a part in some tiny village panto, I had no idea.

'Excuse me. I need a word with someone.' I nodded to Gavin. 'Um, excuse me.'

Inside the Temp, I headed backstage. Lana, Stewart and a handsome, flaxen-haired man I recognised as TV's Harper Brady were whispering ferociously together in a corner.

'For God's sake, Harper,' Stewart was saying. 'Why didn't you tell me you'd be filming?'

'What does it matter? I brought consent forms, and we can pixelate anyone who doesn't want to be in it.'

'You could've bloody said something! Bad enough you dragged Maisie along.'

'Come on, Stew, don't be a dick. Just let her audition.'

'Can she act?' Lana demanded.

Harper shrugged. 'She's got amazing legs.'

'That's not what I asked.'

'Well, she is a bit on the stiff side,' he admitted. 'But she's learning.'

I cleared my throat.

'Oh. Hi, Becks,' Lana said. 'Er, this is Harper.'

'I'd gathered.' I gave Harper a curt nod. 'What the hell's going on, you guys? I just had a conversation with Maisie Moorhouse that basically made it sound like she'd been guaranteed the lead role in our panto.'

Stewart glared at Harper. 'You didn't.'

Harper looked guilty. 'I didn't guarantee it, exactly. I just said you and Lana were involved so she had a good shot.'

'If she can't act, what can she do?' I demanded. 'Dance? Sing?'

'She's got amazing –' Harper began.

'– legs,' I finished. 'Yeah, we know.'

He shrugged. 'Was going to say boobs that time.'

'We know that too. Everyone knows, they've been on the covers of all the lads' mags.'

'Well, isn't that enough? It's only a village panto. Stick a pair of tights on, slap your thigh and look sexy. That's all the principal boy has to do.'

'Why are you so keen for her to audition?' Stewart demanded. 'This is the Egglethwaite panto, not the RSC.'

Harper lowered his voice. 'It's part of our plan. I'm helping her break into acting.'

'And this is the best you could do?' I said. 'Bloody hell, your stock must've fallen a bit since the BAFTA.'

Harper drew himself up. 'My stock is higher than – Knorr, I'll have you know. Who the hell are you, anyway?'

'I'm in charge.' I glanced at Lana and Stew. 'Um, am I?'

Lana nodded. 'This panto was her idea,' she told Harper. 'And she's my sister-in-law so be nice.'

'Oh. Right,' Harper said, regarding me with a modicum more respect. 'Well, the problem is, Maisie's got no experience. We thought this'd be a great in. Win for everyone, isn't it? You lot get a sexy celeb for your panto, Mais gets Brownie points for helping out a local village hall once the reality show hits screens, and any talent scouts out there will see her acting.'

'I thought you said she couldn't act,' I said.

'Like I said, I'm working on it.'

Stew shook his head. 'You're using this to get yourself back in the papers, aren't you? Post-wedding comedown now *OK!* aren't constantly on the phone. You swore this marriage wasn't another PR stunt, Harper.'

'It isn't, honestly! I love her. Really this time. Don't you think if I wanted a fake wife I could've got someone a bit more high-profile?'

'Then what's this all about?'

'It's about Mais,' Harper said. 'I mean, not that I mind her getting her tits out for a living, I'm an enlightened guy. But they won't stay firm forever. She'll need something to fall back on when her figure goes.'

Lana rolled her eyes at me. 'Harper Brady OBE, the nation's sweetheart. Swoon, eh?'

'And you think a reality show's the start she needs?' I asked Harper.

He shrugged. 'Well, who was Kim Kardashian? Just a nice arse that got on telly. Trust me, Maisie's got a great arse.'

'We don't need to trust you. We've seen it.'

Stewart groaned. 'You're not going to do a sex tape, are you? Because it'll be me who has to break it to Mum and Dad when your backside's on the front of *The Sun* again. The Sunday dinner after the pair of us got papped in that strip club was awkward enough.'

Lana raised her eyebrows. 'You let him take you to a strip club?'

'I was just picking him up, all right?'

'Mmm. You're all heart.'

'We'll save the sex tape for a last resort,' Harper said, grinning. 'Gav'd do that one for free.'

'I bet,' Stew muttered.

'But I've got high hopes for *The Brady Bunch* – that's what we're calling the show. Especially with this panto plotline showcasing Maisie's talents.'

'This isn't a plotline, mate, it's our actual lives,' Lana snapped. 'We could lose our community centre.'

'I know.' He sighed. 'Ok, fine. If I really have to... look, if you let Maisie play one of the leads, I'll do you a cameo. Then you can put my name on the posters.'

'You're in a panto already, aren't you?' I said. 'I thought you were playing Dick Whittington at Bradford Alhambra.'

'That was last season. I'm Aladdin in Leeds this Christmas.'

'They're still talking about Harper's Dick in Bradford though,' Stewart told me. 'One to rival Barry Chuckle's, apparently.'

Lana nodded soberly. 'I've always said there's no Dick quite like Harper.'

Chapter 12

Harper glared at them. 'All right, guys, enough with the dick jokes.'

Lana shrugged. 'Just getting into the panto spirit.'

'Look, do you lot want me in your sodding pantomime or not? I can do two, long as the dates don't clash,' Harper said. 'You know my name'll sell it. And Mais too, she's a star in her own right. She's been on ITV4.'

'Oh, yeah. We've all been on bloody ITV4,' Stewart muttered.

'If she's such a star, how come she's not doing Aladdin with you?' I demanded. 'You must've put a word in.'

Harper looked uncomfortable. 'Well, I did, but it's kids, isn't it? Snotty bastards organising it were a bit weird about what she does for a living.'

'What makes you think we won't be?'

'Ah, little place like this, people'll love it. She's a celebrity, that's all they care about.'

'Hmm.'

'She's not exactly a porn star, is she? I bet Sam Fox never gets this shit.'

Stewart turned to us. 'Ok, executive huddle, guys. Harper, bugger off over there.'

'Ugh. Fine.' Harper wandered off to give us some privacy.

'He's not wrong, reluctant as I am to admit it,' Stewart said when his cousin was out of earshot. 'We'd sell out with his name on the bill. And Maisie might not be Leeds material, but she'd be massive here.'

'A Page Three girl though?' I said. 'We could get complaints.'

'I'd tend to side with Harper,' Lana said. 'People care more about saying they've seen a celeb than what she's famous for. And it's like the innuendo, isn't it? Kids won't know who she is.'

'Casting vote, Stew?'

He sighed. 'Go on, let her audition. We do need to make money. A Page Three girl and a BAFTA winner go a long way towards making this an event. And you never know, she might actually be good.' He turned to Lana. 'When you tell Harper about this, make it sound like I was a really hard sell, will you?'

She squeezed his arm. 'Don't I always?'

'Harper!' Stew called.

His cousin swaggered over, looking smug.

'Good news, Stew?'

'You know it is. Go on, tell Maisie she's first up to audition for principal boy. But she still has to properly audition, mind. Organiser decision is completely objective.'

Lana nodded. 'Stew was a really hard sell. I only just convinced him not to chuck you both out on your arses.'

'Argh, really? I mean, I knew you would, but –' Harper gave Lana a hug, then punched Stew on the arm. 'Thanks, guys. I'll go tell her to change.'

I frowned. 'What does he mean, change?'

Chapter 13

Lana was right, most of the crowd didn't stick around after Harper had done his autograph-signing. By the time we were ready to start, there were about 25 left.

It took ages to get to the auditions. Once Harper had finished basking in the adulation of his fans, he had to get everyone present to sign consent forms for his bloody reality show, which he did with the nonchalance of a man who had all the time in the world. I was starting to see why Stew had said getting his cousin involved in village events was a double-edged sword.

Finally, the panel was seated ready to start. We were auditioning the two leads first, Jack and Jill, then the minor parts – giant's henchmen, juvenile chorus and the two halves of the cow – and finally the other big parts of the Good Fairy, Dame Trott and Sleepy Steve.

I was sitting between Marcus and Deano, whose eyes were glittering with their familiar insane spark.

'You're looking forward to this, aren't you?' I muttered.

'You kidding? This is going to be better than sex.'

'Then you aren't doing it right, mate.'

'Hey,' Marcus said, nudging me. 'Brought you something.'

He handed me a little zipped pouch from his pocket.

'What is it?'

He grinned. 'My balls.'

'Oh, right. Aren't you using them?'

'I always keep a spare set.'

I unzipped the case and examined the red-and-yellow juggling balls, nestled together like peas in motley.

'Thanks, Marc. I'll give them back when I get a set of my own.'

'No, keep them. I'd hate to think I was depriving you of apples. You might get Juggler's Scurvy.' He shook his head. 'Nasty way to go.'

Deano nudged me. 'Shush, you two. We're starting.'

I glanced up to see Cameraman Gavin installing himself on one side of the stage. Sure enough, a few seconds later Maisie emerged.

'What the hell is *that*?' I hissed to Deano.

'Bloody hell,' Billy muttered. 'I don't care what the others are like. This one gets my vote.'

'Um, Maisie. What exactly are you wearing?' Deano called out.

She glanced down at her costume. 'It's right, isn't it? I thought this was the sort of thing people wore in pantomimes.'

'Yeah, if they were getting costumes supplied by Ann Summers,' I said.

Maisie was in the shortest, tightest silk tunic I'd ever seen, cut into a low v to expose her cleavage. She'd accompanied it with a pair of spike-heeled thigh-high boots in black PVC.

'She looks good to me,' Harper said, scanning the low-cut tunic appreciatively.

'Why does that not surprise me?' Stew muttered.

'Sorry, Maisie, you can't wear that, it's too revealing. We'd have parents up in arms,' Lana said. She paused. 'Well, the mums, anyway. If you get the part, we'll sort you out a proper Jack tunic.'

'Spoilsport,' Billy grumbled.

Deano went to join Maisie on stage and thrust a copy of the audition scene into her hands. 'Ok, have a quick read of this then I'll run through it with you.'

She took one look then handed it back. 'Wrong part, honey.'

Deano glanced at it. 'No it isn't. Jack and Steve sell the cow.'

'But where're the girl's lines?'

'You're auditioning for Jack, aren't you?'

She laughed. 'You want me to play a bloke? Why?'

'Oh God.' I dropped my head to the table. 'She's never seen a panto.'

'Has she?' Marcus asked Harper.

He looked embarrassed. 'No. Her parents were dead religious. Didn't believe in them.'

'Can't act, can't sing, never seen a panto,' I muttered to the table. 'Why us, table? Why did she have to happen to us?'

'It's all right, babe,' Harper called. 'Girls always play the principal boys in panto.'

Maisie frowned. 'But you're playing principal boy in Aladdin.'

'It's different in the big ones, sometimes. Traditionally girls play the boys.'

'Oh.' She glanced down the script. 'Can I be Steve then? He's got better lines.'

'No, Steve has to be played by a boy.'

'But you said girls play the boys.'

I lifted my head, trying to keep my voice even. 'Only some of them.'

'So there aren't any girls in the story?'

'Three. But one of them has to be played by a man.'

She looked thoroughly confused now. 'What about the other two? Are they played by girls?'

'Yes. There's the principal girl, Jill, and the Good Fairy.'

'Oh, a fairy?' Her eyes sparkled as she looked at her husband. 'I'd love to be the fairy, Harper.'

'The fairy's part is taken,' Yolanda announced stiffly. The curl of her lip suggested she wasn't a fan of Maisie Moorhouse.

'No it isn't,' Deano said. 'But, er, in this village it is usually played by a more mature lady, Maisie.'

'Ah, right.' She smiled sweetly at Yolanda. 'Sorry, I didn't realise. It's all yours, honey. I don't want the granny part.'

Yolanda's cheeks were about the same shade of pink as her hair now. Billy laughed, then hastily turned it into a cough.

'She's trying out for Jack,' Harper announced firmly. He raised his voice. 'Honestly, Mais, it's the best part. Principal boy gets all the sexiest outfits. And you want to play the lead, don't you?'

'Hmm. Suppose.'

'Right,' Deano said, looking relieved there was finally consensus. 'Five minutes to read the lines, Maisie, then I'll do Steve so you can show us your Jack.'

'Ok, I'm ready,' Maisie said after she'd scanned the script. 'Oh, but can Harper be Steve? I'm used to practising with him.'

Deano let out a defeated sigh. 'Whatever you like, kitten. Harper Brady, come on down.'

Harper went up on stage and took Deano's script.

'Hello, you,' Maisie said, beaming at him.

'Hello, you.' Harper leaned forward so they could rub noses.

Deano pulled them apart. 'Oi. You're supposed to be brothers, for Christ's sake.'

'But we missed each other,' Maisie said, pouting.

'Don't care. Get on with the audition and stop making me nauseous.' He guided Harper to a respectable, brotherly distance. 'Ok, Jack and Steve have been sent by their mother Dame Trott to sell the cow. Off you go.'

Harper cleared his throat. 'Hey, Jacky Boy! I've just been offered an awesome deal. The man at the pet shop says we can swap old Daisy for a goldfish.'

'That doesn't sound like such a great deal, Harper... er, Steve,' Maisie said in a stilted, quavering voice.

'But he says we can have an aquarium.'

'I don't think Mum'll care what star sign it is.'

'That was a joke, Mais,' Harper whispered. 'Slap your thigh.'

'Oh.' She gave her thigh a half-hearted pat. 'I don't get it.'

'You know, aquarium? Sounds like Aquarius?'

'I thought fish were Pisces?'

Harper looked thoughtful. 'S'pose they can be any sign, can't they? I mean, they're not all born in the same month.'

Deano groaned. 'Right, that's it. I can't work under these conditions.' He snatched Maisie's script off her. 'Don't call us, love. See you later.'

'Come on, Deano, let her do a bit more,' Stew called out. 'She's nervous. And it was a pretty groanworthy joke.'

'It's panto. That's how the jokes are meant to be.' Deano wagged a finger at him. 'And no cousin favouritism. You swore an oath, remember?'

'I'm on Stew's side,' I said, taking pity on Maisie. 'She's only done two lines. Anyway, Deano, we all need to vote on it. You don't just get to dismiss people.'

Deano's brow lowered. 'Look, who's directing this panto?'

'And whose idea was this panto?'

'Oooh. Did Becks just pull rank on you?' Marcus said, laughing. 'Go on, bruv, let her do the rest of the scene.'

'Fine.' Deano grudgingly handed back Maisie's script. 'Make it good.'

'Read this bit,' Harper said, pointing out some dialogue. 'You get the straight man lines here.'

'Ok.' She raised her voice. 'You're so lazy, Steve. When are you going to get a job?'

'I had a job, but it didn't work out,' Harper said.

'Did you?'

'Yeah, I was a human cannonball.'

'So what happened?'

'I got fired.'

Even Deano had to work hard to suppress a groan at that one.

'Was that it?' Maisie-Jack asked.

'No,' Harper said. 'After that I went to work at the origami factory.'

'Let me guess. They had to let you go?'

'That's right. The business was folding.'

Marcus cringed.

'Did we really write this stuff?' he whispered to me.

'I'm ready to deny everything if you are.'

'All right, Maisie, that was... better,' Deano said.

She beamed. 'Thanks. I do see myself as more of a serious actor.'

'Er, yeah. Ok, off you go. We'll let you know when we've seen the others.'

She looked at Harper. 'Why do they need to see the others? I did it good, didn't I?'

'Perfect, babe. They have to do things by the book, that's all,' Harper said.

'Sorry,' he mouthed to Deano as he led her backstage. 'I'll have her spot on for opening night, I swear.'

Another four aspiring principal boys tried out, and to give Maisie her due, they were all pretty poor. By the time they'd finished, I was heartily sick of slapped thighs, incompetent cannonballs and horoscope-obsessed sealife.

When the hopefuls had disappeared behind the screens, we went into a huddle.

'Ok, Harper, I'm voiding your vote on this one,' Deano said. 'You're too biased.'

'Oh, what? What was the point me sitting through all them then?'

'You're supposed to be giving us tips,' Lana said. 'You know, on what to look for? That is why we invited you.'

'I told you what to look for. Nice legs and big boobs and... my wife, basically. Go on, you know she was best.'

'We'll see,' Deano said. 'Go wait backstage. We'll get you when we've decided.' He nodded to Gavin. 'And take sex, lies and videotape with you. This is private.'

'Whatever.' Harper stood up. 'Come on, Gav. You can get some close-ups of Mais in her costume.'

'Ok, votes?' Deano said when they'd gone.

'Maisie, every time,' Billy said promptly. 'She looks best in tights, plus she's famous. That's what our public wants.'

'You mean it's what you want, you dirty old man,' Yolanda said. 'I don't see that she had such an amazing figure. Personally I'm voting for Sally Horsfall.'

I frowned. 'The girl who mumbled all her lines?'

'Yes, she's a sweet little thing. Anyway, her grandmother's one of my ladies.'

'I'm going for Maisie too,' Stew said, grimacing. 'Sorry, guys, but she is family.'

'You what?' Deano stared at him in disbelief. 'The oath, Stew! You solemnly swore there'd be no nepotism in favour of friends or relatives.' He wagged a finger at Yolanda. 'And that goes for you too, Yo-yo. Pulling in favours for your WI mates.' He turned to Lana. 'Back me up, treacle.'

'Sorry, Deano. I love you, but you know I have to vote with Stew,' she said, squeezing her husband's arm.

He shook his head. 'Et tu, Lanasaurus?'

'It's not just because she's family. If we get her we get Harper, don't we? He's the best asset we've got if we want to make money for the Temp.'

'In blood. Next time I draw up an oath, I'm making everyone sign it in blood,' Deano muttered.

'Well I'm voting for Tilly Stanbury,' Marcus said.

Deano nodded. 'Knew I could count on you, bruv. Me too.'

'She can't do it,' Billy said. 'She's five foot one with dumpy legs. Principal boy needs sex appeal.'

'I liked her,' Yolanda said. 'Actually, can I change my vote? She was certainly the best actress.'

'I agree,' Marcus said. 'Not that any of them were great. But she was better than Maisie.'

'So you've got casting vote, Becks,' Lana said. 'Three votes for Tilly, three for Maisie. Who's it going to be?'

I shot Deano an apologetic look. 'Sorry, Deano, but I'm with Lana. Maisie's name's the biggest draw, especially if we get Harper Brady with her.' I patted his arm. 'Hope you can forgive me.'

'It's fine, Becks. Obviously it was absurd to expect you all to care more about art than money.' He shook his head darkly. 'I'm too bloody good for you.'

Marcus laughed. 'All right, Deano, don't milk it. We lost, fair and square.'

'Honestly, I didn't think she was all that bad,' I said. 'Ok, Tilly was slightly better – very slightly – but with enough practice I think Maisie could make something of it.'

Lana nodded. 'Becks is right. Yeah, ok, she was kind of wooden, but some of that was nerves. And she's got a BAFTA winner giving her private tuition, hasn't she? None of the others can say that.'

'Fine, have it your way,' Deano said. 'But don't say I didn't warn you.' He leaned round to Stew. 'All right, go let Tits and Twat know they're in. I can't bear to do it.'

Chapter 13

Principal girls auditioned next. I was last up, and my stomach was in a flutter.

We'd included a singing element to the Jills' audition, since that was going to be an important part of the role. I didn't have a bad voice, but after the first couple of girls I was getting nervous. The standard was really high. And there were six of them plus me, nearly twice as many as there'd been for Jack.

After the last one had finished her rendition of Copa Cabana, Marcus squeezed my arm.

'Stop worrying. You'll be fine.'

'Dunno, Marc. That lass had some voice.'

'So do you. Belt it, that's my advice. Her voice didn't carry like yours.'

I smiled. 'You calling me loud?'

'Yep, loud and lairy. That's why I like you.' He nodded to Deano, beckoning me up on stage. 'Just remember, in panto there's no such thing as overacting. Serve it with plenty of ham.'

I made my way to the stage.

'Um, hi,' I said, giving the panel a bashful wave. It felt weird, being on the other side.

'Here's your lines, Becks,' Deano said.

I pushed the script away. 'No need. I memorised it.'

'Trying to impress us, eh? Good girl.' He glanced at his script. 'When will you marry me, Jill? I've asked you a hundred times.'

I let out an involuntary snort.

'Sorry,' I said. 'Just nervous. Do it again, Deano.'

'When will you marry me, Jill? I've asked you a hundred times.'

I stared at him, wide-eyed.

'I've asked you a hundred times,' he repeated patiently.

'Oh God,' I hissed. 'I've forgotten the part!'

Deano sighed and thrust a script towards me. 'Here, just read it.'

'Let me do it with her,' Marcus called. 'She knows it, promise. It's just nerves.'

'All right, come on.' Deano turned to me. 'But we couldn't have nerves shutting you down during the run, Becks. So stop being nervous right now, ok?'

'Really not helping, Deano.'

I smiled gratefully as Marcus joined me. 'Cheers, Marc.'

'Call me Jack, please. I'm in the moment.' He cleared his throat. 'When will you marry me, Jill? I've asked you a hundred times.'

With Marcus opposite me, the lines I'd memorised came back easily.

'How could I marry you? You're so poor.'

'Not for long. When my magic beans grow, they'll make my fortune.'

'Magic beans. Magic beans. Magic beans aren't a sound financial plan, Jack.' I turned to the audience. 'I got an email yesterday from a prince in Nigeria who wants to give me a million dollars. Now *that's* a plan.'

Lana laughed, which was pretty encouraging given it was the seventh time she'd heard the joke.

'That was fab, Becks. Do the song now.'

'Belt it, remember,' Marcus muttered.

We'd told auditionees they could pick any song they liked and I'd chosen Gloria Gaynor's I Will Survive. Shutting my eyes and pretending it was karaoke night at the Sooty Fox, I launched into it.

When I opened my eyes again, Deano and Marcus had their hands over their ears.

'Oh God, was it bad?' I asked Marcus.

'It was great. But Christ, when I said belt... I think you might've broken all the windows.'

'My ears've popped,' Deano said, jiggling his head about.

I turned to the panel, who were staring at me. Slowly, they started to clap, and I flushed with pride.

'You're a dark horse,' Lana said. 'Where've you been hiding that voice?'

'The shower, mainly. Cole reckons I sound like a drowning cat.'

'Cole's wrong.'

She turned to the others and they held a brief whispered conversation.

'All right, the part's yours,' Stew said. 'Unless Marcus and Deano want to object.'

'No argument from me,' Deano said. 'We'll need earplugs for the rest of the cast though.'

Marc slapped me on the shoulder. 'See? Knew you'd get it.'

After that we auditioned the minor parts. The juvenile chorus was for kids under 14 and we approved all seven who sang for us. Then we had a couple of burly lads from the Fox's pool team try out for the giant's henchmen, and Roger Collingwood. He recited the whole of the comic monologue The Lion and Albert from memory, which was odd as he was only auditioning for the cow. He made a good job of it though. We decided to let him be the front end as a reward.

After some discussion, Harper was allocated the voice of the giant, whose presence on stage was going to be represented by a huge papiér maché foot. He also said he'd cameo as one of the henchmen, so the audience would know we'd got the real Harper Brady and they weren't being fobbed off with a recording.

Then we auditioned for the Good Fairy, which, as it turned out, only Yolanda wanted anyway. I suspected she'd been sending out death threats to other potential auditionees via the underground network of her Ladies Who Lunched.

She was great though. The Good Fairy had to narrate the plot in verse, and she trilled her lines with just the right blend of sweetness and sarcasm before rounding off with a rendition of Nobody Loves a Fairy When She's 40.

Billy snorted. 'Forty, all right. We'll have to tell the audience she was born in a leap year.'

After Yolanda's audition, Deano called for the next lot.

'Dame Trotts!' he shouted. 'To the stage please!'

We couldn't hear any movement in the hall.

'Dames!' he called again. 'Any wannabe dames?'

He came back behind the screens. 'Well this is embarrassing.'

'Really, there's not a single one?' I said.

'Nope.'

'Well we can't manage without a Dame Trott. I mean, a panto without a dame: we might as well give it up as a bad job.'

'Let's not worry about it now,' Lana said. 'We'll have to ask around, that's all. There must be someone who'll do it.'

'So that just leaves Sleepy Steve,' Deano said. 'Marc, you can go last.'

There were three other hopefuls for the idiot sidekick role, but none of them was a patch on Marcus. He delivered his lines with a deadpan confidence that completely suited the part, and when Deano, as Dame Trott, jammed the bowler hat we'd provided down on his head – not filled with shaving foam as it would be on the night, luckily for him – the expression of comic gormlessness on his face had us all crying with laughter.

It was only when the gales died down that I realised Lana was actually crying.

'You ok, kid?' Stew asked in a low voice.

'Yeah. Marc reminds me of Dad, that's all.' She laughed, wiping her eyes. 'Daft cow, aren't I?'

'But you're my daft cow,' he said, kissing the top of her head.

'Got anything else for us, Marc?' Deano asked when they'd finished the scene.

He shrugged. 'I could do some magic.'

'Now who's breaking the oath, Deano?' I called. 'You didn't ask the others for extra material.'

'You lot voided the oath. Now it's every man for himself.' He nodded to Marcus. 'Go on, bruv, show them what you've got.'

Marcus ran through a few tricks, some from his current act plus some that went wrong from his old uni act, which had everyone laughing again.

'Here, Becks, lend us your balls,' he said, approaching the table. I handed him my juggling balls and he paired them with his own set to perform an impressive six-ball juggle as a finale.

He got a standing ovation. Easiest casting decision of the night.

Chapter 14

Well, it looked like tonight was the night Cole had finally become so wrapped up in his painting he'd forgotten I existed. But it was curry and a pint night, according to the menu I'd been staring at for quarter of an hour, so swings and roundabouts.

'You ready to order?' the bored-looking waitress asked.

'Ten more minutes, please. I'm waiting for someone.'

I'd only been mildly annoyed when Cole admitted he'd forgotten to book the tapas restaurant I'd wanted to go to for our anniversary, despite repeated promises he'd sort it. He'd managed to get us a table at a restaurant called The Adelphi instead, an old Victorian theatre, so at least we'd be in gorgeous romantic surroundings.

It was a lovely building, I had to give him that. It was also a bloody Wetherspoon's.

I tapped out an angry text.

Where the hell are you?

'You ok all on your tod, love? Not been stood up, have you?'

I looked up from my phone to see who the voice belonged to. A swaggering lad in a high-vis vest had wandered over.

'I'm fine,' I said, forcing a smile. 'I'm meeting someone. He's running late, that's all.'

'Course he is,' the man said with a grin. He nodded to a table where his mates were seated. 'Why don't you come join me and the boys? You won't have to buy a drink all night, I guarantee it.'

Chapter 14

Oh God. So this was it, rock bottom. Stood up in a Wetherspoon's, being offered a pity foursome by a bunch of guys on an after-work drinking bender.

'Oh!' I held up my phone so he couldn't see the screen. 'There's my boyfriend now. Felt it buzz.'

I held it to my ear and performed a quick fake conversation.

'Held up at work? Well, can't be helped, sweetheart. I'll just go on home.'

Gathering up my bag and my blushes, I hurried to the door.

By the time I'd driven home, I was seething. Cole had promised this anniversary meal would be special, and where was he? In his bloody studio, forgetting I existed, like pretty much every evening for the last two months. Maybe our anniversary had clashed with some sentimental date he was sharing with his sodding oil paints.

I marched in, kicked off my high heels and jogged upstairs to the attic.

He chucked a sheet over the painting he was working on when he heard me storm in.

'Hello, darling.' He took in my little black dress, the necklace dripping over my collarbone. 'Have you been somewhere nice?'

'No, mate. I've been to fucking Wetherspoon's.'

He frowned. 'There's no need for language, Becky.'

'There bloody is!' I hissed. 'Do you know what day it is?'

'Well, it's...' He hesitated. 'It's Friday, isn't it?'

'That's right. Friday fourth of May. Sound familiar?'

He slapped his forehead. 'Oh God.'

'Four years since our first date. Where the hell were you?'

'I just got so absorbed, I... I'm sorry, Becky. It won't happen again.'

'How many times have I heard that since you moved up? God, even down in London you managed to ring me every night.' I squeezed out an angry tear. 'I thought when you got here, it'd be the start of our big future together. But ever since you came up, it's like... like you're bored of my company.'

'Becky, I love your company.'

'Not as much as you love that thing's company though, eh?' I snapped, nodding to the shrouded painting. 'Do you know how humiliating tonight was? Tarted up to the nines in bloody Wetherspoon's, getting offered pity drinks by random blokes who thought I'd been stood up?'

'I'm sorry. I didn't know it was a Wetherspoon's.'

'It's not that, Cole. It's everything. You forget the names of my friends, my family. You never come when they invite you places. You're a virtual stranger to everyone I love.'

'That's not –'

'And I know why,' I went on. 'Because you don't want them, do you? You just want me, and they're an inconvenient extra that comes with the package. And you only want me when it suits you.'

'That's not true, Becky.' He came over to take my hands, but I pulled them away.

'Then where were you tonight?'

I waited for an answer, but he was silent.

I shook my head. 'Suppose I should've known you'd never be able to put me ahead of your precious painting.'

'I do! I mean, I will,' he said. 'Becky, I love what I do. But I'd give it up tomorrow if I had to choose between painting and you.' His anxious face lifted into a smile. 'Here. Let me show you something.'

I glared at him. 'What're you smiling about? We're having a blazing row here.'

'I'm declaring a row timeout. Please, darling, it's important.'

'What's important?'

'The reason I've been distracted. The thing that's been taking me away from you.'

'This commission, you mean?'

'Well, I'm afraid that was a bit of a fib.' He pulled the sheet off his painting. 'This wasn't a commission.'

I stared at the canvas, shining in places where the paint was still damp. 'Wow,' I whispered. 'It's... gorgeous, Cole.'

He flushed. 'I'm glad you think so. I am proud of it.'

'Pagans' Rock. How did you...'

'I've been sneaking up there when you've been out doing pantomime things. I took a few photos as aides-memoire, and, well, this is the result.'

It really was an impressive piece. It was in Cole's surrealist dreamscape style: Egglethwaite's famous viaduct and reservoir viewed from the beauty spot of Pagans' Rock, strongly invoked with vibrant twilight blends and a dizzyingly liberal take on proportion.

'Is it for me?' I whispered.

'It's your anniversary present. I wanted to give you a little piece of this place you love.' He took me in his arms. 'I am sorry I forgot about the restaurant, darling. I got so absorbed putting the finishing touches to it... I just wanted it to be the best thing I'd ever done. For the best thing that's ever happened to me.'

'It really is beautiful,' I murmured, my eyes still fixed on the arches of Cole's viaduct over his shoulder. 'The times I dreamt about that view when we were down south... it was like it was calling me home.'

He planted a soft kiss on my lips. 'So am I forgiven?'

It was a beautiful gesture. A beautiful painting. It reminded me of how we'd first met, and the stunning Westminster view Cole had given me as his way of asking me out. Big, romantic gestures appealed to him, I think. To the artist in his soul.

But I couldn't help feeling that a big, romantic gesture, wonderful as it was, couldn't compare with the little ones. A coffee in bed, or an unexpected takeaway when you knew the other person had had a rough day. A hand slipped into yours when you needed a reassuring touch. A willingness to get to know each other's loved ones, to be a part of each other's lives with all their ups and downs.

Cole couldn't help the person he was. He had to think big because his mind was filled with big ideas, the gorgeous landscapes he felt compelled to bring to life. He tried to hide it, but I knew that the minutiae of day-to-day life bored him. That was part of what had drawn me to him, and it was hardly fair to complain, now, that he was the way he'd always been.

And after all, perhaps I'd been as guilty as Cole, I thought with a prickle of shame. Badgering him to get involved with a pantomime I knew he wasn't interested in. Silently resenting the intrusion of his friends Ryder and Ali into our lives just because their personalities weren't to my taste. Trying to drag him into my world while not making enough effort to fit into his.

'You're forgiven,' I said, managing a smile. 'And thank you for my painting.'

'You really like it?'

'It's perfect.' I planted a soft kiss on his lips. 'But no more disappearing acts, all right? A surprise is lovely, but I'd prefer knowing you hadn't forgotten me.'

'You know I'll do whatever makes you happy, Becky. Just let me know.'

'Ok.' Still, I couldn't help feeling it might be nice if Cole was interested in getting to know the people in my life for their own sake, rather than just to please me.

He put a finger under my chin. 'Still my girl?' he asked softly. 'Yes.' I took a deep breath. 'Yes. I love you, Cole.'

Chapter 15

'Cole really did that?' Lana said as we made our way up Egglethwaite's steep cobbles the following day.

'Yeah, he can be very sweet. I mean, he can also disappear for weeks and forget my friends' names and not turn up to dates we've arranged. But then just as I'm about ready to bloody throttle him, he'll do something totally adorable and I'll remember exactly why I fell in love with him.' I sighed. 'That's real life. No relationship's perfect, you take the rough with the smooth.'

'Hmm,' she said.

'What?'

'Just something I've been noticing recently. About you.'

'Me?' I looked out over the fields to avoid her stare. 'Well stop noticing me. I hate being noticed.'

'Want to hear a story, Becks?'

'You what?'

'Go on, it's dead short. Pip told it me.'

'Lana, what are you waffling about?'

She ignored me. 'Right, so once upon a time there was this rabbit, the prettiest little rabbit in all the forest, with the fluffiest, wuffiest cotton-wool tail –'

'Eurghh.'

'Shush. And the rabbit lived in the forest with a, um… badger. A handsome, intelligent, romantic badger who loved the rabbit very much in his stripy badgery way. And Becky – this rabbit's name was Becky –'

'Mmm. What a coincidence.'

'I know, right? So anyway, Becky Rabbit loved, ooh, let's call him Cole Badger, too. But even though he was practically perfect in every way, he wasn't perfect for her. They were just too different. You know, what with her being a rabbit and him being a badger. I mean, the cooking arrangements alone must've been a nightmare.'

'Wrap it up, love.'

'But Becky Rabbit just couldn't see that this badger wasn't the one, even though there was some really top rabbit totty right under her stupid twitchy nose. So she married Cole Badger and they all lived miserably ever after.'

'Right. Pip told you that, did she?'

'Yeah.' She fixed me with a shrewd look. 'It's just, there's this little part of me that keeps whispering in my ear. Whispering things about you and Marcus Teasdale and the possibility you might fancy him a tiny bit.'

'What? Don't be daft.'

'Come on, Becks, it's me.'

'I don't fancy him. I... look, it's just hormones, ok? Mine are all over the place at the moment.'

Lana looked triumphant. 'I knew it! I knew there was something between you two.'

'There's nothing between us, Lana.' I held up a hand to stop her interrupting. 'All right, so sometimes I dream about us wandering along a wildflower-strewn path and picnicking naked in the grass. I have the same dream about Ryan Gosling on a semi-regular basis. So what? Doesn't mean anything.'

'Does he know you think that way about him?'

'Gosling? Unlikely. He never answers my letters.'

'Marcus, funny lady.'

Chapter 15

'You kidding? Look up the word "oblivious" in the dictionary, there'll be a picture of Marcus Teasdale next to it.' I jabbed a finger in her direction. 'So keep your gob shut, all right? Marcus hasn't noticed anything and I plan on keeping it that way till I'm over it. Dreams are just dreams. They're not real.'

'And what about Cole?' she asked. 'We've all noticed how quiet you've been lately.'

I winced. 'You all noticed?'

'Yeah. Tom, Cam, Deano. Sorry.'

That was sort of sweet. As irritating as it was that Lana always seemed to know what I was feeling before I did, it was touching to be part of a group who cared.

'No need to worry about me,' I said. 'It was just miscommunication, that's all. We've talked it out and everything's back to normal.'

She still looked concerned. 'I'd hate to see you unhappy, Becks.'

'Look, it's sweet of you all to care, but I love Cole. Honestly I do,' I told her. 'I want to spend the rest of my life with Cole, who despite you and your bloody woodland tales is 100% quality rabbit.'

'And Marc?'

'He's a mate, that's all.'

'A mate you've been having sexy dreams about.'

'That's nothing,' I said, heartily wishing she'd change the record. 'Come on, we all have those. Tell me you've never had a sexy dream about Deano.'

She snorted. 'Deano, are you kidding?'

'Well, you must have had one about someone. Everyone does.'

We reached Pie and a Pint, waved through the window to Tom and Stew, then carried on into open countryside.

'Not me,' Lana said.

'You must do.'

She shrugged. 'Nope. Why go window shopping for Dairylea when you can have camembert at home, right? Stew's enough for me.'

'Ugh. I bet you're the kind of couple that actually kisses at kissing gates, aren't you?'

'Yeah, we're pretty sickening.'

We reached Holyfield Farm, Gerry's big blue tractor parked outside and his Swaledale sheep grazing placidly nearby. Lana rapped at the farmhouse door, and it was soon filled by Sue's plump frame.

'Delivery for Mr Lightowler,' Lana said, nodding to the brown paper parcel under my arm. 'We've come to do a fitting.'

'Hiya, girls.' Sue ushered us in. 'I was just cooking the old man's tea. No one wants a skinny Santa, do they?'

We followed her into the living room, where Gerry was watching rugby.

'So what trouble have you come to get me into today?' he asked, standing up.

'Who says we've come to get you into trouble?' I said.

'A house full of women always means trouble for some poor bugger.' He pointed at my parcel. 'Is that it then?'

'Yep. One jolly fat man, as requested.'

He groaned. 'How did I get roped into this again?'

'You volunteered.'

'Doesn't sound like me. What size did you bring?'

'Extra large with the reinforced waistband,' Lana said, patting his beer belly.

'Less of the cheek, young lady. All right, let's get this over with.' He took the parcel and left the room to go try it on.

When he came back in, Lana stared. Sue stared. Not wanting to feel left out, I had a good old stare too.

'Bad Santa,' Lana muttered. 'That is a bad, bad Santa, Gerry.'

'Fits, doesn't it?'

'You've got the beard on wonky. And those fake eyebrows – you look like a drunken old letch.'

'Well, if the suit fits...' Sue said.

'And your moustache is poking out. Here.' Lana went over and rearranged the false beard, removed the dodgy eyebrows, tightened the belt and put the hat at a slightly less jaunty angle, then stood back to survey her work. 'That's better. Now you look like a man people might be marginally happier to have sneaking down their chimneys.'

'Can I take it off then? I'm sweating like a bitch on heat in here.'

'Yeah, go on,' I said. 'We'll stay for a cuppa.'

'How's the panto?' Sue asked when Santa had re-Gerried himself and we were all furnished with a mug of tea. She nodded to her piano. 'Roger dropped the score off last week.'

'Not bad,' I said. 'We've cast all the parts but one, script's shaping up, Guides and Scouts are working on props. We'll be starting rehearsals soon.'

'Who's in it other than Yo-yo? You two?'

'Not me,' Lana said. 'Don't think I got the acting gene from Dad, sadly.' She nodded to me. 'Our Becky's a sly one though. Turns out she's a great little actress. And you should hear the voice on her.'

I flushed. 'It's nothing amazing.'

'She's lying,' Lana mouthed.

Sue smiled. 'Good for you, love. Let us know if we can do anything.'

'She's volunteering me for stuff again,' Gerry muttered. 'I'll never get a moment's peace while I'm married to that woman.'

'You'll get plenty of peace when you're dead,' Sue told him.

'I bet even then I won't be allowed. I bet you'll be there, standing over the fresh-shovelled earth.' He put on a high-pitched voice, jamming his hands on his hips. '"Gerald! What're you lying about down there for? Don't you know it's lambing time?"'

Lana laughed. 'Come on, Gerry. You enjoy it really.'

'I might enjoy peace and quiet, if I ever got to find out what they felt like.'

'You ok, Becky?' Sue said.

I didn't answer. I was too busy staring at Gerry.

'Do that voice again,' I said.

He frowned. 'What voice?'

'The one you did when you were taking the piss out of Sue.'

'Eh? Why?'

Lana turned wide eyes on me. 'Oh my God! You're right, he'd be perfect.'

I nodded vigorously. 'He's got everything. He's hairy –'

'– grumpy –'

'– overweight –'

'– takes himself too seriously –'

'What are the pair of you on about?' Sue said. 'I hope you're not insulting my better half when you know that's my job.'

'The part we haven't cast,' I said, eyes glittering. 'It's the dame.'

Gerry shook his head. 'Oh, no. Not a chance, love.'

'Please, Gerry! You're just what we're looking for.'

He snorted. 'You what? Dress up like a lass and make jokes about knockers? Being Santa's bad enough.'

'You're a morris dancer, aren't you?' Lana said. 'That's more embarrassing than being a pantomime dame.'

'That's different. That's an ancient tradition that needs to be kept alive for future generations.'

'Well, so is blokes dressing as women on stage. Ask Shakespeare.'

He folded his arms. 'Nope. You're not bullying me into this one, ladies.'

'See, this is why he'd be perfect,' I said to Sue. 'He's so grumpy. It'd be hilarious in drag.'

'You're on our side, aren't you?' Lana said.

'Always, chicken.' Sue turned to Gerry. 'Why can't you do it then, you miserable old giffer?'

'Because I'll look a tit, that's why.'

'Well why break the habit of a lifetime?' Sue said. 'Go on. Do it for our Pip.'

'Oh, no. That was how I got talked into the Santa thing. You can't guilt-trip me with the grandkid this time, I'm ready for you.'

'Then do it for the Temp,' I said. 'This panto could be our chance to get her safely in the black.'

His expression softened slightly. 'Is there really no one else you can ask? I can't act for shite, you know.'

'Course you can,' Lana said. 'What about that double-act routine you did with Dad at Christmas when me and Tom were kids? We fell about laughing.'

'Trust you to remember that.'

'I remember because you were good. Better than Morecambe and Wise.'

'Flattery'll get you nowhere, petal,' Gerry said. 'Anyway, it was a completely different pot of tea, that.'

'Why was it?'

'Because I was a bloke playing another bloke. What do I know about being a woman?'

'It's not about being a woman, Gerry.' I stood and went to rest my hands on his shoulders. 'It's about being *all* woman.'

Lana nodded. 'You just need to get in touch with your feminine side. It'll be behind your moustache somewhere if you've lost it.'

'So, will you?' I said, sensing he was weakening.

He let out a sigh of surrender. 'I'll give it a go. But don't think it's because you ganged up on me. I fancy myself in the wig, that's all.'

Chapter 16

I hadn't realised just how invested I'd become in the panto until the night before our first rehearsal. Thirty years earlier, I'd felt exactly the same staring at the silhouette of an empty stocking: stomach fluttering so much with anticipation about the bulges that would be there on Christmas morning, I couldn't sleep.

Deano wanted to take it easy for the first one – just run through a few key scenes, help the actors get a feel for their parts (innuendo entirely intended). It still felt like a pretty big deal though. It was the first time the group would get to see the script Marc and me had worked so hard on, for one thing. It was also the first time we'd be able to judge how the bunch of misshapes who made up our cast could work together.

The only person more excited than me was Deano. I could tell when I arrived at the Temp that he was all the way up to 11 on the crazyometer. If the panto had a physical presence, he'd be stroking it inappropriately.

'Where've you been?' he demanded. 'You're half an hour late.'

'I'm fifteen minutes early. 2pm, you said.'

'That might be what I said, but those of us who're properly dedicated have been here ages.' He shook his head. 'Thought I could count on you, Becks.'

'What did that letter call you again? "Utter, utter bastard"?'

'That was when I was being nice,' he said, grinning. 'I'm hoping for a "complete and total fucker" by the time you lot are ready to write me a letter. Go on, get backstage. We just need Gerry.'

I waved to Stew and Lana, seated out front playing the important role of 'the audience', and headed through the stage door.

All the main cast members apart from Gerry, the reluctant dame, were there: Marcus, Maisie, Yolanda and Harper. Oh, and Gavin with his camera. The man had a chameleon knack for blending into the background.

Maisie was rehearsing with Harper, Yolanda was reading her script and Marcus was juggling. He stopped when I joined him.

'Don't need to practise that, do you?' I asked.

'No, but it's therapeutic. Calms me down.'

'You haven't got stagefright?'

'It's not the acting.' He lowered his voice. 'It's the script. What if they think it's crap, Becks? They might boo us off stage.'

I scoffed. 'Stew and Lana? I'm sure they'll be constructive.'

'They'll have to be. Because they might go easy on us, but trust me, the kids won't,' he said. 'There's no more savage critic than the average six-year-old. They'll eat us for breakfast if we don't deliver. I mean, literally eat us.'

'Ah, that's nerves talking. They won't eat us,' I said. 'It's a great script. It's got everything. Cheesy jokes, innuendo, slapstick...' I glanced around the rest of the cast. 'It's not the material I'm worried about, it's this lot.'

'God, don't even get me started on that.' Marc nodded to Maisie and Harper. 'Have you heard these two? If his BAFTA's listening, it's weeping for the acting profession.'

'It can't, it doesn't have eyeballs. It's just a creepy gold face staring in empty-socketed horror for all eternity.'

'Yeah, and these guys're why.'

I tuned into the conversation going on a little way from us. Harper was getting impatient.

'It's a joke, Mais. For Christ's sake, stop saying it like you're reading a eulogy.'

'How can I say it like a joke when it's not funny?' she demanded.

'It's not funny to you because you're not a little kid. You don't have to find it funny. You have to bloody act.'

She stuck her bottom lip out. 'I can't do it if you're being mean, Harper.'

I was sure I saw a muttered 'for fuck's sake' on the corner of Harper's lips, but he quickly rearranged his face into a simpering smile. 'Sorry, baby girl. I don't mean to be cross. I just get frustrated when I see the obvious talent you're not using.'

'Bloody hell, he really is a good actor,' Marcus whispered in my ear.

Maisie lifted her petulant frown a little. 'Well, I'll try again. But be nice, ok?'

'Ok.' Harper took a deep breath. 'Have you ever had a pet apart from Daisy, Jack?'

'I had a pet rock once.'

'What happened to him?'

'He died.'

'Jesus, he's right,' I muttered to Marcus. 'She sounds like she's reading the news.'

'Hmm. I'm not sure her dire performance at the audition was completely down to nerves, you know.'

'She just needs practice. I hope. I'm going over, before that vein in Harper's temple pops.'

I strode over and tapped Harper on the shoulder.

'Can I rehearse with her? It'd be good for us to get used to working together.'

'Er, yeah,' he said. 'Becky, right? Be my guest.'

Maisie looked me up and down, then turned to her husband. 'Do I have to do it with her?'

'What's wrong with doing it with me?' I demanded.

'Oh, no offence, honey,' she said, giving my elbow a patronising squeeze. 'I'm used to acting with Harper, that's all.'

I fought down a swell of annoyance. 'But he's not going to be doing the lines when we perform it, is he?' I said. 'I am. We might as well get used to each other now, before we've got Deano bawling us out.'

'The guy with the bright red hair?'

'That's him.'

'Hmm,' she said. 'He was pretty scary.'

'Ok.' I summoned the lines she'd been practising. 'So. Have you ever had a pet apart from Daisy, Jack?'

'I had, um... a fish?'

Harper mouthed the word 'rock'.

'Oh, right, different pet bit,' she said. 'Yeah, I had a rock.'

'And what happened to him?' I asked, waggling my eyebrows encouragingly.

'He died.'

'That was great, Maisie. Really good,' I lied. 'The thing is though, it is supposed to be funny. So what you need to do is make it not funny at all.'

Harper nodded vigorously. 'Yes! Deadpan, Mais. That's the thing I've been trying to explain.'

'So it's funny but it's not funny?' Maisie asked, looking puzzled.

'It's funny for the audience,' I said. 'For you, it's serious as hell. Your poor pet rock's dead, for God's sake! How does that make you feel?'

'Well, fine. Because it's a rock, isn't it? They don't die. They're made of rock.'

'All right, then pretend it's not a rock. Pretend it's an adorable little puppy, called, um, Woofy. The cutest little pup in the whole world. A pug, probably, or a chihuahua: something small and needy with massive soul-wrenching eyes. And he just dropped dead suddenly of, er... dogpox. Now how do you feel?'

'Oh God! Awful!' she said. 'Poor Woofy.'

'Right, that's it! Really get into your head, Maisie. Dig deep into those emotions. Anything else?'

'I feel... like when I watched *Wall-E*. I was in bits for a week, I swear. Wasn't I, Harper?'

'Mais is very sensitive,' Harper said, giving her bottom an affectionate pat.

'Harper, she's making me feel sad on purpose,' Maisie said in the pouty infant voice that seemed to work so well for getting her own way.

'She's right to, babe. It'll expand your emotional range. That's how us actors learn our craft.' He gave me an approving nod. 'You know, you're good at this, bringing out the best in her. I remember when I was starting out and Kev did the same for me.' He glanced at Maisie. 'Kevin Bacon. Great guy. We shot a mobile phone ad together. By the time he'd put me through my paces, I really believed a Samsung Galaxy could feel ennui.'

'Oh. Thanks,' I said, flushing. That was no small compliment. Harper was actually pretty talented.

'Hmm. Well, if you think she's like Kevin Bacon,' Maisie said, casting a doubtful look my way. 'Oh, Harper?'

'Yeah?'

'Can we get a puppy?'

Chapter 17

'Slosh scene first!' Deano called through the stage door. 'Marc, Gerry, you're up.'

The slapstick 'slosh scene', which usually involved copious amounts of shaving foam, flour and other mess, was a key part of any panto. Traditionally it occurred before the interval so the stagehands would have a 15-minute break to get cleaned up. It was also the kids' favourite bit, and me and Marc had given a lot of time to it in our scripting sessions. We'd spent hours doing research together, watching Laurel and Hardy shorts for material we could borrow and combing through old Egglethwaite Players scripts for ideas.

Classic moves from previous village pantos included the hat full of shaving foam jammed down on someone's head, a hole in the centre causing it to spurt fountain-like out of the top; the idiot sidekick offering his belt to hold something in place, with the result that his trousers fell down, and lots of comedy violence. Poor old Phil Donati, Egglethwaite's slapstick king, seemed to have a stage direction instructing another actor to either kick him in the pants or whack him over the head every other line. Kids loved that stuff apparently, the little psychopaths.

The scene we'd written featured Gerry as Dame Trott, Marcus as Sleepy Steve and a volunteer from the audience, all getting nice and messy as they did some 'baking'. We'd stumbled over a winning formula for custard pies in an old script too, with a note in the margin suggesting mushy peas mixed with the shaving foam made for a satisfyingly gruesome splat in the face. Luckily for Marc and Gerry, this first rehearsal we'd decided to let them mime.

While they joined Deano on stage, I snuck out to sit with Lana, Stewart and Sue in the audience.

'Here we go,' I whispered to Lana. 'Time to find out if we've got a dame who can actually act and a script that's actually funny.'

'It'll be fine,' Lana said. But she sounded anxious.

The stage was bare apart from a table bearing a bowler hat and paper plates representing custard pies.

'Gerry, you're here,' Deano said, guiding his Dame Trott into position. 'Here's a script.'

'Don't I get a costume?' Gerry asked.

'Becks is still sorting them. For now, just imagine yourself in fishnets and try to channel Danny la Rue.'

'Oh. I was looking forward to a bit of dressing up.'

'He's changed his tune,' I whispered. 'What did you do to him, Sue?'

She scoffed. 'The man's a fraud. Pretends all he wants is a quiet life, but he loves being the centre of attention.'

'That explains the morris dancing then,' Stew said. 'It's a confident man who'll willingly dress up in knickerbockers and skip round a giant cock every May Day.'

'He has been getting a bit... committed to this dame business,' Sue said. 'Caught him staring at the fashion section in my *Woman's Weekly* the other day, fascinated by a cowl-neck jumpsuit. A sequinned cowl-neck jumpsuit.'

'Bloody hell.' I stared at Gerry. I felt like I'd discovered a whole new side to him.

'When's the moustache coming off then?' Marcus asked him.

Gerry looked horrified. 'You what? Nobody told me that was part of the deal.' He gave his soup-strainer an affectionate stroke. 'I've had this since I was twenty-seven.'

'We can't have a Dame Trott with facial hair,' Deano said. 'She'll look like a cross-dressing trucker.'

Gerry clamped one hand over his moustache, as if he was afraid the lads were going to pin him down and shave it off right then. 'I grew this as a present for my missus on our fifth wedding anniversary. It's got sentimental value.'

'Not to me,' Sue called out. 'I knew it was a mistake, telling him I fancied Tom Selleck,' she muttered to us.

'Oi. No heckling from the stalls,' Deano said, shooting her a look. He turned back to Gerry. 'Come on, mate. It'll only be for a week, then you can grow it back.'

'Why though? Clean-shaven or not, no one's going to think I'm really a lass, are they?'

'The kids will, long as you're in a dress,' Marcus said. He tossed his head. 'That's what we actors call the willing suspension of disbelief, luvvie.'

'It's the unwilling suspension of my moustache that worries me,' Gerry muttered.

Deano sighed. 'All right, if it means that much to you, keep the thing. Let's start the scene.'

'Right.' Gerry cleared his throat and trilled a few scales.

'What's the singing in aid of?' The little twitch in Deano's eye was starting.

'Warming my voice up, aren't I?'

'You're not bloody Julie Andrews. Get on with it.'

'Don't you take that tone with me, laddie,' Gerry said, glaring. 'I'm old enough to be your father.'

'And you're also in a panto I'm directing, so get used to obeying orders.'

Gerry cast a wary look at Sue. 'Believe me, that's one thing I am used to.' He glanced at the script. 'Ok. Stage left, it says here. Is that my stage left or your stage left?'

'For God's sake,' Deano muttered. 'Just do the line, Gerry. The pub's open.'

Gerry's lips moved as he read the scene's opening line to himself. Then he looked up, pursed his lips and put his hands on his hips in traditional high-camp fashion. Deano breathed a sigh of relief and retreated to the wings.

'Now then, you idle beggar,' Gerry said in a sonorous lady opera singer voice to Marc, wobbling his hips. 'Are you going to help me get these pies on for our Jack when he gets home?'

'Awww, Muu-um,' Marc said with teenage belligerence. 'You know I'm supposed to practise my recorder this afternoon. It's the village music recital tomorrow and I'm playing solo.'

'I've told you about that before, my lad. It'll ruin your eyesight.' Gerry assumed a dreamy expression. 'Ah, music, the food of love. How I adored it in my youth.'

Marcus-Steve scoffed. 'What, you?'

'And why not, you great lumpy... lump? Do you think just because we're poor I've got no culture?' Dame Trott fanned herself with one hand. 'I'll have you know that as a gel I once enjoyed an evening of delightful oral entertainment from the Harrogate Male Voice Choir.'

Me, Lana and Stew all laughed. Gerry was great with the innuendo, just the right mixture of deadpan and coy.

Sue wasn't laughing though.

'Well, there goes what was left of our sex life,' I heard her mutter. 'RIP, anniversaries and birthdays.'

'Now then,' Dame Trott said to Steve. 'Try one of the custard tarts I made this morning.'

Marcus-Steve took one of the paper plates and mimed taking a bite. He pulled a disgusted face.

'What do you think I'll get for them when I sell them at the recital tomorrow?' Dame Trott asked.

'About five years?'

'Cheeky beggar. I was thinking £1 each for these cakes, £2 for a slice of this one.'

'Why does it cost more for that one?'

'Oh, that's Madeira cake.'

I groaned internally. I'd contributed that.

'Cut!' Deano yelled. He beamed at them. 'That was great, guys. Gerry, you're a natural.'

'You sure it was ok?' Gerry said in his usual gruff voice.

'Honestly, mate, I'd swear you'd been doing it years.'

'What, panto or the Harrogate Male Voice Choir?' Marcus asked innocently.

'Let's move on to the cooking,' Deano said.

Gerry slipped back into character. 'Right, our Stephen. Let's get the ingredients.' He glanced at his script, then shuffled sideways across the stage.

'Cut!' Deano shouted. 'Ok, Gerry, what the hell was that?'

'It says here "Dame Trott crosses stage to cupboard".'

'Yeah, and if Dame Trott was a species of crab that'd be fine. Just walk over naturally, stop creeping about.' He clapped his hands together. 'Right. Let's try it again.'

But no matter how many times they ran through the scene, Gerry couldn't get it. His delivery was perfect, but when it came to physical comedy he just couldn't manoeuvre his bulky frame around the stage without looking self-conscious. His custard-pieing was stiff, and when they reached the finale, where he was supposed to jam the bowler hat on Marc's head, he perched it there like he worked in a gentlemen's outfitters.

'You're not in a sodding Moss Bros, Gerry. Proper slam it down,' Deano said. 'Don't worry about our Marc, his skull's thick enough to take it.'

'What, like this?' Gerry said, balancing the bowler jauntily on Marcus's head.

'No, like this.' Deano took the hat off his brother and jammed it down with force, covering Marcus's eyebrows and most of his eyes.

'Ow,' Marc said, taking the hat off and rubbing his crown.

'Yeah, ow. That's what I want you to aim for, Gerry. A good, solid ow.' Deano waved a hand. 'Ok, let's move on.'

***

'Well, I have to say that was the worst display of so-called acting I've seen in my long and distinguished showbiz career,' Deano said in the pub's function room afterwards. Hiding out in there was the price of having Harper Brady come for a pint with us, apparently. 'We've got a lot of work to do here, you lot.'

'Come on, Deano. They weren't that bad,' Lana said.

'Weren't that bad, are you kidding?' Deano reached for his notebook. 'You'll be pleased to know I've graded you all.'

I cocked an eyebrow. 'Seriously?'

'Of course, seriously. It's me.' He scanned down the list. 'B-plus for you, Becks. Good delivery, great job on the singing. I want you to work on your arms though. They just seem to dangle there.'

'Yeah. I never really know what to do with them.'

'We call that "stage business" in the trade,' Harper said, sipping his beer. 'Watch some of the greats, that's my advice. Bogart's good.'

'Harper, A-plus for your giant. Nice job,' Deano said.

'Cheers, mate. I'll hang it up next to the BAFTA.'

'And another for you, Yo-yo,' Deano said, ignoring him. 'Top work.'

Yolanda beamed. 'Thank you, darling. Nice to know I've still got the touch.'

'Probably helps your grade if what you've touched is the director,' Sue muttered.

'Marc, A-minus,' Deano said. 'Just need to practise your singing so you can hold your own against Becky and Yo-yo.'

'Pfft, what, A-minus? I'm your brother.'

'When I'm directing, I have no brother.' He moved a finger down his list. 'Gerry. A on delivery, no problem there. But I'm sorry, it's an F on the stage business.'

'Blocking,' Harper said.

'What?'

'Moving around the stage is called blocking. Stage business is body language.'

'Well whatever it's called, Gerry's shit at it.'

'How is that fair?' Gerry said, his pitch almost matching his opera-singer dame voice. 'There wasn't even a set! How am I supposed to move naturally without a set?'

'All right, lad, wind your neck in,' Sue said. 'Remember last week when you didn't want to do this?'

'Well thanks to you I am bloody doing it, aren't I? And since I am, I want to do it properly.'

'And you will, Gerry,' I said in a soothing tone. 'We've all got things to improve. It's only the first rehearsal, there's loads of time.'

'Says swotty Miss B-plus,' Gerry muttered.

'That's the spirit, Becks,' Deano said. 'Next rehearsal's in a week and I want all of you to have done your homework. Practice, practice, practice, so good they named it three times. 110%, folks! 150%!'

'Oh God. The stress is affecting his maths.' Lana went round to massage his shoulders. 'Calm down, eh? We don't want this to be another *HMS Pinafore*.'

'No.' He reached up to pat her hand. 'Thanks, Lanasaurus. Was getting a bit carried away there.'

'And what about me?' Maisie asked brightly.

Deano's eye twitched. 'What about you?' He glanced up at Lana, who was about to sit back down. 'Don't go anywhere. You may be needed.'

'Well, what's my grade?'

Deano subtly turned over his notepad. 'Er... just keep practising, Mais. Two hours a day. Three. Even four.'

'But I was good, wasn't I?' She turned to Harper. 'I was, wasn't I?'

'You know what worries me?' I said, jumping in before Harper had to answer.

'Gerry's moustache?' Stewart said.

'That's always worried me. But I actually meant the script.'

'What about the script?' Marcus looked panicked. 'Everyone liked the script, didn't they? Because we worked bloody hard on that script.'

'There weren't many laughs though,' I said. 'I was sitting in the audience. The innuendos got a few guffaws, but not much else.'

Stewart shrugged. 'We're not five, Becks. Pet rocks might make Pip wet herself, but we're big boys and girls. Knob gags all the way for us, I'm afraid.'

'Seems risky waiting till opening night to find out if we're going to be dying on our arses out there though,' Marcus said. 'You know what I'm thinking?'

I took a sip of my wine. 'I do actually, you dirty git.'

He laughed. 'Apart from that. I'm thinking, test audience. Try some of the material out on actual kids, make sure we've pitched it right.'

'Could we ask your Pippa?' Yolanda said, looking from me to Lana.

'One's a pretty small sample,' I said. 'We could do with a few.'

'What about Beavers?' Lana said.

Yolanda snorted.

'Oh, I am sorry.' She forced a straight face. 'I think I'm still in pantomime mode.'

'That's right. Pip's just started Beavers,' I said, ignoring another titter from Yolanda. 'They might let us perform a scene or two.'

'Right.' Deano swallowed back the last of his Boltmaker. 'You get onto that then. And everyone: 180%, don't forget. Class dismissed.'

Chapter 18

'Why're you coming to Beavers, Aunty Becky?' Pip asked, sulky at the grown-up intrusion into her new club. 'You're too big.'

'I'm not coming to all of it.' I gripped her hand tightly as we crossed the road and started making our way up the cobbles. 'Me and some other people are going to act a bit of our pantomime.'

'What people?'

'Grandad Gerry, Aunty Yo-yo. And Marcus – remember him, from your birthday?'

She brightened at once. 'Will he do magic?'

I laughed. 'You'll have to wait and see.'

When we arrived at the Temp, Pip skipped off to play, acting like she'd never seen me before in her life. I joined Marcus and Gerry, who were talking to Otter, aka Colin, the leader.

'Thanks for doing this, guys,' he was saying.

'We should thank you for providing our test audience,' Marcus said.

I nodded. 'Just hope they don't hate it.'

'Oh, they'll love it, I'm sure,' Colin said. 'You're Jack, I'm assuming?'

Marcus and I exchanged a look. We'd decided it was best not to involve Maisie in a public performance until she'd had more time to work on her lines. Bringing a Page Three girl to a Beaver Scout meeting might've caused a few raised eyebrows too.

'Er, no. I'm Jill, the principal girl. Jack... couldn't make it.' I nodded to Yolanda, who'd just joined us. 'Hiya, Yo-yo.'

'Hello everyone.' She grinned at the leader. 'Hello Colin. Fancy meeting you here.'

He flushed. 'Yo-yo. Long time no see.'

'Well, I'm almost a married woman now, darling,' she said, wiggling her ring finger.

'I heard. Congratulations.'

I shook my head. 'Come on. Not him too.'

She shrugged. 'We were working on the joint Guide/Scout gang show together. It got a bit sexy.'

'All right, well never mind your love life,' I said hastily, before she started going into details. 'Let's go change.'

Yolanda clapped her hands. 'Oh goody! Have we got costumes?'

'Not the proper ones. These're from my stock.'

The four of us headed backstage while Colin and the assistant leader got the kids together for their opening ceremony.

'We'll need a separate changing area for boys and –' Marcus began. But Yolanda had stripped to her bra before he could finish the sentence.

She shrugged when she saw us staring. 'What? I've got nothing to hide.'

'You never did,' Gerry said. He beckoned to me. 'Come on then, pet, give us whatever monstrosity you've got for me to wear.'

I went to the clothing rail where the costumes I'd dropped off earlier were hanging.

'Ok, Gerry, this is yours,' I said, handing one to him. 'Yo-yo, a ballerina costume and some fairy wings, and Marc, this is you. I didn't have anything suitable so it's a loan from Tom. His old work uniform from when Pie and a Pint was a medieval restaurant.'

'Might be a bit tight,' Marcus said. 'I'm broader than he is.'

'Well, just manage as best you can.'

My costume was a ragged Cinderella dress. I sidled into a corner and turned my back to the others while I changed, hoping no one was looking. Not that there was anything particularly exciting to see, I thought, glancing down at my far from voluptuous curves. Not everyone was a Maisie Brady.

On turning back round, I was struck by an eyeful of Marc struggling to fasten Tom's leather jerkin over his bare torso.

I tried not to, but I couldn't help having a bit of a stare. His chest was smooth and sinuous, a faint dimpling defining the abdominal muscles above the waistband of his trousers. A small tattoo of a flaming sun sat just over his hipbone.

'It's not a bad view, is it?' a whisper near my ear observed.

I jumped. Yolanda, looking like a pink-haired Christmas tree fairy in her sparkly tutu and wings, had crept up beside me.

'I wasn't –'

'Oh, no need to deny it, darling. We're both spoken for, aren't we?' She examined the diamond on her third finger complacently. 'Perfectly natural to look. It's only touching that's not allowed.'

I dragged my gaze from Marc to look at her.

'Do you miss it? The touching? I'm sensing it used to be your favourite hobby.'

She shrugged. 'Sometimes. It was rather fun. But it could be lonely too, flitting from one man to another.'

'You were lonely?'

'Let's say it wasn't the way I wanted to spend my declining years. So when Billy asked again, the third time in ten years... I said yes.'

I blinked. I'd never heard Yolanda open up like that before. Or come quite so close to admitting her age.

'Do you love him?'

She smiled, turning away. 'I think you'd better give Marcus a hand, darling. He appears to be struggling.'

'Er, right.'

I headed over to Marc, who was making a last valiant effort to fasten Tom's jerkin.

'It's no good, Becks,' he panted, letting it drop. 'I'm too wide.'

'You'll just have to leave it open then,' I said, trying not to let my eyes linger on the contours of his chest.

Marc snorted. 'I can see that going down well. "So what did you do at Beavers tonight, sweetheart?" "Oh, Otter booked a male stripper and he twerked for us."'

I winced. 'Forgot about the twerking bit.' I nodded at his pile of discarded clothes. 'In that case, put your t-shirt back on. You can wear the jerkin open over the top.'

A throat cleared behind me. I turned, and choked on a giggle at Gerry in his dress and ringleted wig.

'Oi. Rebecca. Do you want to explain why there're glacé cherries on my nipples?'

'Because you're a lovely little cupcake, cupcake,' I said. 'That's our Cherry Bomb dress. We get a lot of demand for that.'

'From burly blokes in their late fifties?'

'Almost exclusively.'

'Well well. Aren't you a pretty little thing?' Marcus said, winking at Gerry. 'What are you doing tonight, darling?'

'You want a slap, son?'

'Dunno. Does it cost extra?'

'Um, Gerald,' Yolanda said. 'I don't mean to be personal, but aren't you a little flat?'

'Oh! That's right.' I went to my rucksack to fetch the other part of Gerry's costume – a bra that'd been stuffed with socks and sewn up. 'Here's your tits, Gerry.'

Everyone tried to keep a straight face while Gerry fed them up through his dress and fastened them on.

'They're halfway round your chest, darling,' Yolanda said with a giggle.

Marcus grinned. 'Here, let me.'

He went over to Gerry, who lifted his arms while Marcus adjusted the new boobs. Once they were in place, Marc gave them a squeeze and nodded appreciatively.

'Firm yet supple. You'll have all the lads after you, Gerry.'

Gerry was examining the additions to his body with interest. He jiggled about a bit to try them out.

'Big, aren't they?'

'All right, darling, no need to brag,' Yolanda said. 'Hadn't we better join the children now?'

'Just a sec.' I reached into my rucksack again and handed some paper plates to Marcus. 'For the cooking scene. And –' I fished out a can of shaving foam.

Marcus shook his head. 'You never said we had to do it properly.'

'They're kids, Marc. Miming won't cut it.'

'Hmm.' He looked at Gerry. 'What do you think? Can the moustache stand it?'

Gerry glanced down at the enormous fake breasts behind his cherries. 'In for a penny, in for a pound.'

Colin poked his head round the door. 'We're ready for you out here.'

'Right.' I beckoned to the others. 'Break a leg, you lot.'

I followed Colin out into the hall, where a group of bewoggled six-to-eights were waiting, their fixed stares saying this had better be good. Suddenly Marcus's fear they might eat us didn't seem so ridiculous. I tried to focus on Pip, but her glare was even more terrifying than the others. She had family honour to maintain.

When we were up on stage, facing the sea of hungry infant eyes, I realised we were missing someone.

'Where's Gerry?' I muttered to Marcus.

'Dame Trott!' he yelled over his shoulder. 'Come on out!'

'I can't! I feel daft!' a Gerry voice called back.

'Come on, gorgeous. You're beautiful.' Marcus turned to the Beavers. 'Isn't she, boys and girls?'

Pip giggled. 'It's my grandad,' she whispered proudly to the boy next to her. 'He has to dress as a lady.'

Gerry finally emerged, shuffling bashfully. The kids were laughing their heads off. Even I didn't know if he was playing it for laughs or genuinely embarrassed. The fact you couldn't tell his deadpan from his grump was one of the things that made him such a perfect dame.

Marcus launched the two of them straight into the pie-making scene.

'Heyup, Mum,' he said. 'You ready to cook some sausage pies?'

Gerry picked up on his cue at once, crooking one arm against his hip. 'Right you are, young Stephen. To work!'

Marcus immediately turned and started wiggling his bum at the kids, who laughed fit to burst.

'What're you doing, you daft beggar?' Gerry said.

Marcus carried on with his dance. 'You said twerk.'

'Nice, isn't it?' Yolanda muttered, her eyes fixed on Marcus's gyrating posterior.

'You're the connoisseur,' I whispered back.

Still. I was starting to feel the heat a bit. I was glad when Marcus and his shapely arse gave over and they moved on.

I didn't know what was wrong with my hormones lately, they seemed to be all over the place. I put it down to getting older, and the fact my sex life had gone a bit quiet. I was so often tired after long days at work and long nights working on the panto, it was hard to summon the energy for much more than a bedtime cuddle.

The performance was a riotous success. The kids screamed when Marc got a plateful of shaving foam in the face, yelled when Gerry knocked merry Sunday out of him with an inflatable sausage, and practically keeled over at the pet rock gag that'd got such a lukewarm reception from our grown-up audience. Marcus's magic tricks held them rapt. And even with an act like that to follow, the song number Yolanda and me did as a duet still kept their attention. A few jokes fell flat, but overall we were definitely onto a winner.

'Thanks, guys,' I said after Colin had led them in a round of applause. 'You promise you really like it?'

Pip turned to the other kids with her bossy face on. 'I did. Did everyone else? That's my aunty so you gotta say yes.'

'Yes,' the other Beavers chorused dutifully. 'It was *brilliant!*' one little lad piped up, and I treated him to a warm smile.

A hand shot up. 'Miss! Miss!'

'Hiya,' I said to the bright-eyed little girl with a shock of wild ginger hair demanding my attention. 'What do they call you then?'

'Tinuviel, Miss.'

'Tinuviel, that's unusual. Is it French?'

'Nah. S'Elvish.'

'Oh. Right. Sorry, my Elvish is a bit rusty,' I said, smiling. 'What's up, Tinuviel?'

'Why's that lady got a moustache?' she demanded, pointing at Gerry.

Gerry rubbed his lip. 'I, er, lost my razor.'

Colin frowned. 'That's bad manners, Tinuviel.'

'It's ok. She didn't mean to be rude,' Marc said. He hopped off stage and dropped to his haunches to bring him level with the kids. 'All right, tiny person. What did you like?'

Tinuviel tilted her head with the air of a true critic. 'Well...
I liked when you did magic.' She giggled. 'And when the
moustache lady kicked you inna bum.'

Marc nodded gravely. 'Good, because it hurt. Anything else
you think we should do when we act it at Christmas?'

Tinuviel pondered.

'Pokémon,' she said.

'Pardon?'

'You should of had Pokémon in it. Oh, and Octonauts!'

'We'll see what we can do.' Marc looked round the group.
'What about the rest of you? Any suggestions?'

'Good with them, isn't he?' Yolanda whispered to me.

'He listens to them,' I said. 'Kids want to feel they're being
taken seriously.'

'T-Rex,' Pip's friend Harry said.

'What, T-Rex the dinosaur?' Marc asked.

'Yeah. That's the best dinosaur. T-Rex means king of the
dinosaurs so you know it's the best one. Everyone'd be like,
arghhh!' Harry clawed his fingers and bared his teeth. 'Like,
arghhhhhhh!'

'You getting this, Becks?' Marcus said. I nodded, jotting
down 'T-Rex, like arghhh!' on my notepad.

'Any more?' Marcus said to the kids.

'Baby Jesus,' one little lass said. 'You gotta have him if it's
Christmas.'

'That's for nativities, sweetie,' Yolanda said.

'You gotta have Baby Jesus at Christmas,' the child repeated
stubbornly. She puffed herself up. 'Last year I was Mary and I
had him. Hid him in my dress so's he could pop out when Miss
said and I put him in his manager.'

'Manager?' Marcus said.

''S'like a cot what cows eat their tea off.'

Chapter 18

'Oh, right. That sort of manager.'

'And there was a donkey that done a poo,' the child said gravely. 'And it chewed our Jackson's tea towel. He was a shepherd.'

Marcus shot a questioning glance at Colin, who nodded. 'The primary got a real donkey for last year's nativity. It, er, didn't go so well.'

'Will there be a donkey what poos in the pantomime?' Tinuviel asked hopefully.

'We've got a trumping cow,' Marcus said. 'Any good?'

'S'pose that's funny too,' she conceded.

'Well, thanks, 1st Egglethwaite Beavers,' Marcus said, giving them a three-fingered Scout salute. 'See you all again at Christmas.'

By the time we left, our list of 'would like to see' consisted of a T-Rex, the Baby Jesus, a pooing donkey, a full chorus of Pokémon, Craig Revel Horwood from *Strictly Come Dancing* and Billy Bantam, the Bradford City FC mascot. This was shaping up to be one hell of a surreal pantomime.

Chapter 19

With some of the cast away on their summer hols, there was no panto rehearsal the following week, which was a shame. It was Cole's dinner party on the Friday, and I could have used something to take my mind off it.

The guest list now consisted of my brother and Tom; Patrick, the classics lecturer at Cole's college, and his wife Gala; and the ones I was really dreading, Cole's snotty friend Ryder and his even more horrific wife. Lana couldn't come – my parents, Gerry and Sue were all away so she was needed for babysitting duty while Stew manned the restaurant. On reflection, that was kind of a relief. She wasn't noted for her tact, and it was going to take all of mine just to get through the night.

I'd spent all week planning the menu. Gala was a vegan, Ali gluten-intolerant, and then there was our Cam, a picky little bugger who claimed mushrooms made him gag. I decided to play it safe: melon boat starter, lentil and butternut squash roast and a vegan, gluten-free chocolate tart.

'How's it going? Can I help?' Cole said when he came into the kitchen, smart-casual in a shirt and dark jeans. It was a bit of a contrast with my tomato-splodged sweatpants and frazzled hair.

'Not dressed like that you can't. Why don't you set the table in the living room?' I cocked an eyebrow. 'We are ok with living room, aren't we? Ryder and Ali won't expect me to call it the day parlour or something?'

Cole smiled. 'Come on, they're not that bad.'

Chapter 19

They were worse, but Cole had a massive blind spot when it came to his best friend. I suppose when you've known each other since you were 11, away at boarding school without your parents, it's bound to form a pretty strong bond. Cole didn't talk about it much but I guessed it had been a lonely time for him. As fantastic an opportunity as a scholarship to the country's top public school must've seemed to Cole's parents, if he'd been my little boy, I'm not sure I could've let him go.

'If you say so,' I said, determined to stay diplomatic. 'You go do the table. I'll just finish preparing the roast then get myself dressed.'

An hour later, everything was set. We'd told people 7pm, and sure enough, at practically seven on the nose there was a knock at the door.

I straightened my grey lace cocktail dress, pushed on the sequinned flats that I hoped were both practical and glam, and went to answer.

Tom and Cam were there, looking flustered and very much not dressed for a dinner party. Between them, in her favourite princess skirt and the top half of a Spiderman costume, was Pip.

'Becks, I am *so* sorry about this,' Cam said, leaning forward to peck my cheek. 'Lana's got a tummy bug. We would've sent apologies, but we didn't want to let you down when you'd been cooking all day.'

Pip hopped up on the step and threw her arms round my legs. 'So I can come to the party too.'

'You won't like this party, Pips,' Tom said. 'It's just boring grown-ups talking. But I brought your new colouring book and pencils. And if you're quiet playing in Aunty Becky's room on your own for a little while, we'll bring you up some pudding.' He shot me a pleading look. 'Do you mind, Becks? We didn't know what else to do. We'll just have to eat quickly then shoot off so she's not up too late.'

'Of course not.' I lifted Pip up in my arms and gave her a kiss. 'Since when do I mind my favourite niece coming to visit?'

'If the party's boring, you can come upstairs and play too, Aunty Becky,' Pip told me earnestly. 'We can make dens.'

God, I wished I could. Making dens with Pip sounded ten times more fun than making worthy conversation with Cole's friends.

'I can't, sweetie. It's my party, so it'd be bad manners.' I lowered my voice. 'But I'll try to sneak up while everyone's having pudding and we can have a quick game.'

"K.'

I ruffled her hair and put her down.

'Go in the kitchen and get yourselves a drink,' I said to the lads. 'There's Ribena for Pip. She can say hello to everyone before she goes upstairs.'

Professor Patrick arrived next, along with his wife Gala. They were rather a surprise. I'd been expecting a couple around our age, but these two must've been well into their seventies. Patrick sported a pointed grey goatee that extended down to his chest, and Gala's hair fell around her bare shoulders in long, blue braids. Both seemed very big on crocheted hemp and tie-dye. I would have bet good money they could've sold my dad some weed.

The pair greeted me with a warm hug each, and Gala handed over a bottle of wine.

'Cole said there was no need, but you can never have too much, that's our philosophy,' Patrick said.

'Thank you, that's very kind. Go through to the living room, please,' I said. 'Oh, and if a small thunderbolt hurtles into your legs, don't worry. That's just my niece, Pip. Bit of a babysitter cock-up so she'll be joining us for part of the evening.'

'Oh, how lovely,' Gala said, beaming. 'What age is she?'

Chapter 19

'Six.'

'The same as Royle – that's our grandson. He's a handful, but we can't get enough of him.'

Ryder and Ali arrived last, fashionably late to the point of rudeness. We were all on our second glass of wine, wondering whether they were coming at all, when a knock finally sounded at the door.

Patrick was kneeling on the floor, letting Pip plait his goatee while he taught her the lyrics to Let It Go in Latin. Cole and Gala were chatting like old friends, having discovered a shared love of Dalí, while I talked pantomime with Tom and Cam. It was all so cosy and nice, I was actually disappointed when the last two guests arrived.

Cole and I went together. It took a good minute for him and Ryder to get the back-slapping out of their systems.

'Thanks for coming all this way, Ryd,' Cole said at last.

'How could I resist? I couldn't wait to see this so-called "rural idyll" that had lured my best friend away from the bright lights.'

'We've been doing a tour of the village,' Ali said, with no apology for the fact they were nearly an hour late. 'Quaint little place, isn't it?'

Not waiting for an answer, she leaned forward to air-kiss me on each cheek. 'Well, Becky, I can see the country air is certainly agreeing with *you*. You're looking positively buxom.'

Ah, buxom, that old chestnut. Backhanded body-shaming was a speciality of Ali's. But I was on best behaviour, so I just smiled politely.

Cole led us all through to the living room. Ryder and Ali blinked with surprise at the strange little scene in front of them.

'This is Patrick, a colleague of Cole's.' I nodded to the professor, who'd taken his seat at the table and was chatting to Tom and Cam. His wife, on the other hand, was lying face down on the floor with Pip sitting on her back, piling her blue braids on top of her head. 'And his wife Gala.'

The old lady looked up and grinned. 'How do you do? I'm sorry, you've just caught me at the salon.'

Pip giggled. 'Her hair is like snakes.'

'Er, my niece, Pip,' I said. 'She's just going upstairs to do some lovely colouring for us. Aren't you, sweetie?'

Pip nodded happily, not taking her eyes off her hairdressing.

'And her dads, my brother Cameron and his husband Tom,' I said. 'Everyone, Ryder and Ali.'

Ryder subjected Tom and Cam to a curious inspection, and they sent a pair of puzzled smiles back.

'Well, I must say, I had no idea you were so forward-thinking up here.'

'I'm sorry?' Gala glanced up at him from under Pip.

'Oh, don't get me wrong, I think it's fantastic.' Ryder pulled up a chair. 'I just thought... well, in London, you know, it's part of the fabric. But it's great to see the modern world has reached as far as this.'

I saw Tom glance at Cam, who looked like he was about to say something, and give his head an almost imperceptible shake.

Gala's smile had taken on a dangerous quality. 'Oh yes, we're very modern – Ryder, is it? We even manage to eat with knives and forks these days. Of course, there's still the odd virgin sacrifice, these high-spirited yokels –'

Cole laughed loudly. 'How funny. Er, Becky. Why don't you take Pippa upstairs while I start serving the food?'

'Come on then, tiny,' I said, holding a hand out to Pip. I nodded to Cam. 'Can you come help, please, Daddy?'

'I am so sorry about this,' I whispered to him when we'd installed Pip on mine and Cole's bed with her colouring book.

'If I punch that guy Ryder, how long would it take for you to start speaking to me again?'

'Are you kidding? I'd give you a bloody Brother of the Year medal.'

He shook his head. 'Tell you what, you're lucky we've only got the quiet Donati here.'

'I'm not sure Gala isn't channelling Lana for tonight. It was about to turn a bit nasty there.'

'Why is Cole friends with these people, Becks?'

'Him and Ryder were at school together,' I said, feeling defensive of Cole even while I was annoyed with him for not telling his stupid friend to shut up. 'I get the sense it's kind of an unbreakable bond.'

'Then thank God Mum and Dad never sent us to boarding school. Imagine having an unbreakable bond with a tit like that the rest of your life.'

I sighed. 'I'm sorry I made you come, Cam. I had no idea the concept of "northern and gay" was going to be such a bloody novelty to him.'

'Let's just get through the night.' He went over to the bed and kissed an oblivious Pip. 'Be good, Pips. Try to stay in the lines. I'll check on you after the first course.'

'And bring pudding?'

He smiled. 'And bring pudding.'

'And you play with anything you like,' I said. She was round often enough that I kept the place kiddy-safe. 'Make a den if you want. I'll come up and see it when it's done.'

"K. Bye bye.' She was only half listening. Her tongue was poking out of the corner of her mouth as she focused all her attention on her colouring.

Downstairs, Cole had served everyone their melon boat but I noticed a few empty wine glasses.

'Ryder. Ali. You haven't got a drink,' I said. 'And it looks like everyone else could use a top-up. Let me get another bottle open.'

I uncorked a couple of bottles of red wine and plonked them in the middle of the table for everyone to help themselves. The look Ali shot Ryder suggested this probably wasn't good host-essing etiquette, but it was a white tablecloth and I was so on edge by this point, my hands were trembling.

'Darling, you did chambrer the wine?' Cole asked when he'd poured himself a glass, swilling it about.

I blinked at him.

'I mean, you got it to room temperature before you served it?' he said patiently.

'Well it's been sitting in the same Morrison's bag on the kitchen counter since I brought it home yesterday, so yes, guess I did.'

Ali trilled with laughter. 'Becky, you are priceless.'

'Yeah. With material like that, you should be on the stage,' Cam muttered in my ear.

'We did bring a bottle of the good stuff for you actually,' Ryder said. 'I know you two have limited funds.' Ali reached in her handbag and handed Cole some wine. 'Château Pape Clément.'

Cole shook his head. 'Honestly, Ryd, you shouldn't. Not at £120 a bottle.'

Tom nearly choked on his Morrison's rioja. 'How much?' he gasped.

'It might be £120 a bottle at Harrod's, but not to me,' Ryder said. 'My father got cases of the stuff when he was in Bordeaux last month. Come on, old man, have a glass with me.'

And this, *this* was what he was like. I'd never realised until I'd started seeing Cole that there were people outside PG Wodehouse who called each other 'old man'.

It wasn't that Ryder was posh. Cole was posh, but other than the occasional miscommunication over what the hell chambrering was, the fact we had very different backgrounds didn't really cause problems. It's that the man was so bloody *rude*. The one thing you could say in his favour was that at least he didn't seem to realise he was doing it, which was more than I could say for Ali, who was a terrible snob. The whole time I'd known the pair of them, she'd actively gone out of her way to make me feel small.

'And how are your parents, Becky?' she asked. 'Still in their – what was it, a fish and chip shop?'

And off she went again...

Cole caught my eye, noticed it glinting dangerously and turned immediately to Patrick.

'How's the masterpiece progressing, Pat?'

'Oh! Do you paint too?' I asked, genuinely interested. Not to mention relieved, because if Ali opened her mouth again I was going to shove my bloody melon into it.

'No, I compose,' he said. 'Not professionally, of course. Still, there's something about the creative process I find very soothing.' He laughed. 'But I'm preaching to the converted here, aren't I?' He nodded to Ryder. 'Cole tells me you run an art gallery. Do you paint yourself?'

Ryder managed a civil answer, and I breathed a sigh of relief as the conversation turned to art and everyone finished their melons in a spirit of relative bonhomie.

'How long has the roast been on?' I whispered to Cole when it looked like everyone was nearly done.

He blinked at me. 'What?'

'The roast. I asked you to put it on when you'd finished serving the melon.'

Cole stared for a second, then dropped his head to his hands. 'Oh no.'

'You're not serious? Cooking time's an hour, Cole!'

'I'm so sorry, darling. Isn't there anything quick you can knock up instead?'

'Like what, beans on toast? I spent most of the afternoon preparing that.' I glanced around the table, where the conversation was limping a bit. 'Jesus. Ok, keep everyone busy. I'll sort this.'

Dashing into the kitchen, I dug out my mobile and pulled up the number for Pie and a Pint.

'Stew? It's me. Look, I know it's last-minute, but can you do us a big favour?'

Twenty minutes later, there was a tap at the back door. Stew was outside in his cycling helmet, holding a couple of carrier bags.

'One vegan, one pork, one gluten-free cheese and onion and four chicken and mushroom, plus seven cartons of mushy peas and seven of mash,' he said.

'Oh God, you're a lifesaver. Thanks, Stew, I owe you.'

'Thank Deano, he made them. How's it going anyway?'

'This is the single worst night of my entire existence,' I told him fervently. 'Remind me never, ever to host a dinner party again.'

He grinned. 'That well, eh?'

'Well, at least it can't get much worse.'

Talk about famous last words...

Chapter 20

When Stew had gone, I started dishing up. It was then I realised the problem.

There were only seven portions. I'd been so busy making sure we had all the dietary requirements covered, I'd forgotten to order myself a bloody pie.

Fine. Right. Ok. I'd just tell them I was on a diet. I could always make a sandwich later.

When I went back in, I found Ali eyeing Tom and Cam like exhibits in a museum.

'It's amazing what they can do these days, isn't it?' she was saying.

Tom blinked. 'Sorry – what who can do?'

'Well, doctors. So which of you is the child's real father?'

Cam glanced at Tom. 'Um, we both are?'

'Oh, yes, yes, of course,' she said, waving a hand. 'But biologically speaking. Or did you mix the sperm so you wouldn't know?'

'Did we...'

'Pip's adopted, actually,' I said, grabbing the rioja and filling my glass to the brim. *Not that it's any of your fucking business...* 'And I'm not sure my brother's sperm's really a suitable topic for the dinner table, thanks, Ali.' I downed a large mouthful of wine, meeting her eye defiantly.

Cole looked horrified, but Gala nodded her approval. Anyway, it wiped the smirk off Ali's face.

'We'd, um, better check on Pip,' said a shellshocked Cam. 'She's suspiciously quiet up there. Come on, Tommy.'

'Well, it must be time for the main,' Gala said from behind a forced smile. 'Becky, let me give you a hand in the kitchen.'

'No need. It's all served up.' I glanced round the table. 'Er, I thought that since we had friends from out of town here we'd have a proper northern tea. Pie and peas.'

Ali's eyebrows raised. 'Pie and...'

'Mushy peas. Yep. Oh, and mash too.'

Patrick grinned. 'Now, that's just about the best news I've heard all night.'

A worried Cameron appeared at the living room door.

'Um, Becks?' he said in a low voice. 'Could I borrow you a minute please?'

'Excuse me,' I said to the guests. 'Gala, Cole, would the two of you mind serving up? There's none for me. I'm on a diet.'

I found Cameron at the foot of the stairs, looking guilty.

'There's been a bit of a problem.'

'Problem? What is it?'

'Well... you'd better come and see. Brace yourself.'

I followed him upstairs to my bedroom. Inside, I discovered my white duvet suspended from a couple of chairs to make a den. Only it wasn't white any more – oh no, it was all the colours of the rainbow. Little handprints in red, yellow and blue were all over it, not to mention the walls, the carpet... and in the middle of the carnage was Pip, covered in paint and sleeping like an angel.

'She found some of Cole's paints in the cupboard,' Tom whispered. 'Becks, I'm so sorry. We'll pay for the damage.'

I stared for a moment, struggling to take it in. Then the bossy big sister in me kicked in.

'Never mind that now,' I said. 'You'd better wake her up and get her straight into the bath. That stuff won't be child-safe, it probably isn't good for it to be in contact with her skin.'

'Right.' Cam went to set the taps running, then came back in.

'Oh my... *God!*' Cole had appeared at the door. 'What the hell happened?'

Pip chose that moment to wake up. She was about to rub her fists in her eyes when Tom dived forwards to stop her.

'Don't, sweetie. It'll hurt if you get paint in your eyes.'

She grinned sleepily at me. 'Hello, Aunty Becky. Look, I made us a princess castle to play in.'

'It's very pretty, my love,' I said. 'But you need to get in the bath now. Go with Daddy and Papa.'

Cole was staring at her, anger and horror in his eyes.

'But look at the mess she's made!' he said to me.

'She's a child, Cole.'

'You know those oils cost £20 a pot?'

'Cole, mate, I'm so sorry,' Cam said. 'We will pay for everything.'

Cole shrugged off the conciliatory hand Cam rested on his shoulder. 'I do wonder, Cameron, why you can't supervise your daughter adequately if you will insist on bringing her.'

Cam, taken aback, withdrew his hand.

Tom frowned. 'There was no need for that.'

'Don't have a go at them. It was me,' I said to Cole. 'I told her she could play with anything in the room. I didn't know you had paints in the cupboard.'

'Am I in trouble, Aunty Becky?' Pip whispered, still half asleep.

'No, sweetheart. You're not in trouble.'

'Can I still have pudding?'

'Course you can.' I summoned a smile. 'Go on, have your bath. Then pudding after.'

'Why the hell did you have paints in here anyway?' I hissed at Cole when Pip's dads had taken her into the bathroom to scrub off all the paint. 'Why aren't they in the attic?'

'You're really going to make this my fault? I didn't know there'd be an unsupervised child running around the place.' He shook his head. 'Who the hell brings a child to a dinner party? What was your brother thinking?'

'He couldn't get a babysitter.'

'Then one would think he'd send polite apologies rather than letting the girl run riot.' He took another sweep of the room. 'It'll take an eternity to get this cleared up.'

'She might've made a mess, but she's a damn sight better-mannered than your bloody awful friends,' I snapped.

He frowned. 'What?'

'Ryder and *fucking* Ali. They've been nothing but snotty all night – about the food, my family, even my weight. And borderline homophobic into the bargain. Actually, no, scrub the borderline.'

'Ryder went to an all-boys boarding school, Becky. Trust me, he's far from homophobic.'

'He's downright rude, whatever else he might be. And Ali's even worse. You don't ask strangers about how they conceived their kid over dinner. You don't remark on what an amazing thing it is that the north's now so advanced, it even has its own homosexuals. Nice people, polite people, don't say those things.'

'He doesn't mean to be rude,' Cole said, looking ashamed now. 'He's just led a rather sheltered life.'

'Yeah, yeah. Because my parents run a chip shop and his dad's the Duke of bloody Pembrokeshire or whatever.'

'Cultural attaché.'

'Exactly. That's so posh, I don't even know what the hell it is. But it sounds like the family should be able to afford a few manners.' I nodded to Pip's den. 'Whereas this is Pip's idea of making something pretty for us, in her little six-year-old head. Can't you get that?'

'It's just... such a waste.'

'You can't expect her to think like you do, Cole. She's a baby.' I shook my head. 'How are you going to cope when it's our kid? Because I can tell you now, there will be stuff like this.'

'I wish you'd stop with that, Becky.'

I frowned. 'I'm sorry?'

'It feels like you're eternally pushing me to start a family at a pace I'm simply not comfortable with. Who knows where we'll be in a year's time?'

'Are you saying... you can't mean you don't want to? We've been talking about it for years!'

'I'm not saying that. I just don't want to be rushed. I've got my career – you know I've always dreamed of being able to paint full-time. I think we should play it by ear, that's all.'

'Right.' I marched out of the room, Cole following like a naughty puppy.

'Are we ok, Becky?'

'Never mind that now. We've got a bloody dinner party to get through. And as dreadful as Ryder and Ali have been all night, I don't want to be rude to Patrick and Gala.' I knocked on the door of the bathroom, where I could hear Pip giggling and splashing. 'I'll bring your food up, lads. Sorry for an awful evening.'

***

Mine and Cole's bedroom was declared off-limits until it could be de-Pipped the next day. When our guests had left, I curled up in the spare room with a book and a glass of red (the Morrison's stuff, not Ryder's Chateau de Thingy). But the words swam before my eyes. Exhausted by the world's most horrific dinner party, miserable because Cole and I weren't speaking and with a rumbling stomach because I'd missed out on my main course and pudding, I felt close to bursting into tears. I couldn't even offload on Lana, who was still ill.

I was just toying with the idea of ringing Marcus for a nice, cathartic rant when Cole poked his head round the door, looking penitent.

'What do you want?' I said.

He came in, bearing aloft a plate with a generous wedge of chocolate tart on it.

'You didn't have dessert.'

'I wasn't hungry.'

He sat down beside me and pushed the tart tantalisingly into my eyeline. I was angry with him, but I was also starving. Unable to resist the prodding of my stomach, I grabbed the spoon and tucked in.

'But don't think this means I forgive you,' I said through a mouthful of chocolate.

He smiled. 'Here,' he said, wiping a smudge of chocolate from my mouth. 'I can see which aunty young Pippa learnt her messiness from.'

'So is this an apology?'

'Yes.' He took my free hand. 'I was wrong and you were right. As usual.'

'Good start. Go on.'

'I shouldn't have been so angry at Pippa. Pip. I know children do these things.'

'And?'

'And I shouldn't have snapped at your brother. I'll call him tomorrow to apologise. That was £100's worth of oils, that's all.'

'Pip didn't know that. To a kid, paints are for painting with.'

'No, I know. I just... I saw red. I'm the adult and I should know better. Sorry.'

I relented slightly. 'Well, then I guess I'm sorry I was rude to Ryder and Ali.' I paused. 'Actually, no I'm not, they had it coming. But I'm sorry it upset you.'

'No, you're right. They were out of order to talk to Cameron and Tom that way. I'll have a word, see if I can make Ryder understand.'

'What's to understand?' I muttered. Then I remembered we were building bridges and gave his hand a squeeze. 'Thank you.'

'I know you wonder why I'm friends with him. We go back a long way, Becky.'

'But he's such a... you know. Knobhead.'

'Put it this way. If Cameron was a... you know, would you still want a relationship with him?'

'Well, yeah. He's my brother.' I smiled. 'Ok, I see. Point taken.'

'Becky, the other thing...'

I winced. I'd been wondering when he'd get to that.

'You do still want to, don't you?'

'I want to if you want to. I want you to be happy, darling.'

'But not just because of that, right? I mean, you want to be a dad?'

'Of course. When the time's right. I just don't want to feel it's a race against the clock, that's all.'

'That's... fair enough. I never meant you to feel I was putting pressure on you.'

He took my empty pudding plate away and pulled me into his arms. 'Friends again?'

'Friends again.' I planted a chocolatey kiss on his lips. 'Let's get some sleep. It's been a long night.'

Chapter 21

'I thought you'd be at rehearsal by now,' Cole said one evening when he descended from his studio to find me opening that morning's post on the sofa.

'Marc and Gerry are going through their slapstick routine first so they don't need me yet.'

'Do you want a glass of wine?'

'Dunno, has it been chambrered?'

He smiled. 'Will you ever stop teasing me about that?'

'Nope.'

'So do you?'

'No, I'd better get going. Just checking if the catalogue I sent for from a panto costume specialist is in this lot. If it is, we can have a look through in the pub after.'

Cole went into the kitchen. 'Are rehearsals going well?' he called.

'Pretty well. There's still the Maisie problem, and Gerry's blocking's not improving as quickly as we'd like, but –' I broke off, staring at the letter I'd just opened.

Cole poked his head through the door. 'What's the matter, darling?'

'This,' I whispered.

'Is it your catalogue?'

'No, it's... oh God. I have to get to the Temp.'

'Becky, what is it? Becky!'

But I was already out of the door.

Chapter 21

I could've rivalled Usain Bolt racing to the hall, the letter gripped in my fist.

'Oh good, you're here,' Deano said when I burst in. 'You and Maisie are up next. The Tomorrow scene.'

'No we're not,' I panted, clutching my stomach. 'Panto's off.'

***

It was a subdued group of amdrammers who stared into their beers in the pub function room.

'Bloody hell, what's up with you lot?' asked Billy, who'd come in to collect our empties. 'Someone died?'

'Just our theatrical hopes and dreams,' Deano said.

I took a glum gulp of my wine. 'And the Temp. That's looking a bit moribund.'

'What's moribund mean?' Marcus said.

'Fucked.'

'Oh.'

Billy cast a concerned glance at Yolanda. From the look on her face you'd think someone really had died.

'You ok, love?' he said gently.

She choked back a sob. 'It's the panto,' she whispered. 'Becky got a letter.'

I handed it to Billy. 'From the management of the Hyperion.'

'That theatre in town?'

'Yeah.'

'"Dear madam,"' he read. '"It has come to our attention that your amateur dramatics group is planning to stage a version of Jack and the Beanstalk that will be in direct competition with our version of the same pantomime. If you do not wish to face legal action, we politely request you immediately desist."'

'Pathetic,' Gerry spat. 'Since when have the big-budget pantos given a shit what village halls do? I bet there's plenty doing Jack and the Beanstalk.'

I cast a look at Harper, who smiled sadly.

'She's right. It's me,' he said. 'Sorry, everyone.'

'It's not your fault. And we're glad to have you, darling.' Yolanda sighed. 'But that is the reason, isn't it? That's why they think we're competition.'

'This is bollocks though!' Billy said. 'Threatening to sue. They'd never have a case.'

Yolanda squeezed his hand gratefully.

'They're just trying to scare us, I think,' I said.

Lana pulled the letter towards her. 'Mmm. It does read a bit "nice little panto you've got there, shame if anything happened to it".'

'So what can we do?' Marcus asked.

'I'll drop out if you want,' Harper said.

Yolanda shook her head. 'Oh, we couldn't let you do that, darling. You're our big selling point.'

'Too late anyway,' I said. 'Publicity's gone out so the damage has been done. No, I think the only solution is either to brazen it out and hope they're bluffing, switch pantos or... well, give up.'

'I don't think we're in a position to call their bluff, are we?' Stew said. 'Let's face it, we're the underdog here. And underdogs only come out on top in films.'

'We change pantos then,' Deano said. 'Buggered if I'm giving up on this after all my hard work.' He glanced round the table. 'Er, our hard work.'

'Change pantos?' Maisie said. 'But I've spent ages learning my lines!'

'Plus there's only four months,' Marcus said. 'That's not long to write and rehearse a whole new script.'

'And then there's the props the children have been making, and Rita's choreography,' Yolanda said. 'We'd have to start everything again from scratch.'

I shook my head. 'Yo-yo's right, it's too late to start all over again. Let's face it. Unless someone comes up with some miraculous brainwave, we're screwed.'

Billy looked thoughtful.

'Oh God, please say that's your miraculous brainwave face,' Marcus said to him.

'Here. You lot know Jimmy James?' Billy said.

Lana frowned. 'What, the milkman?'

I cocked an eyebrow. 'Jimmy James? Seriously?'

'Yeah,' Billy said. 'One in a long line. His dad was a James James, and his dad before him. Someone's idea of a family joke.'

'But what's this milkman with the daft name got to do with us?' Marcus asked.

'Because he's not a milkman,' Billy said. 'Not by trade. He went a bit funny ten years ago and bought himself a round, reckoned he wanted to live the quiet life out here in the sticks. But before that he was a hotshot lawyer over in Leeds. Competition law was his specialty.'

'And you think he'd help us?' Stew said.

'I can ask him to take a look at this letter, see if he thinks it's above board,' Billy said. 'Jim's one of my regulars, I bet he'd do it for a free Boltmaker. If they're bluffing and we call them on it, maybe the underdog actually can come out on top for once.'

Chapter 22

'So? Any news?' I asked Billy when I dropped into the Fox on my way home from work the following week for an update. Jimmy James the Milkman had been on his holidays, so he hadn't been in for his regular evening pint for a bit. Everyone was on tenterhooks waiting to see if there was anything he could do for us.

Billy shook his head, and I knew in an instant that there was news, and it wasn't the good kind.

'Sorry, love. Jimmy wanted to help, and he took a look, but...'

'You can't mean it's legal? They couldn't actually sue us, surely?'

'It seems they could make a case if they were minded, yeah.'

'No, come on. Not a big theatre like that and a little village panto.'

'That's what Jimmy thought at first. Said they wouldn't have a leg to stand on if they tried it. Then I mentioned Brady and suddenly he seemed to think it was a problem. You've got a bigger star than them at a third of the ticket price.'

'He's not the star though, he's a cameo. Maisie's the star.'

'Yeah. Jimmy seemed to think she might be a problem too. Two celebrities for the price of one.'

'So... is he saying there's really nothing we can do?'

Billy shrugged. 'Jimmy offered to talk to them, see if they'd see reason. But you'd probably have to ditch Brady and his missus to have a chance of getting them off your backs.'

I hesitated.

'No,' I said at last. 'No, there must be another way. We don't want to lose Harper.'

'Another way such as what?'

'God, I wish I knew. I was really hoping Jimmy might be able to make it all go away for us.' I sighed. 'So that's it then. Unless one of us thinks up a miracle, it looks like when it comes to underdogs there's a clue in the name.'

***

And bloody hell, I only did. Think up a miracle, that is – or at least, a workable compromise. It was pitch dark when I woke three days later with a sudden epiphany.

'Becky?' Cole mumbled. 'What's wrong?'

'Nothing, love. I just have to make an urgent call. You go back to sleep.'

I grabbed my mobile, tiptoed out of the bedroom and pulled up Marcus's number.

'Y'm?' he answered groggily.

'I've got it, Marc!'

'Becks, it's midnight.' There was a pause. 'Wait, are you saying you know what to do about the panto?'

'Yeah, it just came to me. Listen, can I come over?'

'Now?'

'Come on, you might as well now you're up.'

'Thanks to you bloody getting me up.' He sighed. 'All right.'

'Get your script ready.'

I was so excited I didn't even get dressed. Just jumped straight in the car in my ladybird pyjamas and burned it over to Marc's flat.

I beamed at him when he answered the door, topless in just a pair of lounge pants.

'Nice,' he said, taking in my PJs.

'Thanks.' I bounced past him into the flat.

'Come in the bedroom and tell me this brilliant idea then.'

I followed him into his room and jumped on the bed. Marc sat cross-legged opposite.

'Right. You ready for this?' I said.

'If it'll get me back to sleep faster, yes.'

'Ok. So here's what we do.' I took a deep breath. 'Cinderella.'

'What?'

'We change pantos to Cinderella. The Hyperion can hardly complain, when we've gone out of our way to accommodate them. Plus I checked on my phone and no theatres in the area are doing that one.'

'But we talked about this. Writing a whole new script, getting everyone to learn new lines, starting again with the props – it'd be practically impossible.'

'That's why this is such a great idea.' I leaned forward eagerly. 'Because it wouldn't be a whole new script, Marc! What's Jack and the Beanstalk about? Hero trapped in poverty, looking for a better life. And what's Cinderella about? Heroine trapped in poverty, looking for a better life. Instead of a comedy sidekick brother she's got a comedy sidekick mate, Buttons. Instead of a bullying mum in drag she's got a couple of stepsisters. With a few tweaks we can use nearly all the existing material, plus most of the props. Everyone's roles switch to the nearest equivalent, then we just need to write a couple of new scenes.'

He looked thoughtful. 'So I'd be Buttons?'

'Yeah, but you can use nearly all Sleepy Steve's material.'

'Hmm. We'd be a dame short though. There're two ugly sisters. And we had enough trouble getting the one we've got.'

'Let's not worry about that for now,' I said. 'If we really can't find anyone, we can always pass it off as a budgeting joke.

Pogley are doing Snow White and the One Dwarf this year. And he's six-three.'

'Be better if we can get someone. The sisters work best as a double act.'

'Well, we can try.'

'So Maisie would be – what, the prince?'

'Guess so.' I brightened. 'And that fixes another problem, doesn't it? The prince gets less stage time than Jack. People might not notice how awful she is.'

'And you'd have more stage time. Assuming you're Cinders.'

'S'pose I would.'

''Fess up, Becks. Was this whole thing a stunt to build up your part?'

I laughed. 'Busted.'

He passed me his script from the bedside table. 'So talk me through it. How would we adapt the scenes to fit the new story?'

I flicked through, looking for a good example. 'Ok, so the Tomorrow scene, where Jill comforts Jack about being poor and they do a duet.'

'I don't see how that could that be adapted for Cinders and the prince.'

'She could do it with Buttons though. And that stops Maisie having to sing.'

'But it's a love scene.'

'It can still be a sort-of love scene. There is that whole subplot of Buttons being in love with Cinders. We just make it so that instead of them kissing at the end, he tries to kiss her and she lets him down gently.'

Marcus laughed. 'Poor old Buttons. You know, I used to get really upset about that panto when I was a kid. I could never get why Cinders didn't go for Buttons rather than the prince.' He started counting on his fingers. 'They're best mates, he makes her laugh, he obviously cares about her. And she rejects the poor bugger in favour of some rich, handsome knobhead she met for five minutes at a party.'

'Yeah. She is a bit of a golddigger, isn't she?'

'She wants out of her miserable life,' he said, shrugging. 'Understandable. Still, seems a bit hard on Buttons.'

I smiled. 'You put a lot of thought into this, didn't you?'

'I was an emotionally sensitive child.'

I gave his knee a pat. 'Well, if it makes you feel better, I'd pick Buttons over Prince Charming every time.'

'Sweet of you.'

'So you think it's a plan?'

'It'll be a lot of work, Becks. We'll have to go back to weekly scripting sessions.'

We'd cut back to meeting once a fortnight now rehearsals were advanced, just to see if there was anything that could be fine-tuned.

'Fine by me.'

He smiled. 'All right. But I'm letting you break it to the cast.'

Chapter 23

S witching pantos at this stage was no small thing. As well as a new version of the script, there was the dame problem. We needed another ugly sister, and as Marc had pointed out, finding the one we'd got had been hard enough. Apparently the menfolk of Egglethwaite were not big on frocks.

Not only that, we needed another principal boy. Cinderella had two – Prince Charming and his right-hand man, Dandini. But every girl who'd tried out for Jack had been nearly as hopeless as Maisie. We couldn't have two abysmal principals.

Finally, there was the baddie issue. In Jack and the Beanstalk the giant was only ever a foot and a voice, a cameo for Harper Brady. But Harper couldn't do the Wicked Stepmother part. We needed a lady who could cackle and scheme, who'd be booed and hissed with a good grace.

I broke the news to everyone next day. There was the predictable grumbling about the months we'd wasted on a panto that'd never be performed, but they grudgingly accepted it was the best plan we had. I suggested a two-week hiatus while me and Marc turned our Jack script, pumpkin-like, into a Cinders script, then we'd get back on the pantomime horse.

The first rehearsal after the switch, there was drama as soon as I walked through the door.

'Ok, Becky, what the hell happened to all my lines?' Maisie demanded, waving a copy of the new script. 'I've got half as many, and you've got loads!'

'That's just the story. Cinderella's the focus. Sorry, Mais.'

'Then I want to be Cinderella. I'm the star.' She turned to her husband. 'Tell her, Harper.'

Harper looked embarrassed. 'Thing is, babe, this is all kind of my fault,' he said in a low voice. 'I don't think you should be too high-handed.'

'High-handed?' Maisie said, her voice getting shriller. 'I'm never high-handed. Everyone loves me because I'm so bloody... low-handed!' She glared at me. 'You did this on purpose, didn't you? Couldn't bear me stealing the limelight.'

'I didn't, honestly! I hate limelight.'

'Right, then give me your part. I'll learn all the new lines, I don't mind.'

I exchanged a look with Harper. Cinders had even more lines than Jack, not to mention a load of song numbers, and even Harper, much as he kept trying to convince himself his wife had hidden talents, seemed to recognise there was no way she could carry the part.

'You don't want to be Cinderella,' he said soothingly. 'She's a drudge. If you're the prince you get to –'

'– show my legs, I know. That's all I am to you people, isn't it? A nice pair of legs.'

Harper glanced at her chest. 'No. Not just that.'

Yolanda stormed into the hall, brandishing her own copy of the script. 'What's all this, Rebecca? Where are all my lines?'

I groaned. 'Oh God, another one.'

'What's going on, Becks?' Deano said, strolling over with Marcus.

'Maisie and Yo-yo have got issues with their parts.'

'What's wrong with them?' Marcus asked,

'I've got hardly any lines!' the two women said, practically in unison.

Deano shrugged. 'Sorry, ladies, that's just the story. The Fairy Godmother only has one big scene, getting Cinders ready for the ball. And the prince –'

'– has got about five lines in the whole thing!' Maisie snapped.

'Rubbish. It's one of the biggest parts.'

'Not as big as Jack. Or Cinders.' She folded her arms. 'If I can't play her, I won't do it.'

'Don't be hasty, Mais,' Harper whispered. 'You need this.'

'Look, you talked me into this. Well now I'm having my say, and I bloody well want a decent part or I'm out.'

Yolanda shot her a sideways glance, a smidgeon of admiration thrown in with the dislike. 'Er, yes. Me too,' she said, folding her arms. The pair of them faced off against us side by side.

Marcus glanced at me, and I nodded.

'Actually, Yo-yo, we were hoping you might play another part,' Marc said with a winning smile. 'One with loads of lines.'

'But I'm the fairy. I'm always the fairy.'

'And you can still be the fairy,' I said. 'But there's another part we need to cast. It doesn't share scenes with the Fairy Godmother so you can do both.'

She looked suspicious. 'What part?'

I tried not to flinch. 'We, er... we were hoping you'd be the stepmother.'

Her eyes widened. 'You want me to play the *witch*?'

Maisie snorted.

'She's not a witch, Yo-yo,' Deano said soothingly. 'And you'd be great. Just channel that inner bitch we all know and love.'

'I will not. I'm the fairy. I'm not the witch.' She jerked her head towards Maisie. 'Let *her* be the witch, since she's so desperate for lines.'

'Maisie can't be the witch.'

'Why?' Yolanda demanded. 'Because she's young and I'm – less young?'

Deano took her by the elbow. 'Don't get upset, love. Here, let's talk in private.'

He guided her out of earshot, over by the stage. We saw them talking, Deano at his most charming, smiling and squeezing her arm; Yolanda's black expression gradually lifting until she was smiling too. Finally she gave him a hug and disappeared backstage.

'Sorted,' Deano said when he came back. 'She'll do both parts.'

'I'm impressed,' I said. 'What did you say to her?'

He shrugged. 'I told her she's the best actress we've got and it was too important to let anyone else play that part. That she'd get more stage time than in any panto since she was a principal boy. That we'd get her a sexy black dress for her wicked step-mother costume. Oh, and I reminded her about all the times I did that thing she likes.'

Marcus shook his head. 'TMI, Deano.'

He grinned. 'All right. Let's just say she owes me a few favours.'

'And what about me?' Maisie demanded. 'Because that thing I like is more bloody lines.'

'Well, and that other thing,' Harper said.

'Ok, and that other thing. But you can't buy me off with that.'

I shot a panicked glance at Marcus. We hadn't planned for this.

'What if... ok, what if we wrote the prince another scene?' I said.

She narrowed one eye. 'What scene?'

'Maybe you could be, um...'

'Having dancing lessons,' Harper said brightly. 'Ready for the ball.'

I shot him a grateful look.

Chapter 23

'Hmm.' Maisie didn't look convinced.

'It'd be just like *Strictly*,' Harper said. 'You've always wanted to go on that.'

'Who would I dance with?'

'Well, me. I could play the dance instructor. I need a new part.'

'We were hoping you'd play Baron Hardup though, Cinders' dad,' Marcus said.

'He could give the lessons, couldn't he?' Harper was warming to his theme now. 'It's a great idea, Mais! You get a bigger part but you still get to wear the sexy costumes, and you can show off your best skill. Maybe the *Strictly* people'll be watching our show.' He looked at me and Marcus. 'Mais is a great dancer.'

'Are you?' I asked her.

She shrugged. 'I've had some training. I was in this girl band for a bit. Slut Drop.'

'You were in a band?' I wasn't sure how that could've happened, given she was practically tone-deaf. On the other hand, with a name like Slut Drop it didn't sound like it had selected its members for their musical talent.

'No need to sound so surprised, honey.' She drew herself up proudly. 'We made the top 100 in Ukraine, you know. I swear, we were this close to getting picked for Eurovision.'

'Show them,' Harper said.

'All right. This was our signature move.'

She performed a stripperesque dance move, dropping to the floor and writhing sensuously.

'That's... er, great, Mais,' Marcus said. 'But you couldn't do that with kids in the audience. You look like you're trying to pick up a penny between your buttocks.'

She giggled. 'Funnily enough, that's what they used to tell us to think of when we were practising.'

'He's right, that's not for pre-watershed,' I said. 'Have you got anything else?'

'Oh, I can do loads of stuff. I can even waltz. Tango, salsa...' She did a few ballroom steps for us. 'When the band split I made it part of my exercise routine.'

'Great,' I said, relieved we'd found something she was good at. 'So we'll write a dancing scene, then everyone's happy.'

'Hmm. I'd still rather play Cinderella.' She narrowed her eyes. 'You better not have done this to get the best part, Becky.'

'I honestly didn't.'

Still, there was a distinctly frosty atmosphere as we started rehearsing. Yolanda had been appeased by Deano and that thing he used to do, but Maisie was glaring daggers at me the whole time.

Deano sighed, for the umpteenth time, as we made a total hash of the new ballroom scene.

'Maisie, you've just seen your true love for the first time. Can you not glare at her like she's spilt your pint?'

'I wasn't!'

'Yes you were. Look, we decided all this. You're the prince, Becky's Cinders, I'm in charge, deal with it. Now try again.'

'Fine.' She nudged Lana, who was filling in as Dandini until we had chance to recruit someone. 'Who is that mysterious stranger, Dandini?'

'I couldn't say, sire,' Lana said, reading from her script. 'She must be a young lady of quality to carry herself with such grace.'

'She's a great beauty.' The way Maisie put the emphasis on 'great' made the line sound more than a little sarcastic, and she accompanied it with a look that suggested she found me as beautiful as a damp slug.

Deano groaned. 'Ok, cut.' He walked over to Maisie and grabbed her by the shoulders. 'Look, love. I don't know where the chip on your shoulder's coming from and I don't care. Get rid of it.' He nodded to me. 'When you're on my stage, that lass is the love of your bloody life and I don't expect you to forget it. Get it sorted for the next rehearsal.'

'Yes, Chef,' Maisie muttered.

'All right.' He patted her arm as she made her way backstage. 'Just keep practising.'

When Maisie had gone, he turned to Lana. 'You were pretty good. Don't suppose you fancy the part, do you?'

'Me? I'm just supply Dandini.'

'He's right, you were better than anyone at auditions. Even Tilly Stanbury,' I said. 'Why don't you? We can rehearse together, it'll be a laugh.'

'Dunno, guys. I'd get nervous in front of an audience.'

I snorted. 'Who, you?'

'Hey. I'm a delicate little blossom.'

'Course you are.'

'Come on, treacle,' Deano said. 'You spent years as a medieval tavern wench, didn't you?'

'It might be nice to have a Donati in the cast,' I said. 'I mean, with your dad being such a favourite back in the day. Sort of like Egglethwaite Players: The Next Generation.'

'Well... for Dad's sake then,' she said. 'But I reserve the right to drop out if I'm awful.'

'That's ok,' Deano said. 'If you're awful, I'll kick you out.'

'Ta, mate. I bet you would as well.'

'Ok, great. Another problem solved,' I said. 'So all we need now is a dame. Again.'

Chapter 24

The chalkboard had been up outside the Fox for a fortnight. *Teenage Kicks, LIVE!!! 7.30pm, Saturday 8th September. Don't miss this exciting new band!!!!* I couldn't walk past it without wincing.

Now the night had finally arrived. The first, and quite possibly last, performance of my dad's new band.

'Who's in the lineup?' I asked Cameron as I walked to the pub with him, Tom and Cynthia.

'Dad's on lead vocals, there's Mr Page on guitar, Billy on bass, and Brad from the butcher's on keyboard. Oh, and I think they've got Dave Grohl on drums.'

Lana and Stew were babysitting so the four of us could go to the gig. Cyn wanted the family to put on a united front, ready to lie through our teeth if necessary about how fantastic they were.

Cole had offered to come too, but I'd begged him not to. Having his face hovering in my peripheral vision, filled with excruciating embarrassment, would make the whole thing ten times harder.

'You never know,' Tom said. 'They might be good.'

'What do you think?' I asked Cynthia.

'I think I love your father very much and if he says they're going to be good, they're going to be good.'

'So it's total denial for you then, is it?'

'Pretty much.'

Chapter 24

When we got to the pub, Dad was with Billy, getting the equipment set up. We bought drinks and went to join Yolanda, sitting up front near the speakers.

'Isn't it exciting?' she said to Cynthia. 'Who knew we'd get another chance to be groupies at our time of life?'

Cynthia raised an eyebrow. '*Another* chance?'

'Oh, Billy's not my first musician, of course.'

'Have you heard them?' I asked.

'No, but I'm sure they'll be wonderful.'

'We're sure they will too.' Cynthia glanced round. 'Aren't we, kids?'

'Oh, completely,' Cam said.

'100%,' Tom said.

'Never been more positive of anything in my life,' I said.

Dad had spotted us. He left his mike stand and headed over.

'Hiya Dad,' Cam said, 'Nervous?'

He took a seat next to me and dropped his head to the table. 'Bricking it. Talk me down, family.'

I gave his dazzlingly bleached hair a pat. 'Come on, it's only the Fox.'

'Today it's the Fox,' Tom said. 'Tomorrow, who knows? Wembley Stadium! The Superbowl! Egglethwaite Temperance Hall!'

'Funny,' Dad mumbled, not lifting his head.

'Just enjoy yourself.' Cynthia reached over and yanked the collar of his leather jacket to pull his face up. 'That's why you started this, isn't it, for fun? I figure you're not really counting on the Superbowl this time next year.'

'Yeah, but it'd be nice if I didn't get booed off stage by my own darts team.' He glanced at the bar. 'Oh God, there's Gerry Lightowler. Kit Beeton, Roger Collingwood... shit, everyone I know's here!' He squared his shoulders. 'Right. I can do this.' He stood up, then immediately sat back down. 'I can't do this.'

'Oh, of course you can,' Yolanda said, flicking a hand. 'Honestly, Danny, don't be such a drama queen.'

That seemed a bit rich, after her diva strop at our last rehearsal. I swallowed the comment I was tempted to make concerning pots, kettles and their relative colours and nudged my dad.

'Go on, Billy's waiting. You've been rehearsing for months, how bad can you be?'

The answer to that, we quickly discovered, was pretty damn bad.

It wasn't long into Teenage Kicks' first number, a cover of The Beatles' Twist and Shout, that we realised the full horror of the evening ahead. It was worse than the worst we'd thought it could be.

Dad's singing was jarringly off on the high notes, his voice cracking like a teenage boy struggling through puberty, while the backing vocalist seemed to be performing some harmony that went with an entirely different song. The drummer wasn't even a Ringo, let alone a Dave Grohl. Only Billy on bass managed to hold his own.

Once they'd finished slaughtering The Beatles they gave the Rolling Stones a trouncing, followed by a kick in the nuts for poor old Lynyrd Skynyrd. Chuck Berry, The Sex Pistols, even Slade – no artist, genre or era was sacred.

'Your old man'll put his back out if he keeps jumping like that,' Tom said, watching Dad bouncing about like Sid Vicious.

'At least then it'd stop.' I groaned. 'Oh God, will no one make it stop?'

No one did make it stop. It went on for another hour, not even granting us the small mercy of a break for half-time.

'Bloody hell,' Cameron muttered when the band finally played the last chord of Purple Rain and downed instruments – well, what would've been the last chord if Hendrix had decided to play it flat for a wheeze. 'Think I just felt the ground move while everyone who played Woodstock span in their graves.'

'Billy was fabulous though, wasn't he?' Yolanda said, waving to her fiancé.

Cynthia glared at her. 'Oh yes, it's all very well for you, isn't it, Yo-yo? You don't have to pretend your other half was amazing when clearly he was even better than that. Oh hello, sweetie, never saw you there.'

I had to marvel at how seamlessly she'd segued into a fib when she sensed Dad behind her. Years of practice, presumably.

'So, what did you all think?' Dad asked.

Yolanda stood up. 'I'd better congratulate Billy. Well done, Danny. That... took a lot of nerve.' She grabbed her G&T and flounced off.

That was one way to avoid answering. Unfortunately for the rest of us, we were stuck there: fixed in the glare of my dad's hopeful, puppy-dog eyes.

'So?' he said.

'Excellent,' Cynthia answered promptly. She waggled her eyebrows at us.

'Five stars,' Cam said.

'I'll recommend you to all my friends,' Tom said.

'Modern-day Bowie,' I said.

Dad sighed. 'We were terrible, weren't we?'

Cynthia looked pained. 'No. We were a little close to the speakers is all.'

I nodded vigorously. 'I bet it sounded amazing at the back.'

There weren't many people at the back to ask, as most of them had sneaked out during the gig. Gerry and Kit, old friends of Dad's from the darts team, were still there in a show of middle-aged solidarity, but the looks on their faces said the music hadn't sounded any sweeter from the pool table.

'Come on, guys, I'm not stupid,' Dad said. 'We've emptied the place. You can admit it.'

Cam winced. 'It... wasn't great. Sorry, Dad.'

'But it's only your first one,' Tom said. 'Live performance isn't like rehearsal: that's when the nerves kick in. Trust me, I've got experience.'

I raised one eyebrow. 'What, you were in a band?'

'No. Nativity.' He nodded encouragingly to my dad. 'You just need time to find your sound, Danny.'

Dad sank down next to Cynthia and buried his fists in his cheeks. 'Oh, who am I kidding? We're duds. I've been wasting my time.'

'It's not a waste of time if you've enjoyed it,' I said. 'And Tommy's right, you'll get better.'

'I get it. Pension the old man off with a hobby he's shite at, keep him out of mischief. Well, suppose I'm at that age now.' He smiled sadly. 'I'd better go say hi to Gerry and Kit. Seems only right I buy them a pint after they stayed through that racket.'

We watched in silence as Dad went to join his friends.

'Poor Danny,' Cynthia said, sighing. 'The thing is, it actually did make him happy, this little mid-life crisis club. It'd be a shame if he abandoned it just because they sound like they're murdering a rhino.'

'I thought you were worried about him staying out so late,' I said.

'I'm more worried about his moods. Having something creative to focus on really seemed to pep him up.'

'What made him decide to start a band?' Tom asked.

'Reminds him of being young, I think,' Cameron said, draining his pint. 'He was in one when he was a teenager.'

'Were they as bad – I mean, were they anything like this one?'

Cam shrugged. 'No idea. He used to love it though, gigging on the pub circuit. Whenever he gets nostalgic he'll get the photos out and force me and Becks to look through them with him.'

'Are you ok, Becky?' Cynthia asked.

I was only half listening. My eyes were fixed on Dad laughing with Gerry at the other side of the pub.

'I'm... fine,' I said absently. 'Cyn, it'd be nice if Dad had something he actually felt he was good at to focus on, wouldn't it?'

'Such as?' Cynthia said.

'How long've Dad and Gerry been mates?'

'Oh God, she's obsessed,' Cam muttered.

'You what?' Tom said.

'Nothing. Just realised where this is heading.'

Cynthia frowned. 'I don't know, twenty-five years?'

'So they're pretty close, right?' I said. 'I mean, they've got a sort of natural rapport?'

'Um, yeah,' she said, looking puzzled. 'Where are you going with this, Becky? I know I was worried for a while your dad might've met someone else, but Gerry Lightowler wasn't who I had in mind.'

'Wasn't a romantic relationship I was thinking of,' I muttered.

'What relationship were you thinking of, as if I couldn't guess?' Cameron said.

'Well, look at them, Cam. Wouldn't you say that in a lot of ways, they're just like sisters?'

Chapter 25

Yolanda nearly knocked me down when I arrived at the Temp for the next rehearsal.

'Did you bring them? Are they here?'

'Yours are. Deano's bringing the dames' stuff.'

'Oh, goody goody!' she squeaked. 'Costumes! I've been so looking forward to this bit.'

'I really haven't,' Gerry muttered.

Everyone was there except Marcus and Deano, including my dad, who'd been a lot keener than I'd anticipated on doing a stint as an Ugly Sister now he realised there was no future in rock-and-roll stardom, and Lana in her new role as Dandini. It was our first dress rehearsal and excitement was high.

The only people missing were extras – the adult and juvenile choruses. They were rehearsing separately with Yolanda's line-dancing friend Rita, ready for the all-singing, all-dancing rehearsal.

It wasn't like our director to be late – in fact sometimes I'd swear he camped outside with his Thermos, just so he could be first.

'You haven't heard from Deano, have you?' I asked Lana.

'No, I –'

She was drowned out by a series of phuts and bangs outside, and a minute later the Teasdale brothers burst in, Marcus in his blue Buttons costume, Deano's hair blazing red, like Egglethwaite's answer to Batman and Robin.

'Sorry we're late,' Deano panted. 'Car trouble.'

'What was all that noise?' I asked.

'We came in the Morris.'

My eyes widened. 'What, you two actually got that thing roadworthy?'

'We got it road,' Marc said. 'I'm staking nothing on worthy.'

'Just a few teething troubles,' Deano said, waving a hand airily. 'She's a little tease.'

'Cough. Scrapheap. Cough cough,' Marc said from behind his hand.

Deano glared at him.

'Nasty cough, that, Marc.'

'That'll be the exhaust fumes from your bloody car.'

'You know what's good for tickly coughs? Walking home.'

Marcus grinned. 'All right, little brother. Come on, let's get the dresses.'

My Cinders costumes were pretty straightforward. There were just two: a ragged dress with patched tights and long blonde wig for the kitchen scenes, and a huge white evening gown for the ball. I wasn't looking forward to acting with that thing on. It was like wearing a tea tent. Plus there was a heavy Regency wig that felt like it was going to crush my brain.

Marcus just had the one outfit, his bellboy-esque Buttons uniform. Maisie and Lana had short silk tunics and knee-high boots, of course, and Harper was in a frock coat and breeches as Baron Hardup.

Yolanda, having been so reluctant to play the part, totally fell in love with the Morticia Addams-style black velvet number we'd picked for her Wicked Stepmother. Once she got that on, the poofy Fairy Godmother dress barely got a look-in.

But it was the dames who got the really interesting outfits. There were a matching pair for each scene the Ugly Sisters appeared in: pie-sprigged dresses with Danish pastries over the nipples for the baking scene, huge chandelier dresses for the ball and a load of others equally outrageous. I'd got them a pair of decent breasts each too, better than the lumpy bra Gerry had worn to Pip's Beaver meeting: inflatable, with a built-in pump.

The first scene we were rehearsing was the sisters ordering Cinders and Buttons to scrub the house. Me and Marcus were kneeling by the fireplace Cole had painted onto a curtain backdrop when my dad burst through the door at one side of the stage, Gerry emerging from the other.

Dad walked up to Gerry and scanned his Shirley Temple sailor smock, identical to his apart from being a few sizes bigger.

'Well this is embarrassing.'

'I told you *I'd* be wearing this,' Gerry said. The pair of them stared at each other for a moment then cracked up laughing.

'Not sure I didn't prefer it when he was in the band,' I muttered to Marcus.

'He looks happy though.'

'Does, doesn't he?' I smiled at Dad and Gerry honking each other's boobs. 'Hopefully this'll be just what he needs to grab life by the fake knockers again. Plus we get our dame, Pip gets to see both grandads making prats of themselves: everyone's a winner.'

'Hmm. Not everyone.' Marc nodded to Maisie in the wings. 'She's giving you evils again. Don't think she's managed to forgive you for not letting her be Cinderella.'

And that wasn't the only problem. It soon became clear that Lana was going to be an issue too.

It wasn't her delivery, that was fine. It was her memory that was bloody awful.

'Oh, Dandini. If only I could find a girl I could marry for love. Sigh,' Maisie said.

'Don't say "sigh", Mais!' Harper's voice came from off-stage. 'Actually sigh.'

'Oh, right.' She sighed, a pathetic little 'huh'.

'Perhaps you will, sire,' Lana said. 'I only wish... I only... wish...' She grimaced. 'Line?'

'I only wish your father wasn't in such a hurry to have you married,' Deano hissed from the wings.

'Right. I only wish your father wouldn't marry you in such a hurry.' She flinched. 'No, that's not it, is it? I only wish you could marry your father in a hurry. Oh God.' She plucked her feathered hat off and held it in front of her face.

I had to feel for Deano. When someone's both your best mate and your boss, obviously you want to go easy on them, but as he marched onto the stage, the twitch in the corner of his eye told me it was going to be a struggle holding back.

'Sorry,' Lana mumbled from behind her hat.

'You're trying your best, love,' Deano said. 'Here, take the script. You'll have to read it until you've had more time to learn the lines.'

'What if I can't do it, Deano?'

'Just keep practising with Stew. I believe in you.' But he looked worried.

'I was great though, wasn't I?' Maisie said, beaming at Deano. 'I remembered all my lines.'

'Er, yeah. Well done.'

'Sigh,' I said to Marcus from our position in the wings. He snorted.

The dames had their getting-ready-for-the-ball scene next, with Yolanda as the stepmother, and I felt a glimmer of hope. It was a baptism of fire, for Dad especially, but he took to it like a duck to hoisin.

Deano had been spot on about Yolanda. She was perfect, just the right bitch factor. Even Gerry's blocking, now he had a partner he could double-act with, was vastly improved. His and Dad's duet of Sisters, heavy on the bum-bumps and bloomer-flashes, was fantastic.

But there were still a couple of little problems...

'Cut!' Deano shouted mid-way through the song.

'What's wrong, darling?' Yolanda said, patting her towering Bride of Frankenstein wig. 'I thought the boys were doing brilliantly.'

'Gerry, mate,' Deano said. 'You're, er, a bit lopsided there.'

Gerry glanced down at his bosom, which had deflated on one side. 'Oh. Right. Just a sec.' He started pumping his arm like a one-winged chicken, and Yolanda giggled as his left breast grew before our eyes. I could see Sue, playing piano at the side of the stage, leaning her forehead on her music and groaning.

'Now you've got one bigger than the other,' my dad told Gerry.

'You're just jealous.'

'Mine might be smaller but at least they match.' Dad patted his boobs proudly. 'Some girls have got it, some girls haven't.'

They resumed the scene, but Deano was soon shouting 'cut!' again when my dad started looking deflated. All together, there were five scene interruptions due to collapsed-booby incidents. Deano's eye-twitch was off again, and I was starting to think we'd been safer with sock-stuffed bras.

Chapter 26

Me and Marcus were up next with the Tomorrow scene we'd upcycled from Jack and the Beanstalk.

It was my favourite scene of the show, at least of the ones I was in. Roger Collingwood had picked the song Tomorrow from *Annie* based on my ability to belt, and it worked brilliantly.

Plus I loved acting opposite Marcus. He was so natural, it brought out the best in me too.

'What's up, Cinders?' Marcus said when he found me crying over the remains of my ballgown on the hearth.

'It's my sisters,' I sobbed. 'Oh, Buttons, I did so want to go to the ball. But they've ripped my dress to pieces, and now I'll never get to meet the prince.'

'Here. Pretty flower for a pretty girl.' He made a pure white rose appear from behind my ear. I smiled through my tears as I tucked it into my buttonhole.

'What's so great about a silly old ball anyway?' Marc said, sinking down next to me. 'We've got the whole house to ourselves. Let's get this mess cleaned up, then we'll have a wonderful evening just us.'

I sighed. 'It's so horrible to be poor. To be always dirty and in rags, running round after Griselda and Tabitha from morning until night.'

'Things'll get better, you'll see. There's always tomorrow, Cinders. And tomorrow's a brand-new day.'

That was the cue for the song. Marcus put one finger under my chin and sang the opening lines softly to me: *The sun'll come out tomorrow, bet your bottom dollar that tomorrow, there'll be sun...*

I wiped away my tears and joined in, and soon we were dancing round the kitchen hand in hand, joyously singing our hearts out.

When we were done, I sank back onto the hearth to stare at my torn dress again.

'But tomorrow won't really be any better than today, will it, Buttons? Nothing ever gets better here.' I dabbed at my eyes with the hem of my rags. 'All I wanted was to go to the ball. Who knows? Maybe the prince would have fallen madly in love with me, and I could have lived at the palace and worn fine silks instead of crawling around in the cinders for my keep.'

Marcus cast his eyes down. 'And what about me? Would you be too fine a lady to remember your old pal Buttons?'

'Of course not! You're my best friend. I wouldn't go to the palace without you.'

He took my hands. 'Don't go to the palace, Cinders,' he said earnestly. 'Run away with me. I'll take care of you, and you'll never have to rake out a grate again.'

I laughed. 'Run away with you? But you're as poor as I am. Where would we go?'

'Anywhere. Then we could get married and...' He flushed. 'I love you, Cinderella. I always have, you know.'

He looked deep into my eyes, leaning towards me slowly with my two hands still gripped in his.

I don't know what happened. I knew this scene perfectly, we'd rehearsed it a million times. I was supposed to push him away and say 'Oh Buttons, you know I love you as a friend, but I could never see you that way'. Then he'd say he understood, there'd be a chummy hug and a reprise of Tomorrow, and Buttons would stalk sadly away before Sue played Dance of the Sugarplum Fairy to herald the arrival of Godmother Yolanda.

But for some reason, as Marcus's dark eyes looked into mine and his lightly parted lips got ever closer, I froze. Every line went straight out of my head.

'Ok, cut!' Deano shouted impatiently. Marcus pulled back at once. 'What was that, Becky?'

'Sorry,' I said, flushing. 'Mind went blank for a sec.'

'I swear, between you and Lana I'll be in an institution before we get this bloody panto to the stage.' He tapped my temple. 'Mind on the job, Becks. 210%, remember.'

'Yes, Chef. It won't happen again.'

We picked up from where we'd left off, and, thankfully for Deano's mental state and grasp of maths, I was able to do the rest without a hitch.

After that we moved on to the ball, which most us appeared in at some point: the two dames, Yo-yo as the Wicked Stepmother, both principal boys and me, of course. Only Marcus as Buttons and Harper as Baron Hardup would be off-stage.

The prince was last to enter the ballroom. He was supposed to stride on stage, slap his thigh, and instantly inspire lust in all the female characters and love at first sight in Cinderella. Assuming Maisie could manage to stop sneering at me.

Deano had let me off wearing the heavy hooped petticoat and whipped-cream wig that went with my costume for now, so the ballgown was just about manageable. I made my grand entrance stage right, to the hushed whispers of the Ugly Sisters as they wondered who the mystery girl could be (despite the fact they saw me every day, the idiots). Then Lana announced the prince.

'His Royal Highness, Prince Charming of Rummancoke!'

But no Maisie appeared stage left so our eyes could meet across the crowded room.

Lana tried again. 'His Royal Highness, Prince Charming of Rummancoke!'

Still nothing. Deano poked his head through the stage door.

'Maisie? You've missed your cue.'

Silence.

'For Christ's sake,' he muttered. 'Anyone know where she is?'

'I'll check the Ladies,' I said. 'Deano, you try the kitchen. Maybe she went to make a brew.'

I headed backstage, where Marcus was studying his script.

'What's wrong?' he asked.

'Have you seen Maisie? She's missed her cue and we're all waiting.'

He frowned. 'No. I thought she was on stage.'

'Ugh. Well she must be somewhere. Come help me look.'

'What the hell is that noise?' Marc said as we headed down the stairs that led to the Ladies' loos. 'Sounds like someone punching a gibbon.'

There was an odd noise, like some sort of trapped animal.

'It's coming from that cleaner's cupboard,' I said.

I marched to the cupboard and peeked round the door, then quickly slammed it shut.

'Oh my God!'

'What? What is it?'

'Unless I'm much mistaken, it's the frantically bobbing arsecheeks of Harper Brady OBE.'

'Jesus Christ.' Marc slapped his forehead. 'Couple of legs wrapped round?'

'Funnily enough.'

He rapped on the door. 'Harper! Maisie! Get your clothes on and come out.'

There was the sound of whispering, and a Maisie-ish giggle, then Harper's breathless voice rang out.

'Can you give us ten minutes, mate? We're nearly there.'

'For fuck's sake,' Marc muttered. 'Never work with children, animals or randy bastard celebrities.'

'No we bloody can't give you ten minutes!' I said. 'Maisie's due on stage. Out, now.'

Marcus put a hand on my arm. 'Oh, let him finish. We can't have Baron Hardup wandering round with a tentpole in his breeches for the rest of the rehearsal.'

'Hmm. S'pose.' I raised my voice again. 'All right, guys, quick as you can. Then we'll be having words.'

'Cheers,' Harper called. Marcus grabbed my hand and led me hastily upstairs, away from the disturbing grunts now emerging from the cleaner's cupboard.

'Well? Did you find her?' Deano demanded when we joined him on stage.

'Yeah, she's just in the middle of someone – er, something,' I said. 'She'll be here in ten. I'll go wait backstage till she's ready, then we can start again.'

'I'm so grassing him up to Stew,' Marcus said as the pair of us waited backstage for Harper and Maisie to come get their bollocking.

The young lovers emerged 15 minutes later in their now very dishevelled costumes, flushed and shame-faced. Well, Harper was shame-faced. Maisie just looked amused.

'Sorry,' Harper mumbled, scuffing at the bare boards of the floor.

'For Christ's sake, Harper!' I said. 'You're supposed to be Baron Hard*up*, not Baron –'

'What the hell did you think you were playing at?' Marc demanded.

'It's the tights,' Harper said. 'They... kind of have an effect on me.'

Maisie giggled. 'He asked to see how my thigh-slap was shaping up. Next thing I knew he was tearing my clothes off in the cupboard.'

'It is much better,' Harper muttered.

'What's he like?' Maisie flashed an indulgent glance at her husband.

'Come on, you're not teenagers,' Marcus said sternly. 'Can you not save the tight-based role play for when you get home?'

'We'll be good from now on,' Maisie said, although I could tell she was struggling to keep a straight face. 'It was the first time he'd seen me in them, that's all. We are newlyweds.'

'Promise?' I said.

'Promise.' She nudged Harper, who looked up from examining his boots.

'Er, yeah. Promise.' He leaned over to Maisie. 'Worth it though, babe,' I heard him whisper.

'You getting all this?' Maisie said to someone behind me. I turned to see Gavin with his trusty video camera, trained on the Bradys as usual. We'd got so used to him lurking around the place that he'd almost become part of the furniture.

'Yes, Mrs Brady.'

'And you got us coming out of the cupboard, didn't you?'

'Course.'

Harper patted his wife's pert backside fondly. 'That's my girl, Mais. Now you're thinking like a star.'

Marcus shook his head. 'This is unbelievable,' he muttered to me. 'They're only putting it in their daft reality show.'

'That's not why you did it, is it?' I demanded.

Harper shrugged. 'No, but there's no point wasting good material.'

'You're getting dangerously close to that sex tape, Harper.'

Chapter 26

Marc nodded towards the stage. 'Maisie, go let Deano know you're ready. And bloody well behave from now on. We can't afford cock-ups like this during the run.'

'No pun intended, eh?' Harper said. Maisie snorted.

'Just do as you're told, you,' I said. 'I don't want to be standing here in December, explaining to a bunch of three-to-eights why Baron Hardup's been caught trousers down showing his future son-in-law his magic pumpkin.'

'You know, honey, that innuendo doesn't really work,' Maisie said. 'Harper's willy doesn't look anything like a pumpkin.'

'Yeah, sorry. Was on the spot a bit.'

'All right, it won't happen again.' Harper took Maisie's hand. 'And I'd say it was more of a marrow,' I heard him whisper as he led her to the wings.

'I'd better get ready for my cue,' I said to Marcus. 'Jesus, what a mess. If the live run is anything like tonight, there'll never be another panto in Egglethwaite.'

We managed to struggle through the rest of the rehearsal, although Maisie and Harper's dancing lesson was looking a bit precarious. He really did seem to have a thing for tights.

'Does it feel to you like there's something wrong?' I whispered to Marc as we watched the cast file out at the end of the night.

'What, apart from the principal boy who can't act, the other one who can't remember her lines, the Baron Hardup who's permanently on heat and the dames who can't maintain a full set of tits between them?'

'Yeah, apart from that.'

'Bloody hell, love. I would've thought that'd be enough catastrophes to be going along with.'

'There's something else. The script – I can't put my finger on it. It seems flat somehow.'

'I know what you mean,' he said. 'It does feel like something's missing.'

'Just wish I could work out what.'

He slapped my back. 'Well, we can work on it at mine next week. Scripting team to the rescue, eh?' He grabbed Harper's arm as he made his way past. 'Oi. You. If you're feeling randy before the next rehearsal, do you mind giving your wife a good seeing-to before you leave the house so you can behave like bloody professionals?'

'Yeah, yeah. I told you, it won't happen again.'

'It better not, because next time I'm setting Deano on you.'

My dad stopped to give me a hug before he left. 'Thanks for talking me into this, Boo. Most fun I've had in ages.'

So Dad was happy. At least one thing about the rehearsal had gone right.

I wasn't sure Deano agreed though. 'Shambles,' I heard him mutter as he passed. 'We'll never make it.'

Chapter 27

'Ok, so I think I've worked out what's wrong with the script.' Marcus reached across me for the bag of Doritos we were sharing. 'Too cautious,' he said through a mouthful of corn snack.

'How d'you mean?'

'Not enough innuendo. Our village panto when we were kids was proper filth.'

'We've got innuendo.'

'Not much.' He flicked through the script. 'Woodcutting scene, the baron compliments Buttons on his big chopper. Pie-making scene and the hilarious erect sausage. Couple of jokes about your dad being jealous of Gerry's firm, juicy dumplings, and that crack about the Harrogate Male Voice Choir. That's it.'

'Say chopper again.'

'Chopper. Why?'

'Turns me on.'

He laughed. 'So am I right or am I right?'

It was a point. We'd thought up loads of good dirty jokes while we'd been working on the script, but when it came to writing them in we'd come over a bit coy.

'You're right,' I said. 'We can probably let our knickers down a bit more without offending people.'

'Here, Becks. You've got Dorito crumbs on you.' He reached over to brush them off my neck, and I tilted my head to one side.

'Right,' he said, picking up the script again. 'So the Fairy Godmother scene's got potential. A few one-liners for Yo-yo about the prince having big balls, what do you think?'

'Um, Marc?'

'Yeah?'

'I think you've got all the crumbs off now.'

His fingers were still trailing over my skin. I needed him to stop. The patch of flesh behind my ear was one of the most sensitive parts of my body, and his touch was starting to have a stirring effect.

He glanced up and frowned at his own fingers, as if he didn't know they were still there.

'Oh. Sorry,' he said, pulling them away. He stared at me with a puzzled expression, like he was seeing me for the first time. 'Hey, Becks. Anyone ever tell you you're kind of pretty?'

I laughed. 'Thanks.'

'You are, you know. Cole doesn't tell you?'

'Sometimes.'

His fingers found their way back to my neck. He put down the script, and with his other arm he drew me closer. 'Well, now I'm going to tell you. You're a beautiful woman, Becky Finn.'

'Cheers,' I mumbled. I cast about for something suitable to say back. 'Er, you too.'

'Did you just call me a beautiful woman?'

I shrugged. 'My perception of gender's become very flexible since I got involved in the pantomime scene.'

'Going to kiss you now.'

'Not going to stop you.'

But before I had time to really savour the cheesy Dorito flavour on his lips... I woke up.

'Shit!' I muttered, sitting up with a start.

Cole blinked at me sleepily. 'Everything ok?'

Chapter 27

'Yes... yes, fine. Sorry for waking you.' I settled back into bed, hugging myself.

Ok, so this was new. New and bad.

I mean, it wasn't like I hadn't had sexy dreams about Marcus before, but this one had seemed so... real. Away from the realms of fantasy and into something I could actually imagine happening. The Doritos were a nice touch too, kudos to my subconscious for that.

'Cole?' I whispered.

'Hmm?' He was nearly asleep again.

'Love... you ever have dreams? About other people?'

'What other people?'

'You know, like people you... maybe that you're attracted to. Not me. Celebrities or colleagues or whatever.'

'I love you, Becky.' He nuzzled my nose with his. 'And I love you most when you feel insecure during daylight hours. Go to sleep, darling, I'll give you all the reassurance you need over breakfast.'

'I'm not insecure. I just want to know, is that normal? For people to dream about people who aren't their partners sometimes?'

He blinked himself awake. 'Is that what woke you up?'

I flushed. 'Yeah.'

'Who were you dreaming about?'

'Someone I know from the panto,' I said. 'Other times it can be film stars, or... you know, other people. That's ok, right? I mean, you have that?'

'Well yes, sometimes.' He drew a finger down my cheek. 'Why the worry? Dreams like that don't mean anything.'

I exhaled with relief. 'Yeah, that's what I thought. This one was just... dunno, it seemed really vivid. Shook me up a bit.'

I could see his eyes searching mine in the darkness.

'Who from the pantomime?' he asked quietly.

'Oh, no one. It doesn't matter.'

'Was it Marcus?'

I blinked at him. 'Well... yeah, it was. But I guess it could've been any of them, the amount of time we've all been spending together.' I paused. 'Possibly not Gerry.'

He was quiet for so long, I thought he'd fallen asleep.

'Cole? You upset?'

'No.' He kissed my nose. 'No, of course not.'

'It was just a daft dream. I've got panto on the brain, that's all.' I laughed. 'Plus me and Marc caught a couple of cast members bonking noisily in a cupboard at rehearsal last week.'

'You didn't?'

'Yeah, bloody Harper Brady. Anyway, my subconscious obviously made some sort of Freudian connection.' I gave him a kiss. 'Night, Cole. Love you.'

***

'Ok, so I've had an epiphany,' I said in the pub the following evening. I'd called an emergency script-fettling meeting, and me, Deano, Marcus, Lana and Stew were sitting behind our copies of the script. 'It's not rude enough. We need more innuendo, guys.'

'When did you decide this?' Marcus asked.

I flushed. 'It... came to me in a dream.'

'She's not wrong, you know,' Deano said. 'I've thought these last few rehearsals the Cinders script was lacking oomph.'

Stew grimaced. 'Do you have to do the hip-thrust when you say "oomph", Deano?'

'Yeah, you know you get off on it.'

'Oi.' Lana held up a warning hand. 'No sexy talk till we've got pens out, lads.'

'She's right,' I said. 'We need to stop using up our best filth in real life and get it onto the stage where it can do some good.'

'Next rehearsal is tomorrow though,' Lana said. 'Becks, you and Marc are script gurus. You weren't thinking we could make big changes by then, were you?'

'I don't think it needs big changes, just a few gags scattered here and there. We don't want people having to learn too many new lines.' I shot her a wary look. 'Especially you.'

'Well, I'm ready to pull an all-nighter if you are,' Marcus said to me. 'You bring a bottle, I'll get the Doritos in, see you at mine after tea?'

'No.' God, him and his bloody sexy Doritos. 'I mean, um, I thought at this stage it'd be good to expand the scripting team. Five dirty minds are better than two.'

'S'pose.' He was frowning at me, and I felt my cheeks heat. 'Everything ok?'

'Everything's fine.' They were all staring now, wondering what'd happened to turn me such a fetching shade of lobster. 'I'm going to get a round in. You guys get thinking.'

I was leaning against the bar watching the barmaid pour our drinks when someone tickled my hips from behind.

'God, Marc,' I said, patting my heart. 'You nearly finished me off then.'

'I often have that effect on women. Usually have to put a bit more effort in than that though.' His grin disappeared when I didn't smile. 'You sure everything's ok, Becky? You seem on edge.'

'Bad night's sleep, that's all.'

'You're not pissed off with me, are you? You were a bit quick to turn down my offer of a script date.'

'I just think we need all the help we can get.'

'That's all?'

'Yes.' I sighed and turned to look at him. 'No.'

'What is it?' he asked, looking concerned.

'It's... well, it's what you just said. It does sound like a date, doesn't it?' I held up my hand to stop him interrupting. 'I know it isn't. But you're a man who likes women and I'm a woman who likes men and people might, you know, talk. About us spending so much time alone together.'

'Who might talk?'

'People round here,' I said. 'You know what they're like. Our sordid affair could be the next Kit Beeton's hot-tub parties. I'd hate Cole to think there was anything... you know.'

'But there isn't anything you know.'

'All the same. I just...' I trailed off, registering his hurt expression. 'I think it's better this way,' I said in a small voice.

'So are you saying we can't be mates any more?'

'God, no, that's not what I meant at all!' I said, horrified. 'I just think, from now on, it's better if we hang out as part of a group.' I nodded to the table of our friends. 'With these guys. I'm sorry, Marc.'

He still looked hurt, but he made the effort to fix on a smile. 'We're ok though? Because I really like spending time with you. I'd hate to lose that.'

'Course we're ok.' I gave his arm a playful punch. 'I mean, we've juggled together, you don't forget a bond like that. BFFs forever, pinky swear promise and all that Nickelodeon bollocks.'

'Eurghh. Do we have to make each other bracelets?'

I widened my eyes. 'What, you don't want to? I've been braiding for days.'

He laughed. 'All right, love. Let's go fix this script, before the others think we've gone for a quickie.'

'Ok.' I grabbed his arm before he could walk off. 'Marc?'

'Yeah?'

'I just want to say, before we go back... I really like spending time with you too. I mean, I'd miss you. If we couldn't be mates any more. I want you to know that's the last thing I'd ever, ever want.' I pinkened in the face of his stare. 'So... there.'

He broke into a warm smile. 'Thanks, Becks. I'd miss you too.'

'You understand then?'

'Yeah, I can see Cole's point of view. If you were my girlfriend I'd probably feel weird knowing you were alone with another bloke all the time. Just as long as you're not friend-dumping me.' He looked at me keenly. 'You actually are kind of my best mate, you know. Is that a bit sad?'

'No. Not at all.' I gave him a swift one-armed hug. 'Come on then, bestie. Let's innuendo.'

Marc grabbed the drinks and we headed back.

'Right. We think we've got one,' Lana said as she took her Guinness.

I sat down. 'Ok, entendre me up.'

Marcus didn't go back to his old seat. Instead he sat next to me, where he could look at my notes over my shoulder.

I subtly shuffled so his warm breath wasn't on my neck. I didn't want to feel him there if we were about to do sexy jokes.

'How about this for the dancing lesson?' Lana said. 'The prince and the baron start waltzing and the prince forgets to take his sword out of its sheath. So then it pokes Harper in the hip and he says "Oooh, that's a big one".'

Me and Marcus stared at her.

'"That's a big one",' she repeated. 'You know, like a cock,' she added helpfully.

'Yeah, we got it.' I shook my head. 'You'll have to do better than that, love.'

'Plus if it's anything like the first dress rehearsal, the last thing we want Harper and Maisie thinking about is cocks,' Marcus muttered to me.

'All right, how about "Is that a sword in your tights or are you just pleased to see me?"' Lana said.

'Too old school,' Deano said. 'We need something cheekier. Think *Two Ronnies*. Think seaside postcards. Think 1970s sitcoms.'

'Here's one,' Stewart said. 'Gerry comes into the kitchen holding two jugs of milk. Then you can get a line in about him having a great pair of jugs.'

Lana raised her eyebrows at him and he shrugged. 'What? I watched a lot of *Carry On* films as a kid.'

'Hmm. Slightly better,' I said, jotting it down. 'Any more for any more?'

'Rude poems where you don't say the ending are good,' Marcus said. 'You know the sort of thing. "There was a young barmaid from Pogley, the lads all said she was canny. See her all right on a Saturday night and she'll give you a flash of her –"'

'Yeah, we get the idea,' I said hastily. 'Ok, a few of them. Oh, and how about this for the Ugly Sisters? Tabitha could tell Griselda she once acted in a play, then Griselda could ask if she had a large part.'

'Oh! Like a cock,' Lana observed cheerfully.

I frowned at her. 'Yes, Lana, like a cock. But the whole point of a double entendre is you have to let the audience work that out by themselves.'

By the time we'd finished our second round of drinks the script was riddled with things that were secretly cocks, apart from the things that were secretly boobs, and even Deano, the hardest to please when it came to innuendo, agreed it was looking a lot more colourful. Whether the knob gags were going to stand up during performance, though (pun entirely in-tended), was something we wouldn't find out until our second dress rehearsal the following day.

Chapter 28

'Oh. Hullo,' Cole said when he came into the kitchen later. 'I didn't expect to run into you tonight. Aren't you going to Marcus's?'

'No,' I said, rummaging the cupboard for quick meal options. 'No, not tonight.'

He frowned when he opened the bin to empty the dregs of his Thai curry into it. 'Why is there an unopened bag of crisps in here, Becky?'

'I'm on a healthy-eating kick. Doritos are full of salt.'

He quirked an eyebrow. 'What, the queen of junk food is going on a diet?'

'Better late than never, right?' I selected a Pot Noodle and flicked the kettle on. 'I'll start as soon as I've eaten this.'

'So why aren't you going to Marcus's? It's his night to have you, isn't it?'

I winced. Of all the ways he could've phrased it...

'I'd just rather spend the evening with you,' I said. 'I mean, if you're not busy.'

'That sounds nice.' He put his arms around me from behind and started kissing the sensitive spot on my neck. 'Don't you need to work on your script though?'

'It's finished. Tonight's group meeting at the pub was the last lot of changes we're making.'

'Marcus's loss is my gain then,' Cole mumbled between kisses. 'Hey. We could always have an early night. What do you think?'

'No... not tonight,' I said, tilting my neck away from his lips. 'Bit tired.'

'You're tired a lot lately.'

I wiggled out of his arms and turned to face him. 'What's that supposed to mean?'

He blinked. 'Becky, it wasn't an accusation. No need to be so touchy.'

'Look, I know it's been a while. It's just... the panto and everything. Once it's done, everything'll go back to normal.'

'I wasn't trying to make you feel guilty,' he said earnestly. 'I'm just as happy with a cuddle. I'm worried about you burning out, that's all.'

'I'm fine.' I sighed. 'Sorry, love, didn't mean to snap. I'm just tense this evening. Couldn't get back to sleep after I woke up last night.' I let him absorb me into an embrace. 'Oh, guess what? I was looking at wedding venues in the shop today.'

'It's going to be a little while until we've got enough put away, Becky. Late next year at the earliest.'

'I know, but it gives me something to look forward to.'

He smiled. 'Well, I'm glad you're excited. I am too. I can't wait to wake up next to my beautiful new wife.'

I looked up into his face. Cole hadn't changed much in the four years since we'd met. A couple of little crinkles bracketed the blue eyes, but they still held that absent, slightly baffled innocence that had first drawn me to him. They looked permanently far away, full of deep thoughts, as if the real world was the one in Cole's head – the one where his paintings lived – and everything outside was a dream.

I felt a surge of affection as I thought about every sacrifice he'd made for me, his love for me; the man himself. All mingled with a crushing guilt over the attraction that, try as I might, I couldn't help feeling for Marcus.

I'd just have to conquer it, that was all. I loved Cole. Whatever I felt towards Marcus would soon go away once the panto was over and we stopped seeing so much of each other.

I reached up to draw a tender finger down his cheek.

'Cole, you know that I... I mean, I want you to know I'd never hurt you. Not on purpose. You know that, don't you?'

'Yes, darling, of course I do,' he said. 'What's brought this on?'

'Oh, nothing. Hormones and sleep deprivation.' I smiled. 'Sorry, didn't mean to be weird. Why don't you go find something on TV while I get us drinks? Then we can have a nice evening snuggling.'

Cole went into the living room while I poured a couple of glasses of wine.

'Anything decent?' I asked as I handed him his drink and joined him on the sofa with my Pot Noodle.

'Not really. I'm assuming you wouldn't be interested in *Hockney: A Retrospective* on the Arts channel?'

I grimaced. 'Honestly?'

'I'll keep looking.'

TV was always hard work. Nights in front of the telly usually involved a compromise that left one or both of us asleep before the end of whatever we were watching.

'Oh! Stop there,' I said as Cole channel-hopped. 'No, down one – that's it!'

He frowned. 'A reality show? You don't like those, do you?'

'It's *The Brady Bunch*. Don't you remember me telling you? Some of it was shot at our panto rehearsals. Didn't realise it was already airing.'

'You mean you and Marcus and the others are in it?'

'Yeah, bits of it.'

The early scenes were all of Harper and Maisie, playing with their puppy, entertaining their celeb pals, going to photoshoots and acting jobs. Gav's shaky fly-on-the-wall footage was interspersed with talking-head interviews, where either Harper, Maisie or one of their mates would get dragged into a private room and asked questions.

The show was minutes in when a face I recognised popped up.

I giggled. 'Oh God, it's Stew. Doesn't look right happy, does he?'

'Who's Stew?' Cole asked.

'Lana's husband.' I shook my head. 'You've met him a dozen times, Cole.'

'What's your relationship to the Bradys?' the muttered voice of Gavin asked TV Stew.

'Professional gimp,' Stew said gravely. 'They don't let me out normally. Not in daylight, anyway.'

'This will be broadcast nationally, Mr McLean. Could you spare the levity?'

Stew grinned. 'All right, I'll do it properly. I'm Harper's cousin.'

'Are the two of you close?'

'Yeah, suppose we are.' He turned to call over his shoulder. 'Harper, do I have to do this?'

'Yes!' the voice of Harper sailed back from somewhere. 'Aunty Heather said there'd be trouble if you didn't.'

Stewart sighed. 'Go on, Gav. Apparently I'm under orders from my mum.'

'It sounds like the two of you have more of a sibling relationship than cousins,' Gavin observed. 'Why is that?'

'Er, that's kind of personal.'

'That's the whole point!' Harper's voice called again. 'Get on with it, Stew.'

'Stop eavesdropping!' Stewart yelled back. 'This is the private bit.'

Cole nudged me. 'Didn't your actor friend think to edit this before it went out?'

I shrugged. 'Probably thought it'd show his human side, that rapport with Stew. Harper doesn't seem to recognise any boundary between his private life and his public image.'

'Harper's mum died when he was eighteen, and she was bringing him up alone before that,' Stewart told Gavin, and several million viewers. 'We were both only children, and we grew up together.'

'Harper's mum being Sonia Brady?'

'That's right.'

'Millionaire sauce bottle inventor Sonia Brady?'

'The money came later,' Stewart said. 'When Harper was little they were pretty broke.'

'What do you think of Maisie?'

'I think she's a lovely girl. Perfect for him.'

'Mr Brady once dated the lady who's now your wife, I believe. Did it cause any tension between the two of you?'

Stew laughed. 'Now that I'm not answering or I'll have Lana on my case. Let's just say we're all friends now.'

'Bloody hell,' I muttered. 'She never told me that.'

'How are you finding Maisie's acting?' Gav asked Stew. 'I believe it was you who recommended her for your village pantomime.'

'Her approach is certainly... creative,' Stew answered diplomatically.

His interview faded and the backstage area at the Temp came into focus.

'Oh! It's me!' I said, grabbing Cole's arm. 'Ugh, is this really going out nationally? The state of my hair.'

'What on earth are you doing?' Cole said.

I laughed at the little person on TV, bouncing on her haunches with her mouth wide open. 'Watch and see.'

Sure enough, a second later a Malteser sailed through the air and landed right in TV me's gob. Catching it made me lose my balance and I rolled over backwards like a Weeble, giggling.

'Oh God,' I groaned. 'I look a right tit.'

'Where did that chocolate come from?' Cole asked.

'Marc chucked it. It's a game we invented to amuse ourselves between scenes. We call it Human Malteser Pong.'

Cole blinked. 'How bizarre.'

'We've got a million of them. Human Buckaroo's my favourite, but we only get to play that when Gerry falls asleep.'

Next the camera cut to me and Maisie performing one of our scenes. Oh God, it was excruciating.

Was that really what my voice sounded like? And was my head that enormous in real life? Ugh, and there was a song number coming up...

'The lady playing Jack isn't very good, is she?' Cole said.

'No. She has improved a bit since then though. And she's Prince Charming in the new script so she hasn't got as many lines.'

'You're wonderful though, darling,' he said as I started belting out my song. He leaned over to peck my cheek. 'I'm very proud of you.'

The camera cut again, to Harper this time in a private interview.

'What made you and your wife decide to perform in a little production like this?' invisible Gavin asked.

'Maisie and I are both very socially conscious,' Harper said. 'When my cousin told me his village hall was at stake, of course we had to get involved.'

'You do a lot for this village, don't you?' Gav said.

'I do what I can,' Harper said, spontaneously sprouting a halo and wings. 'But it was Maisie's idea to volunteer for the pantomime. She's the best-kept secret in showbusiness, the greatest little actress. It's like my girl to use that to help people.'

What Harper seemed to have forgotten was that the TV audience had just watched Maisie acting, so that really wasn't going to wash.

Harper faded and Maisie herself appeared, her Yorkie pup Teddy tucked under her arm.

'How do you find the other pantomime actors to work with?' Gavin asked her.

'Oh, I've been very impressed,' Maisie said, beaming. 'At the end of the day it is just a tinpot village production, even with the two of us involved, but these people could hold their own against the best in the business.'

'Such as?'

Maisie, not actually having worked with the best in the business, looked lost for a moment. 'Oh, well, Harper, of course,' she fumbled. 'And, er... Kevin Bacon.'

'And your leading lady – Becky Finn. Do you like working with her?'

'She's wonderful, honey, just wonderful. Of course she's an amateur, she doesn't have that star quality that my Harper, or –' she coloured prettily – 'or perhaps I have. But she does perfectly well for a little thing like this. She's so eager to learn too, I've enjoyed mentoring her.'

'Do you think you'll stay in touch?'

'Oh, no. I shouldn't think so.'

Cole examined my scarlet cheeks with concern. 'Are you all right, Becky?'

'No I'm bloody not all right!' I exploded. 'And neither will Maisie Brady be when I get my hands on her!'

Chapter 29

I marched backstage next evening with just one aim. To give Maisie Brady a massive piece of my mind.

'Ok, Maisie, what the hell?'

She glanced at the puppy by her feet. 'Do you mean Teddy? We couldn't find a sitter so Harper said I could bring him.'

'Well Harper's not in charge! I am! Nominally,' I said. 'Anyway, I didn't mean the dog, I meant your bloody TV show.'

'What about it?'

'That bitchfest last night. You're still sulking because I didn't let you play Cinders, aren't you?'

'Oh no, honey. Last night's episode of *The Brady Bunch* was finished long before we switched pantos.'

'Right. So you just don't like me then.'

Maisie fixed her face into a patronising simper. 'Well, you have to admit, Becky. You're not the easiest leading lady to work with, are you?'

'You've got to be kidding! After all the times I've stayed late to rehearse with you when everyone else was in the pub?'

'Exactly. Quite the little martyr about it.' Her gaze flickered momentarily to Gavin, filming us from a corner.

'Oh for God's sake, love, switch that thing off and be a real person,' I snapped. 'I just want one nice, ordinary row without feeling like a bit player in your bloody life.'

Gav looked unsure. 'Shall I, Mrs Brady?'

'No,' Maisie said. 'She signed the consent form, she can't object.'

'Fine. Film this then.' I rubbed a v-sign against my cheek. 'Do you know who had the deciding vote when we cast you, Maisie? Me. I was the one who voted against a better actress when it was three-all on the panel, because I thought that with enough commitment you could make something of the principal boy part.'

She laughed. 'You?'

'Yes, me. And what do you do? Let the other cast members carry you while you're slagging them off behind their backs. That might be the way it works in Celebrityville, but here in... Realworldsville, we look out for each other. Right?'

'Look –'

'And don't pretend you're giving it your best, I know you're not,' I snapped. 'Harper might be deluding himself when he rates you as the showbiz world's best-kept secret but he's right about one thing: you're better than this. So get it sorted, ok? Ask yourself what Kevin Bacon would do.'

'Maybe I could Bacon it, if I had a decent part,' she snapped back. 'But you wouldn't let me be Cinderella, would you?'

I held up a hand. 'You know what? I'd rather save my stock of drama for the panto. Stay away from me, Maisie, and keep bloody Blair Witch Gav out of my face. From now on we're professionals working together and that's it.' I glanced down at her puppy, who was sniffing my shoes suspiciously. 'That goes for you too, dog. Nothing personal.'

I stormed off to get changed, leaving Maisie scowling in my wake.

'You ok?' Marc asked when he found me ten minutes later in my bra and tights, struggling to get into my giant ballgown with a black look on my face. Any modesty-related commitment to boy/girl changing areas had gone out of the window pretty early on.

'No I'm not ok. Did you see that poisonous bollocks on telly last night? Bloody Maisie, I could strangle her.'

'Here. Keep still.' He helped me pull the dress over my shoulders, then turned me round so he could zip me up. 'Yeah, I saw it.'

'Can you believe it? God, she made me sound like such a... such an amateur.'

'But you are an amateur. We're all amateurs. That's why they call it amateur dramatics.'

'I don't mean amateur as in not getting paid, I mean amateur as in unprofessional. I sounded like some fawning hanger-on.'

'Oh, she's just trying to keep it interesting for viewers,' he said, turning me back around. 'That's reality telly for you, everything has to be melodrama.'

'What, you're defending her?' I said, feeling aggrieved. 'Do you know how humiliating it was? Don't know why I ever signed that bloody consent form.'

'Sorry, Becks,' he said gently. 'Just trying to make you feel better. I'm on your side, promise.'

'You know, it's not even the fact it was on telly, really. It's that she made me sound like she thought I was nothing.' I looked up at him. 'I mean, it wasn't like I thought we were best friends, but I did think she respected me.'

'Here. Get your hair on.' Marc placed the heavy Marie Antoinette wig on my head. 'She does respect you, that's why she's behaving like this. She's jealous of you.'

I snorted. 'What, long-legged, big-boobed Maisie Moorhouse, object of lust for every red-blooded man with access to a copy of the *Sunday Sport*? Do me a favour.'

'Not every red-blooded man.' He reached round to fasten the necklace that went with my costume, and I lifted the ringlets of my wig for him. 'Honestly, Becks, I've seen how she looks at you. She's jealous. It's a compliment, I promise.'

'Jealous of what?'

'Your acting? Your singing voice? Your general Beckyish charm?' He gave me an encouraging peck on the cheek. 'Just be a pro, eh? Maisie's your prince, you're her Cinderella, you're madly in love, and until we get out the Temp door that's all you need to know. You can have a bitch fight in the pub after if you really want. Hell, I'll even provide the baby oil.'

Deano poked his head through the stage door and clapped his hands. 'Right, everybody out here for a director's pep talk.'

'Since when do we have director's pep talks?' Lana asked.

'Since now. Come on, out.'

The assembled cast – our two dames, Yo-yo, Harper, Maisie, Marcus, Lana and me – traipsed dutifully onto the stage. Deano was marching up and down with his rolled-up script under his arm, doing his best impression of a sergeant-major.

'Right then, you 'orrible lot,' he barked. 'Today is the sixth of October. Know what that means?'

'Sixty-four shopping days till Christmas?' my dad said.

'It means forty-five rehearsal days till opening night, that's what. So I want you all giving it...' He hesitated. 'Infinity per cent, all right? We can't afford another rehearsal like the last one, people.'

'Infinity per cent?' Lana muttered. 'Fuck me, it's happened. The last sane braincell's popped.'

'Pantomime is a magical box of wonders in which anything can happen, you maggots!' Deano went on, waving his script at us with a crazed look in his eyes. 'Where even the roughest old scrubbers can wear pretty dresses and get laid. Where boys have short tunics and great legs and lady parts. Where mice can turn into horses and pumpkins into coaches.' His voice rose to a shout. 'I want everyone feeling the magic, and I want them feeling it 24-7 from now until panto! I want pep! I want ginger! I want –'

'You want to get a shift on,' Gerry called out. 'This bloody chandelier dress is killing my old shoulders.'

'Quiet, dame. I'm inspiring you.' He paused. 'Where was I? Oh yeah. From now on I want everyone immersed in the golden, enchanted world of fairytale at all times, on pain of... me.' He glanced over the line-up. 'Becky. No more script blackouts. That Tomorrow scene had better go without a hitch. Lana-banana, I expect those lines to be perfect. And Maisie...' He winced. 'Just do your best, love. Let's try the ballroom scene, then we'll go through some of the others you made such a hash of last time.'

The scene got off to a good start. Maisie managed to come in on cue, and Dandini's crack about the prince having the biggest balls in the kingdom, which we'd written in during our emergency innuendo session, got a snort out of Sue Lightowler on piano. The main problem this time round was me. Or more specifically, my dress.

'May I have this dance?' Maisie-Charming asked when we'd done our eyes-meeting-across-a-crowded-room bit and duetted to Some Enchanted Evening.

'I'd be honoured, your highness,' I said, fluttering my fan coyly.

Maisie bowed, put her arms round my waist, and Sue struck up a waltz. I tried to move but the bloody velvet ballgown was like wearing a bus shelter. I could barely lift my feet. Maisie was reduced to dragging me around like a sack of spanners while I tried desperately not to send us both flying.

'So... are your family... here?' Maisie puffed as she tried to make dancing smalltalk while supporting the full weight of both me and my dress.

'My sisters and stepmother are.'

'And are they as... Christ! Are they as... lovely... as you?'

'Ok, stop!' Deano shouted. Maisie let me go and sagged in relief.

He jumped up on stage. 'What the hell's wrong with you, Becks? Maisie's about to have a coronary.'

'It's the dress,' I said. 'It's too heavy, Deano. I can hardly walk in it, let alone dance.'

'You managed last time, didn't you?'

'I wasn't in the underskirts then. Or the wig, that weighs a ton as well.'

'The dames are coping. Their dresses are bigger than yours.'

'But they're big strapping blokes, aren't they?'

'Ok, now you're just ruining the magic.' He sighed. 'All right, go take the wig and petticoats off so we can rehearse properly. We'll have to sort you another costume.'

After the ball, Harper and Maisie were due to rehearse their dancing. That, at least, had little scope for disaster, since Harper could actually act and Maisie could actually dance. The biggest risk was that close proximity to his wife in tights would have Harper dragging her off to the nearest cleaner's cupboard.

Sue opened the scene with a snatch of Shall We Dance?, then Maisie got the ball rolling.

'Are you sure you can teach me to dance in time for the ball, Baron?'

'Ahh, that I can, boyo. Look you, we'll have you tripping a hornpipe with the best of them by the –'

'Cut!' Deano shrieked. The vein in his temple looked like it was approaching critical. 'Ok, Harper. What the hell's that accent?'

'It's Welsh, isn't it?'

'Bloody hell, is it? I had my money on Tasmanian,' Deano snapped. 'Why've you suddenly started playing it with an accent?'

'Just trying to give the character a bit of depth, that's all,' Harper said sulkily.

'He doesn't need depth. He needs to say his lines properly.' Deano groaned. 'One decent actor, is that too much to ask?' he muttered, turning his eyes skywards in an impassioned appeal to the gods of theatre. 'Now even my BAFTA winner's taking the piss.'

'Well, I'm bored,' Harper grumbled. He was clearly in the mood to let his ego off the lead. 'This bloke Hardup winds me right up. How am I supposed to get into his head when I don't know what his motivation is?'

'He's a minor character in a pantomime, mate. You're not playing King sodding Lear.'

'I think he's right,' said Marcus, who was watching in the wings with me.

Deano stared at him. 'You think what?'

He shrugged. 'Well, what is Hardup's game? He marries this awful woman, lets her and her daughters bully his kid without a word, and yet we're still supposed to believe he's a nice guy. Sorry, but I'm not buying it.'

If Deano had slumped face-first onto the stage and started beating it with his fists, it wouldn't have surprised me. But he managed to stay upright, just.

'My point exactly,' Harper said.

'He's sort of wet, isn't he?' I said. 'He loves his daughter, but he's scared of his terrifying wife.'

Marcus shook his head. 'Not strong enough. His only child's being abused: you'd think that'd make him grow a pair if anything would.'

'I can't believe you lot!' Deano said in a shrill voice, grasping his hair like the *Sesame Street* version of a mad scientist. 'We open in less than two months and you're trying to find motivation for a cameo character with about ten bloody lines!'

'What if we introduce mind control as a factor?' I said, ignoring him. 'Maybe the Wicked Stepmother's controlling him with hypnosis.'

'No good,' Marcus said. 'Baroness Hardup's not a witch. Ask Yo-yo.'

'Ok, then maybe some mind-altering substance. A potion or, um...'

'What about just good old-fashioned booze?' Harper said. 'I do a great drunk.'

Maisie nodded. 'He got a fab write-up for playing an alky in *Silent Witness* once.'

'And if Hardup was a lush, that could explain why he doesn't get his house in order,' Harper said. 'Plus it'd be funny.'

Deano narrowed one eye. 'All right, give us your drunk.'

Harper slurred his way through a few of Baron Hardup's lines, reeling all over the stage.

'And if I let you play it like that, will you be happy?' Deano demanded. 'No more Welsh?'

'Promise. I'm just trying to keep it interesting, that's all.'

Deano's eye twitched. 'Fine, fine, it's all fine. Be the drunk then, if you must. That's just so bloody... fine,' he muttered as he strode back to the wings.

Chapter 30

After the dancing scene, the dames performed their duet of Sisters. Despite the fact it'd been carefully examined for punctures, one of Gerry's breasts would keep deflating at regular intervals, but apart from that the scene was spot on. It certainly cheered Deano up.

The Ugly Sisters were in perfect harmony as they bumped their padded backsides and lifted their skirts to flash their bloomers. By the end of it, Deano looked like he was close to bursting into tears.

'That was beautiful, boys. Beautiful,' he said, coming out of the wings to give his two dames a big hug each. 'Gerry, Danny: if it ever doesn't work out with Sue and Cynthia, I'll marry either one of you. I don't even mind that you've only got three tits between you, that's just how much I love you.'

'Steady on, son,' Dad said, holding Deano back from a hug that was giving every indication of going on for some time. 'I'm not that kind of girl.' He jerked his head at Gerry. 'He is.'

The smile got wiped off Deano's face pretty cleanly in the next scene we rehearsed though, the shoe-fitting. I could see right away that my barney with Maisie earlier had been festering. Prince Charming entered stage left with a glance at me that didn't say future bride so much as future murder victim.

'There's one young woman who hasn't tried the shoe,' Marcus-Buttons said when both dames had failed to get the size five glass slipper onto their honking great man feet. 'My friend Cinderella.'

Chapter 30

'Buttons! How can you be so absurd?' Stepmother-Yolanda snapped. She simpered ingratiatingly at Prince Maisie. 'Pay no attention, your superlativeness. The girl is a mere servant.'

'Let me have another go at that glass slipper,' Dad-Tabitha said, barging Gerry out of the way. 'I was using my big foot before.'

'If anyone should get another go, it's me,' Gerry-Griselda said. 'My toe was still swollen from when you stamped on it, Tabby, you big galumphing elephant.'

'Ooh! I'll get you for that, Grizzly.' Dad got Gerry in a headlock and the two started wrestling. We hadn't written that into the script, but it was a good bit of comedy adlibbing and Deano let them carry on for a minute before he waved to Lana to move the scene forward.

'Ladies, ladies, you, er...' Lana-Dandini flinched, but she managed to fumble out her lines. 'You had your chance. Show some, um... some decorum in front of his highness.'

'Is there another young lady in the house then?' Maisie asked in a can't-really-be-arsed-with-all-this tone. She was staring straight at me kneeling by the grate, so I don't know why she bothered to ask.

'Yes. My youngest daughter,' Harper said, stretching out his hand to guide me to my feet.

'Then she must also try the shoe,' Maisie said stiffly.

I sat on a stool and stretched out my foot. Maisie jammed the shoe onto it with force.

'Oh look. It fits,' she said through gritted teeth.

'Ow! Jesus Christ, Maisie!'

'Er, Becks, your line is "Yes, I was the mysterious stranger you danced with last night",' Deano hissed.

'She's bloody crippled my toe, Deano!' I glared at her. 'You did that on purpose, didn't you?'

'My hand slipped.'

'Look, if the pair of you can't –' Deano stopped and sniffed the air. 'What's that smell?'

Marcus peered round the stage. 'Oh God. It's the bloody puppy.'

'Oh!' Maisie jumped off stage and ran to Teddy, who was standing by a suspicious-looking puddle looking mightily pleased with himself. 'Naughty Teddy. See what you did?'

'Why the hell did you bring him if he isn't housetrained?' Deano demanded.

'Well I can't leave him home alone, can I?' Maisie said. 'He'll be good from now on – won't 'oo, Teddy Bear?'

Deano groaned. 'Right. Get that cleaned up, Maisie, and in future we're having a No Dogs policy. And you and Becky are doing extra sessions together from now on, till you can act a bit more like a couple in love and a bit less like women's prison inmates.'

'What, I'm getting detention?' I said. 'She's the one who –'

Deano held up a hand. 'Don't want to hear it. Right, the Schrödinger's Behind You.'

The Schrödinger's Behind You was Deano's theory that until Cinders turns round and actually sees the Ugly Sisters, they're simultaneously both behind her (Oh No They're Not) and not behind her (Oh Yes They Are), the point being to keep the audience in a state of suspense for as long as possible. Which was a typically Deano way of saying he thought I turned around too quickly.

'Right, Becks. This time I want at least two "Oh No They're Nots" before you look round, ok?' he said.

'Got it.'

'And try not to look quite so much like you know they're there.'

'It's not my fault. I can feel Gerry's moustache tickling my ear.'

'Don't care. Grin and bear it, like Sue has to.'

I cleared my throat to deliver my woe-is-me monologue to the girls and boys in the audience – well, to Stew, who was playing the role of the girls and boys for today.

'Oh, I am unhappy,' I sighed. 'My sisters make me slave away from morning until night, and now I have to help them get ready for the ball. I do wish they would let me go! The prince said every unmarried lady of noble family in the kingdom was invited.'

I felt Dad and Gerry creep up behind me and fixed my face into a wide-eyed stare.

Deano cleared his throat pointedly at Stew, who was fiddling with his phone.

'Oh, right,' he said, glancing up. 'Er, boo. Hiss. Boohiss.'

'Do you know what, boys and girls?' I said conspiratorially from behind my hand. 'Griselda and Tabitha think the prince will marry one of them. Can you believe that?'

'Um, no?' Stew ventured.

'I mean, fat chance, right? Griselda looks like a warthog licking a nettle, and as for Tabitha, I've seen prettier toads. And not the front end.' I laughed. 'I'm sure the prince isn't *that* hard up.'

'Oh,' Stew said in response to another signal from Deano. 'Er, they're behind you, Becks – I mean, Cinders.'

I cupped a hand to my ear. 'What's that, boys and girls?'

'Behind you. Your sisters.'

'They're not behind me, are they?'

'Yeah. Turn round and have a look.'

'Do it properly, Stew!' Deano hissed.

'Do I have to?' Stew said. 'I feel daft.'

'Yes. Get on with it.'

'Oh, all right.' He raised his voice. 'Oh yes they are!'

'Oh no they're not! You're teasing me, aren't you, you naughty things?'

'Oh yes they... look, how long do I have to do this, Deano?'

'Two more,' Deano hissed.

'Right. Oh yes they are.'

I opened my eyes wide. 'Oh no they're not!'

'They are. Oh yes. They really, really are. You'd be amazed how much they are behind you right now.'

'A bit less of the sarcasm, mate,' Deano whispered.

'What, they're really behind me?' Slowly I turned around, then staggered theatrically when I discovered Dad and Gerry with their hands on their hips.

'So I'm a warthog, am I?' Dad said, grabbing me by the shoulders and pushing me to Gerry.

'And I'm a toad's bum, am I?' Gerry spat, pushing me back.

'Oh my God, this is it!' Stewart yelled suddenly.

'We're done with the audience participation bit now, Stew,' Deano said. 'Appreciate your enthusiasm, but can we have some hush?'

'Not that, this,' he said, brandishing his phone. 'Where's Lana? Lana!' He jumped up, almost tripping over his chair, which he kicked to the floor impatiently. 'Lana! Where are you?'

Lana's head poked out of the wings. 'Someone call me?'

Stew ran down the hall, leapfrogged onto the stage and swung his wife round in his arms, kissing her heartily. Everyone had come out now to see what the shouting was about.

'Um, missed you too, Stew,' she said breathlessly when he put her down. 'What's the public display of affection in aid of?'

'This is it, kid,' he said, hugging her tight. 'I just got the email to say we're through to stage three. You're going to be a mum.'

***

Lana and Stew's news put paid to rehearsals for that day. Our panto cast was dismissed to the Fox for a celebratory piss-up, not even bothering to change. Me and Marcus said we'd lock up then meet the others there.

'Happy days, eh?' Marcus said as we put chairs away.

'Yeah, so pleased for them.'

'What happens next, do you know?'

'The agency has to match them to a kid,' I said. 'Then they set up some play dates, make sure they're compatible, then presto: they're a mum and dad.'

'How long will that take?'

'It took three months till Cam and Tom were matched with Pip. Cam told me it could've taken up to two years though.'

'Oof, two years? Hope they don't have to wait that long.' He cocked his head. 'Hey, did everyone go to the pub?'

'I think so, why?'

'Thought I heard something.'

I groaned. 'It's not Harper and Maisie, is it? It'd be nice to end one rehearsal without the image of his arse seared onto my retinas.'

'It can't be, I saw them leave.'

I listened. There was a sort of shuffling, and a low, whispered moan.

'Sounds like it's coming from the meeting room.'

Marcus followed me out of the main hall to the room next door.

'Jesus! Deano?'

The red-haired figure lying face down on the floor gave a high-pitched laugh.

'Oh God. We broke him,' Marcus muttered. 'Ok, Becks. One arm each.'

We guided him up into a chair.

'It's no good,' he was muttering. 'It's no good. *Titanic*. Glam Rock. The *Joey* spinoff. Pick your disaster.'

'What's up, love?' I said gently.

'What isn't up? Christ, Abe Lincoln's had better nights at the theatre.'

I shook my head. 'Too soon, Deano. Too soon.'

'Come on, little brother,' Marcus said, resting a reassuring hand on Deano's shoulder. 'So there're a few little problems to iron out. We can do it.'

'A few little problems?' Deano said, fixing glazed eyes on Marcus. 'My principal boy can't act, Marc. Not even enough to summon the basic level of make-believe needed to pretend she doesn't want to bitch-slap the supposed love of her life with a heavy-duty anvil.' He groaned. 'Oh God, I'm going back to the floor.'

We held his arms to stop him sliding out of the chair.

'Don't worry about Maisie,' I said. 'Me and her can do some extra sessions, build a rapport. We'll sort it.'

'Yeah? How's your foot?'

I wiggled my toes. 'A bit sore. But... we'll sort it.'

'You know just saying that doesn't actually sort it, right?'

'We'll sort it,' I repeated helplessly.

'I wouldn't mind if that was the only problem,' Deano said. 'But then there's everything else. Lana still can't remember her lines. Harper's liable to throw a hissy fit at any moment, just because he's Harper Brady and he knows he bloody can. Yo-yo's a ticking bomb of age paranoia. And then there's you two.'

I frowned. 'What about us two?'

'You're a bad influence on each other.' He jerked his head towards his brother. 'He's a distraction. So are you to him. I've a good mind not to let you play out any more.'

I laughed. 'You what?'

'You're forever corpsing each other. That or he's fluttering his eyelashes and making you forget your lines.'

'That was a one-off. It won't happen again,' I said, avoiding Marc's gaze.

Deano plonked his cheeks glumly onto his fists. 'Even my dames can't manage to maintain a full set of tits between them. We're jinxed, guys.'

'Oh, never mind Gerry's boobs, they're the least of our worries,' I said. 'We'll just go back to sock-stuffed bras. A bit lumpy, but they stay up.'

Marc snorted. 'It was bloody funny though, watching him pump himself up every five minutes.' He nudged his brother. 'Come on, our Dean, snap out of it. Prosecco's flowing at the Fox. Let's go raise a glass to Lana and Stew, eh?'

'Yeah.' Deano roused himself. 'Yeah. Something to celebrate, at least.'

'You coming, Becks?' Marcus said as Deano stood to leave.

'Hmm?'

'You coming to the pub?'

'It was funny, wasn't it?' I said absently.

Marcus frowned. 'What was?'

'Gerry's tits. When he had to keep pumping them up with his arm. We were cracking up in the wings.'

'I know, I was there. Come on, love, let's go get a drink.'

'And when Lana kept shouting "line!", that was pretty funny. And Maisie dragging me round the stage in that horrific dress. Even when the puppy piddled in the corner, everyone was laughing.'

'I'm glad my distress provides such entertainment to the rabble,' Deano said darkly.

'I mean, it was funny. All the stuff that went wrong was funny. And pantos are supposed to be funny.' I stared at them.

'What if we worked some of it in? Like, had things go wrong on purpose?'

'You what?'

'Well, we found it funny. Who says the audience won't? We could make our weaknesses our strengths.'

'Gerry's deflating knockers, maybe,' Marcus conceded. 'I don't see how we're going to make Maisie a strength though. There's nothing funny about bad acting.'

'Ok, maybe not that,' I admitted. 'But the other stuff. If we can't fix it, why not play it for laughs? Then if anything goes wrong by accident we can pretend it's part of the show.'

'She might be right, you know,' Deano said slowly. 'It was pretty funny. I mean, not to me, I wanted to cry, but all you other sadistic bastards seemed to be pissing yourselves.'

'Ha! Yes we were!' I slapped him on the back. 'Tell you what, I'm a bloody genius. Let's get to the pub. You both owe me a drink.'

Chapter 31

'Here, try this one,' Lana said, pricking a piece of pastry off the paper plate.

I leaned over to bite it off her fork. 'Mmm. Just like Mother used to defrost.'

'What is it?'

'Peach, I think.'

We were at Fancypants, playing Pie Russian Roulette with some of Deano's latest tasters for the Pie and a Pint menu.

'Doesn't Deano get bored making nothing but pie?' I asked.

'You'd think. But no, he seems to enjoy the challenge.'

'Not sure this panto isn't a challenge too far, you know. That meltdown he had at the last rehearsal was a bit full-on.'

'Oh, he thrives on meltdown. Meltdown's his middle name. Well, Kevin.'

'Ooh!' I said, catching sight of a gorgeous cerise dress on the website I was browsing. 'Lana, you'd look great in this.' I twisted the laptop screen to show her.

She blinked. 'Yeah, lovely. I could keep it handy in case I got invited to an embassy ball.'

'For the wedding, you turnip. I'm after matching bridesmaids' dresses for you and Cole's sister.'

'You're not buying them now, are you?'

'No. Just bookmarking a few things.'

'Why the wedding fever suddenly? Seems a bit premature, picking out bridesmaids' dresses when you haven't fixed a date.'

'I just want to feel like plans are under way, that's all,' I said. 'Makes it seem more real.'

She stared at me for a moment, and I flushed.

'What?'

'Nothing.' She gagged on a bit of pie. 'Ick. Beetroot.'

'So come on then. What's next in your daft perfect-partner quiz?'

Lana glanced at the magazine on her lap. 'Is your perfect partner a) your best friend, like Ryan Reynolds in *Just Friends*; b) a hopeless romantic who treats you to thoughtful gifts, like Ryan Reynolds in *Definitely, Maybe*, or c) a sexy hunk who looks great in lycra, like Ryan Reynolds in *Green Lantern*?' She glanced up. 'Think they might've run out of ideas on that last one.'

'What if my perfect partner isn't Ryan Reynolds?'

'I don't think the quiz writer allowed for that possibility.'

'All right, B. No, A. A or B.'

'You have to pick one, Becks.'

'Oh, I don't know. A then,' I said. 'Here, there's a load of naff Christmas jumpers on this website. What do you say to getting the lads matching ones for Christmas Day?'

'Hmm?' she said, ticking the A box on her quiz.

'His-and-his Christmas jumpers for Cam and Tom. Come on, Lana, pay attention.'

'Ok, ok. Yes to jumpers.' She scanned the mag again. 'Right, last question.'

I sighed. 'Go on.'

'What's your perfect date? Is it a) a night in with a takeaway and a Ryan Reynolds film, snuggled on the sofa; b) an evening at a swanky restaurant, or c) a delicious meal cooked by your partner?'

'A I think, long as I can pick the film. Hey, did you really go out with Harper?'

She laughed. 'Yeah, once.'

'Didn't shag him, did you?'

'God, no! I only did it to make Stew jealous.'

'Did it work?'

She examined her wedding ring. 'Something obviously did. Right, Becks. You got... let's see, mostly As.' She skimmed to the bit at the end. 'Your perfect partner will be your best friend, the love of your life and the person you feel happiest vegging in your PJs with,' she read. 'They'll always be the first person you call when you're feeling blue, the one whose jokes can make you snort wine out of your nose and the person you'd rather spend time with over everyone else. Your strong friendship will make for a loving and lasting romantic relationship.'

I shook my head. 'Where do they get this bollocks?'

'I think they make the work experience kid write it between tea runs as some sort of penance.' She looked up. 'So is that Cole?'

'Course. Hey, is there any more of Deano's peach pie? It's kind of moreish.'

'I'll tell him. It can go on next season's dessert menu.' She passed the plate. 'What time's Yo-yo getting here?'

'Seven.' I smiled at her. 'Thanks for staying. I think an evening of watching my old Brownie leader parading around in fishnets all on my own is more than my constitution could stand.'

'Hey, you had me at free prosecco.'

I'd never meant to run a costume shop. My original plan after leaving uni and moving south was to be a full-time photographer.

But I'd soon found there wasn't much money in it. I'd ended up working retail jobs on the side to make ends meet, and eventually I'd realised I wasn't a photographer who worked in a shop any more. I was a shop girl who took a few photos.

That was when it'd occurred to me I could do the same thing a lot more cheaply back in Yorkshire. Cole could paint in the sort of beautiful countryside that would really inspire him, I could come home to my family, and the giant playground of the Dales would be the perfect place to raise a child.

Dad and Cynthia had offered me work in Your Plaice or Mine, their chippy, till I got on my feet, but I'd really wanted my own business. So I'd looked around and found Fancypants, or Willy's Wacky Warehouse as it was then. Running a costume shop sounded fun, plus I could still do a bit of photography on the side.

It was Lana who'd had the big brainwave. There was an empty storeroom adjoining the shop, just going to waste. Lana suggested it was the perfect size for a photography studio, and my business within a business, Fancysnaps, was born.

The idea was that people could book a professional photo-shoot in any of my costumes, without having to hire them. It was popular too – in fact I made my living from it, far more than the pittance I got hiring out fancy dress. Some people came for period photos in Victorian or Edwardian gear, all printed in classy sepia. Sometimes it was fanboy couples wanting photos as their favourite characters from *Game of Thrones* or the Marvel universe. But most popular of all were the boudoir sessions.

They were for ladies only and made use of my saucier burlesque-style costumes, for women who wanted to give their partners a cheeky set of prints as a present. They often came in groups after hours, with me providing the prosecco to get their Dutch courage up before they stripped off. All the clothing was for sale too, so I made a bit flogging pants on the side.

Somehow Yolanda got to hear about it, and the next thing I know she's booking a session to get some sexy pics done for Billy as a wedding present. I wasn't sure there was enough prosecco in the world to block out the sight of my old Brown Owl prancing around in lacy knickers like Gypsy Rose Lee, but Lana had offered to keep me company, and Sue, as maid of honour, was coming too.

'Evening, ladies,' I said when they arrived, handing them a glass of prosecco each. 'Come on through.'

'You got roped in too, did you?' Sue muttered to Lana as they followed me into the studio.

'Yeah, I'm Becky's moral support. You?'

'I'm Yo-yo's Something Old.' She shook her head. 'Never thought I'd be on maid of honour duty at fifty-eight.'

'I heard that, Susan,' Yolanda said. 'My official age is forty-five, thank you, and I plan on keeping it that way until I'm at least seventy. Which means you do too. Oh!' She clapped her hands when she caught sight of the rail of clothes. 'Oh, aren't they gorgeous?'

'Think you'll ever grow out of playing dress-up?' Sue said.

'Oh no, I shouldn't think so.' She drew a hot-pink showgirl basque from the rail. 'Isn't this fabulous, girls?' she breathed. 'It just matches my hair.'

'You'll need the accessories.' I nodded to the plush armchairs next to the changing screen for Lana and Sue to have a seat, then went to rummage in the box next to the rail. 'Long silk gloves, fishnets, ostrich-feather fascinator.'

'Ooh, I love a fascinator! Can I try them on?'

'Course. The screen's there if you want to –'

'Oh, no need for screens. We're all girls, aren't we?'

I don't know why I'd even bothered suggesting it. She was already taking her top off in front of the full-length mirror. There was blushing maiden modesty, and then there was Yolanda Sommerville.

'What's the wedding dress like, Yo-yo?' Lana asked.

Yolanda smirked. 'I'm afraid you'll have to wait and see. It's gorgeous, that's all I'm at liberty to say.'

'Virginal white, I assume?' Sue asked innocently.

'Wait and see, Susan. Wait and see.' She hooked the stockings to the basque's suspenders, attached the fascinator and turned to beam at us. 'Well, how do I look?'

'Great,' I said. She did too, with her shapely legs and the basque cinching her waist: still every inch the principal boy she'd been 40 years earlier. 'You certainly don't look, er, forty-five.'

'You're sweet,' she said, patting my cheek. 'Could I have a photo in this one please, Rebecca?'

I placed her in front of the black curtain I used as a backdrop then put her into the preferred showgirl position, one leg kicked back at the knee, hand on hip and the other behind her head, face fixed into a come-hither pout. She was soon cooing over the monitor I'd fixed up for customers to review their shots.

'Don't I look fantastic? Billy will adore them! Thank you, darling.'

'He's a lucky man,' I said, smiling. 'Does he know you're doing this?'

'Oh, no. These are a wedding-day surprise.' She started browsing the rails again. 'It's really as much for me as him. There's something terribly liberating about it, isn't there? And at my age, it does no harm to remind yourself you can still be sexy.'

'What, forty-five?' Lana asked.

'Well, I think I can pass for forty if the lighting's right.'

'She means if there's a blackout,' Sue whispered to us.

Lana nodded. 'She'll remember those from the war. Getting felt up by GIs in air-raid shelters.'

'You're a cheeky pair. But I'm in such a good mood, I'm going to let it slide.' Yolanda beckoned to the three of us. 'And now you all must have a turn. Come on, up up up!'

Sue shook her head. 'You're not getting me up like a Wild West brothel madam at my age, love. I'll leave the daft costumes to the hubby.'

'But you must have a photo. Just imagine what Gerry will say.'

'I am imagining it. That's why I'm not doing it.'

'You have to. I'm the bride and I say so,' she said, pouting. She grabbed the bottle of prosecco and refilled everyone's glasses. 'Have another drink, girls. Then I'm giving every one of you a makeover. I am the Fairy Godmother, after all.'

'Don't think we've forgotten you're the Wicked Stepmother as well,' Sue muttered as she was dragged reluctantly to the clothes rail.

Chapter 32

'Glad you came?' I whispered to Lana while we watched Yolanda lacing Sue into a huge leather basque.

Lana shook her head. 'Never thought I'd see the basque that could take on that bosom.'

Sue pushed her cleavage up a bit. 'Not sure I could wear it every day, but it's good to feel the old girls are getting some support. They're a bit nearer the floor than they were thirty years ago.'

'I'll never forgive you for this, Becks,' Lana muttered.

'It suits you, Susan,' Yolanda said. 'How about that photo? A little early Christmas present for Gerry?'

'In this? He'd be off over the moors.'

'Nonsense, you look fantastic.' Yolanda turned to us. 'Doesn't she, girls?'

'Er, yeah,' I managed to mumble. 'Very... striking.'

'I can't believe Tommy got out of seeing this,' Lana said. 'Not fair.'

Sue grinned. 'Well if you can't embarrass the kiddies at my age, what else is there to live for?' She refilled her prosecco, then topped the rest of us up. 'It's nice to have a bit of girl bonding, I must say. Most of the female company in my line of work comes covered in wool.'

'Did you and Gerry not want kids?' I asked. 'Swaledales don't seem like much of a substitute.'

She came over to Lana's armchair and squeezed her shoulder. 'We did try for a while. But when Phil lost Paula, and this one and her brother were short of a mum, it felt like fate had fixed us up with a different kind of family. Takes all sorts, doesn't it?'

'Thanks, Mum,' Lana said, smiling. 'Don't lean down again though, eh? You're going to smother someone with those things.'

I giggled. 'You look like one of them Viking goddesses, Sue. Valeries.'

Lana nudged me. 'Valkyries, you div. Valerie's that woman at the bakery.'

'Oh yeah.' I giggled again when Lana started humming Ride of the Valkyries. 'Hey, this is good prosecco.'

'Valkyrie, eh?' Sue shrugged. 'I've been called worse.'

'How long were you trying for a baby?' I asked.

'Until we lost one. Stillbirth. Too painful to go through it all again.'

'Bloody hell,' Lana said, blinking. 'You two lost a baby? I never knew that.'

'No.' Sue grabbed a blue feather boa from the accessories box and wrapped it round her, staring thoughtfully at her reflection. 'Not many people do.'

Yolanda reached out to take her hand for a moment, and I saw Sue give it a grateful squeeze.

'At least me and Stew never had to go through that,' Lana said. 'Trying was bad enough. Every month another disappointment.'

'How come you never went for IVF?' I said.

'We talked about it. But then Tom and Cam adopted Pip, and she was just so perfect and so... theirs, you know? And we thought that there was a kid out there who needed a mum and dad, and there was a mum and dad with a lot of love to give, so why not go find them? There's all sorts of ways people become parents.' She smiled at Sue. 'Wouldn't swap the mum I ended up with.'

'What about you, Yo-yo?' I said.

'Oh, no,' she said, wrinkling her nose. 'Children are lovely, of course – that's why I did Brownies for so many years. But I wouldn't want one I couldn't give back.'

'Even if you'd met the right man?'

'Not even then, darling. I'd have been a miserable failure as a mother, you know.' She laughed and turned back to the clothing rail. 'Now, let's not have our girl talk getting too serious. This is really my hen night. And I'm not letting you and Lana get away without a makeover.'

I groaned. 'Do we have to?'

'You certainly do.' She picked out a long, fitted evening gown. 'Rebecca, this will be just gorgeous with your colouring.' She took my hand to guide me to my feet. 'Come into the other room so you can have a mirror of your own, and we'll leave Susan to choose something lovely for Lana.'

She led me through to the shop, and after some arm-twisting I nipped into the changing room to put on the evening gown. It was new in: a sheer, shimmering thing in baby-blue, strapless with a plunging back.

'Sit down, dear, so I can do your make-up,' Yolanda said, guiding me to a chair and producing a little case from somewhere.

'So did you never fall for any of them? The blokes?' I asked while she applied some foundation. Tongue loosened by too much prosecco, I was quite enjoying a bit of female bonding. 'Not sure I could stop myself getting emotionally invested if I tried that friends-with-benefits thing.'

'Of course, darling, I loved every one of them. And yet I never loved any of them. That was the freedom of it.' She sighed. 'And the loneliness. Close your right eye for me and keep very still, I want to do your eyeliner.'

I did as she said. 'But wasn't there anyone a bit special?' I asked, squinting with my one eye. 'Before Billy, I mean.'

Chapter 32

She smiled. 'There was one I fell rather hard for, a long time ago. Before you were born, although I'd appreciate it if you didn't spread around that I was old enough for love affairs in those days.'

'How come it didn't work out?'

'Oh, he wasn't a lover. Just a friend. He's gone now.'

Her eyes had clouded with nostalgia. I felt an urge to press her hand, so I did.

'Didn't he know how you felt?'

'No, I never told him. He was in love with someone else, a girl from the village. I don't think he ever saw me as anything more than a good friend.'

'What happened to him?'

'He married her, the other girl. They were happy together, had a couple of children. Like I said, he's gone now.'

'Gone as in...'

'Yes. Passed away.' She blinked back a tear. 'I think about him sometimes. Miss him. Close your other eye there, could you, darling?'

'What was it about him over the others?'

She was silent a moment. 'Well, he was very handsome. But I suppose really it was that he made me laugh. He was in the Players too, and when we used to act together... I've never known a man who could have me in stitches the way he could.' She smiled. 'And the accent helped. It sounded so sexy and exotic compared to the boys I'd grown up with.'

'Oh. Oh!' My gaze flickered to Lana. I could see her through the open door of the studio, trying on fascinators with Sue. 'You don't mean –'

'Phil Donati. Yes, I'm afraid so.'

'Do Tom and Lana know?'

'Of course not, darling. No one knows but Susan. And you, now,' she said, fluffing out my hair. 'It's my guilty little secret. Every girl should have one, it adds mystique.'

I looked up into her sad blue eyes. 'But why are you telling it to me?'

She smiled. 'Do you remember when you were seven and I took you and the other girls to Ilkley on pack holiday?'

'Er, vaguely.'

'Some of you had stayed up after lights-out to tell ghost stories. It was all part of the fun of being away, so as long as you didn't get too loud we Owls used to turn a blind eye.'

'I... yes, I remember,' I said slowly. 'Kylie Petrescu told this story about a ghost trying to find his hairy toe. God, I was terrified.'

'That's right, it was your first time away from home. You came to the leaders' room in tears, and I took you to the kitchen to make you a hot chocolate. Then you crawled onto my knee for a cuddle and I sang to you until you stopped crying. Oh, you were a sweet little thing. I almost wished for a moment I could keep you.' Her voice shook slightly. 'It was the first thing I remembered about you when you turned up at the village society meeting.'

'You said I was always covered in jam.'

'And so you were, my lovely. Children often are, you know. But I still remembered you as one of my favourites.' She added a smear of pink lipstick and stepped back. 'There. You're a beauty, Rebecca.'

I flushed. 'Me? Don't be daft.'

'Now, you mustn't insult my fairy-godmother skills. When I send someone to a ball, they go looking like a princess.' She nodded to the long mirror. 'Take a look at yourself and tell me I'm wrong.'

Chapter 32

I stared at the girl in the mirror, with her soft blonde hair and her soft grey eyes, shining with emotion and wine. The dress clung flatteringly to every curve, flowing out behind her like a river, making her look willowy and fluid and like she didn't have any feet. But in an attractive way.

'I don't look much like me,' I murmured, reaching out to rest my fingertips on the glass. Everything seemed dreamlike, Yolanda behind me looking elfin and otherworldly with her pink hair glowing in the low light.

'You look more like you than ever, my love.' She squeezed my arm. 'Fit for a prince. Or anyone you choose.'

Impetuously, I threw myself at her for a hug. 'Thank you,' I whispered. 'I hope you'll be happy with Billy, Yo-yo. You deserve it. And for what it's worth, I think you would've been a great mum.'

'Godmother, darling. I'm really just the godmother.'

***

There was a knock at the door just as we were finishing the last of our prosecco.

Yolanda had a full set of snaps she was happy with, which I was going to have printed in time for the wedding. Despite her friend's urging, Sue steadfastly refused to have any photos done, although she was still wearing the basque. She seemed to have got quite attached to it. Lana wouldn't have any photos done either, but she did buy some lingerie as a treat for Stew.

'That'll be the old man with my lift,' Sue said.

'I'll get it,' I said. I was still in the long dress Yolanda had put me in. It felt sort of nice, being someone else for the night.

'Hiya,' I said to Gerry when I answered the door. I frowned. 'Bloody hell. What's up with your face?'

He rubbed his newly nude upper lip. 'Aye, shaved it off till after the panto. Young Deano kept staring at it with a murderous glint in his eye.'

I nodded approvingly. 'Takes years off you, Gerry.'

'Cheers, pet.' He glanced at my dress. 'You look nice. What is that, chiffon?'

I laughed. 'Yeah. You know, you've changed since you became a female impersonator.'

Gerry shrugged. 'If you're going to do a job, might as well be thorough.' He nodded to the studio. 'The boss in there, is she?'

'She is. Come on through.'

He followed me in.

'All right, our lass, time to –' His eyes widened when he caught sight of Sue taking a last look in the mirror at her gravity-defying bosom. 'Jesus Christ! What the hell is *that*?'

Yolanda smirked. 'It's a basque. Gorgeous, isn't it?'

'Jesus Christ,' Gerry muttered again.

'I'll just get changed and we can –' Sue broke off when she turned to look at her husband. 'What happened to your face?'

'He's going the full dame,' I said. 'No facial hair till after the panto.'

They walked towards each other slowly, like the last scene in a Hollywood film. I was starting to feel a bit awkward.

'You wore something like that on our wedding night,' Gerry murmured.

'A good few sizes smaller.' She reached up to run her fingers over his lip. 'You know, I never did like Tom Selleck all that much. I just wanted to make you jealous.'

'How much, Becky?' Gerry asked, not taking his eyes off Sue's cleavage.

I blinked. 'Sorry?'

Chapter 32

'The basque thing. We'll take it.' He shook his head. 'Never mind, I don't care. We'll settle up in the pub next week. Bye, girls.'

'See you, everyone,' Sue called as Gerry dragged her determinedly to the door.

'Oh God,' Lana groaned. 'I didn't need to see that.'

'I don't think any of us needed to see that,' I said.

'Do you know how randy a Yorkshireman needs to be not to even wait for the price? Oh God...'

Yolanda laughed. 'Honestly, you young people. Do you really think sex should just stop when you turn fifty?'

'No, I think it should stop when you turn forty,' Lana said. 'Well, I do when it comes to them two.'

'And I'm sure when you and Stewpot have a child they'll think the same about you,' she said. 'But I for one wish you a long, healthy sex life filled with basques and fun. That's my Good Fairy blessing for you.'

Lana shook her head. 'You've actually started to believe you're proper magic, haven't you?'

'Oh, let them enjoy themselves,' I said, recovering finally. I patted Lana's arm. 'Forget about it, love. Take your suspenders and go give Stew a treat. And Yo-yo, if you're not saving yourself for the wedding night, help yourself to whatever you think Billy might like. Apparently tonight the men of Egglethwaite are getting lucky courtesy of my stock.'

'And what about you?' Lana said, nudging me. 'Anything you want to take home and model for Cole?'

I laughed. 'I don't think he'd appreciate being woken up at this time of night, even for fishnets. Maybe another day.'

Chapter 33

'Aunty Becky, can I ride Peppa?' Pip asked, tugging at my hand.

The ride-on Peppa Pig in Egglethwaite Playground had been her favourite thing since she'd joined the family four years ago. I don't suppose she remembered, now, how her Aunty Becky had rushed up from London to meet her beautiful new niece, or the joy and love in her dads' eyes as they'd argued over whose turn it was to give her a push.

But it was a toddlers' toy, and every time I let her have a go I saw the sign clearly labelled 'FOUR YEARS AND UNDER' glaring accusingly.

'You're too big now, Pips. That's for the little kids.'

The bottom lip jutted out, but I stayed firm. There'd been mutterings within the family that our Pip was in danger of getting spoilt.

'It's no good pulling that face, madam. You don't want to break it for the babies, do you?'

I suspected the word 'baby' would do the trick. At six, Pip was very grown-up. She pulled herself up to her full height.

'I bet Harry doesn't play on baby rides,' I said, following up my advantage.

'Bet he does,' she muttered sulkily. 'He's littler'n me.'

'Then you'd better act like the big girl you are, hadn't you?' I nodded to Cole, who'd been reluctantly dragged from his studio to join us for today's play date. 'Why don't you ask Uncle Cole to give you a push on the swings?'

Pip didn't look too impressed by this suggestion.

'No thank you,' she said, using her best manners. 'I'm going on the slide. The big-kid slide.' She ran off to climb the steps.

I nudged Cole. 'What do you think, am I getting the hang of it?'

'Of what?'

'Well, parenting.' I smiled. 'Don't worry, I'm not getting baby fever again. But it does no harm to start practising stern-mum mode.'

Cole didn't answer, just gazed into the distance towards the moors. He'd seemed distracted all day.

'Cole?'

'Hmm? Oh.' He shook himself. 'Sorry, I was miles away.'

'Come on, love. Switch off work brain and try to be in the moment. Your painting'll still be there when we get home.'

'I'm sorry. Just worrying. It's starting to feel lately like it might never happen.'

I blinked. 'What, the wedding?'

'My career,' he said. 'I'll be thirty-six in three months. I like lecturing, but I did hope that by now I'd be in a position to paint full-time.'

I squeezed his hand. 'It'll happen. You're making a name for yourself now, aren't you? It's a slow burn, I know, but –'

'Oi! Finnster!'

I looked over Cole's shoulder and spotted Marcus approaching. He was hand in hand with Pip's friend Harry, and a pretty, dark-haired woman was holding the boy's other hand.

'Fancy meeting you two here,' he said when he reached us. 'This is Livvy. Livvy, Becky and Cole. Becky's in the panto with me.'

'Hiya,' I said, shaking the woman's hand. I smiled at Harry. 'And I think there's someone on the slide who'll be pleased to see you.'

But Pip had already spotted him. She bounced off the end of the slide and came running over, making a noise that sounded like 'Squeeeeeeee!', until she hurtled into her best friend and nearly knocked him to the ground.

There were some fragments of 100-mile-an-hour kid conversation that sounded like gibberish to us but obviously made perfect sense to them.

'– *Moana* stickers swap you –'

'– crocodile tig no den –'

'– trolls –'

Once they'd jabbered out all their incomprehensible six-year-old news, Pip commandeered Harry's hand and dragged him off to play.

'Are you Harry's mum?' I asked Marcus's friend.

'Childminder. Marcus offered to keep us company on a trip to the park.' Livvy flashed him a smile, and I wondered what their story was. Marc hadn't mentioned anything about a new girlfriend.

Pip came bounding back, panting.

'Need pushes,' she gasped. 'Swings.'

'And we also say…?' I reminded her.

'Please, Aunty Becky. We want to go higher than the most highest ever. Higher'n Uncle Stew.'

I nudged Cole. 'What do you reckon? Think you could beat Stew's record as champion swing-pusher?'

Pip looked up at Marcus. 'We want you to do it. I mean, please may you do it.'

'Ok, I think I could give Uncle Stew a run for his money.' Marcus glanced at Cole. 'If I'm not treading on toes?'

'Oh no, please. Be my guest.'

It was an innocent enough comment, but there was definitely a sarcastic note. And I could tell by the way Marc's eyebrow lifted that I wasn't the only one who'd noticed.

'Er, right,' he said. 'Come on, Livvy, we'll take one each.'

'What was that for?' I asked Cole when they'd gone.

'What?'

'You sounded dead snarky then. I think you might've offended him.'

'Oh, I'm sure he'll get over it.'

I glanced over to Marcus and Livvy pushing the kids, all four laughing as they tried to see who could get the highest. Grabbing Cole's arm, I led him to a bench where we'd be safely out of earshot.

'Seriously, what's up with you today?' I demanded. 'You're being a right mardy bugger.'

'Overtired, that's all.'

'Cole, come on. Don't make me play the Honesty Card.'

We'd devised the Honesty Card after we'd nearly fallen out over him not showing up to our anniversary dinner. When played, it meant we had to admit exactly what was bothering us before it festered and caused a row.

'Honestly, Becky, it's nothing. I didn't mean to snap at Marcus. I suppose I just can't help thinking about what you told me.'

'Not jealous, are you?'

'A little. Is that so surprising?'

'We're just good friends, Cole. That's all.' I pressed his hand to my lips. 'You and me have been together four years. I've promised to spend the rest of my life with you. I love you. There's no need to be jealous, of Marcus or anyone else. Ok?'

'Ok.' He sighed. 'I'm being silly, aren't I? I need sleep, I think.'

I patted his knee. 'You've been overdoing it. Let's go join Marcus and Livvy and play with the kids for a bit, that'll get you out of yourself. Then we'll drop Pip off, I'll do steak for tea and we can have an early night.'

'You go. I'll watch from here.'

'You sure? I wanted you to come so you could spend some time with Pip.'

He looked sheepish. 'It's just... I never really know how to talk to her. And I feel so ridiculous, playing make-believe at my age.'

'But Pip's not your age,' I said. 'You need to remember how you saw the world at six.'

'When I was six I tended to have my nose in a book. I didn't have many friends as a child.'

'Well, then it's high time you lightened up and learned how to play,' I said, smiling. 'Come on, you'll enjoy it.'

'No, Becky, I'd feel foolish with the other adults there. You go. Perhaps if I watch you, I can learn how to do it.'

This had been worrying me ever since the way he'd reacted to Pip making a mess at the dinner party. Cole was a grown-up, and in some ways it felt like he'd almost been born a grown-up. Perhaps it was because he was super-intelligent, perhaps it was being sent away from home so young, perhaps it was just the way he was. But I was starting to realise there was more to his awkwardness around kids than just a lack of experience. He actually seemed not to like them.

I couldn't help thinking about the miscarriage I'd suffered in the early days of our relationship. If things had worked out differently, we could have a three-year-old by now. How would Cole cope with a toddler in the house? Would his paternal instinct have kicked in when he'd become a father, or would he be hiding away in his attic, leaving me to parent on my own?

I wondered, sometimes, whether I should tell him about the pregnancy that never was, but something always held me back. I think my biggest fear was what I might read in his face if I did. There was one emotion I particularly dreaded seeing.

Relief.

'Ok, I'm playing the Honesty Card,' I said.

'What is it, Becky?'

'Cole, do you like kids? Because you seem to hate spending time with them.'

'I don't hate it. I just find them... incomprehensible. I'm not used to them, I expect.'

Which was exactly what I'd been telling myself. But he didn't seem in any hurry to rectify that.

'You do want one though?'

'I told you, darling. I want you to be happy.'

'That's not what I asked, Cole.'

For a moment, silence reigned. Then Cole's ringtone went off and he fumbled for his phone.

'Ryder,' he said, scanning the screen.

Only half listening to Cole's one-sided conversation with my favourite person, I went back to watching the children.

Marcus was a natural with them. He and Livvy looked like they were having the time of their lives bouncing about on the trampoline hand in hand with the two kids, and I felt a pang of envy. I'd got so used to us being panto buddies, it actually hurt a bit seeing him having a laugh with someone else. I longed to join in the fun, but I didn't want to go without Cole.

'...no, but there's a Waitrose half an hour's drive away so it's not completely barbaric,' Cole was saying. 'How's the gallery?'

He paused as Ryder jabbered in his ear.

'Gosh, really? Well, I'd love to, of course. Very generous of you to schedule it out of term-time just for my benefit. Yes, I'm sure I – oh no, week of the 24th?' He glanced at me. 'I'm supposed to be going to a wedding.'

He was silent a moment.

'Can you hold a second, Ryd?' he said. 'I need a quick word with Becky.'

He hit the button for mute and turned to me.

'What is it? Another exhibition?' I asked.

'Yes. Much bigger than the last two he invited me to,' Cole said. 'It sounds as though the gallery is really gaining a reputation. He's just been listing the artists he's lured in and there are some real up-and-comers.'

'Sounds like a great opportunity.' I patted his arm. 'Well, go on, love. I'll make your excuses to Yolanda and Billy, I'm sure they'll understand.'

'But I promised to start doing more with your friends, getting to know them better.'

'I think this counts as extenuating circumstances,' I said, smiling. 'You know you have to do it. I'd hate myself forever if you gave it up just to be my date for a wedding.'

'I can't leave you to go alone though.'

'Don't worry about that. My family's going, and loads of people I know.'

To be honest, a short break from each other might be just what we needed. I could feel the weight of the question he still hadn't answered, hanging in the air between us.

'Will Marcus be there?' he asked.

'Guess so. Him and Deano are bound to have been invited.' I smiled. 'You're not going to start being jealous again, are you?'

'No. No, of course not. Sorry.'

I leaned over to kiss his cheek. 'Go on, tell Ryder you're in. I'll be fine.'

He hesitated another moment before he unmuted the phone. 'Hello, Ryd? Yes, I'd love to take part.'

Chapter 34

'So, how was the wedding?' Deano asked.

'Pink,' I said. 'Really, really pink.'

Yolanda and Billy had booked a country house for their reception, Monkton Hall, and those of us who'd been invited to the ceremony had the not-small job of trying to get across to those who hadn't – which included Marcus and Deano, on the basis there wasn't enough room in the church, or even York Minster, for all Yo-yo's former lovers and their families – just how bloody pink the whole thing had been.

'What, the dress?' Marcus said.

'The dress. The hair. Billy's suit. Even the vicar had a colour-coordinated sash.'

'How was the dress?'

'Pink,' Lana said.

'I think we got that much, Lanasaurus,' Deano said. 'Anything else?'

'Tight. So, so tight.' She nodded to the door. 'Take a look. Here come the happy couple.'

Marcus squinted at the door as the very, very pink Yolanda and Billy made their entrance, clinging to each other while those nearest showered them with rose petals.

'Ha! Really loves that Wicked Stepmother frock, doesn't she?'

'Yep,' Stew said. 'She had that specially made in the same style.'

The bride was wearing a figure-hugging dress with a little ruff at the feet, the model of her panto costume but in hot-pink velvet. It was very Yolanda.

'Nice ceremony?' Marcus asked.

Lana grimaced. 'Yes and no. They wrote their own vows.'

He winced in solidarity. 'Shit, really?'

'Well, no, technically Wet Wet Wet wrote the vows,' I said. 'They used the lyrics from that song.'

'Oh God. What, so, I feel it in my fingers...'

'...I feel it in my toes. Yeah. Pretty rough trying to keep a straight face while they stood there soberly reciting it at each other.'

'Still, it was cute,' Lana said. 'Billy started crying at one point.'

'Tears of joy?' Marcus asked.

'Yeah. I'm sure they were tears of joy. Come on, Stew, we'd better hand over our present.' She nudged Deano. 'Want to come with us, give Billy a few tips on how to do that thing she likes for the wedding night?'

'Yeah, go on. There is a trick to it.'

'I'll hang on while the queue goes down,' Marcus said. 'I've not known them as long as you lot. Better let close friends and family get congratulations in first.'

'I'll keep you company,' I said. 'I've got her wedding present to Billy in my bag. Don't really want to hand it over in front of an audience.'

'Is that the sexy photos?' Stew asked.

'Yep.'

'Eesh. Good thing we got them champagne. Sounds like Billy'll need a stiff drink.' He shot me a thumbs-up as Lana took his hand to guide him away. 'Oh, er, thanks for the suspenders, Becks.'

I smiled. 'Glad you enjoyed them.'

When they'd gone, Marcus nodded to Gerry, who was whispering to Sue in a corner with one hand on her backside. 'What's going on with the tacheless wonder over there?'

I laughed. 'Think I accidentally triggered a second honeymoon for them at Yolanda's photoshoot. Basques were involved.'

'Really?' He frowned. 'On which one? You can never tell with him these days.'

'Sue. Lana's traumatised. Still, good for them, I say.'

He turned back to me. 'Did you wear anything sexy?'

'Just a fancy frock.'

'This one?' he asked, scanning my floral cocktail dress. 'It's very pretty.'

'No, an evening gown.' I nodded to what he was wearing. 'Speaking of which, nice to see you dressed like a proper magician for once.'

'Thanks. Although to shatter the illusion, this tie's a clip-on.'

The invitations had said black tie and Marc had gone the full James Bond. It suited him.

'So do you fancy doing the tour of this crumbly old place before we get a drink?' I asked.

'You like a stately home, do you?'

I shrugged. 'Yeah. Must be getting to that National Trust membership age.'

'Heh, me too. Rock and roll, eh?'

He linked my arm and guided me into an adjoining room laid out like a study.

'I think I've still got that Famous Five mentality from when I was a kid,' I said. 'You know, where there might be a smuggler in every suit of armour and a secret passage behind every bookshelf.'

'It's more Scooby Doo for me. That haunted-house feeling the paintings' eyes are following you round the room.' He nodded to a portrait of a formidable old gent with God-like facial hair over the fireplace. 'Like that terrifying bastard.'

I shuddered. 'He is a bit scary. Wonder who he was.'

'Thaddeus Monkton, local mill owner. He was an illiterate woolcomber who worked his way to the top. New money, darling.'

'Oh, how terribly vulgar,' I said, turning up my nose. 'How'd you know that?'

'I know a lot of things. Come on.'

We toured the plush, elegant rooms, examining the old furniture and paintings. I loved the portraits particularly. Perhaps it was my photography background, but I couldn't help being fascinated by every face, every untold story. The painters always took such pains with the eyes.

Marcus really did know a lot of things, especially about the paintings. He seemed to have an endless supply of trivia – not technical stuff to do with technique or blend, like Cole, but little facts about what the colours meant or why someone was dressed a certain way. If the magic didn't work out, he'd make a great tour guide.

'Wonder what her story was,' I said, gazing dreamily at a painting of a young girl.

'Well, she was married. This is probably her bridal portrait. And when it was painted, her husband loved her very much.'

I shook my head. 'You can't know that.'

'Course I can. Magician, remember?'

I cocked an eyebrow and he grinned. 'Ok, if you promise not to tell I'll let you in on the secret.' He nodded to the girl's colourful gemstone necklace. 'It's all in the jewellery.'

'What is?'

'Her story.' He pointed to the gems. 'The deep red's a jasper. Purple, that's amethyst. Then a diamond, the jet black one's an onyx, ruby and emerald. It's an acrostic necklace. There was a fad in Victorian times for people to give them as wedding gifts, with the first letter of each stone spelling out a secret message.'

I followed the stones with my eyes. 'Jasper, that's J. J-A-D-O-R-E... Jadore. Was that her name?'

'*J'adore*, you plum. They didn't have a gem beginning with V easily available at the time. If you wanted to tell your wife you loved her, it was easiest to do it in another language.'

'Aww.' I looked at the woman's expressive green eyes. 'I'm glad she was happy. How did you know all that?'

He shrugged. 'Geology graduate, aren't I? I know rocks.'

'But how did you know about it being a bridal gift?'

'Promise you won't tell anyone? Because it could seriously damage my street cred.'

'I promise.'

'I'm a bit of a history buff,' he said, with the faintest trace of a blush.

'Not really?'

'Yeah. It's fascinating, entering another time. I like to read up on it between card tricks.'

'You're a surprising man, Marcus Teasdale.' I tugged his arm. 'I think we've seen everything. Let's go congratulate the new Mr and Mrs Yo-yo. I need to hand over these sexy pics before they burn a hole in my handbag.'

The queue of well-wishers had gone down now, and we discovered Yolanda and Billy sipping champagne by the bar with Gerry and Sue.

'Congrats, guys,' I said, giving them both a hug. 'Lovely ceremony. Very pink.'

'And from me,' Marcus said, shaking Billy's hand and planting a kiss on Yolanda's cheek. 'You look great, love.'

'Ta,' Billy said.

'I actually meant your missus. But yeah, you too. It's a very secure man who can pull off a suit like that.'

Billy glanced down at his pink tails, which came with a matching dicky bow and top hat. 'I don't half feel a tit.'

Gerry patted Sue's bum. 'Start married life as you mean to go on, lad, that's my advice. I'd get into the habit of doing as you're told now.'

Sue nodded. 'Saves time later.'

'This is a bit posh,' Marcus said, glancing round the red velvet drawing room. 'Didn't know they did wedding receptions here.'

'They don't usually,' Billy said. 'Your telly man sorted it as his present.'

'Harper?' I said. 'That was nice of him.'

'Aye, knows the owners. Personally I'd have been happy with the pub.'

'Well I wouldn't.' Yolanda rolled her eyes at me. 'Honestly, these boys. I've a good mind not to let him have his present.'

I smiled. 'Oh, go on. You worked so hard on it.'

Billy frowned. 'Present?'

'Have you got them, Rebecca?' Yolanda asked.

I handed over the packet of photos.

'What is it?' Billy said. 'Why're you all smirking at me?'

'Here you are, darling,' Yolanda said, giving him the packet. 'A little keepsake for our special day.'

Billy took one out to examine it, and his eyes went wide. 'Jesus Christ, lass!'

'That's what I said,' Gerry said.

'What's that you're waving about? A riding crop?'

Yolanda grinned. 'Certainly is.'

'The woman'll be the death of me,' Billy muttered. He held one of the photos up to examine it more closely. 'Er, did you hang onto the stockings, by any chance?'

'You'll find out later.'

Chapter 35

It was warmish, despite being late October, and some of the party had spilled out onto the lawn. When we'd done our congratulating, Marcus and I grabbed a champagne each and made our way out in search of friends.

We soon spotted Lana and Stew, talking to Harper and Maisie near a sort of folly. As usual, Gav was there, getting it all on film. You stopped noticing him after a bit.

'I think we need to change the dames' second song number,' Harper was saying when we joined them. 'It's not nearly as strong as the first.'

I smiled. 'Are you lot talking panto again? You're obsessed.'

'Says you,' Lana said. 'You're the worst of all of us. Apart from Deano, obviously.'

'Harper's right,' Marcus said. 'I'm Too Sexy is a weaker number than Sisters. Not enough melody.'

'You're getting a bit into this,' I said to Harper. 'What about your proper panto?'

He shrugged. 'I like ours better. They don't let me have any creative input with Aladdin.'

'Another creative input like that Welsh accent and I can see Deano lamping you one,' Stew said, laughing.

Maisie gave her husband a loyal squeeze. 'I liked your Welsh.'

He planted a kiss on her cheek. 'Thanks, Mais. It's sweet when you lie to me.'

'So what about the number then?' Marcus said. 'Maybe we could do a community song instead, get the audience involved. Agadoo or something.'

Stew's eyes widened. 'Oh God, no. If you're going to inflict Agadoo on me, you can find yourself a new audience.'

'We've already got Funky Gibbon. We can't have two community songs,' I said. 'Know what I think?'

Marcus took a sip of champagne. 'I do actually, you dirty mare.'

I elbowed him. 'That's my joke.'

'Don't see your name on it. So what do you think?'

'I reckon we should write something. We could make it local, like an in-joke for the village.'

'Such as?'

'I'm not sure yet,' I admitted.

'Have we really got time to –' Stew began, but he was interrupted by Lana grabbing his arm.

'Oh God,' she hissed.

'What?'

She nodded to a man making his way towards us. 'Jamie Collingwood.'

'Ugh,' Stew said, grimacing. 'Who invited him?'

'Yo-yo, probably. Suppose she couldn't not when the rest of the Collingwoods were asked.'

'Who is he?' I asked.

'Roger's great-nephew. He's that obnoxious prick you never want to invite to your wedding but you have to invite to your wedding. Every couple's got one.'

'Looks like he might be a pissed obnoxious prick too,' Marcus said, squinting at the squat, meaty figure weaving unsteadily over the lawn.

'I was at school with him,' Lana said. 'He hasn't changed a bit. And trust me, that's not a compliment. He hasn't even managed to move out of his mum's spare bedroom.'

'All right, Lana?' Jamie said when he reached us, his speech heavily slurred. 'Thought it was you I spotted hiding over here.'

'Jamie.' Lana's tone was distinctly chilly.

'How's the pie restaurant going? Managed not to eat all your stock?' He nudged Maisie, who was next to him, in a matey sort of way. 'She was a right little fatty at school. You could've boiled a couple of puddings in her gym knickers.'

Maisie didn't seem to know what to say to that. 'Well, er, she certainly looks great now,' she said, sending Lana an apologetic grimace.

Jamie blinked at her through the booze haze, his eyes fixing on her cleavage. 'Here, you're Maisie Moorhouse, aren't you?'

'Maisie Brady, honey.' She cast an affectionate glance at Harper. 'Mrs.'

'Hey, I bought every mag you were ever in, you know. Still got them. I keep them in the shed where my mum won't find them.'

'Oh? Well, always nice to meet a fan.' Maisie waggled her eyebrows at Lana in a desperate plea for rescue.

'Um, I'm just going to the little girls' room,' Lana said. 'Mais, can you show me where it is?'

'Nothing little about those girls,' Jamie muttered when they'd gone, making a chest-weighing gesture to the three lads. 'Funny how they flock together when they go to the bog, isn't it? Lasses, I mean. Like... birds or something.' He blinked like he'd had a sudden epiphany. 'Hey! Is that why they call them birds? Always wondered.'

'Ok, so the kids' big dance number,' I said to the boys, deciding ignoring Jamie till he got bored and went away was probably the best option. 'I was thinking, it'll be easier for them if we pin the tails of their costumes up so there's no chance of –'

'That was your missus, wasn't it?' Jamie said, interrupting me to talk to Harper.

'I'm sorry?' Harper said.

'You're Harper Brady off TV. That Maisie Moorhouse is your missus.'

'That's right,' Harper said, eyeing the staggering Jamie with an unimpressed lip-curl.

I tried again. 'Because Rita told me little Evie Barraclough tripped over hers the other day and nearly broke her glasses. I know it won't look as good, but it would be safer –'

'Christ, you lucky bastard,' Jamie said to Harper. 'Can't believe you can have them legs wrapped round your neck whenever you want.'

'– if we pinned the tails –'

'I bet she's well dirty. I mean, they call them glamour models, but they're just prozzies really.' He laughed drunkenly. 'Well, you'd know about that, you've shagged a few. Seen it in the papers. S'pose that's the best thing about marrying one: you get all the experience without having to pay for it.'

I gave up. No one was listening to me. All eyes were fixed on Jamie, with expressions of mingled shock and disgust.

Except for Harper. He smiled brightly.

'Sorry, I don't think I caught your name?' he said.

'Jamie. Jamie Collingwood.'

'Pleasure to meet you,' Harper said, shaking Jamie's hand.

'You too, mate. Big fan.'

'Right, I'm glad we got that out the way. I'd hate to do this to someone I hadn't been formally introduced to.'

The next bit was kind of a blur. There was a general impression of flying fist, followed by a high-pitched scream, and the next minute Jamie was holding his nose, groaning, as the tears streamed down his face.

Harper grabbed him by the collar. 'And next time you talk about my wife with anything but the most awesome respect, I'll break it for you. Now fuck off.'

'You're mental, you are,' Jamie whispered, backing away. 'I'm going to the tabloids with this. You wait.'

Harper shrugged. 'Go ahead, I've done worse. With my record it probably won't even make page five.'

When Jamie had gone to lick his wounds and see if the editor of *The Sun* was listed in the *Yellow Pages*, Harper turned to Gavin.

'I want that edited out.'

'You sure, Mr Brady? Early feedback did say viewers wanted more conflict.'

'Not that bit. Take it out.'

'You won't be able to cover it up, will you?' Marcus said, the first one of us to recover the power of speech. 'That knobhead'll be on the phone to some hack down in London before you make it home.'

'Don't care if he is,' Harper said, rubbing his knuckles. 'They can put it on the front page if they want. I just don't want Mais hearing what he said about her.'

'Harper, come here,' Stewart said.

Harper hung back, looking wary. 'You're going to bollock me, aren't you?'

'Just come here.'

'I didn't break his nose, Stew. It was a stage punch, that's all. Teach him a lesson.'

'I'm not going to bollock you.' Stew grabbed his cousin for a hug. 'Proud of you, mate.'

Harper blinked. 'Really?'

'Yeah. I mean, don't make a habit of it, for God's sake. But if he'd said that stuff about Lana, I would've done just the same.' Stew let him go. 'Come on, let's go find the girls. If he's already got to a journalist there could be press on the way. We should get you and Maisie out of here.'

'Jesus,' I muttered to Marcus when we were left alone. 'That was a bit exciting.'

'He's got hidden depths, that man, hasn't he?'

I shrugged. 'He loves his wife. They are pretty sweet, in their odd little celebrity way. Even if one of them does hate me.'

'She doesn't hate you. I told you, she's jealous. And I think she's coming round.'

I glanced up at him. 'You ever hit someone defending a girl's honour?'

He laughed. 'No, but someone hit me once. Well, stabbed me with a fork actually.'

'Bloody hell!'

'Yeah, over a girl called Charlotte. Here.' He unfastened his dinner jacket and pulled up his shirt to show me.

'Don't see anything,' I said, squinting at the flat abs of his stomach.

'Under the tattoo.'

I looked more closely at the flaming sun just above his hip. There were four little bumps under the ink that could've come from a fork.

'Must've been deep to leave a scar like that.'

He shrugged. 'You should see the other guy.'

'Who was the other guy?'

'Deano. I said Charlotte was a badly put-together heap of junk so he stuck a fork in me.' He smiled at the look on my face. 'Charlotte was a Meccano truck. He was seven, I was twelve.'

Chapter 35

I shook my head as he tucked his shirt back in. 'There must be a name for whatever his thing is.'

'There is. Deano.' He nudged me. 'Hey. We're all alone and I just flashed you. Aren't you worried people'll talk?'

'Still sulking about that?'

'Not sulking. I miss having you over though.'

'You see me in the pub.'

'Yeah, but it was nice having you to myself.'

I looked at him. From anyone else, that would have constituted serious flirting. But Marc just grinned in his oblivious way.

'What?' he said.

'Haven't you got other girls you could ask round?' I asked, genuinely interested. Marc never talked about his love life. 'Single ones who might want to sleep over and have sexy fun with you?'

'Yeah. They don't half look disappointed when I get the juggling balls out.'

'Seriously. Don't you go on dates?'

'Sometimes. I've got one tomorrow actually.'

I tried to ignore the pang of jealousy I had the hypocrisy to feel. 'Oh. Right. That girl Livvy?'

'Yep. Third date so I might even get lucky if I play my cards right. And I'm a magician so that's one thing I'm good at.'

'She seemed nice.'

'She is. It's going really well.' He gave my arm a squeeze. 'Hey, maybe we could make up a foursome with you and Cole sometime, what do you think?'

'Yeah. Maybe. Come on, let's go find the others.'

Chapter 36

'It's not right, you know,' Deano muttered darkly as he watched me help Roger into his costume.

'We promised Roger he could be the cow,' I said. 'Not his fault Cinderella doesn't have a cow, is it? Here, Rodge, lift your arms.'

'Know what else Cinderella doesn't have? A sodding Tyrannosaurus.'

'The kids asked for a T-Rex. We have to listen to our audience, Deano.'

'Tell you what, why don't we just do Jurassic Park: The Musical instead?' He shook his head. 'A T-Rex pulling the pumpkin coach. I can see the press write-ups now.'

'Wasn't it you who said the Egglethwaite pantomime should be unique, young man?' came the muffled voice of our rather pompous T-Rex.

'There's unique and there's plain weird. And this is me talking.' Deano turned to me. 'And do we have to have the line-dancing Pikachus?'

I shrugged. 'The kids wanted Pokémon. Just be grateful we vetoed Baby Jesus and the pooing donkey. That could've gone a bit *Life of Brian*.'

'You know this is going to be the most surreal panto ever?'

'I'm hoping it'll be remembered as quirky,' I said. 'Come on, Roger, let's get you to your pumpkin.'

I grabbed one of Roger's little dino arms and led him to the painted chipboard coach Yo-yo had brought, lovingly painted by her Ladies Who Lunch. Harper and Marcus were examining it.

Marcus waved to the dinosaur. 'Hi, Rodge. Looking good.'

'Hello Marcus,' Roger said. 'And Mr Brady. I'm told you punched my nephew in the face recently.'

'Yeah,' Harper said, grimacing. 'Sorry. Lost it a bit when he insulted my wife. We don't have a problem, do we?'

'I don't doubt he deserved it. It's been the popular opinion within the family that what young Jamie has needed for a very long time is a punch in the face.'

'Roger!' I said.

The T-Rex shrugged. 'No need to sound so shocked, my dear. You should hear what his mother has to say on the subject.' He turned to examine the coach. 'Oh, now this is rather impressive. The ladies have done well.'

The coach did look good. It was two-dimensional, with a little window and a handle for me to carry it. Swirling tendrils of pumpkin stalk – well, twilling – curled around it, with a simple leather harness to attach it to our dinosaur.

'Ok, Rodge, let's give it a whirl,' I said, guiding him into it. 'Show us your dino trot.'

I moved behind the coach and picked it up, then primmed my lips in my best Victorian-lady-in-the-park expression, which drew a laugh from Marcus.

'Home, James, and don't spare the T-Rexes,' I said, batting the harness imperiously. Roger gamely trotted off, leading me out onto the stage.

Gerry and Dad were there, practising their steps for the new number we'd written to replace I'm Too Sexy while Lana looked on. I put down my pumpkin and joined them.

I couldn't help a snicker at their new costumes. They were in a pair of matching 1920s-style Bathing Beauty swimsuits, each with a lace parasol. The rubber ducky hats were a nice touch too.

'New song's sounding good, Becks,' Lana said. 'You and Marc have done a great job on the lyrics.'

'You don't think Kit'll be offended, do you?'

'Are you kidding? He'll love it.'

'Go on then, Dad,' I said. 'From the top.'

Sue started playing Billy Joel's Uptown Girl and Dad and Gerry launched into their new song, Hot Tub Girls. Marc and I had only written it the week before so they hadn't had long to practise, but they'd certainly risen to the challenge, improvising a pretty hilarious sexy-unsexy dance routine.

When they'd finished, Roger laughed. 'Oh, very good. That's bound to go down well.'

'Er, cheers, Barney,' Dad said, squinting at him.

'That you in there, Rodge?' Gerry said.

'Yes. Hello, Gerry.' He nodded to the other two. 'Danny. Lana.'

'Ha!' Gerry slapped him on the back. 'Beats being a cow's arse, eh, lad?'

'You're very chipper today,' I said.

'Why shouldn't I be? Life's good.' Gerry sent a little finger-wiggle wave to Sue on piano, who blushed and waved back.

'This is all your bloody fault,' Lana muttered to me. 'You and your basques. Now look what you've done.'

We were interrupted by Deano, who was anxious to get things started.

It was the first time we'd done a full run-through with the entire cast and crew, and luckily for Deano's ever-twitching mad eye, it was pretty problem-free. Lana remembered most of her lines without prompts. Harper's drunken dancing went down well with the kiddies in the juvenile chorus, who were allowed to sit in the audience when they weren't needed on stage. The line-dancing Pikachus, with tails pinned up for safety, managed to perform all their steps without incident. Even the new song, the least-rehearsed part of the performance, went well, with the kids cracking up at Gerry's constantly deflating boobies.

The only real problem was Maisie.

'No, no, no!' Deano yelled when for the third time in a row she failed to deliver her pet rock line in a way that would get a laugh.

'Didn't I do it right?'

'No you didn't do it right. You never do it right.' He shook his head. 'Have you practised at all?'

'Of course I've practised,' she said, drawing herself up. 'Haven't I, Harper?'

He nodded. 'We rehearse together every night. That's why she's line-perfect.'

'It's not her memory that's the problem,' Deano said. 'It's her complete inability to bloody act that's going to sink my panto.'

Maisie's face crumpled.

Harper frowned. 'No need, mate.'

'I know. Sorry,' Deano said, pushing his fingers into his hair. 'Sorry, Mais, I didn't mean that. You are getting better. Just... keep working on your delivery, ok?'

'Ok, Chef,' she mumbled. 'I'll try.'

We made it through the next few scenes without incident, and Deano was actually smiling by the time we reached the ball. I sailed on stage in the new, lighter dress I'd borrowed from Fancypants, confident I could manage to glide around the ballroom without giving Maisie an asthma attack. Now that the stage was fully loaded with the eight members of the adult chorus as well as principals, it felt for the first time like I was turning up to a real ball.

It was when Lana bellowed Maisie's cue that we realised we had a problem.

'His royal highness, Prince Charming of Rummancoke!'

And... nothing.

'Oh God, not again,' Deano muttered. 'For fu–' He caught sight of a little Pikachu, picking her nose in the wings, and his eye started going. 'For flipping heck's sake. Will somebody go find the prince and tell him he's missed his blood– his ruddy cue again please?'

'I'll go.' I gave his shoulder a squeeze as I walked past. 'Don't be too hard on her, eh? I think you really hurt her feelings before.'

She wasn't backstage. I knew she couldn't be bonking in a cupboard with Harper this time either. He was in the audience with Stew.

'For God's sake,' I muttered. Deano's head was going to explode if this kept happening.

I headed downstairs to the toilets. There was no sound from the cleaner's cupboard, thankfully, but when I pushed open the door to the Ladies, there was a noise coming from in there. It sounded like... sobbing.

'Hello?'

No answer. I crouched down to look under the doors. Sure enough, a pair of heeled principal boy boots attached to a couple of long, shapely legs were visible in the second cubicle.

I knocked on the door. 'You missed your cue again, Mais.'

'Go... away,' she sobbed. 'I'm not coming.'

'Open the door, love. Let me take you to Harper.'

'No. I'm staying here where Gav can't get at me.'

'You can't hide forever.'

'Can too.'

'Let me in then.'

There was silence, just the sound of gulped sobs filling the empty air. Then I heard the lock slide back.

Chapter 36

Maisie was sitting on the closed loo seat, mascara streaked down her face.

'What's up, Maisie?' I said gently. 'Is this because Deano told you off?'

'Yes,' she sniffed. 'A bit.'

'He does it to all of us, you know. It's nothing personal.'

'He hates me. You all hate me because I've got no talent.'

'Come on, you know that's not true.'

'Yeah? Then tell me which of you voted for me to play this part. I bet Deano didn't, did he?'

'No,' I admitted. 'But that doesn't mean he hates you.'

'What about Marc?'

'He doesn't hate you either.'

'But I bet he didn't vote for me. Because I'm the world's worst actor, right?'

'You're not the world's worst actor.'

She ignored me. 'So that just leaves Stew and Lana, because they're Harper's family, and that pervert from the pub. Real vote of confidence.'

'Not just them. I voted for you.'

'I know. And now you hate me most of everyone.' She looked up through bleary eyes. 'Did you really vote for me because you thought I could be good?'

'Well... partly, yeah,' I said, deciding honesty was probably the best policy at this stage. 'You know, with enough practice. But also because I thought you'd help us make some cash for this place.'

'I thought so. The legs, right? Everyone's a big fan of the legs. Oh, and the breasts. Sometimes even I forget there's a head stuck on top.'

There was a knock at the door.

'Are you two in there?' Harper called.

'Yeah, Maisie's not feeling too hot,' I called back. 'Can you get Deano to call a time-out for ten minutes?'

'All right,' he said. 'You ok, babe? Need me to get you anything?'

'I'm fine,' Maisie said, trying not to sound too choked. 'Er, period pains. Just waiting for the ibuprofen to kick in.'

'Maybe I did mainly vote for you to make money for the Temp,' I said when he'd gone. 'You're famous and Harper's famous, and people like to see famous people. That doesn't mean I think you're a bad actor.'

'I am though. I stopped kidding myself ages ago. Harper's the only person who still thinks I've got any talent, and he's biased.'

'You're better than you think,' I said earnestly. 'You've surprised me, sometimes. You just need to channel the character.'

She laughed. 'In a pantomime?'

'In a pantomime more than anything. Kids need to believe it's real far more than adults do.' I stopped, hit by a sudden idea, and filed it away for later.

'You know why I started modelling, Becky?' Maisie said.

'Because you're gorgeous?'

She smiled. 'You're sweet. But yeah, kind of. Because I looked good, but mainly because I was shit at everything else.'

'That's bollocks,' I said firmly. 'You're an amazing dancer, for a start.'

'No. I'm an ok dancer, and that's after years of practice.'

'Well, that's the same for everyone. Nobody gets good at anything without practice.'

'Maybe. But taking my clothes off was easy money, something I didn't need to work at to do well. It ruined my life for a while, but it was easy money.'

'Ruined your life!'

'Until I met Harper, yeah. I was never ashamed of the work, but when it came to my private life – I mean, my confidence was shot, my love life in tatters. All the blokes I went out with saw in me were tits and legs.' She let out a bleak laugh. 'And because I got them out for a living, some of them thought they were entitled to tell me to get them out for them whenever they felt like it. Some of them were... not nice men, Becky.'

'Hmm. I'm guessing Harper told you what that guy said at Yo-yo's wedding?'

'He told me he thumped someone. I worked out the rest.' She smiled fondly. 'He's so naive. He thinks he can protect me from that stuff, I haven't got the heart to tell him I've been hearing it for years. Trust me, the man he punched was a long way from the first guy to call me a whore.'

I flinched. 'Don't use that word. It's horrible.'

'Not my word, honey. Their word.' She grabbed some loo roll to mop her eyes. 'That's one reason I fell for Harper. Ok, there was that physical aspect to it, when we met. I knew it was my body that first attracted him to me, and vice versa, if I'm honest. But he does love me. For myself, I mean.'

I smiled. 'He really does.'

'I'd never had a boyfriend like him. We'd been together a month when he took me home to meet his aunty and uncle, and Stew and Lana, and he seemed so proud of me – like he really respected me, you know? And his family were lovely. They made me feel like I belonged.'

'Does he get on with your parents?'

She flushed. 'We're not really in touch. They're dead religious. Don't approve of the whole modelling thing.'

'Here. Budge up.' She shifted over on her loo seat so I could plant half a bum down. 'You belong here too, you know. We're your friends now.'

'But I've been so mean to you,' she mumbled. 'On TV and everything.'

'Yeah. Why was that?'

She shrugged. 'Jealous, I guess.'

'Seriously?' I shook my head. 'That's what Marc said, but I didn't believe him. I thought you were just being bitchy.'

'I was really,' she admitted. 'You're so bloody good at everything, aren't you? You can act, sing, juggle. You're funny. I'm just the lass who gets her tits out in the papers.'

'Not to us you're not. You're Maisie.'

She glanced up. 'How do you do it so it feels real like that? The acting?'

'Well, I...' I frowned. 'Dunno really. S'pose it's all about being in the character's head. Feeling what they feel, seeing things how they see them. Accepting a new reality, then chucking a bit of empathy at it.'

'Harper's always saying stuff like that. Sounds like nonsense to me.'

'It's hard to explain. You'll get it though, eventually.' I stood up. 'We'd better go up. Just remember that we've got your back, ok? You can do this.'

'You really believe that?'

'I really do. Now come on, love. Fix your make-up, take me up those stairs and convince me you want to marry me. We shall go to the ball.'

Maisie grabbed my arm as I turned to leave the cubicle. 'Becky, can I tell you a secret?'

'Dunno. Is it something good?'

'I don't know yet,' she said, flushing. 'You can't tell anyone though, ok? Not even Harper.'

I frowned. 'What is it, Mais?'

'It's me.' She took a deep breath. 'I'm going to have a baby.'

Chapter 37

Date: one month until opening night.

It was the second week in November, and in the shop windows and public buildings of Egglethwaite, it was beginning to look a lot like Christmas. Even at the Fox, despite Billy's rumblings that it got earlier every year, there was a smattering of pink tinsel over the quiz machine. The place was looking a lot more feminine since its new landlady had taken up residence.

That Saturday was the afternoon of our big Christmas Fair, and when I arrived at the Temp, it was already in full swing. I fought my way through the throng of villagers browsing stalls to Stew, who was leaning against the wall beaming at Lana while she played a Frosty the Snowman solo with Egglethwaite Silver up on stage.

'Bloody hell. It looks like somebody sicked up Christmas round here,' I said. There were two huge decorated trees flanking the stage, swathed in multi-coloured fairy lights. Giant metallic baubles in red and gold were strung from every beam and the rich scents of cloves and cinnamon and pine mingled in the air.

'Yeah, Yo-yo and the decorating committee went a bit over the top. Happens every year.' Stew glanced at what I was wearing. 'Pretty festive yourself.'

I was in a knitted reindeer jumper, a flashing LED keeping the nose rosy. Posters had said there was a competition for the best Christmas jumper, with the chance to win a pie and a pint at Pie and a Pint, so I thought I'd better show willing.

'Thanks,' I said. His eyes had fixed on Lana and the band again. 'You look very proud today.'

'Why shouldn't I look proud? It's not everyone who's got a tromboning wife. You haven't got one.'

'Ok, you've got me there.'

'Here, Becks. Have a cigar.' He took a large, shrink-wrapped cigar from his pocket and handed it to me.

'Er, thanks,' I said, blinking at it. 'I don't smoke though.'

'Doesn't matter. You can keep it as a souvenir.'

'Oh my God!' I said as the penny dropped. 'Are these new-dad cigars? You two got matched to a kid, didn't you?'

'Yep,' he said, grinning. 'Jay, two years old, cute as a button. We're going to meet him next week.' He took out his phone and showed me a photo of a tousle-haired little boy, grinning at the camera with his teeth and mouth covered in chocolate.

'Awww. What a sweetheart.'

'Isn't he? If it all goes as planned, we'll be mum-and-dadding in the new year.'

'Congratulations, Stew. That's brilliant news.' I grabbed him for a hug. 'You'll be fantastic.'

'Lana will be. I'm just planning to follow her lead.' He nodded towards the floor. 'Someone small seems to be trying to get our attention.'

Pip was smirking up at us, clutching a couple of gift-wrapped parcels. While dressed as a camel, for some reason.

'Hello, tiny,' I said, lifting her up. 'Oof. Getting heavy. Why are you a camel?'

'Because she's got the hump,' Stew said. 'Get it, Pips? That's a joke.'

Pip giggled. 'Yeh, coz camels are humpy.'

'Why really though?' I asked her.

'Beavers're doing a play when Aunty Lana's band stop. S'called an activity.'

Stew looked puzzled. 'Activity?'

'I think she means a nativity,' I said, smiling.

'Oh. Why've you got two presents, Pips?'

'Santa gave them me,' she told him proudly.

'Been to see the big man, have you?'

'Yep.' She pointed through the door to the backstage area, where we'd made a grotto for Gerry and his entourage – one elf, as played by Noah, a spotty teenager who had a Saturday job up at Holyfield Farm, and Rudolph the Red-Nosed Sheepdog, portrayed for the third year in a row by Flash. 'He's in there. He doesn't live there though, he lives at the North Pole.'

'That's a long way to come just to see us.'

'Yeh, but he's magic so he can do it fast.'

'Weren't you frightened?' I asked her. 'Last year you wouldn't say a word to him.'

'He's not so scary now I'm big.' She cocked her head thoughtfully. 'And he smells like Grandad Gerry now, so that makes him not scary too.'

'Roll-ups and beer?' Stew muttered to me. 'I bet he does.'

Pip giggled. 'Santa's got Flash, Uncle Stew. He's pretending to be a reindeer. Santa said his real reindeers weren't allowed in coz they'd poo everywhere.'

'That's right,' Stew said gravely. 'Santa asked me and Aunty Lana and we said Flash wouldn't mind being a reindeer for the day.'

'How come Santa let you have two presents, Pips?' I asked. 'You're only supposed to be allowed one before Christmas.'

'Coz I told him I was getting a new cousin but not till after Christmas and he said I could save a present for him.'

Stew laughed. 'Sounds like a sneaky way to get extra presents to me.'

Someone nudged me. I peered round the bundle of kid in my arms at Cameron and Tom.

'Think you've got something that belongs to us,' Cam said.

'Here you go,' I said, plonking Pip back down on the floor. 'I was getting arm-ache anyway. Heavy things, camels.'

'I actually meant that boxset of *Breaking Bad* I lent you.' He shrugged. 'But go on, we'll take the child while we're here.'

'Look at Papa's jumper,' Pip whispered, tugging at my sleeve. 'It's really silly. Isn't it, Aunty Becky?'

I scanned Tom's Christmas jumper, which bore a knitted Darth Vader and the legend 'I find your lack of cheer disturbing'.

'Nice, Tommy. Geek chic.'

'This is my lucky jumper, I'll have you know, little girl,' Tom said, crouching down to tickle his daughter.

'Why is it lucky?' Pip asked, squirming. 'Does it make you win things?'

He smiled up at his husband. 'Well, I was wearing it when I won one thing I'm quite attached to.' Cam squeezed his shoulder fondly.

'I want hot chocolate,' Pip told them in an imperious little voice, oblivious to any notion of romance between people as ancient as her parents.

Cameron shook his head. 'Try again with the magic word, Pips.'

'Please may I have hot chocolate. With marshmallows.'

'Better. Now we just need to work on turning it into a question.' Cam waved goodbye. 'See you later, guys. Congrats again, Stew.'

'And cheers for the cigars,' Tom said.

They each took one of Pip's hands and half walked, half swung her towards the kitchen hatch, where some Ladies Who Lunch were serving refreshments.

'So did you pick up any tips there?' I asked Stew.

'Yeah, one. Do you think if I told Gerry I was just minding it, he'd let me have Harper's present too?'

The band were downing instruments to take a break. Lana stuck her trombone on its stand and joined us.

'Did Stew tell you the news?' she demanded.

'That he's got a devious plan to con Father Christmas out of two gifts? Yeah.'

She nudged her husband. 'You did tell her, didn't you?'

I pulled out my cigar and gave it a Groucho-style waggle.

She grinned. 'He did tell you.'

'Yep. Congratulations, love. You're going to be amazing.'

She threw herself at me for a hug. 'God, I've got no idea what I'm doing. I was planning on following Stew's lead.'

'Ha! You'll be following each other round in circles.' I patted her back. 'Well, don't worry. Show me a parent who claims they're not making it up as they go and I'll show you a big fat liar.'

'So do you girls want to go see Santa? Becks needs to tell him what she wants for Christmas.' Stew smiled at his wife. 'We already got our present.'

'Yeah, go on,' I said. 'I'm dying to see Gerry in his suit.'

'No Cole?' Lana asked as we queued up behind the excited kids and slightly less excited parents waiting to see Santa.

'No, he's working.'

'How did his big exhibition go?'

I frowned. 'Dunno really. He's been very quiet since he got back.'

In fact, I'd barely seen him. He'd taken to locking himself in the attic until all hours again, which usually meant that whatever he was working on was all-absorbing.

'Not as well-attended as he'd hoped?' Stew said.

'Well, he said it went ok, but he doesn't seem keen to talk about it. Hope there's nothing wrong.'

Gerry's grotto was a simple affair, a sort of den made of white bedsheets, fairy lights and tinsel, with the sullen-looking elf, his green velvet suit rather clashing with his acne, taking money at the door. And yet, basic as it was, to the kids it was magical. It worked like some sort of kiddy happiness factory, children entering through the slit in the bedsheets at one side, gripping a parent's hand nervously, then emerging beaming from the other side five minutes later with a gift-wrapped parcel clutched in their fist.

Eventually we reached the front of the queue.

'50p per kid,' Noah the Elf muttered, voice cracking with sulk and puberty.

'We haven't got a kid. We've come to tell your boss what we want for Christmas.' Stew pressed £1.50 into the lad's unresisting hand. 'We'll show ourselves in.'

'Ho ho – oh, it's you lot,' Gerry said, glancing up. 'In that case, ho ho bugger off.'

Lana grinned. 'Come on, Santa. That's no way to talk to good boys and girls, is it?'

Rudolph, dozing next to the sack of presents, pricked up his ears. He bounced up and headbutted Lana in the leg with his antlers.

I sat down in the little chair next to Gerry's and crossed myself. 'Forgive me, Father, for I have sinned. It's been eleven months since my last Christmas.'

Stewart plonked himself down on Gerry's knee.

'All right, Gerry, how long do I have to stay here for a train set?'

'Oof. Geroff, you big daft lump,' Gerry said, pushing him away. 'You aren't worth the price of a lapdance.'

Lana gave Stew's arm a sympathetic pat as he went back to join her. 'I think you are.'

'Thanks, wife. I'll give you a private performance later.'

'So have you kids just come to take the piss then?' Gerry demanded. 'Because if you want to make yourselves useful, I could murder a beer. Thirsty work, Santaing.'

'Santas don't drink beer. Just sherry,' I said. 'And no, we didn't just come to take the piss.'

'We mainly did,' Lana said.

'All right, we mainly did,' I agreed. 'But we've got a message for you from Deano as well.'

'He's not on about my tits again, is he?'

'Jeez, Gerry, get over yourself,' Stew said, rolling his eyes. 'It's not all about your tits, you know. You aren't that sexy.'

'Not what my missus says.'

Lana curled her lip. 'Can you and Sue please stop talking about your manky sex life in front of me?'

Gerry grinned. 'All right, since I'm in uniform. Go on, what's the message?'

'Deano's managed to arrange some press for our last dress rehearsal, sort of an advance screening,' I told him. 'Get us some reviews ahead of opening night.'

'*Keighley News*, is it?'

'Not just them. The county papers too.'

'What, the *Yorkshire Post* are sending someone out just to write up a village panto?' Gerry said. Then realisation dawned. 'Ah, right. Brady.'

Stew nodded. 'We'll never be short of attention with Harper involved.'

'So best foot forward, Grizzly,' I said to Gerry, slapping him on the back. 'Because from the state of Deano's eye when he told us, I'm thinking it could be painful.'

Chapter 38

The day dawned the same as any other. I was running around like a chicken on speed, late for work as usual. Cole was hiding out in the attic, also as usual.

'Cole!' I yelled up the stairs. 'If you're not going out today, can I borrow your mobile? I can't find mine and I need to let our Cam know I can pick Pip up from Beavers tonight.'

There was no answer.

'Cole?' I called again.

'Yes, darling. Whatever you like,' a distracted voice sailed down.

'Thanks.' I snatched the neglected smartphone from the dresser and stuck it in my jeans pocket. 'I'll ring the landline if I need you.'

It sat in my back pocket for most of the day, silent as the grave. I'd actually forgotten I had it until the ringtone went off at full volume in Fancypants that afternoon, making me jump.

'Sorry,' I said to the customer I was helping, a woman hiring a school assembly costume for her son. 'The Gruffaloes are on the kiddies' rail by the changing rooms.'

When she'd gone to browse, I nipped into the back room to answer the call.

'Hi Ryder.'

'Oh. Becky. Is Cole not around?'

'No, I borrowed his phone for the day. Can I get him to ring you back this evening?'

'Unless you can help me?' Ryder said. 'I was calling for his decision. The patrons are pushing so I need to know ASAP.'

'Patrons?'

'Rather a coup for you, old girl, eh? I expect soon you'll have the sort of life you must have dreamed of back in the old family chip shop.'

'I'm sorry?'

'Oh bugger, I haven't offended you again, have I?' he groaned. 'You really shouldn't be so sensitive. Honestly, I wasn't suggesting you were only with him because you knew he'd make money one day.'

'Ryder. Stop.' I took a deep breath. 'I have literally no idea what you're on about. What patrons?'

'Mine, of course.' He sounded amused. 'You mean Cole didn't tell you?'

'Clearly not.'

'I've wangled him a job, darling. Artist in residence at the gallery, his own permanent exhibition space – it's the chance of a lifetime. The patrons got a raging hard-on for his stuff at the last exhibition. I would have thought he'd have bitten my hand off, but he said he wanted to talk it through with you first.' He laughed. 'As if you were going to object.'

'Artist in residence! You mean in London?'

'Well of course in London, where else? You can hardly expect a talent like Cole to waste his fragrance on the desert air in the wilds of Yorkshire forever.'

'When did this happen?'

'I told you, the exhibition. They spoke to me and I was able to make him the offer on the spot.'

The exhibition. The exhibition... had been over three weeks ago. And Cole had never breathed a word.

'I need to talk to Cole,' I said. 'He'll call you, Ryder.'

I managed to struggle through the rest of the afternoon, but my mind was all over the place. Ryder's words ricocheted around my head: *the chance of a lifetime...*

Cole's dream job, the opportunity to paint full-time, everything he'd always wanted. But what did it mean for us? And the biggest question – why the hell hadn't he told me?

And what would I have said if he had? What would I say, later today, when we had the conversation I knew we needed to have? This was Cole's dream. If I stood in the way, I'd hate myself.

But if he took it...

No. Even with a decent cashflow, even with a house big enough for a family, I couldn't go back to London. I'd left my home once before, when I'd been young and the city had seemed full of bright lights and wonders. I couldn't do it again. My parents were here. Cam, Tom, Pip. Lana, Stew, Marcus... even Deano. I hadn't realised, until I started thinking about it, how painful it would be to leave Egglethwaite now I was a part of the place.

But the alternative... the alternative was losing Cole.

Maybe there was a way out of it. Maybe I didn't need to choose. Cole could commute into town when he was needed at the gallery, and... well, somehow we'd work round it.

But the harder I clutched, the more the straws seemed to slide out of my grip.

I was supposed to be picking Pip up from Beavers, but after ringing round I managed to arrange for Cynthia to do it, mumbling some excuse. As soon as I closed the shop, I rushed home.

Cole was sitting in his studio, staring at a painting he'd been working on: a local landscape, sheep-starred and arteried with our shambling drystone walls.

'Oh. Hullo, darling,' he said absently when he heard me come in. 'What do you think? It still needs work, of course.'

Chapter 38

'It's brilliant. One of your best.'

'Yes. You know, I think it might be.'

'Cole, we need to talk.'

He turned to look at me. 'You heard then.'

'How did you know?'

He smiled. 'I've been with you for four years, Becky. I can tell when there's something wrong.' His expression was strange. Dreamy, wistful. Sad.

'Why didn't you tell me, love?'

'I meant to. I tried to.'

'And yet you didn't.'

'Here.' He drew a spare stool opposite his. I sat down, and he took my hands in his. 'Now let's pretend the Honesty Card's right there on the table, shall we?'

'Ok.'

'Becky, I love you. You know that, don't you?'

'Of course.' I squeezed his hands tightly, fearing what might come next. 'Why are you telling me now?'

'Because I want to hear you say it back.'

'I love you, Cole. You know I do.'

'Yes.' He sighed. 'Yes, I know.'

'So are you going to take it? Ryder said it was the chance of a lifetime.'

'I don't know.' He dropped my hands and went to stand under the skylight, looking up at the star-flecked sky. 'If I did, would you be coming with me?'

'Would you really have to move to London?'

'I'm afraid so.'

'I... Cole, you know I –'

He held up a hand. 'It's ok. I knew you'd have to stay. This place – it's a part of you, I understand that.'

'Yes,' I whispered. 'And you have to go.'

'Maybe I don't. I haven't decided to take it yet.'

'But it's your dream, Cole.'

'One of them.' He came and rested his hands gently on my shoulders. 'The only other dream I ever had was you, Becky. And before I choose one over the other, I think I'd like to get a few things out in the open.'

'Oh, love...' I reached up to squeeze his hand, blinking on a tear.

'Becky, you've asked me more than once recently if I wanted to be a father. And each time I said I wanted you to be happy.'

'Yes.'

He took his seat again, earnest blue eyes searching my face. 'And I do, darling, I really do. I honestly believed when we came here that it would all work out, eventually. That spending time with your niece would help me find the parental instinct I was sure I must have.'

'But it didn't.'

He looked down at his hands. 'I've never believed I was a cruel or an uncaring man. But children, to me, they just seem...'

'You don't like them?'

He met my eyes. 'You want to know the truth?'

'I think I need to.'

'Well then, the fact is... they bore me. There. I said it.'

'What?'

'Children. I just can't think on their wavelength. I don't like being around them because... because I find them tedious. Their conversation, their company, their games. And the more time I spend with them, the more irritating it becomes.'

'So you... that means you'd never...'

'I did want to make you happy.' He sighed. 'But on reflection, I really feel I'm one of those men who isn't cut out for fatherhood.'

I stared at him in disbelief. 'And you tell me *now?*'

'I didn't know before. When we moved here I had some doubts, but I thought... I mean, you wanted it so badly, I believed things would just naturally fall into place.'

'For years we've talked about this, Cole! You told me...' I gave in and let the tears I'd been holding in flow freely. 'You said it was what you wanted,' I whispered.

'I thought it was. It's what we're all told we're supposed to want, isn't it? I didn't realise how much my brain would revolt when confronted with the reality of the thing.' He leaned forward and took my hands again. 'So I suppose what I'm asking is, is it absolutely a dealbreaker for you? Do you want a child more than you want this – us?'

'I... Jesus. That's a hell of a question to spring on me, Cole.'

'Don't pretend you haven't been thinking about it.'

I was silent a moment. I thought about Pip and Cameron and Tom. About Lana and Stew, and the little boy, Jay, who was about to become theirs. About my dad and Cynthia, and the loving, joyful home I'd grown up in. Here in Egglethwaite, the place I'd always known I wanted my own children to call home.

'Yes,' I whispered. 'Yes, it... Cole, I'm sorry. I think, for me... it has to be a dealbreaker.'

'You want a family more than you want to be with me?'

'I want – I did want both. But if you're telling me I can only have one or the other...' I bit my lip. 'Cole, sweetheart, I'm so sorry, but I guess I just am that kind of person. I want to be a mum.'

'I know. I love you for it. I just wish I could be the person you need me to be.' He shook his head sadly. 'But even then, I don't know if it would work.'

'Why?' I whispered, not bothering to check the tears dripping down my cheeks and into the turpentine-stained boards of the floor.

'Honesty Card still on the table?'

'We're breaking up, aren't we? It might as well be.'

He walked over to one of his paintings and started examining the canvas, presumably so he didn't have to look at my tear-stricken face. I could see he was fighting a battle not to break down himself.

'Becky, do you know what I've been doing the evenings you've been at pantomime rehearsals?' he asked after a minute. His voice was trembling.

'Painting?'

'No. I've been watching your actor friend's television show.'

'*The Brady Bunch*? Why?'

'Oh, it's a fascinating study,' he said, turning to face me again. 'The little dog's rather a character. And your director – Deano, is it? But it was you and Marcus I noticed particularly. The way you laugh together. The childish games you play.'

'I told you, Cole, we're friends. That's what friends do. I mean, not your friends. But it's what my friends do.'

'Perhaps. But when you're with him, it's like you're another person to the one I know. I might have liked to know her, but... but you never are that person with me.' He pulled his gaze from the floor to meet my eyes. 'How long is it since we last made love, Becky?'

'What?'

'You and me. How long?'

'God, I don't know... a couple of months?'

'Four. It's four months.'

I flushed. 'Well, I've been tired. With the panto and everything. You said it was ok.'

'But I've been thinking about it more lately. What it means – your body language with him, our sex life, the way you obviously missed him when you stopped going to his house for script meetings. And I finally got it all worked out.'

Chapter 38

I shook my head. 'You're not saying you've been locked up here soul-searching because you think I fancy Marcus Teasdale more than you?'

'No. Not because you fancy him.' He turned away, and I finally saw the flash of the tear he'd been holding back. 'Because you've fallen in love with him.'

Chapter 39

'So Cole's moved out,' Cynthia said as we drank tea together the following week.

'Ugh. You and your bloody lemons.' I plucked the offending wedge off the saucer and put it on the table. 'Yes. He's staying with his friend Patrick while he works out his notice.'

'What happened, Becky? Did you have a row?'

'Not exactly.' I squeezed back a tear. 'He had to make a choice. His dream job in London or me, here.'

'And he chose the job.'

'I chose for him. When he told me he'd changed his mind about having kids, I knew we couldn't have a future together.' The tear escaped and dripped into my teacup. 'I miss him, Cyn.'

'He said that? After three years you've been planning a family?' She shook her head. 'Your father and I always felt he wasn't the one for you.'

'It wasn't his fault. I honestly don't think he knew himself until recently.' I wiped my eyes to bring her back into focus. 'Cyn?'

'Yes, honey?'

I gazed down at the hands twisting in my lap. My finger felt weird without my engagement ring. 'That wasn't the only thing. He said... there was something else. I wanted to talk to you about it.'

Her eyebrows lifted. 'He didn't meet someone else?'

'Not him.' I closed my eyes so I didn't have to read her expression. 'Cole thinks... Cyn, he told me I'd fallen in love with another man.'

'Do you think you have?'

'I... honestly, I don't know. There's someone I can't seem to stop thinking about, just lately.'

'Oh my God!' She paused, watching my twitching features. 'Marcus Teasdale.'

I stared at her. 'How did you know that?'

'Your dad and I have had our suspicions a while,' she admitted. 'Danny told me how close the two of you have gotten. And we've been watching the show.'

'Was it really that obvious?'

She smiled. 'Afraid so, sweetie, to anyone who knows you like we do.'

I sipped my tea to give me an excuse to break eye contact. It was weird to think my one-sided love affair with Marcus, if that's what it was, had been playing out in all its glorious, in-your-face Technicolor for the nation while the two leads remained merrily oblivious.

'Have you told your friends?' Cynthia asked. 'About the break-up?'

'Just Lana. I'd like to keep it quiet until after the panto, if I can. I really can't deal with all the questions and the looks and... you know, everything.'

'You're still going ahead with the pantomime then?'

'Well, yeah. I can't let everyone down now. We open in three weeks and the Temp's counting on us.'

'Will you see Cole again?'

'Yes, tonight. He's coming over after rehearsal to pick up some of his stuff.' I put my tea down. I couldn't drink it with the lump that kept rising in my gullet.

'You know you did the right thing, don't you?' Cynthia said gently.

'Logically, yes. Doesn't stop me missing him though.' I smiled sadly. 'I know you never thought he was right for me, but I did love him.'

'I know you did, my love. But that's not always enough, is it? Not when you want different things.'

I sighed. 'We had so many plans, Cyn. It almost feels like a bereavement, giving up on them all.'

'You're not giving up on them. You just won't be doing them with Cole.' She came to sit on the side of my chair and put her arm around me. 'A relationship has to be a partnership, Becky, or it just won't work. I'm glad you found that out sooner rather than later.'

'Me too,' I said. 'Imagine if he'd only worked out he didn't want to be a father after he was one. What a nightmare for all three of us.'

'So what will you do about Marcus?'

'What I feel for Marc... God, I don't know what I feel for him. What I do know is what he feels for me. Bugger all.'

'You really believe that?'

'Romantically, yeah. It's like... like we're best friends. But he's never given any sign he sees me as more than that.'

'There's no better basis for a solid relationship than a solid friendship,' Cynthia said, echoing Lana's dodgy perfect-partner quiz. 'Do you think you've fallen for him?'

'I don't know. I... I don't know what to feel. What it's ok to feel.' I blew my nose on the tissue she handed me. 'Is that even possible, to love two people at once?'

'I believe it.' She dipped her head to look into my eyes. 'But I think if you're honest with yourself, you'll find the feelings aren't quite the same kind.'

I hid my face in her arm to avoid that shrewd, understanding gaze. Cyn couldn't know, could she, that whenever Cole had tried to initiate anything in the bedroom recently, I'd been unable to go through with it?

And now I really looked into my feelings, I could see what was wrong. It was Marcus. I hadn't been able to bring myself to have sex with Cole because it felt like... like I'd be betraying Marcus.

I burst into tears against her shoulder and she made soothing noises until I was quiet again.

'Oh, sweetie,' she said softly. 'It'll all be ok.'

'How will it?'

'I don't know,' she admitted. 'But I'm the parent and that's the sort of thing I'm supposed to say.'

'Well, Brownie points for trying.' I reached up to squeeze her hand. 'I'm glad I've got the panto to focus on, stop me brooding. It's the last rehearsal before the press showing on Wednesday.'

'Oh yeah, the press showing. Your dad's been talking about nothing else for days.' She patted my shoulder. 'Thanks for getting him involved in this, Becky. It was just what he needed.'

'He was just what we needed. Turns out he's one of nature's dames.' I glanced up at her. 'He'll be a bit bereft when it's over, won't he? Hope he doesn't have an existential crisis relapse.'

She groaned. 'Oh God. You haven't heard then.'

'Heard what?'

'He's found a new hobby. Gerry's talked him into joining the Egglethwaite Morrismen.' She shook her head. 'Now there's another British tradition I'll never understand.'

'Yeesh, really?' I said, grimacing. 'I'd just about got used to seeing him in drag. Not sure I'm quite ready for knickerbockers –' I broke off, glancing at the hand massaging my shoulder. 'Hang on. What's digging in me?'

I grabbed her hand and held it up to examine the ring that had materialised on one of the fingers. 'What's this, Cyn?'

She flushed. 'Present from your father.'

'Oh my God! He didn't!'

'He did,' she said, letting loose the grin hovering at the edge of her lips. 'Next year, you're finally getting your very own wicked stepmother.'

Chapter 40

'Ok, guys, much better tonight,' Deano said at the end of our rehearsal that evening. 'Gerry and Danny, you're pearls of great price and my own true loves, as ever. Rodge, some solid dinosauring, but I want you practising your roar. Lana, good work: only two slip-ups tonight. Next week, I want it down to none.' He shot us all a double thumbs-up. 'Well done though, everyone. I think we're really shaping up.'

'Thank God. We can finally go to the pub,' Maisie said with a sigh of relief. Deano was in a double panic over the press showing and the imminence of opening night and it'd been a long rehearsal, two full run-throughs.

Deano shook his head. 'No pub for you yet. You and Becky are staying after school.'

She groaned. 'What, detention again? I've really been trying, Deano.'

'You're doing a lot better,' Deano said, giving her arm an encouraging pat. 'But sorry, the kiss scene's leaving me cold at the moment. I want another couple of run-throughs for the Happily-Ever-After before pub.'

'Do we have to?' I grumbled. 'My feet are killing me.'

'You want to be perfect for the papers in a fortnight, don't you?'

'S'pose,' I muttered.

Deano grabbed Marcus's arm as he turned to follow the others backstage. 'I want you here too, bruv.'

'Me? Why?'

'Favour. Your love scene with Becks is the most convincing one in the whole panto, you can give Maisie some tips.'

'The Tomorrow bit? It's not really a love scene.'

Deano shrugged. 'It sort of is. So will you?'

Marc sighed. 'All right. But you're buying me a pint after.'

When everyone else had gone, Deano put me and Maisie in position for the Happily-Ever-After, which followed on from the slipper-fitting.

'How's it going with Livvy?' I asked Marcus while Deano was fiddling with the lighting.

'Oh. That. Yeah, didn't work out in the end.'

'Really? Sorry to hear it.'

He shrugged. 'It was mutual, all amicable. Nice girl, but not the one, I think.'

I'd only been making smalltalk, but... did that change things? Did I want it to? Today's heart-to-heart with Cynthia had done nothing to clarify my feelings about Marcus. My current plan was to completely ignore them, whatever they were, until the panto was safely out of the way.

'Get ready, Becks,' Deano said.

I approached Maisie and took her two hands in mine.

'Try standing closer.' Deano guided Maisie further towards me. 'You've just found the love of your life, remember.'

'This is like being on a bloody photoshoot,' Maisie muttered to me. 'Except I'm not getting paid.'

'Right, off you go,' Deano said.

'It *was* you!' Maisie-Charming said. 'You were the mysterious girl who captured my heart.'

'That's right, your highness. It was I.' I glanced at Marcus. 'Is that right? Maybe we should change it to "I am she".'

'They won't be knocking marks off for grammar,' Deano hissed. 'Do the kiss.'

'Oh, Cinderella,' Maisie sighed. 'I'm so happy we found each other. Say you'll be my princess, and you'll never have to clean another fireplace as long as you live.'

'Yes, sire, I will marry you. I love you.'

'I love you too, dear heart.'

Maisie gave me a quick peck on the lips.

'Cut!' Deano yelled. 'Rubbish.'

'I thought it was a lot better,' Marcus said.

'The delivery was better. The kiss was abysmal.' Deano shook his head. 'Not getting it, are you, Maisie? You're supposed to be in love with her.'

'But I'm not in love with her, am I?' Maisie said.

'Yeah, and you're not a prince with his own castle either. It's called acting, sweetheart. Can't you pretend she's Harper?'

Maisie looked me up and down. 'No,' she said flatly.

'Well, there comes a time in every girl's life when she has to learn to fake it.' He nodded to Marcus. 'Show her how it's done.'

'Me? Why me?'

'Who else is here? Go on, be a pro. She just needs to watch the movements.'

'I'm not doing it. You do it, you love snogging people.'

'I can't, I'm directing. Anyway, you've got the most stage experience when Harper's not around.'

I folded my arms. 'Don't all queue up for me at once, lads, eh?'

'Fine, if you're going to get stroppy about it. Honestly, I've worked with some diva-ish leading ladies in my time...' Marcus grumpily took me in his arms.

'You watching this, Maisie?' he said over his shoulder.

'Mmm.' Our principal boy, who'd taken a seat on the stool by the kitchen fireplace, looked up from examining her nails. 'Edge of my seat, honey.'

'Right. So you start with the fingers in the hair.' He placed one hand against my cheek, then started sliding it slowly upwards, the tip of his little finger trailing over my ear.

I laughed nervously at the intimate touch. It reminded me of my sexy Dorito dream.

'Careful you don't knock the wig off, Marc.'

'Hush, you. No talking while I'm cherishing you.' With his other hand he pressed against the small of my back, pushing my body into his. 'Then you can ramp up the sexual tension a bit, Mais. Not too much, remember it's a family audience. Got that?'

'Just the right amount of girl-on-girl for the kiddies. Heard and understood.'

Marcus let me go and turned to her. I tried not to feel too disappointed at my sudden freedom.

'Look, are you taking this seriously or what?'

'I am, honestly!' She grinned. 'But come on, it is pretty funny. You teaching me how to gay up.'

Deano grabbed a notepad and pen from off the piano, vaulted on stage and thrust them into her hands. 'Funny's for the pub after closing night. Funny's not for rehearsal two weeks before we open. I don't care who you are or who you're married to: I want you hanging on to every word of this, and there will be a test afterwards.'

She stuck out her bottom lip. 'Yes Chef.'

'"Yes Chef" is right. And if you think I'm bad now, just wait till we open. This is my show, lollipop, and believe me when I say the son of a bitch has landed.'

'Was he always like this?' Maisie asked Marcus.

He snorted. 'This is him going easy on you. You should see how he gets over soufflé.'

'Never mind soufflé.' Deano nodded to his brother. 'That was cracking stuff, Marc. Go on, please.'

Marcus took me in his arms again, a gentle yet businesslike embrace that set my heart thundering. His heart rate didn't budge, of course. The hot breath on my cheek was as calm as if he was helping Deano make a soufflé.

'Right, Mais,' Marc said. 'Hand in hair – so. Other hand in small of back – so.' He glanced round. 'Now, this is where you go in for the kiss. And in case you were wondering, the right amount of girl-on-girl for a family audience doesn't involve tongues.'

'Oh dear. And I'd flossed specially.'

Deano frowned at her. 'Less sark, more notes, you. Chop chop.' Maisie dutifully started scribbling on her pad.

'You ready?' Marcus muttered to me.

'Yes.' My answer came out more like a squeak.

'So on stage, kisses are carefully choreographed. You just touch lips gently, then Maisie swings you round and you can separate. But, and this is the really important bit, you need to hold your position. The back of her head will block the audience's view of your face so it'll look like you're still kissing.'

'Sounds simple enough,' I tried to say. The actual sound that came out was more of a 'schmuff'.

'Right, here we go.' He pressed me close, and then his lips were on mine.

He spun me round, and I waited for him to pull away. But he didn't. He kept his mouth against mine, and I saw his eyes widen with a look of shock, and something like wonder, before falling closed.

I tried to stop my lips parting, but it was no good. I felt the gentlest touch of his tongue, just brushing mine. It was like I was sinking, losing myself as I gave in and kissed him back...

He drew away, and the spell was broken.

'Um, Becks. What just happened?' he whispered, his arms still tight around me.

I pushed him away. 'What the hell do you think you're doing?'

He blinked. '*Me?*'

'That was not a stage kiss, Marc! That was... real.'

Suddenly, I was angry. Angry with myself, for kissing Marcus. Angry with Marcus, for what he'd just made me feel. And... and for making me realise Cole had been right.

'You kissed me!' he said.

'I was acting.'

Maisie and Deano were staring at us, blinking in shock. But I didn't have time for them.

'Acting?' Marc said. 'Where in the script does it say to stick your tongue in my mouth?'

'You started it!'

'Ok, guys, let's have some calm,' Deano said, but we ignored him.

'Becky...' Marcus reached for my hand, but I jerked it away. 'Please. Let's go somewhere and talk about this.'

'I don't want to talk about it. I want to forget about it. Ok? Just... keep your lips away from me.'

'Look, I know you feel guilty about Cole, but we can't just –'

'Don't you *dare* talk to me about Cole!' I yelled, my voice echoing off the Temp's lofty rafters.

Deano blinked. 'Woah.'

'You're the reason he's gone,' I shouted at Marcus, all the grief, all the anger I felt towards myself spilling out in his direction. 'And no sooner is he out the door then you... we...' Unable to hold back my tears any longer, I burst into sobs.

'Hey.' Maisie approached and rested a gentle hand on my shoulder. 'Come on, honey, let me take you home. You need to calm down.'

'Stay away from me, Marc,' I gasped. I shrugged off Maisie's hand. 'All of you. Just... leave me alone.' Sweeping a frightened-looking Deano to one side, I stormed out of the hall.

***

Back at home, I threw myself down on mine and Cole's bed and let my rage dissipate in a fit of cathartic tears. My eyelids were like golf balls by the time I'd finally got it all out.

I knew I'd been unfair on Marcus. I'd kissed him just as much as he'd kissed me. All my grief about Cole leaving, all my guilt at being drawn into a kiss so soon after, all my confused feelings about my panto co-star and my ex-fiancé, had exploded in one big emotion bomb. And Marc was the one who'd got caught in the shrapnel.

And then there was the kiss itself. I didn't know how to feel about it – how I was allowed to feel. On the one hand I felt guilty, because even though Cole and I had broken up, it still felt like a betrayal to move on so quickly. On the other, I felt... well, pleased. Elated, if I was being brutally honest. Because Marc had kissed me back, which meant the feelings I'd unconsciously been developing over the months spent working on the panto were reciprocated.

But I had a migraine from crying, and Cole was on his way to say a last goodbye, and I couldn't process all the myriad emotions fighting each other for dominance.

What I did know was that I owed Marc an apology.

I tapped out a text.

Sorry. Broke up with Cole last week, you probably gathered. Shouldn't have taken it out on you.

It buzzed immediately with a reply.

Becks, we need to talk. Can I come over?

God, that was the last thing I needed. It was going to be painful enough seeing Cole again. I didn't have the emotional strength to sort through my Marcus feelings as well. Turning the phone off, I stuffed it back in my pocket.

When I felt sufficiently calm I started packing up Cole's things, musing on the remnants of our life together, the paintings in his attic studio. Some were finished, others barely begun.

It was interesting to see how they evolved. The most complete were all London cityscapes, dating from when he'd first moved up. Then, gradually, he'd drifted into local scenes: desolate moorland bruised with heather; sheep-stubbled hills; black, ruinous mills nestled in deep West Riding valleys. A harsh, glorious tapestry of gritstone and graft, scarred with industry and half-healed by nature. It was hard not to get a bit lyrical about it.

I felt a surge of affection and loss as I examined the paintings. I didn't know if the Yorkshire theme meant Cole had come to see the area as his home or if it was an effort to learn to love it for my sake, but it was obviously his best work. No wonder Ryder's patrons were so desperate for him.

There was none of his art in the house itself, other than the view from Pagans' Rock he'd given me for our anniversary and the painting of Westminster Bridge that had been his very first present. In fact, there was nothing much of his in any room but the attic. All the furniture, all the ornaments, had been picked out by me. 'Whatever makes you happy, darling,' had been his standard response when I'd asked for an opinion on anything. The photos on the walls were of my friends, my family, except for one small picture of the two of us taken at some art function years ago. Everything in the home we'd shared seemed to be evidence of two very different people, leading very different lives under the same roof.

It was nearly nine when he showed up. I opened the door to find him looking tired but the same as ever: handsome, faintly baffled, like half his thoughts were somewhere else.

'Hello,' he said.

'Hi.'

He reached up to rub his hair, avoiding eye contact. The awkwardness was painful.

'Um, do you want to join me for a glass of something?' I said, to fill the silence as much as anything. 'It's been chambrered.'

I was hoping that might raise a smile, but the ice remained firmly unbroken.

'No, I can't stop. I've a lot to do before the move.'

'When are you going?'

'Next month officially, but I'm going to start moving my things down tomorrow.' His eyes kindled, and he finally met my gaze. 'Ryder sent some photos of the studio annexe they're preparing for me. You should see it, Becky. It's huge.'

I smiled. 'I'm glad you're excited. Here, come in. I've packed most of your things, and I can send the rest of the paintings down by courier.'

He followed me into the living room.

I gestured to a couple of holdalls containing his clothes, and some canvases leaning against the wall.

'I was careful,' I said, seeing his worried look. 'I know how precious they are. Especially now you're going to be a star.'

'Thank you.'

There was another awkward silence.

'So, um, do you want to take that one too?' I nodded to the Pagans' Rock picture hanging over the fireplace.

'Of course not. I painted that for you.'

I smiled. 'Hoped you'd say that. I do love it.'

He reached out to take my hands. 'Becky...'

'It's ok,' I whispered, blinking back a tear. It was amazing I still had any left in me. 'Cole, it's ok.'

He glanced down at my fingers in his, denuded of engagement ring, and swallowed a sob of his own.

'Be happy, darling,' he whispered. I let him draw me into his arms for a final hug. 'Chase your dreams. Love and be loved. I hope life gives you everything you want.'

'I'll never forget you.' I breathed deeply against his chest, inhaling his scent for the last time.

'And I'll always be grateful to you. I don't believe I'd be the artist I am if I hadn't had you in my life. Or the man.'

He let me go and slung one of the holdalls over his shoulder.

'You should tell him, you know,' he said without looking at me.

'Cole...'

'He loves you, Becky. Any fool can see that. And you love him.' He held up a hand to stop me interrupting. 'Oh, I won't pretend it doesn't hurt. Love doesn't switch itself off overnight. But I really do want you to be happy, I always did.'

'I'm so sorry. So sorry.' I didn't know what I was apologising for, but I felt I needed to.

'Don't be. I'm not.' He planted a soft kiss on my hair. 'Goodbye, Becky Finn. I'll miss you every day.'

I tried to say goodbye back, but the word stuck in my throat.

Half an hour later, he was gone.

Chapter 41

You are coming to rehearsal tonight, aren't you? Worried about you, Becks.

I glanced at the message from Lana. It was the third one this week, not to mention the two from Deano and a load from Marc.

Other than going out to work, I'd been locked in the house for a week now, trying to get to grips with my thoughts. I'd told everyone I'd appreciate a bit of space, but in a village like Egglethwaite, 'recluse' wasn't in most people's vocabulary.

Not tonight, I messaged back. *Can't face it. Ask Deano to do my lines.*

It's been a week. Come on, come out. Pretty hard to rehearse Cinderella without Cinderella.

I'm just a bit emotional right now, that's all. I'll see you at the press showing next week, I promise.

It buzzed again, but it wasn't Lana this time. It was yet another message from Marc, which I didn't need to open to know it said pretty much exactly the same as all the others he'd sent. But I opened it anyway.

Becks, I feel awful. Please let me come over and talk to you. I'm sorry.

A week after our kiss, I still didn't know what it was I wanted – needed – to say to Marcus. My head throbbed every time I tried to think about it. *Not right now, Marc* was all the reply I could manage.

Sleep wouldn't come again that night. I'd been struggling with it ever since the breakup. I just lay, inhaling the faint smell of turps Cole had left behind, thinking about him and Marcus, all the endings and beginnings of my life, crying soft, wistful tears.

I was still awake at midnight when there was a faint knock at the door.

I thought it was the wind at first, it was so quiet. But a minute later, there it was again.

Who'd be calling at this time? Was it Lana, checking up on me? Or Cole?

When I answered the door, I discovered it was Marcus. He was in his motorbike leathers, helmet tucked under his arm and a faint dusting of fresh snow over his shoulders.

'I couldn't sleep,' he said.

'You know, I'm trying to be a recluse.'

'What, that detective from *The Pink Panther*?'

I couldn't help smiling. 'Well, you might as well come in now you're here.'

In the hall, he took his jacket off and came through to the living room. We took a seat next to each other on the sofa, but he kept a respectful distance, his usual touchy-feely body language nowhere to be seen.

'I couldn't sleep.'

'You said.'

He turned to face me. 'Becky, look, I'm sorry. I know you said not to come over, but I needed to talk to you, and when you weren't at rehearsal... I had to see you.'

'To say what?'

'Well to apologise, for a start. You know, about what happened last week.'

'The kiss?'

315

'Yeah. I got carried away in the moment, I guess. Being your Prince Charming. I didn't mean to upset you.'

'And I didn't mean to yell at you. Just with Cole... well, I'm a bit all over the place right now.'

He examined my face. 'You've been crying.'

I brushed the remains of a tear off my cheek. 'Crying for the end of something. That's not the same as wishing it hadn't ended.'

'So it's really over?'

I glanced down at my ringless finger. 'Yes. He's going back to London.'

'What happened?'

'He told me he didn't want kids.' I smiled sadly. 'It was a dream I just couldn't give up on.'

He stretched a comforting arm around my shoulders and shuffled closer.

'I'm sorry, Becky. You should've said something.'

'I just wanted to get through the panto without any additional drama.'

'You know you can tell me anything, don't you?' he said gently. 'I'm your friend.'

I looked up at him, eyes swimming again. 'Marcus, at rehearsal –'

'Honestly, I'm so sorry.' He reached up to wipe a tear from my cheek. 'Once I got you in my arms, I couldn't help it.'

'I didn't know you... um, that you saw me like that,' I said, cheeks flushing with confusion. The look in his eye wasn't one I'd seen there before. It seemed to be a combination of tenderness, puzzlement and... I don't know, something else. And though he could see I was embarrassed, he didn't withdraw his gaze.

'Neither did I,' he said quietly. 'Until last week.'

'Why?' I could feel the arm he had around me trembling.

'Truth is... look, Becks. We're friends, right?'

'Course.'

'This last year working on the panto, it feels like we've sort of become best friends, you know? Even when it felt like the whole thing was a disaster, it was still the most fun I've had with a girl – well, ever. Getting to know you, feeling so comfortable with you...'

'That's how I felt too.'

'But I never really thought about... anything else. You were engaged, so yeah, there was a cheeky flirt here and there, and I won't deny I've had the odd sly look at your legs in those tights when we've been getting changed, but there was this sort of off-limits screen in my brain that stopped me seeing you as anything more than a mate.' His eyes moved over my face. 'When I kissed you last week, it's like that barrier just dissolved. Like I –' He swallowed, and when he spoke again his voice was hoarse. 'I just realised I'd really, really like to see your legs without the tights.'

His gaze was locked into mine, and his lips had parted.

'You said Cole was gone because of me,' he whispered. 'What did you mean?'

'I'm sorry. I shouldn't have said it.'

His other arm slipped round me in a full embrace. 'Tell me what you meant, Becky.'

'Well, he worked out I was... he knew I was... attracted. Um, to you, I mean. That's not the only reason we broke up, but... yeah, it was a factor.'

'You were attracted to me?'

'I couldn't help it.' I let my arms wrap around his neck. 'I thought, after Cole left, that maybe it was my subconscious's way of telling me he wasn't right for me. But...'

'But?'

'I think it was a bit more basic than that.'

'Oh God, Becky,' he whispered, and his voice was shaking. 'Come here.'

Before I had time to process what was happening, his lips were on mine.

And this wasn't stage kissing, cold and choreographed and cautious, but real, full-on, no-holds-barred kissing. There was a determination to the way his tongue parted my lips, a passion that caught me off guard for a second. But I responded. Oh God, I responded, with every fibre and nerve. His hand slid to my back and he pushed my body against his.

Eventually he drew back, his breath coming through in short pants. He slid his hand inside my pyjama top, shivering as he caressed my back.

'Marcus...' I whispered, nuzzling into his neck.

'Becks, can we – I don't know what's happening, and you just broke up with someone, and a week ago I didn't even know this was ever going to be a possibility. But Jesus, I want to be with you now. I want to kiss you again and for you not to tell me to stop.'

'Then you should.'

'You really want me to?'

'Yes. Yes, Marc.' I was too far gone to turn back now.

He gave his head an angsty shake. 'No. You're vulnerable.'

'I'm not, I'm really not.' I stroked his cheek. 'I want to.'

'We should wait. It's not the right time.'

He drew back, panting; holding my gaze. I didn't say a word. Just waited for him to make his choice.

'Oh God, I don't care,' he said at last. 'I don't care.'

He pulled me to him and buried his face in my neck, planting fast, fevered kisses under the collar of my pyjamas.

'Is it ok?' he murmured against my skin. His fingers were already toying with the buttons of my pyjama top. 'I need you to tell me it is.'

'It's ok.' I gasped as he twisted my face around to kiss the sensitive flesh behind my ear. 'Don't stop, please.'

'I don't want to have sex with you because you need to be with someone, Becky. I want to have sex with you because you need to be with me.'

'Are you kidding?' I bit my lip as he unfastened the last button of my shirt and stripped it off me. 'You've been on my mind for months.'

'Seriously?' He dropped to his knees on the carpet and buried his face in my chest.

'Yes. Ah!' I gasped as he flicked his tongue over my nipple. 'Couldn't stop thinking about you, about... this. That's why I had to stop coming round to yours.'

He laughed breathlessly. 'In case you accidentally ravished mc?'

'Something like that.'

He trailed his fingers lightly under my flimsy pyjama bottoms while he explored my breasts with his mouth.

'Why didn't you tell me?' he murmured. He hooked his thumbs into my waistband and guided my pyjama bottoms, the last stitch of clothing I had on, off my body.

'I just wanted it to go away,' I whispered. 'I tried to make it go away, but... well, it wouldn't.'

'Good.' He kissed softly from my knee up my thigh. His fingers mirrored his mouth, sliding up between my legs, and I heard a faint, guttural groan at the back of his throat.

His tongue rolled against the flesh of my inner thigh. I pushed my hands deep into his hair, and he shivered.

'Wait. Stop,' I gasped.

He looked up at me. 'What's wrong? Don't you like it?'

'Yes.' I was panting heavily and it took me a second to get my breath back. 'It's our first time, that's all. I want to... do it properly. Can we go upstairs, Marc?'

He hesitated. 'To your room?'

I knew what he was thinking. My room. My bed. The one I'd shared with Cole.

'To the spare room.'

'Oh. Ok.'

He stood and lifted me easily. I wrapped my arms around his neck and my legs around his waist; clung on tightly, bashful of my nudity, while he carried me up the stairs.

He carried me into the spare room and plonked me on the bed. I pulled him down on top of me, opening my lips to him for a deep kiss.

'You sure it's ok for us to do this?' he whispered when he broke away.

'You couldn't go now.'

'No.'

He stood to remove his clothes, stripping out of his t-shirt, the heavy motorcycle trousers. When he was as naked as me, he stretched himself out on the bed.

I'd seen him semi-starkers plenty of times when we'd been changing backstage. Dreamed about him. But actually touching him made it all so real. I felt a wave of pleasure to think I could finally have him right there, under my fingers.

I ran my hands over his body while we kissed: the smooth chest, the inviting ripples of his stomach, the little sun tattoo with its almost invisible scar, finally trailing my fingertips over the solid erection pressed against my middle.

'Do I get the Becky Finn seal of approval then?' he asked softly when I'd had a good explore.

'I'd say you just about make the grade.'

He traced my shape reverently with one finger. 'Not so bad yourself.'

I rolled him on top of me, legs weaving round his, and he glided over my body, pressing kisses onto every inch of bare flesh. Hot skin against hot skin, backs of his nails trailing along my hips, my thighs, and his tongue, which seemed to sense it was welcome anywhere, teasing at the spot behind my ear that was always a guaranteed winner. I don't know how he knew that, but he did.

'Condom?' he muttered.

'Next door.'

'Ok, go on.'

I grabbed a sheet off the clothes horse in the corner to wrap round me, then went to dig out a condom from my bedside cabinet. When I'd found the foil packet I went back, holding it aloft like a trophy.

He laughed. 'You look like the Statue of Liberty.'

'Do you fancy her too?'

'Never could resist a girl in a toga.' He pulled me unceremoniously back onto the bed, stripped me of the sheet and homed straight in on the skin behind my ear.

'How did you know I like that?' I breathed.

'Lucky guess.'

'Really?'

He rolled his tongue over me, flicking the end like he was getting the last bit of raspberry syrup off a 99.

'All right, no,' he whispered. 'From juggling.'

'Juggling?'

'Yeah. When I stood behind you, if I breathed on you just there, it always made you shiver. Don't think I didn't notice.'

'Bastard! You used to turn me on on purpose?'

He grinned. 'And still never dropped a ball.' He ran one finger down my cheek. 'We've had some fun together, haven't we, Cinders?'

'Let's have a bit more.'

I ripped open the condom and rolled it on. He groaned as he manoeuvred himself inside me, yanking my leg up to wrap around his back.

'Jesus, Rebecca,' he whispered. 'You have no idea how good that feels.'

'You know, you don't have to call me by my full name just because we're having sex.'

'Sorry, love. Just trying to keep it classy.'

He dug his fingers into my buttocks, gliding my body back and forth as we found our rhythm. Rolling, holding, bucking, riding... I felt my nerves start to tremble at the joy of it, the sheer animal joy of giving myself to someone I understood; someone I trusted. Someone I... yes, someone I loved. As he held me tight against him, as our bodies shattered and split into orgasm and we cried out to claim each other through the fog, it felt like everything was finally in its right place.

***

'Well that was bracing,' Marcus panted as we lay cuddling afterwards, his body gilded with sweat.

'Always good to try new hobbies with old friends, eh?'

'I'll never be satisfied with mixed doubles again, that's for sure.' He kissed me softly. 'Glad I know you, Becky Finn.'

'Will you stay?' I asked, burrowing sleepily into his arms. 'It's nice having you here.'

He stroked gentle fingers over my hair. 'If you want me to.'

I kissed his nose. 'Thanks, Marc. And thanks for being with me when I needed you.'

'Now you can never say I don't put the effort in when you need cheering up.'

'Certainly beats a card trick,' I said, smiling.

He grinned. 'I could really freak you out right now if I told you the Three of Diamonds was in your knicker drawer, couldn't I?'

'I'd burn you as a witch.' I sighed as his hand traced idly over my hip, sending a pleasant post-orgasmic tickle over my skin. 'That's nice.'

'So what did Cole actually say?' he asked. 'He didn't think there was something going on between us, did he?'

'Oh, he...' I yawned. 'Yes, he worked it out. A bit faster than I did anyway. I think I was in denial until you kissed me last week.'

'Worked what out?'

'Well, that I love you.' I yawned again. 'God, you've worn me out. Night, Marc. See you in the morning.'

'Yeah,' he said quietly. 'Sleep well, Becks.'

***

I was woken a few hours later by the roar of a motorbike bursting into life outside the house.

'Marc?' I mumbled, groping for him.

He was gone.

Chapter 42

I didn't hear a word from Marcus before the final pantomime rehearsal, the press screening, five days later. Not a call, not even a text, to acknowledge the night we'd spent together. Angry and hurt, feeling betrayed by someone I'd come to think of as one of my best friends and still adjusting to a new reality after splitting with Cole, I didn't know how I was going to react when I saw Marc again. I was genuinely worried I might burst into tears.

I'd been all at sixes and sevens since Cole moved out, and it took me ages to find my ragged Cinders dress. Eventually I discovered it in the washing basket, under one of his old overalls. I just had time to give it a quick Febreze and pull it on before I dashed to the Temp.

By the time I exploded, panting, through the door, I was a good ten minutes late and there were already a load of journalists, being plied with tea and biscuits by some Ladies Who Lunch. I thought I'd be the last one, but when I went backstage I discovered we were still missing Deano and Harper. And Marcus.

'Where's all the menfolk?' I asked my dad.

He shrugged. 'Beats me. I thought young Deano would've set up camp days ago.'

Marc burst in, in costume with his motorcycle leathers over the top, just as I was gathering everyone together.

'Oh good, you're here,' Lana said to him. 'We were starting to worry.'

'Yeah, sorry. Got held up at a job.' He clapped me on the shoulder. 'Hiya, Becks. We all set?'

Right. So we were pretending the other night never happened, were we? I pushed down the waves of grief and anger, reminding myself I had a job to do.

'Where's your brother?' I asked.

'What, he isn't here?'

'No. We still need him and Harper.'

Marc fumbled for his phone. 'Oh God. Yeah, he's texted. The bloody Morris has broken down.'

'Did he have to come in that thing tonight?' I demanded. 'Now what will we do?'

'We can go on without him. We know what we're doing, don't we?'

'We can't do without Harper though,' Lana said. 'Most of those journalists are only here for him.' She turned to Maisie. 'Do you know where he is?'

'No. He went out with Gav earlier to buy my Christmas present.'

'Hang on. That's me,' Stew said as his ringtone fired up. He fished out his phone. 'Harper.'

'I hope he's just ringing to say he's right outside,' I muttered darkly.

'All right, mate, where are you?' Stewart said when he'd picked up. He frowned. 'Gavin?'

He looked serious as Gav talked into his ear. 'Right. Ok. I see. Yes, tell him I'm on my way.'

'Oh God, what?' Maisie said when he'd hung up. 'Harper's ok, isn't he? There hasn't been an accident or... is he ok, Stew? Tell me, quick.'

Stew looked hesitant. 'Harper didn't want me to say anything in case you worried.'

'Well you have to now, don't you? Come on, please!'

'He's ok. I mean, he isn't hurt.' Stew grimaced. 'He's been arrested.'

'*What?*' Lana said. 'Jesus, not again. What for this time?'

'It's bloody Jamie, he's pressing charges over what happened at Yo-yo's wedding. He obviously couldn't sell the story so he's decided he'll get his revenge this way instead.'

'Oh no.' Our T-Rex slapped his head with one of his little arms. 'Oh, I am sorry.'

'Not your fault, Rodge,' Stew said. 'Look, I have to go. He needs bailing out. Soon as I've got him, I'll bring him back here. Until then... God, I don't know. Move the slosh scene earlier on, that'll kill some time.' He patted Maisie on the shoulder. 'And don't worry, Mais. He'll be fine, promise.'

'He won't go to prison, will he? He only hit that man because he called me a – because he was rude about me. Harper's too pretty to be in prison.'

'He won't go to prison,' Stew said. 'Not for something like that.'

'But he's got a record already,' Maisie said, sounding frightened. 'Don't they take that into account, when something's not a first offence?'

'He's not going to prison,' Stew repeated firmly. 'And it's not going in the papers this time either, not if I can help it. I'll be back as soon as I can.' He hurried out, planting a quick kiss on Lana's cheek as he passed her.

I groaned. 'Well this is a great bloody start, isn't it? Right.' I nodded to my dad and Gerry. 'You two, and Marc – Marcus. I'm moving the pie-making before the dancing lesson. If we put the dancing after the long scene, hopefully Stew'll be back with Harper.'

'We'll never get the stage cleaned up in time if we do the slosh scene there,' Marcus said.

I frowned. 'Ok, well how about – what if we do two intervals? One after the slosh scene, then another after Tomorrow and the ball for the finale.'

'Yeah, that'll do it.' Marcus nodded approvingly. 'Nice one, Becks.'

God, would you just listen to him? I tried not to glare.

'Ok, Maisie, you need to get into costume. Dames, go get Yo-yo to do your make-up ready for Sisters.' I clapped my hands together. 'We can do this, people!'

Maisie still looked worried. 'I don't want my baby born while his daddy's doing time for GBH, Becky,' she whispered as I guided her towards the costume rail.

'He'll be fine, Mais. It'll all be fine.'

'You sound like you don't believe yourself.'

'Fine, fine, fine. The more I say it, the more it'll come true. A dream is a wish the heart makes or some bollocks.'

It got a smile, but she still looked anxious. I hoped it wasn't going to affect her performance.

***

When everyone was ready, I poked my head through the curtain to check on the audience. All the seats were filled, about ten journalists with notepads perched expectantly on knees, plus Tom and Pip, who I'd invited to help me out with something. They could only stay an hour before it was time for Pip's Beaver meeting, but I was hoping that'd be long enough for what I had in mind.

After I'd done my opening monologue, I went backstage. There was still no Deano, and I seemed to have stepped into the role of director temporarily.

'Ok, Lana, Maisie, you're up. Good luck.'

A couple of stagehands finished fixing Cole's palace backdrop in place, then the curtain rose on our principal boys. There was an appreciative murmur from the journalists, mainly blokes and clearly fans of the tits-tights-and-tunics look, and a giggle from Pip when she recognised her aunty pretending to be a boy. I watched from the wings, fingers and toes crossed.

'Oh, Dandini. If only I could find a girl I could marry for love,' Maisie said, looking out over the audience as she gave a deep, heartfelt sigh.

'Hey, that was a bit better, wasn't it? Sounds like our Prince Charming's finally found his muse.'

I started. I hadn't noticed Marcus sneaking up behind me.

'I've been giving her a few pointers,' I said. 'We're trying something new tonight.'

If he picked up on the frostiness in my tone, he didn't let on.

'What are you trying?'

'I told her to focus on one member of the audience and pretend the whole play's for them. That's why Pip's here. I had an inkling that if Maisie had to convince a kid, she'd naturally channel the character.'

'Seems to be working.' Marcus put one arm around my waist, and I stiffened. 'Becks – we are ok, aren't we? Me and you?'

'Why wouldn't we be?'

'It's just, the other night... look, it was a mistake. I shouldn't have taken advantage like that when you were upset. I've been beating myself up over it ever since.'

'Mistake. Right.'

'Then we're still friends?'

'Mmm.' I glanced at the stage, where Lana was staring at Maisie with a panicked bunny look. 'Oh God, she's forgotten her line again. Do you remember it?'

'No. Deano's the prompter. Hang on.' He disappeared and came back with a script, rifling through to find the scene. 'I only wish your father wasn't in such a hurry to have you married.'

'I only wish your father wasn't in such a hurry to have you married,' I mouthed to Lana.

She managed to repeat the line, then froze again, gaping.

'Shit!' I whispered to Marc. 'She hasn't just forgotten her line, has she? She's forgotten her whole bloody part!'

'Bollocks, I think you're right. The nerves must've got to her. What do we do, Becks?'

'Hang on. Maisie's trying to claw it back.'

'You know what would be wonderful?' Maisie said, waggling her eyebrows at Lana. 'Some sort of ball.'

'Yes.' Lana seized the prompt with relief. 'A ball for all the maidens in the land. Maybe then you could, um... could, um...'

'You're so right, Dandini!' Maisie slapped her thigh with vigour, which provided a handy distraction from her co-star's distress. 'Maybe then I could meet the girl who deserves my heart instead of being matched with some foolish, shallow princess.'

And so through a combination of unsubtle prompts and stealing Lana's lines, Maisie managed to get her through. It was painful to watch, but they did it.

Deano arrived in the wings just as the scene was ending.

'Where the hell have you been?' I muttered.

'Car trouble, sorry. Old girl likes to keep me on my toes.'

'Did you see any of that travesty?'

'Enough,' he said darkly.

The curtain fell, and Lana and Maisie came to join us. Lana looked mortified.

'I'm sorry, guys,' she said. 'Deano, mate, I'm so sorry. It was the stagefright. Every word just went out of my head.'

Deano patted her bum, but he didn't seem quite able to find the words to tell her it was ok. She nodded once, then made her way backstage looking thoroughly miserable.

He had a few words for Maisie though.

'Mais, I never thought I'd say this, but you're a real pro,' he said. 'Finest incarnation of "the show must go on" I've ever seen.'

Maisie beamed. 'Thanks, Chef. That's what we do, isn't it? Help each other through.'

'Your delivery was much better too. Been practising?'

'Becky's been helping me.' She nodded gratefully to me. 'And it did work, Becks. With the little girl looking at me, it felt like it had to be more real, somehow. Like it was part of a game. Cute little thing, isn't she?'

'Yeah.' I patted her arm. 'You did great, love. I'm proud of you.'

'Right. So it's kitchen scene, Sisters number, then the dancing,' Deano said. He peered behind him into the backstage area. 'Where's Harper?'

I grimaced. 'That's the other thing. You won't like this, Deano.'

'Oh God, what?'

'Our Baron Hardup's been banged up.'

***

I'd never had to bail someone out of the slammer before so I didn't know how long it usually took, but as we approached the first of our two intervals, there was still no sign of Stew and Harper. The dancing scene had to come after the break, there was nowhere else it could logically go, and we couldn't do it without Baron Hardup.

Deano grabbed my arm as I went to chat to the journalists, mingling with the cast while they drank tea and gobbled Jammy Dodgers. 'Spin it out,' he muttered. 'Half an hour.'

'We can't do two half-hour intervals, Deano. They'll be here all night.'

'We have to give Brady chance to get here. Otherwise we might as well send them all home now.'

'All right, all right. I'll keep them talking.'

I approached a couple of blokes who were sipping tea out of paper cups near the kitchen hatch.

'Um, hi. Thanks for coming.'

'Hello,' one of them said. He scanned my costume. 'Cinderella, right?'

Nice to know they'd been paying attention to something other than Maisie's legs.

'Just Becky off stage,' I said, smiling. 'So what paper are you from?'

'Ade. *Telegraph and Argus*,' he said, shaking my hand. He nodded to the other man. 'This is Freddy. He's a researcher from BBC Radio Leeds.'

'Oh,' I said, blinking. 'Didn't know we had anyone in from the radio.'

'Yeah, my producer sent me,' Freddy said. 'Once he heard you had Harper Brady, he insisted we had someone here. Should be good for a segment in our quirky local news roundup.' He glanced around the room. 'Is he here?'

'He's, er... somewhere about.'

'How've you found him to work with?' Ade asked. 'Bit of a handful, I imagine.' I was guessing by the suspiciously casual tone that this wasn't off the record.

'Mmm. But when he's not punching people or bonking in a cupboard or getting himself arrested, he's actually a pretty decent guy.'

Ade stared at me for a moment. Then he laughed. 'No, but seriously. Has it been a good experience?'

'Absolutely. Harper's a talented lad, it's been an honour for us to have him.' I smiled. 'Although if you want a tip, never ask to hear his Welsh accent.'

With help from the rest of the cast, I managed to spin the interval out for a good 25 minutes. But the audience were soon getting antsy, and we still had no Baron. Deano beckoned us backstage for an emergency meeting.

'I just rang Stew,' he told us. 'He's got Brady but they're stuck in heavy traffic.'

Everyone looked concerned, apart from Maisie, who seemed understandably relieved that her husband was no longer being detained at Her Majesty's Pleasure. I think in her mind's eye she'd been picturing Harper in a dingy barred cell, being asked by a beefy bloke called Chunk with tattoos on his eyelids to help him find the soap.

'So what can we do?' Marcus said. 'We can't cut the dancing scene now. Too many others refer to it.'

Deano's twitchy eye took on a grimly determined expression. 'Chuck us Harper's costume, will you, Yo-yo?' he said to Yolanda, who was nearest the rail. 'Honestly, if you want a job doing...'

And that was it. From that point on, we were jinxed. The whole performance was a catalogue of disasters from start to finish.

Deano did his best with the scene. He really wasn't a bad actor, although he wisely decided not to play it drunk, plus he was line-perfect after months on prompt duty. The big problem was, he couldn't dance.

'I do hope I won't – ow! – I won't embarrass myself at the ball,' Maisie said, wincing as Deano stepped on her feet yet again.

There were some mutterings among the journalists. I could hear Harper's name being whispered as people questioned why our star still hadn't made an appearance.

'Nonsense, sire – oof, sorry,' Deano said as he managed to knee his future monarch in the stomach. 'The women of Rummancoke will fall at your feet.'

'Oh God,' Maisie said, turning a bit green. She stopped dancing and took a queasy step back.

Chapter 42

'I don't want them to fall at my feet. I want them to see the man behind the crown,' Deano muttered without moving his lips.

'I know the line, Deano,' Maisie said. She made an unpleasant bubbling noise, and one hand flew to her mouth. 'Oh God, get out of my way. I'm going to be sick...'

She pushed Deano to one side and ran off stage.

'Flipping heck, boys and girls,' Deano said, turning in deadpan mode to the audience. 'I didn't think my dancing was *that* bad.'

That got a laugh, at least. I had to admire his quick thinking, registering no surprise as he pretended it was all part of the show.

'What's up with her?' Marcus asked me.

'Stagefright, I guess. Drop the curtain, Marc.'

There was a five-minute break while we waited for Maisie to stop vomiting. Marcus and Lana were in favour of stopping the performance all together, but Mais promised she was fine to go on, blaming her dicky tummy on nerves.

After the dancing scene came the Schrödinger's Behind You, then the dames' Hot Tub Girls number. My next big scene after that was Tomorrow, followed by a second interval before the Fairy Godmother turned up to send me to the ball.

The Tomorrow scene. More than all the others, I'd been dreading it. After the night we'd spent together, the thought of Marcus touching me, telling me he loved me, filled me with horror.

We managed to get through the song, although I could tell from the way Deano's eye was going that my voice wasn't up to its usual standard. But then it was the kiss.

Marcus was sitting by me on the hearth, and I mentally steeled myself as he took my two hands in his. He looked like the same old Marc. He even smelled the same. But he wasn't the same, because he'd done something I'd never thought he was capable of. He'd hurt me.

'Don't go to the palace, Cinders,' he said earnestly. 'Run away with me. I'll take care of you, and you'll never have to rake out a dirty grate again.'

I gave a mirthless laugh. 'Run away with you? But you're as poor as I am. Where would we go?'

'Anywhere. Then we could get married and...' He gazed into my eyes, like the silver-tongued, bungee-boxered lothario he was. 'I love you, Cinderella. I always have, you know.'

My stomach lurched. He started leaning towards me and I hesitated, for what seemed like forever. I could see Deano nervously mouthing my next line from the wings. *Oh Buttons, you know I could only ever love you as a friend...*

I don't know what made me do it. Seeing Marcus there, so close, pretending he cared about me just like he'd pretended when he'd talked me into bed, something snapped.

'Ok,' I said.

Marcus blinked. 'What?'

I shrugged. 'Ok. I'll run away with you.'

In the wings, Deano started banging his head against the wall.

'Er, will you?' Marc said at last.

'Yep. I mean, you're completely right about that prince. Why should I go to the palace in the hope some over-entitled chinless wonder might deign to marry a common slob like me? Who the hell does he think he is, anyway?' My voice was getting shrill. 'Just sending out to bloody Dial-A-Bride like every woman in the land's his personal property. Who wants to be with a bloke like that, right? I'd much rather marry you, Buttons: someone who actually loves and respects me. You wouldn't treat me like a sodding takeaway pizza.'

'But, er... don't you want to be rich?' Marcus fumbled. 'Leave this awful life behind?'

Chapter 42

I folded my arms. 'No. I want to be with you.'

'Oh no you don't, Cinders,' he hissed, jerking his eyes towards the puzzled-looking journalists in the audience.

'Oh yes I do.'

'Oh no you *don't*. Trust me, you really don't.'

'Oh yes I do. You aren't the boss of me, mate.'

'You don't though,' he said from behind a fixed grin. 'You want to marry the prince. Seriously, you're always wittering on about it.' He lowered his voice to a whisper. 'Get back on script, Becks. Please.'

'Right, I get it,' I said, ignoring him. 'You don't want me any more. It's just wham, bam, thank you Cinders, right? Get what you want then bugger off, when you know I –' To my disgust, I burst into tears – 'when you know I've been falling for you for months, you bastard, when you know I – I miss you, and I wish I'd never... oh God.' I took the flower he'd given me earlier in the scene out of my buttonhole and threw it in his face. 'Don't come near me. Don't speak to me. I can't stand the sight of you.' I ran off stage, past a horrified Deano, sobbing my heart out.

Chapter 43

'**B**ecks!'

I heard Marcus before I saw him. His voice soared up the street as I strode past Pie and a Pint, no idea where I was going except that I wanted to be away. Away from my house, with its memories of Cole. Away from the Temp, with its memories of Marcus. Away from bloody Egglethwaite all together.

'Becky, wait! Please!'

I quickened my step, but his legs were longer than mine. I felt his hand on my shoulder just as I passed Holyfield Farm.

'What do you want, Marc? I don't want to talk to you.'

'But I want to talk to you,' he panted. 'Please, just let me – we can't leave it like this.'

'You were happy enough to leave it like this last week.'

He flushed. 'I'm sorry about that. When you fell asleep, I just felt so... so guilty. I'd gone round to apologise, to – God, I don't know why I went round, except I had to see you.' He shook his head. 'It wasn't right. It was a mistake.'

'Yeah, so you said. Well this is one late-night booty call you don't need to worry about any more. The panto'll be over in a fortnight and then you can forget you ever met me.'

'Please don't say that.' He reached out to take my hand, but I jerked it back. 'I've missed you, Becks. I wanted to call you. It was so hard to know what to say.'

'What do you usually say to mistakes?' I said. 'Surely you've got a neat little one-night-stand speech saved up to let me down gently? I mean, I'm guessing I'm not the first.'

He shook his head. 'You're taking it all wrong. I don't mean *you* were a mistake. I mean what we did – well, no, what I did. You were upset, you needed to be with someone and I took advantage. That was the mistake.'

'Not just someone.' I blinked back tears. I wasn't going to cry again, not for him.

'Yes you did. You were hurting, and I'm supposed to be your friend and I did a bad thing. I wanted you and I was too weak to... Becks, I'm so sorry.'

'I'm not,' I tried to say, but the words stopped in my throat.

'And then when you said what you said – God, I felt like the worst kind of lowlife bastard,' Marc said, staring at the ground.

'Well thank Christ you handled it so well,' I snapped. 'I mean, running out on me and not getting in touch. Nice job.'

He flushed. 'I know. I thought... I don't know what I thought. My head's been all over the place since that night.'

'And yet you just waltzed into rehearsal like you'd forgotten it'd even happened, didn't you? Do you know how painful that was?'

'I'm sorry. I didn't know what else to do. Everyone was there, and there was the panto –'

'Oh, bugger the panto,' I snapped. 'And bugger you, Marcus Teasdale.' I turned to do the dignified exit thing, then changed my mind and spun back round. 'And the pathetic thing is, there was nothing to feel guilty about. I had sex with you because I wanted to have sex with you, pure and simple. Because I actually fucking do love you, you bastard. I thought you felt the same.' I gave in and let the tears pooling in my eyes slide down my cheeks. 'I was wrong, wasn't I?' I whispered.

'I... no. I don't know.' He rested a hand on my shoulder. 'You have to give me time, Becks. I never realised you thought about me like that, or I thought about you like that, and now... I mean, this time two weeks ago you were engaged to someone else, I was still seeing Livvy and we were just panto buddies.'

'So?'

'So I need time. Can't you get that? Time to work out what's happening in here.' He tapped his head. 'And here, I guess,' he said, punching his chest where I assumed he thought his heart lived, although his biology looked a bit off to me.

'You hurt me, Marc. I never thought you could do that.' I pulled my hand away. 'Maybe you're not who I thought you were.'

'I am, honestly! I just... you said scary words and I panicked, all right? If it makes you feel better, I hate myself for it.'

'I needed you. I needed you and you shagged me and then you fucked off. That's not nice.'

He cast his eyes down. 'I know it isn't.'

I sighed. 'Well, take your time to think or whatever. I'll see you next week for opening night. Let's try to stay professional for that, at least.'

'Are we still friends?'

'Not right now, Marcus. No.'

***

'Thought we might find you here.'

Lana took a seat next to me on her dad's memorial bench up at Pagans' Rock, Deano plonking himself down on the other side. I ignored them and kept on juggling.

'Why did you think you might find me here?' I said, watching one beanbag ball sail into the air as another landed in my gloved palm. Marc was right, it was good for stress relief. Focused the mind.

Lana shrugged. 'Pretty much because we'd tried everywhere else. You going to put your balls away?'

'No. It's relaxing me. Ugh!' I reached down to pick up the one I'd dropped. 'Fine,' I said, putting them back in my jacket. 'What do you two want then? Come to bollock me about cocking up the press showing?'

'Come to see if you're ok,' Lana said, putting her arm around me.

The clawing wind, blowing across the moors from Lancashire, filled my eyes with tears. Below me, hardy walkers, huddled in fleeces, made their way over Egglethwaite's famous viaduct, and a thin crackle of ice glazed the reservoir behind.

I choked back a sob. 'Been better.'

'So we all noticed you seem to have shagged my brother,' Deano said, putting his arm around me from the other side to create a sort of three-man cuddle.

'Yeah. Sorry it ruined your panto.'

'It's fine. Well, no, it's not fine because I bloody love that panto. But you're upset so I'm lying to you.'

'Great job,' I said, smiling weakly. 'What do you think the papers'll print about my little meltdown then?'

'Don't worry about that, I squared it,' Deano said. 'They're holding back on write-ups in exchange for a free ticket to opening night.'

'Seriously? How did you manage that?'

'Begging on my knees may've been involved. I had to offer them my body, obviously.'

'Any takers?'

'One. I'm sending him a voucher.' He shrugged. 'They were pretty amenable to coming back another time, to be honest. Most of them only turned up to see Brady. When he wasn't there, your thing barely registered.'

'Is he ok?'

'Yeah, Jamie Collingwood's dropped the charges now,' Lana said. 'Rodge told his mum what he said about Maisie and she's grounded him until he can learn to treat women with a bit of respect.'

I couldn't help smiling. 'Good for her.'

'So what about you and Marc?'

'There isn't a me and Marc. There's just me and then Marc.'

'You looked ready to lamp him at the end of that Tomorrow scene.'

I gave a wet laugh. 'Felt like it. Sorry I made such a mess of things, guys. I'll be fine for opening night, I promise.'

'What happened, Becks?'

'It was the other week. He came round to apologise for something and... one thing led to another, kind of thing.'

Lana was smirking.

'Sorry,' she said, forcing her face straight. 'I know it's not funny. Just wondering how the pair of you managed to turn an apology into foreplay.'

'I was upset. He was comforting me.' I blinked hard. 'Truth is... I've kind of been falling for him for ages. I didn't realise quite how hard until Cole made me face up to it, the day we – when he left.'

'Yeah, we worked it out too,' Lana said.

'You and everyone else apparently. Everyone but me and Marc.'

'What does he think about it?'

I poked my finger into a rip in my Cinders tights and wiggled it, watching the hole grow. 'Says he wants time to think. Trying to let me down gently, I guess.'

Deano shook his head. 'He's not like that.'

'Like you, you mean?'

'Yeah. It's little brother's prerogative to be sexily irresponsible and devil-may-care. Marc doesn't get his magic wand out for just anyone, you know.'

'Then why'd he walk out on me straight after, Deano? Why didn't he call? Even if he did see it as a casual thing, I thought we'd still be mates.'

'He's confused,' Deano said. 'Honestly, before he kissed you in rehearsal I don't think he realised he had any romantic-type feelings for you. The rest of us did, but not Marc.'

'Talk to him,' Lana suggested.

I shivered, hugging myself. There was an icy tang in the winter wind that was freezing the tears to my eyeballs. My legs, sheltered from the elements only by my thin panto tights, had gone numb.

'I did. I told you, he asked for time to think.' I gave a damp snort. 'God, how could I let myself get into this mess?'

'Really got it bad, haven't you?' Deano said gently.

'Yeah. Fucking true love, isn't it ridiculous?' A tear dropped onto the patched skirt of my Cinderella dress. 'I guess that's what you get for immersing yourself in fairytales.'

Chapter 44

I stared up at the towering sandstone front of the temperance hall, blackened by centuries of mill smoke.

'This is all your bloody fault,' I muttered to it.

I'd always thought of the Temp, austere and bleak though it might seem to outsiders, as a happy, welcoming place. But not today. Today, it loomed. The huge wooden doors looked maw-like and hungry.

This was it. Opening night.

My nerves were in my throat as I made my way in, past the volunteers selling tickets, through the fast-thickening crowd of excited kids and families, to the backstage area.

Top of my worry pile was Marcus. I hadn't heard from him since the last rehearsal, and my feelings towards him were currently ticking between anger and bereavement. How I was going to get through our week-long run without either slapping him or bursting into tears I didn't know.

Second in the pile was – well, everything else. Maisie's burgeoning morning sickness. Deano's burgeoning insanity. Lana's inability to remember her lines. The kids in the juvenile chorus and their Pikachu tails. Harper. The journalists in the audience. Everything.

When I got backstage there was one weight off my mind, at least. Harper was already there, perched on a stool with Maisie on his lap.

'Becky!' He beamed round the throng of cast and crew. 'Hey, it's Becky, everyone! Here, love, have some of this.'

He poured me a fluteful of something fizzy from a bottle under his stool. One of several, I noticed.

'Er, thanks,' I said as I took it from him. 'I think we might be a bit premature with the bubbly though, Harper. I'm as chuffed as anyone that you've managed to get here without being arrested this time, but not sure it really warrants –' I glanced at the bottle by his feet – 'bloody hell, Veuve Clicquot?'

'Well I'm not going to celebrate with that dishwater prosecco from the Fox – er, no offence, Yo-yo,' he said, nodding apologetically at the pub's new landlady. He leaned forward to rub noses with Maisie, in a way that would've been nauseating if they hadn't looked so blissfully happy. 'Not when my beautiful wife here's having our baby.'

Ah. So Maisie's secret was out. She sent me a raised-eyebrow look, and I fixed my face into my best expression of shock. I was an actor, after all.

'Wow, that's amazing news!'

'Isn't it?' Stew clapped his cousin on the shoulder. 'Both of us graduating to proper grown-up in the same year. Mum'll be so proud.'

I came forward to give Harper and Maisie a hug each. 'Congratulations, guys. So pleased for you.'

Maisie beamed. 'Thanks, Becky.'

I jerked my head at Stewart. 'Stew, can I have a word in private?'

He followed me into the wings. 'Everything ok, Becks?'

'Yeah. I mean, great news, obviously.' I held up my glass. 'But this stuff's bloody strong. How much has everyone had?'

'Only a glass each. Maisie just told him so he's all excited.' He smiled fondly in Harper's direction. 'Look at his little face.'

'I am looking at his little face. And what I'm seeing are the saggy features of a man who's half-cut. He has definitely had more than a glass.' I groaned as Harper topped up his champagne. 'Oh God, he's having more.'

'Give him a break, Becks. It's not every day you find out you're going to be a dad.'

'Can't he do his celebrating afterwards? We've got a panto to get through, and there's a load of journalists who've come for the sole reason that we've got Harper Brady on the bill. I can't see them being too impressed if we have to drag him out unconscious.'

'He'll be fine. He's a professional.'

'A professional actor or a professional Champagne Charlie?'

'Both.' Stew slapped my back. 'I'll have a word, ok? You try to relax.'

'Right. Yes. Relax.'

I threw my shoulders back and tried a few breathing exercises. They didn't help much.

I was on first with my opening monologue. Peeking through the curtains, I could see we were looking at a full house. Cynthia was there, and Tom and Cam and Pip, Kit Beeton, Gav with his video camera capturing it for the nation, plus all the journalists from the last rehearsal. If this panto was going to die on its arse, it was going to make sure it achieved maximum humiliation in the process.

'Nervous?' a voice at my ear asked.

I jumped. 'God, Marcus. Don't do that.'

'Becks, can we talk?'

'No we bloody can't talk! I'm on in five minutes.'

'I need to tell you something. Please.'

'I don't want to be told things. I want to be left to panic in peace.'

'It'll only take a second.' He moved in front of me and dipped his head to look into my face. 'I just wanted to say I'm sorry. I said that already, but I mean it. And I care about you, I do, and in the last year I've come to feel that... you're very special to me.' He shook his head impatiently. 'God, this wasn't how this was supposed to go. Look, I don't want to lose you, Becky. It did mean something, that night. I'll never forget it, ever. I just... I wanted you to know that.'

I frowned. 'Sorry, what?'

'I guess what I really want to say is, I hope we'll always be friends.'

Ah. It was the just-good-friends speech. So that was the outcome of his time to think.

'Yeah. Great,' was the best I could manage.

I went through the stage door and waited for my cue: Sue tinkling out the final notes for Some Enchanted Evening. Once I heard that, I had to come out in front of the curtain and address the audience, leaving the stagehands to finish fixing the palace backdrop behind.

When the last note died in the air, I came out and blinked at the audience.

There were at least 60 people there – maybe more. With the lighting rigged to cast a spotlight right on me, the expectant eyes of dozens of Egglethwaitians fixed on me and Marcus's words, *I hope we'll always be friends,* still ringing in my ears, I goggled, fishlike, for a moment. Suddenly it was all very real, and I was in serious danger of losing my lines in the fog.

Then I remembered my tip to Maisie. I sought out Pip and fixed my gaze on her.

It was ok. It was just play. Just acting out stories, like me and her did all the time.

'Why, what a lot of people!' I said in mock surprise. 'Hello, boys and girls. My name's Ella.' I smiled warmly. 'But round here, most people call me Cinderella.'

I told them about my hard life. How I was made to live as a servant in my own home, the cruelty of my stepmother and her two daughters, and how my kindly but drunken father was powerless to prevent it. How I dreamed of marrying the handsome Prince Charming and leaving this life behind. The kids were sympathetic and I got a few *aww*s, which was more than I could say for Stew and Lana in the wings. She was miming playing a tiny violin while he boo-hooed theatrically, rubbing his eyes with his fists.

'What're you even doing here?' I muttered to Stew when I came off. 'You're not in this panto.'

'I've done my share of audiencing. Thought it'd be more fun from this side.'

'All the better to take the piss, yeah?'

He grinned. 'Something like that.'

The prince and Dandini were up next, planning the ball. Deano, in a last-minute brainwave, had provided Lana with a prop – a scroll, appropriate to Dandini's job as the prince's herald, with a few prompts written on in case she forgot her lines.

She kept it tucked under her arm throughout the scene, but to my relief, she remembered her part perfectly without a single peek. Once the curtain dropped, she marched smugly back to me and Stew.

'See?' Stew said, giving her a kiss. 'I knew you could do it.'

'Yeah, nice work,' I said. 'How come you didn't get stagefright this time?'

She shrugged. 'Had my scroll, didn't I?'

'But you didn't even look at it.'

'I knew I could if I needed to though. It's my magic feather.' She nodded to the stagehands fitting the next backdrop. 'Our old men are up, Becks.'

Chapter 44

The curtain rose on Yolanda in her towering black step-mother wig, the backdrop and props announcing to all that this was the boudoir of some rather tasteless aspiring ladies of fashion. There was a big cheer from the audience. Everyone knew Yolanda.

'Griselda! Tabitha!' she called. 'Now come along! There's only –' she looked at her watch – 'three days until the ball. You must begin getting ready, my dears.'

Dad and Gerry trudged sullenly out from each side of the stage. There was a massive laugh from the audience at their matching little-girl sailor dresses, and a shriek from Pip.

'They're not ladies!' she yelled. 'They're my grandads!' That got a big laugh too.

'Oh, my girls, my girls,' Yolanda-Stepmother said, pinching their cheeks. 'Thank goodness you inherited your mother's looks. No lady in the kingdom will come close to two such beauties.'

I heard Pip's friend Harry, who'd come with her and her dads, titter. 'They're well ugly,' he whispered.

Gerry picked up on it at once. 'And who said *that?*' he snapped. He raised an opera glass to his eyes to peer at Harry. 'How dare you call my sister ugly, little boy?'

'*Me?*' Dad fluttered his hands in comic surprise. 'I believe he was talking to *you*, Grizzly.'

'Oooh. Come here and say that.' Gerry got Dad's head under his arm and started mercilessly nuggying his wig, with enough realism that Dad actually started turning purple.

'Girls, enough!' Yolanda snapped, pulling them apart. 'As if I haven't got enough to worry about with that idle, good-for-nothing Cinderella to keep my eye on.' She cupped a hand to her mouth, oblivious to the boos being aimed at her. 'Cinderella! Come here at once!'

That was my cue. I darted onto the stage.

'Yes, Stepmother?'

'Tabitha and Griselda will require your help getting ready for the ball.'

Gerry, who was leaning over the painted sink pretending to wash his face, sprang up, grasping his buttocks, as Dad kicked him in the rump. 'Oooh! Right in the middle of me ablutions! Tell her, Mummy!'

'Now, Tabby, do behave,' Yolanda said, cuffing Dad indulgently.

Dad rummaged out a gigantic pair of bloomers from the chest of drawers. 'You'll need to help me get into these, Cinderella.' He waggled his eyebrows at the audience. 'My lucky knickers, folks. The prince won't know what's hit him.'

Gerry leaned round to look at his sister's enormous backside. 'I'll say he won't. He'll think it's an asteroid.'

Dad tossed his ringlets haughtily. 'My bottom has been admired in five counties, I'll have you know.'

'True. They can bask in the shade of your left bumcheek as far away as Lancashire.'

The audience guffawed appreciatively. That was the secret of a good bawdy joke. Adults laughed at the punchline, kids just laughed because someone had said 'bum'.

'Now, now, girls,' Yolanda said. 'You mustn't tease one another so at the ball. Whatever would the prince think? Remember you are sisters and should love one another.'

That was the lead into the song. Off the dames went, really giving it everything.

Sisters, sisters, there were never such devoted sisters...

The pair of them seemed to be constantly trying to outdo each other: Gerry kicking his legs up in a cancan motion, Dad bending over to waggle his bloomered backside at the audience. And every now and then, Gerry would glance down at his deflated left breast, raise his eyebrows suggestively, then pump it back up with his arm. It was a wonderful bit of comic theatre. I could see Cynthia crying with laughter, and Pip was bouncing up and down with glee. Cameron and Tom looked a bit traumatised, but you couldn't win them all.

'Please, Tabitha, please, Griselda,' I said shyly when they were done. 'I'm your sister too. May I not go to the ball? The prince did decree every single woman of good family should –'

'Good family!' Yolanda said, patting her heart. 'My dear girl, how dare you presume to put yourself on a level with me and my daughters? You, who sleep among the ash, who consort with that lazy little boot boy as if he were an equal –'

'Buttons is not lazy,' I snapped. 'He's my best friend.'

Yolanda shot a knowing look at her daughters, and the three of them laughed nastily.

'Aww,' Dad said, pulling my hair. 'Little Cinders has got herself a friend.'

'A boyfriend,' Gerry said. 'Isn't it adorable? Our sister, the boot boy's girl.'

I flushed. 'He's not my boyfriend.'

Gerry-Griselda sent a malicious smile to her sister. 'I think we should take Cinders to the ball, Tabby.'

Dad-Tabby nodded. 'She has a right to go.'

Yolanda looked like she was about to object, but Dad held up his hand. 'Now, Mummy, we must not be cruel. If Cinders can get us and herself ready in time, then of course she may go.' He scanned my ragged dress. 'Perhaps the palace has some skivvying for her to do.'

'She could even bring the boot boy as her date,' Gerry sneered.

'May I really go?' I asked, wide-eyed.

'Of course.' Dad thumped a fist against his inflated bosom, which let out a comedy raspberry. 'A Hardup's word is her bond.'

'Oh, thank you, thank you!' I seized his hands gratefully. 'I'll be ready. And I'll have a dress fit to be seen in, I promise.'

Poor Cinders. She really was a naive little soul.

Chapter 45

Next up was the dancing lesson.

'Are you sure he'll be ok?' I whispered to Lana when I got backstage, indicating Harper on his stool by the costume rail. He was nodding groggily, glowing with a combination of impending fatherhood and champagne.

'God, I hope so,' she said. 'The last thing he needs now he's going to be a dad is a "Harper Brady pissed on stage at family panto" headline.'

'Eesh, yeah. Didn't think of that.' I grabbed Maisie's arm as she walked past. 'Can you wake the father of your child up, Mais? You're on.'

'Jesus. Look at the state of him.' She went over and prodded him. 'Harper!'

He grinned sleepily. 'Hey, beautiful.'

Harper tried to guide her onto his lap but she stood firm. 'We don't have time for that. It's our scene.'

He blinked. 'Scene?'

'You know, the panto?'

'Oh yeah.' His voice was pretty slurred. 'Is it old lamps for new?'

'Not that panto. The other panto.' She patted his cheeks, trying to wake him up a bit. 'You're Baron Hardup, all right? You're the baron, I'm the prince, you're teaching me to dance.'

'Baron.' He blinked. 'Ok.'

'Just wait till I get you home,' she muttered.

He smirked. 'That a promise, babe?'

'It's a promise you're sleeping on the settee.' She slapped him a few more times. 'A lot of people have worked hard for this. There are a lot of kids and a lot of journalists out there waiting for you to impress them. Don't you dare let me down, Harper Brady.'

'God, Mais. You're scary.'

'Bloody right. Now get your arse in gear before I really slap you one.'

'Is this pregnancy... things? Will you be scary all the time now?'

'I'll be worse.' She cocked her head to listen. 'Come on. Sue's playing the intro.'

She dragged him on stage.

Yolanda smiled after them. 'You know, I wasn't a fan to begin with, but I've grown to rather like that girl.'

'Me too,' I said.

And then it was the moment of truth. Time to find out just how genuinely pissed our supposedly fake-pissed baron really was.

The curtain went up, to a big cheer from the audience when they saw Harper.

'Oh. Hiya,' he said, giving them a matey wave.

Maisie launched them into the scene.

'Are you sure you can teach me to dance in time for the ball, Baron?'

Harper beamed, wavered, then flicked her ear. I could see a terrified-looking Deano watching from the wings.

'You're pretty,' Harper whispered, in full hearing of the audience. There were some titters, and frantic scribbling from the journalists up front.

Maisie looked irritated. 'Um, that's very flattering, *Baron Hardup*. But what I really want is to learn to dance in time for the ball.'

Chapter 45

Harper blinked. 'Are you going to a ball?'

'Yes,' Maisie said through gritted teeth. 'At the palace. Where I live. Because I'm the prince.'

'You're a princess. My beautiful princess. I always said so.' Harper leaned forward unsteadily, and it really looked for a moment as if he was about to give his prospective son-in-law a massive smacker on the mouth. Maisie froze, panic-stricken.

'Oh Christ,' I whispered to Lana. 'He'll ruin the whole thing. I'm going in.'

I grabbed one of the empty champagne bottles and marched out.

'Father? Father!' I called. I pretended to clock Harper and put my hands on my hips. 'Now, Father. Was it you who drank all the champagne Stepmother bought to bring to the ball?'

Harper blinked. 'What?'

'It was, wasn't it?' I curtsied to Maisie. 'You must excuse my father, your highness. He, er, drinks to block out the reality of his miserable life.'

'Bit bleak,' Maisie muttered.

'Sorry,' I mouthed. 'Improvising.'

I grabbed Harper's shoulders. 'Now pull yourself together, Father. The prince needs you to show him how to dance. And if you don't, you'll make him very unhappy. You wouldn't want that, would you? You know how much you love... your prince.' I grinned at the audience. 'As, um, we all do. Loyal subjects to a man.'

'Oh. Oh!' Harper glanced down at his frock coat and breeches, as if he'd suddenly remembered where he was. 'Dancing. Right.' He blinked for a moment. 'We'll... we'll have you dancing a hornpipe by Saturday, sire, no problem.'

He grabbed Maisie's waist and started swaying her drunkenly around the stage. That, at least, was in the script, and the audience were soon laughing again.

'Right. I'll leave you to it then,' I said, sidling off. 'Bye, Dad. Bye, Prince.'

'Nice save,' Marcus whispered when I got back to the wings.

Deano came forward to give me a big hug. 'I love you, Becky. You know that, right?'

Wrong brother, came a thought in the back of my mind. But out loud I just said, 'You think they noticed?'

'Course they noticed. But the show went on, that's what counts. And he is Harper Brady, half the press probably only showed up in the hope he'd do something like this.' Deano glanced at Harper and Maisie drunkenly waltzing. 'He seems to be doing ok now. I think the actor gene's kicked in.'

Marc laughed. 'I wouldn't want to be him tomorrow though. If he survives the hangover, Maisie's going to throttle him.'

I was half worried Harper's antics, showstopping in the absolute worst sense of the word, heralded more disasters to come. But as we moved from scene to scene, I started to relax. Just a blip, that was all. Everything was ok. Everything was better than ok, in fact.

Lana remembered all her lines. Maisie was chipper and nausea-free. Yolanda, despite her initial horror of playing the baddie, seemed to revel in being booed and hissed by old friends. Everyone, especially Kit Beeton, cracked up at the Hot Tub Girls number, which the dames performed complete with tin bath on wheels.

But it was the slosh scene, with added mushy peas, that was our biggest triumph: just a disgusting, joyous, roof-raising success, with Gerry and Dad on top form as they baked innuendo-filled sausage pies to take to the palace banquet. Marcus was a big hit as he joked, juggled eggs and made things appear out of thin air with imperceptible sleight of hand, and their little assistant, Pip's friend Tinuviel, grinned happily while she delivered lumpy green custard pies to the ugly sisters. The laughter must've been audible from across the road at the Fox.

After sausage pies came the interval while our volunteer stagehands cleaned up the mess.

'Going well, isn't it?' Marcus said when he joined me backstage. I was sitting on a stool having my makeup topped up by Deano, who'd decided Yo-yo was being too sparing with the blusher and had taken it upon himself to pinken everyone's cheeks.

'Yeah,' I said. 'So far.'

Marcus had grabbed a shower after getting all messy in the slosh scene and he was currently in just a dressing gown, hair soaking wet. It might've been sexy if I wasn't still so bloody pissed off with him.

'You'd better get into costume,' I told him. 'It's Tomorrow soon.'

'That's right.' Deano nodded to his brother. 'Good luck, Marc.'

I'd been rehearsing this for days. Not rehearsing the lines, I knew those inside out. Rehearsing my reactions. Pretending not to care when Marc brought his face close to mine, when he told me he loved me.

It didn't get off to a great start. Marcus, line-perfect usually, seemed to have forgotten that he was supposed to magic me a flower. He just blinked when he got to that bit, fumbled, then moved on to his next line – 'What's so great about a silly old ball anyway?' But the audience didn't notice, and he quickly recovered.

We did the song, then I braced myself as we got into position for Buttons's love declaration. I was determined not to cock it up this time, no matter how angry I was at the man currently gazing at me with the fake love-light in his eyes. Again.

'And what about me?' Marcus-Buttons asked. 'Wouldn't you miss me at the palace, Cinders? Or would you be too fine a lady to remember your old pal Buttons?'

'Of course not!' I said with as much vehemence as I could muster. 'You're my best friend. I wouldn't go to the palace without you.'

He hesitated, and I thought for a second he'd forgotten his lines. I was about to mouth a prompt when he reached behind my ear for something.

'Something to give you,' he said softly. 'Pretty thing for a pretty girl.'

He'd remembered the flower? There didn't seem much point working it in now. Perhaps it was getting tickly, hiding up there in his sleeve.

He opened his clenched fist. Something shiny slipped through his fingers, catching around them to dangle in front of my eyes. I blinked at it in surprise.

'It's gorgeous,' I breathed.

'It's for you.'

He reached round me to fasten it on, and I glanced down at the four colourful gemstones set into a golden filigree pendant.

'What does it mean?' I murmured. Then I remembered the panto, the eyes of the audience fixed on me, and I raised my voice. 'What does it mean, er... Buttons?'

Marc traced the gems with his fingertip. 'The deep blue stone is lapis. Then opal. Garnet, which is sometimes called vermeil.' He glanced up. 'And emerald last of all.'

'Loge. Um, loge?'

Marcus smiled. 'Love.' He took my hands, his deep brown eyes searching my face. 'I love you. I always did, you know.'

And we were back on script. Except for one thing. He hadn't called me Cinderella.

I glanced at Deano in the wings, who nodded encouragingly.

'Oh Buttons. You know I only love you as a friend.'

The rest of the scene played out as planned.

Chapter 45

As soon as the Tomorrow scene ended, Marcus exeunted stage left while I waited for the Fairy Godmother to turn up with my ballgown and pumpkin and Pikachus and T-Rex, those must-have accessories for any girl going to a royal ball.

Yolanda was really a natural in the Fairy Godmother parts. She just played herself.

'Oh, darling, no no no no, absolutely not,' she said when she'd appeared in a cloud of dry ice provided by our special effects department (aka Billy). She fingered my ragged dress in disgust. 'Oh heavens, now you're quite a horror, aren't you? We can't possibly have you seen in public like this. I'll have my Fairy Godmother licence revoked.'

'Is it really that bad, Godmother?'

'Bad? You're a fright, my love. Honestly, you need to fire your stylist immediately.' She clapped her hands, and a couple of little Pikachus in sparkly tiaras and tutus arrived on stage, bearing something long and gauzy.

'Now this is much more like it,' Yolanda said, fluttering her fairy wings in excitement. '*This* will turn heads, my dear Ella.'

She held up the dress, and I stared at it. It wasn't my costume, the uncomfortable Regency meringue that made me feel far from the belle of the ball while being dragged around by Maisie sweating like a hog. It was the sophisticated figure-hugging ballgown I'd worn the night of Yo-yo's photoshoot. How she'd got her hands on it I had no idea. A lady had hired it from the shop a few days ago for her daughter's prom.

'I'm wearing this?' I said, running my fingers over the soft material.

'You are,' Yolanda said. 'Tonight, you need to be completely and essentially you.' She gripped my shoulders. 'Be true to yourself, Ella. And remember, not every girl needs a Prince Charming.'

Ok, what the hell was going on? That most definitely was not in the script.

Chapter 46

When I got backstage, it felt like everyone wanted a piece of me – well, everyone except Harper, who was having a little lie down by the costume rail. As soon as I emerged from the wings, Yolanda grabbed me.

'We must do something with your makeup,' she said. 'Your cheeks are awfully pink.'

'Where's Marcus?' I asked as she attacked my face with assorted brushes. I fingered the necklace with its hidden message. 'I need to talk to him.'

'He's not in the next scene, darling. Taking a break in the fresh air, I imagine.'

'Oh. Ok.'

Next I was commandeered by Deano, who barked instructions at me while I blinked dazedly, then Lana, who helped me into my dress. Pushed from one friend to the next, there was no time to look for Marcus.

The ballroom scene went ok, although Maisie was a bit odd. Her prince seemed sneery all of a sudden, curling his lip at his female guests in a very unchivalrous manner. He chucked me about pretty unceremoniously while we danced too. I don't know what version of the character Mais was channelling, but he seemed like a right dick to me.

When we got backstage, Lana grabbed me. 'You need to be in your rag dress for the shoe-fitting.'

'Where's Marc?'

'On stage, I think. Here, lift your arms.'

After she was done I was shoved to Yo-yo in makeup, then I headed to the stage.

'Here,' Deano said as I passed him in the wings. He pushed a coal scuttle into my arms.

'What do I need this for?'

'Look inside.'

I glanced into the scuttle. There were a few sheets of paper stuck around the sides, handwritten in biro.

'What is it?'

'Script changes.' He waved a hand in a most unDeano-like way. As a rule, unexpected script changes found him curled in the foetal position, groaning. 'Nothing major,' he said breezily. 'Last-minute improvements.'

'It's a bit late for that, isn't it?'

'It's never too late to be the best we can. Just remember, when Mais asks for your hand in marriage, take it from the notes. You can hold onto the scuttle to cover the fact you're reading.'

'People'll notice, Deano.'

'Just do it, there's a good girl.' He patted my backside. 'Make Chef proud.'

I wandered dazedly onto the stage, clutching my scuttle.

Everyone was there – Dad and Gerry as the sisters, Marcus in his Buttons uniform, Wicked Stepmother Yolanda, and a still wobbly Harper Brady as my father. They stared at me expectantly.

Oh right. My line.

'Did you have a nice time at the ball, girls?' I said, falling to my knees at the fireplace.

Dad clasped his hands. 'Cinders, it was wonderful. The prince and I were twin souls. I knew as soon as our eyes met that it was him I was destined to be with.'

'So did I,' Gerry said. 'As soon as my eyes met his bank balance, it was love at first sight.'

Yolanda gave their shoulders a sympathetic squeeze. 'Oh girls, it was so unfair. I feel sure he would have fallen in love with one of you, if it hadn't been for that floozy and her wiles.'

'Oh?' I said, sweeping round the grate.

'Such a dreadfully tacky woman, Cinderella. She just threw herself at the prince, no shame at all. All fur coat and no knickers, as my mother used to say.'

Marcus-Buttons winked at the audience. 'And trust me, her mother'd know.'

'Buttons! How dare you insult dear Mama!' Yolanda said, drawing herself up. 'I've a good mind to hand you your notice.'

'You don't scare me,' Buttons told her. 'I've worked for people from Pogley.'

Gerry's hand flew to his mouth. 'Not Pogley!'

'Yep. Where men are men and sheep are nervous.'

There was a solitary boo from what I assumed was our only Pogley audience member, and riotous laughter from everyone else.

In burst Lana, bearing aloft the glass slipper nestled on a cushion.

'His royal highness, Prince Charming of Rummancoke!'

Maisie entered with a haughty look on her face, still apparently channeling the dick version of the prince.

'Attention, womenfolk of Rummancoke,' she said imperiously. 'I hereby decree that whoever this shoe fits shall be my bride.'

Then came the shoe fitting, with some typically damey antics from the dames. Finally, it was my turn.

'Oh! It fits,' Maisie breathed as she slid the slipper gently onto my foot.

'That's right, your highness,' I said. 'I am she, the mysterious stranger you danced with last night.'

'Oh, Cinderella, I'm so happy I found you,' Maisie said, guiding me to my feet. 'Say you'll be my princess, and you'll never have to clean another fireplace as long as you live.'

There was a snort from Dad-Tabitha. He elbowed Buttons maliciously.

'Oh dear, boot boy. Looks like you've lost your one true love. Well, tough luck.'

'Perhaps when Cinders is queen, she might let you clean grates for her,' Gerry-Griselda said. 'Every girl has her price, you know, Buttocks.'

'It's Buttons,' Marcus said, glaring at him. 'And I hope Cinders will always choose what makes her happiest.'

That was all new material. It seemed to be rubbing salt in the wound for poor old Buttons, but I guessed Deano knew what he was doing.

My next line was supposed to be 'Yes, sire, I will marry you.' I glanced down into the coal scuttle to see what'd changed.

'Um, no?' I said in a faltering voice.

There was a gasp from the audience. There was a gasp from the Ugly Sisters. There was a gasp from Yolanda. Harper just grinned.

Maisie drew herself up. 'What do you mean no, wench? I am heir to this kingdom, you know.'

'I mean, no. I don't want to marry you.'

'Look, I may have phrased it as a question – I mean, just to be polite – but I do have the power to command. Marry me, Cinderella. That's an order.'

I squinted at the handwritten sheet in my scuttle. There was a stage direction.

[Cinderella puts her hands on her hips defiantly. PS Hi, Becks. It's me.]

I smiled at the familiar scrawl. I'd worked on too many scripts with that man not to know Marc's writing.

The adults in the audience were looking puzzled, but the kids seemed fascinated. Who doesn't love a twist, right?

I put my hands on my hips. Defiantly.

'You can command my body, your highness, but you can't command my heart. And that belongs to another.' I stretched out a hand to Buttons. 'To this man. My best friend. The one I realise now I was always meant to be with.'

Marcus-Buttons pulled me to him. 'Oh Cinders, sweetheart. Although we must be poor, I promise I'll always respect you and do my best to make you happy. Prince Charming might be able to offer a life of wealth and glamour, but he could never know and love you like I do.'

'You would choose this – this servant, this *slave*, over a prince?' Maisie-Charming hissed at me.

I gripped Marcus's hand and we faced her proudly. 'I would. I do.'

'Cinderella. Buttons. You needn't be poor,' Lana-Dandini piped up. 'I've always been the prince's man, but dash it, the beauty of your love compels me to speak.'

Marcus grimaced at the cheesy line. 'Sorry,' he mouthed to me.

'Whosoever shall defeat the prince in single combat becomes heir to the kingdom in his place,' Lana said. 'It is written into the constitution of Rummancoke, the long-forgotten rule of, er... Droit du Seigneur.'

Harper looked thoroughly confused now. He leaned over to Yolanda. 'What the hell is going on?' I heard him slur. 'Am I in the right panto?'

'True love, darling,' Yo-yo whispered back. 'Shhh.'

'Here,' Deano whispered from off stage, sliding a couple of costume fencing swords our way.

'Ha ha! Have at thee, prince!' Marc said, grasping for one of the mysteriously materialising swords. Maisie reached for the other and they fought, with Maisie eventually falling to her knees, Marcus's blade at her throat.

'Oh! I am beaten! Cinderella shall never be mine!' she cried, with some pretty strong hamming.

'Good!' Pip's little voice rang out from the audience. 'You're mean and nobody likes you so ner.'

Maisie blinked at me and Marcus, and we nodded.

'Um... oh no I'm not?'

'Oh yes you are!' the kids chorused.

'Oh no I'm not!'

'Oh yes you are!'

'Ok, Mais, wind it up,' Marc muttered.

'All right, I am then,' she conceded. 'Oh, go on, take my kingdom. I never liked being a prince anyway.'

'Cracking,' Marcus said, shooting a thumbs-up to the audience. 'Tabitha, Griselda, Baroness: consider yourselves banished. Baron, your money worries are over. I'll pay off your debts and, er, we'll get you into AA or something. Dandini, have a knighthood. Boys and girls, these are for all your help.' He reached into his pocket and chucked a handful of sweets into the audience, to delighted squeals from the kids. 'And Cinders...' He turned to me. 'It's your choice. Will you have me?'

'Yes, Buttons. I'll marry you.'

'Not just because I'm rich now?'

'Because I love you. Because I always loved you, really. I just didn't know it.' I stood daintily on one leg to kiss his cheek.

I held my position, freeze-frame, and Lana stepped forward. She unfurled her scroll and began.

'So good has won in Rummancoke

Now Buttons is our man
It's ta-ra Wicked Stepmother
And mutton dressed as lamb.' She jerked her head towards
the dames.

'We've got ourselves a brand-new prince,
A really smashing feller
And best of all a happy end
For our girl Cinderella.'

She beamed at the audience. Maisie nudged her, nodding at
the scroll.

'Oh right, yeah. So thanks for being, one and all,
An audience that rocks.
That's all, folks, and till next year
You'll find us in the Fox.'

There was a loud cheer from the crowd.

'Nice,' I muttered to Marcus.

'Cheers. Billy owes us a pint for that.'

As soon as the curtain dropped, he pulled me to him for a
kiss. When he released me, I laughed breathlessly.

'You didn't really do all that just to –'

'To show you I love you? Yeah.'

'Why?'

He flushed. 'Buggered up, didn't I? I knew it had to be
something a bit spectacular. A bit... well, a bit fairytale.' He
drew a finger down my cheek. 'Did it work?' he asked softly.

'Course it worked, you ridiculous sod.' I glanced round the
rest of the cast. 'And you lot were all in on it, were you?'

'Yep,' Dad said, grinning.

'Marcus talked us into it,' Yolanda said. 'Well, what self-
respecting Fairy Godmother can resist a real-life love story?'

'Come on, no time for cuddling.' Deano came out of the
wings and guided us apart. 'You need to get into your posh gear

Chapter 46

so you can take a bow. Becks, back in the ballgown. Marc, I've got something for you.'

Lana dragged me off stage and helped me, trance-like, into my frock, then pushed me back on. Marc stumbled through from the other side, looking like a sexy toy soldier in a military-style red blazer, blue sash and white trousers. He took my hand, lifted it, and as the curtain came up we bowed in unison to the wild claps of the audience.

'What do we do now?' I whispered.

'We kiss, I think.'

'Stage kiss?'

'No, love. Not today.' He leaned me back over his arm in true fairytale fashion and planted a soft, lingering kiss on my lips. There were loud cheers, and a few 'yucks!' from the kids.

'Is it real?' I whispered when he drew back.

'It's real.' He cupped my cheek. 'I'm so sorry, Becks. I think I must've loved you for ages, only I was too thick to realise it until I'd made such a massive mess of everything. Do you forgive me?'

'Have to, don't I? I love you.'

And the thunderous applause rang out.

***

The show was over. The fat lady had sung. Our revels now were ended, our T-Rex had turned back into a Roger Collingwood-shaped mouse and the coach was back in the pumpkin patch.

'You two coming to the Fox?' Lana asked me and Marcus.

He glanced at me. 'Give us half an hour.'

She squeezed his arm. 'Course.'

I smiled at a frazzled-looking Deano, arm in arm with Lana like he needed the support.

'So how was your first panto-directing experience?'

'Nightmare. Living, breathing nightmare.' He grinned at us with dazed, shining eyes. 'When can we start the next one?'

'Let's see if we survive the rest of the run first, eh?' Marcus said, laughing. 'See you in the pub, guys. Get us some drinks in, we won't be long.'

When they'd gone a de-damed Dad, hand in hand with Cynthia on one side and Pip on the other, came over to say goodbye, along with Tom and Cam.

'Great show, sis,' Cam said, slapping my arm.

Tom nodded. 'I can honestly say I did not see that ending coming.'

'That's not the proper Cinderella story, Aunty Becky,' Pip informed me loftily.

'You liked it though, didn't you?' I asked.

'I liked it better.' She looked up at Marcus. 'Do you really love my aunty or was it just pretend?'

The grown-ups all laughed.

'I think that's six-year-old for "what are your intentions?"' Dad said to Marcus.

Marc dropped to his haunches to talk to her.

'No, kid, that bit was real.'

'Will you get married now like Cinderella and Buttons?'

He laughed. 'Well, I was hoping she might agree to be my girlfriend first,' he said, glancing up at me. 'I mean, if you say it's ok. She's your aunty.'

Pip pondered a moment. 'Ok,' she said with a magnanimous nod. 'If you do magic at my house sometimes I'll let her be your girlfriend.'

Marcus shook her hand solemnly. 'It's a deal.'

Dad came forward to give me a hug. 'Well done, Boo,' he whispered. 'Think you're onto a winner with this one. In fact, you can have my blessing in advance.'

I smiled at Cynthia over his shoulder, proudly sporting her new engagement ring. 'You too. Congratulations, Dad.'

'Well. Time I stopped worrying about what might've passed me by and started appreciating what hasn't, eh?' He kissed my forehead as he released me. 'Something my little girl taught me. That and a bit of festive cross-dressing.'

'Bye guys. Becky, we'll see you Sunday,' Cynthia said as they prepared to go. She looked at Marcus. 'How about you? Would you like to join us for Sunday dinner?'

'Me?' He blinked. 'Er, yeah, I'd love to. Thanks, Cynthia.'

'Chucking you in at the deep end there,' I said when we were left alone. 'Sorry.'

He shrugged. 'I just half-improvised a pantomime in front of a crowd of feral kids to impress the girl of my dreams. Think I can manage a family dinner.'

'We're not doing the new version for the whole run, are we?'

'I do prefer it,' he said. 'And why not? It's our panto.'

'Yeah, you're right. Let's give Cinders and Buttons the happily-ever-after they deserve.'

'Like we got ours,' he said, leaning down to kiss me.

'What do you think the press write-ups'll say?'

'What, the Cinderella with the line-dancing Pikachus, T-Rex-drawn coach, drunken TV star and very unorthodox happy ending?' He shrugged. 'I'm banking on a "memorable".'

'Tickets went well anyway. £480 on the door and £126 on refreshments, according to the Ladies Who Lunch, and that's just tonight.' I glanced round the tinsel-festooned hall. 'Looks like this place is safe for another year.'

Marcus took my hand to guide me to the stage. He swung me up, then himself, and we sat with our legs dangling off the edge.

'Why'd you do it, Marc?' I whispered, nestling into the arm he slung round me. 'Walk out on me?'

He sighed. 'I failed, Becks. Like we all sometimes fail. I'm sorry.'

'But why?'

'It's like...' He paused. 'Ok, I've tried three times to say this and it's always come out wrong. Let me break it down.' He nodded to me. 'Here is Becky. She is my friend.'

'Am I a rabbit? In Lana's stories I get to be a rabbit.'

'No, in this story you're a sexy lady,' he said. 'Right, so I kissed my friend Becky and was all confused, because it turned out I really fancied her, only I'd been hiding it from myself.'

'Then what?'

'I found out that my friend Becky's fiancé, who was the reason I'd been hiding the things I felt from myself, had moved out, and Becky was single again and fancied me too.' He took a deep breath. 'Here's the bit where I sound like a prick.'

'Go on. I can handle it.'

'So my friend Becky looked pretty hot in her pyjamas with the ladybirds on, and she'd been crying, and I...'

'Kissed her?'

'And the rest. Hey, did you hear this story before?'

'One a bit like it, yeah.'

'And afterwards I felt bad, because friends don't kiss friends – and the rest – when they've been crying. And then... then Becky said this thing that made me feel infinity per cent worse.'

'What?'

'That she loved me. Only I didn't know if she meant it or she was just upset. And that made me feel awful about the kissing and the rest. Especially when I realised.'

'Realised what?'

'That I didn't just fancy her at all. I loved her. That I had for ages, and I'd been lying to myself about that too. And then I felt even more confused than before the kissing.'

'And the rest.'

'And the rest, even though at the time the rest had actually been the best bit. And that's when I did the Bad Thing.'

'What was it?'

He flushed. 'Ran away. Like a cad and a coward. Scared stiff of what I'd done and what I felt.'

'Then what happened?'

'I made it worse. Panicked. Avoided you while I tried to get to grips with this massive thing I'd just realised I was feeling.' He wrapped both arms around me. 'Can't believe I nearly lost you,' he whispered. 'Oh God, Becky, I'm sorry.'

'I know you are,' I said gently, stroking his hair. 'When did you rewrite the panto?'

'Couple of days ago. We had an emergency summit in the pub and I managed to get everyone on board.' He reached up to finger the necklace he'd given me. 'And I got your Christmas present. Genuine vintage, 1847. Same age as the Temp, I thought you'd appreciate that.'

'I do,' I murmured. 'Thank you, Marc. It's beautiful.'

'You're beautiful.'

I guided him down so we were lying on the stage and pulled him to me for a kiss.

'You really forgive me then?' he whispered.

'Don't have much choice after all that, do I?'

'And you'll...' He laughed. 'Sounds daft asking this at thirty-four. Will you go out with me, Becky Finn?'

'You know I will.'

He ran his finger down my cheek. 'Kiss me again, Becky,' he said softly. 'That's the proper way to end a fairytale, isn't it?'

Everything was hushed and sleepy, only the Christmas tree lights twinkling in the gloom. The seats were empty. But when he kissed me, I could still hear the applause.

Acknowledgements

Once again, an enormous thanks goes to my agent Laura Longrigg at MBA Literary Agents for her unfailing cheerleading and support, and to the team at Mirror Books for going above and beyond to make this book the best it can be – Jo Sollis and Paula Scott doing a fab job on the editorial side and Cynthia Hamilton and Mel Sambells working ultra hard on promotion. Not to mention the sterling editorial work done by Annabel Wright and Donna Cordon of Whitefox, which was invaluable in helping me to polish the story and characters.

Thanks too to all the panto performers over the years who helped me fall in love with the quirky British pantomime tradition and made me determined that, one day, I would write a book about it. The Townfield Players of Wilsden Village Hall; the panto gang at Wilsden Con Club – both now sadly gone, but never forgotten; David Brett and the team at Parkside Middle School who produced our annual show, and the Harden Players troupe, especially my lady on the inside, Vicky Foster, for her helpful advice on how it all works. A special mention to Amy Smith, to whom this book is dedicated, and the Laycock Players for many happy and inspirational hours spent watching them being daft.

All my lovely, supportive Firths, Brahams and Anslows need a big thank you as always for putting up with me in writerly recluse mode, as does my first and most exacting beta reader, my partner Mark Anslow.

A big shout out to all my author pals in the real and digital world, especially Kate Beeden, Rachel Hawes, Rachel Dove, the Authors on the Edge gang, my fellow Wordcount Warriors on Facebook, and the Airedale Writers' Circle. Thanks for all the support, encouragement and bribes as I staggered to the finish line. And big thanks to the talented Phillipa Ashley, who first suggested The Perfect Fit as the title of this book.

Eternal gratitude on behalf of all authors to the book bloggers and reviewers for the time they dedicate to helping us promote our books. We do appreciate it.

And as always, my long-suffering friends, Bob Fletcher, Nigel and Lynette Emsley, and my colleagues at Country Publications Ltd. I promise I'll shut up about this one now. Maybe. For a bit.

Finally, Billy Pearce, Bradford Alhambra panto stalwart. Because it wouldn't be panto season without Billy...

Book club
discussion questions

Finished the book? Use the questions below to spark your discussions.

1. What did you think of Cole's character within the novel?
2. Do you feel Becky ended up with her "perfect fit" in the end?
3. What parallels are there between events in Becky's life and the Cinderella story?
4. Did your perception of the relationship between Harper and Maisie change by the end of the novel?
5. Which character could you most relate to?
6. Discuss the role of Becky's niece Pip in the plot.
7. Do you think if Cole and Becky had both wanted children, their relationship would have worked?
8. Discuss the character of Yolanda and her relationship with Becky.
9. Do you agree that Becky should have forgiven Marcus for the way he behaved?
10. What are your thoughts on the relationship between Gerry and Sue?

Also by Mirror Books

A Bicycle Made for Two
A Love In The Dales story…
by Mary Jayne Baker

In a lost corner of the Yorkshire Dales, Lana Donati runs a medieval theme tourist trap restaurant with her brother. As a distraction to help them get over losing the father they loved dearly, and as a tribute to his passion for the beautiful area they live in, Lana hatches a plan to boost business for everyone by having the Grand Départ route pass through their village.

This means getting the small community to work together to make it happen – including arrogant celebrity Harper Brady and Lana's (attractive) arch-nemesis – the former pro cyclist turned bike shop owner Stewart McLean, whose offbeat ideas might just cost them everything.

Also by Mirror Books

All That Followed
by Emma Campbell

Emma bravely shares her uplifting true story of triplets(!), the embrace of friendship, losing love, finding love, the kindness of strangers, a constant fear of death mixed with the joy and relief of living. The anxiety of cancer returning… and then facing it head on when it does.

"There wasn't one chapter that left me dry-eyed, it's a love story… a full on rollercoaster read"– *Grace Timothy (author Mum Face)*

"Extraordinary" – *Clover Stroud*

"Warm, funny… unflinchingly honest" – *Amy McCullough*

"… a true fighter, survivor and inspiration… she is someone I'll remember for a lifetime." – *Peter Andre*